MW00814648

GYM BUDDIES & BUFF BOYS

An Erotic Anthology
Edited By

Mickey Erlach

Herndon, VA

Published in the United States by STARbooks Press, PO Box 711612, Herndon, VA 20171. Printed in the United States

Cover Photo Model: www.justinwoltering.com

Cover Photo Courtesy of www.photosbyjae.com

Cover Design by Emma Aldous: www.arthousepublishing.co.uk

Herndon, VA

Titles Edited by Mickey Erlach

CONTENTS

GYM DANDY
By Landon Dixon

The guy strode into the gym like he owned the place, slammed his bag down on the floor and bellowed, "Not bad! Not bad at all! I think I can get even bigger here!"

Then he ripped off his sweatshirt and started crunching out poses in the wall of mirrors – double biceps, side triceps, most muscular – right there in front of everyone in his jeans.

"Who's this douche?" Larry said to me, halting his progress on the lat machine.

"Damned if I know," I replied, watching the workout intruder take narcissism to a whole new level, a pair of dumbbells hanging mute by my sides.

The new guy finished off his routine with a peak of the biceps and a twist of the torso, screaming his abs out in stark relief. Then he threw us a sneer and ambled off in the direction of the locker room.

"Christ," Larry grunted. "There's a guy who needs to be taken down a notch or ten."

"Yeah," I murmured, a plan already forming in my mind. Alongside some other visualizations – of me and the big, blond-streaked muscleman getting it on.

I'd liked everything I'd seen of the guy: his tanned, ripped torso with the bulging chest plates; his huge, vein-striated arms that peaked up into the clouds; his cleft chin and square jaw and bright blue eyes. Yeah, I liked everything about the dude, except his 'tude; that did need a whole hell of a lot more work. And, I was just the horny man to do some honing, since I worked part-time at the gym.

All of our initial misgivings were confirmed when Dexter started working out for real. He hogged barbells and dumbbells, posed in front of other guys doing the same, failed to wipe down the machines after using them, derided people by offering unsolicited 'advice' on their 'weak spots.'

He even threw a huge arm around my shoulders when I was curling a barbell and said, "Been watching you, little guy. I think that's way too much weight for you to handle. Try less, more reps. You're never going to get the mass, anyway."

"I'll try and forget that, thanks," I growled, vowing right then and there to take my plan out of my brain and put it into action.

It's not hard to get into the head of a muscleman; slightly harder to get into his shorts. And, I was going to do both, so help me, or risk a beating trying.

I rolled things out the following Monday. First, using my master key to open up Dexter's locker, I replaced his sweatshirt, muscle-shirt, and shorts with larger versions of the same. His originals were all well-used, with the tags faded, so I washed and faded the new duds, too, before slipping them into position.

Dex wasn't the brightest bulb in the sunlamp. I watched him from around the corner, as he stripped off his street clothes and put on the new gym clothes I'd bought for him. The look on his rugged mug in the full-length mirror attached to his locker door was priceless, as he saw himself practically swimming in his duds, his fragile ego instantly flashing onto the apparent fact that he was getting smaller, not bigger. That's crushing news to a mass-man.

Since I'd gone to so much time and trouble in arranging the 'ol switcheroo, I decided I deserved to squeeze some additional fun from it. I was actually wearing Dexter's old muscle-shirt and shorts, the muskily-scented garments draping my tight, toned, but rather small body. And now I slid a hand under the shirt, cupping my left pec, pinching my pink nipple. As I slid my other hand down into the drawstring-tight shorts, gripping and ripping the heavy metal that had swelled up there as a result of watching Dexter change.

The befuddled guy even put on a show for me, spurring me on to greater flows of testosterone. He stripped off his oversized togs and threw them down onto the floor, then stared at his naked bronze body in the mirror, trying to figure out where he'd gone wrong, what had shrunk.

The light gleamed off his gloriously rounded glutes, his thick, high-toned traps and delts, his breathtakingly broad shoulders and lats and perfectly powerful legs. And when he spun around for a rear view, I got a good gander at the snake-like muscle dangling down from his loins. He was hung like he was huge, his cock four inches of smooth, tan shaft and meaty hood, un-erect.

The gym was empty that early in the morning, just me and Dexter – just Dexter, as far as he was concerned – as he went through his erotic routine, searching for his shocking loss of muscle mass. My hand and cock bulged his shorts, my other hand roaming all over my clenched chest. While big stud was fired by anger and frustration, I was fired by lust and desire, my cock raging in my stroking hand, nipples stiff and tingling.

I filled my eyes with the hunk's beefcake body and jumping cock, as he bounced from one rippling pose to the next. My balls filled with semen, cock humming cum-hard in my hand. It seemed entirely appropriate – jerking off in the guy's shorts – since the big jerk was the source of my arousal.

I twisted a nipple 'til it screamed, fisting wildly, feasting my eyes on Dexter, my nostrils sucking in the smell of him in his gym clothes. Then I bit my lip, and whimpered, jerking, jetting. He topped off his hasty routine with a full-blown most muscular, his ass cheeks clenching hard enough to break any man's resolve. I stained his shorts with my appreciation over and over and over.

I wasn't done with him there, though. I had a couple more surprises waiting for the big guy out in the gym.

He had a favorite weight belt, and after reluctantly putting on his baggy new clothes, he walked out into the gym and plucked the belt off the wall, curved it around his waist. Only this was a smaller version of the same belt, and the hole that normally cinched him up tight and trim was now beyond even his strength to reach.

I walked up to him wrestling with the heavy leather support and slapped him on the shoulder. "Looks like you're putting on a few pounds, huh, Dexter? Better be careful about what you eat."

He stared at me with a look of pure horror, then down at the belt that just wouldn't hook up. I moseyed on by, swishing my hips.

3

And, Dexter dropped the belt and ran for the wall where the scales normally stood. Not today, however, since I'd removed them. He looked around, lost.

That's when I loaded three-hundred pounds onto a benched barbell and slid in underneath, pounded out twenty straight reps. Dexter watched me, as I finished the set off with a flourish by sitting up and exhaling, "Getting strong now!" to the tune in the *Rocky* movie.

Normally, as he and I both knew, I can barely push two-hundred pounds off my chest maybe six or eight reps. But, thanks to the twin Styrofoam seventy-five pound 'plates' I'd inserted into the middle of the other plates, I was suddenly appearing a whole lot stronger, much to Dexter's chagrin.

He gave me an angry grimace and tried to hoist his own favorite, pre-loaded one-hundred-twenty-five-pound barbell off the floor, to crunch out some curls. But today the guy staggered under the weight, his arms shaking like a ninety-eight-pound weakling as he tried to raise the bar.

"Looks like you took on more than you can handle, Dex!" I yelled. "Better take it down a notch."

There were more guys in the gym now, getting a big kick out of the big man fighting the barbell – little realizing that I'd replaced the normal iron barbell with a lead version, adding another twenty-five pounds or so to the mix. It was a sight to behold, and everybody got a good laugh, except the body on the end of the lesson in humility.

He cornered me in the shower an hour later, as I was soaping myself up with pride.

"You've been screwing around with my stuff, haven't you!?" he accused, jabbing a thick finger backed up by a thick fist into my face.

He was as nude as I was, his burnished body beaming, heavy cock hanging. "Go soak yourself," I responded. "There's too much blood in your muscles and not enough in your head."

I had to give the guy credit, though, for pointing the finger at me so quickly. He obviously wasn't as dumb as he acted.

Now he acted with rage, flattening out his hand and swinging it at my face. I caught the edge of it in my hand, hooked his little finger and bent it backwards, bringing the muscleman down to his knees on the slippery tiles. He stared up at me, water streaming off his handsome, anguished face. My cock rose up to console him, the naked stud at my feet putting me on full arousal.

He looked at my prick, lengthening, thickening right there in front of him. Then he looked up at me again, something besides anger and pain showing quite clearly in his blue eyes now. I released his finger, and he shook out his right hand, grabbed onto my cock with his left.

"Yessum!" I gulped, jumping at the man's hot, wet touch.

He pumped my cock, the water deliciously lubricating his actions. My dick quickly poled out full-length in his tugging hand. He liked what he saw, and felt, expressed it by sticking out his neon-pink tongue and flicking the tip against my swollen hood.

I was jolted again.

Down on his knees, with my hard cock in his huge hand, his thick tongue swirling around my cap, Dexter wasn't such a bad guy. A great guy, in fact, when he slid his plush lips over my cockhead and sucked, still pumping my shaft with his hand.

I shot my own dripping hands into his hair, grabbing hold, urging him on. He responded enthusiastically, gripping my dick at the base and sliding his lips and mouth down my shaft until they met up with his hand. I was buried in the guy's velvety-wet, furnace-hot mouth; he obviously knew how to handle all types of iron.

I curled my fingers in his hair, clawing at his scalp, as he kept me locked down in the wicked man-eating pose. My cock throbbed in his mouth and throat, beating time to my heart thumping away in my chest. I felt my balls boil, the deep-throat pressure getting intense.

Dexter pulled back, releasing my dong from its heavenly home in a gush of hot air and saliva. Then he was all over it again, swallowing me up again, pulling back tight and quick, pushing forward, deep-sucking my cock. The water streamed, and we steamed, my brains and body ablaze with the awesome sensations of the muscle hunk wet-vaccing my dick.

He squeezed my balls with one hand, head bobbing fast and furious. He snaked his other big mitt up onto my water-sheened chest and clutched a pec, spun a nipple. I full-body shuddered, staring down at the guy with his mouth full of my cock. His heartfelt sucking up was getting to me, apology accepted.

I helped him to his feet. Then I threw my arms around his hulking body and showed my admiration and appreciation for his noble change in attitude, kissing him hard and hungry on the mouth. He squeezed my naked body tight, our cocks pressing together along with our lips. The temperature skyrocketed another hundred degrees or so, the both of us blowing off steam in the best way known to man. Dexter shot his tongue into my mouth, twirled it around my tongue.

We Frenched, kissed, fondled; devouring each other's mouths and getting a real good feel for one another's bodies. I slid my hands down off the big guy's muscle-bunched shoulders, down his long, strong back to his tight, trim wasp-waist, and then onto his ass cheeks. I gripped the tawny pair, and he moaned into my mouth, undulating his butt, his cock against my cock.

He was all ready to assume the ultimate posing position against the wall of the shower room, and I would've loved fucking that hard ass as I stared at that chiseled body. But, I owed the guy something for all the aggravation I'd caused him. So, I wheeled him around and slapped my own hands up against the tile, stuck out my bubble-bum, waving it like a white flag in front of the bull. Besides, I wanted to feel that eight-inch ball-bar he possessed pumping me to supreme peakness.

Dexter gripped my narrow waist with one hand, soaped up his dong and my crack and butthole with the other. His thick fingers felt great scrubbing my rear entrance, his bloated hood even better, squeezing against my pucker.

"Fuck!" we both groaned, as he popped through, slid shaft into my anus. He went in slow and sure and all the way, swelling my shimmering butt, turning my vibrating cock steel-hard.

He planted both of his hands on my hips and planted his feet, started rocking, gliding his rod back and forth in my chute. Fuck, it felt wonderful! His corded thighs smacked against my rippling cheeks, fingernails biting into my flesh, cock delving deep as a man can go, sawing pure pleasure all through my trembling body.

He was used to performing, before a crowded auditorium or a crowd of one. So, he really worked my anus, pumping slow and long and sensuous, then hard and fast and savage. I bounced with joy on the end of his thumping dick, up on my toes, scratching at the tile and flooding with water and heat.

I tore a hand off the wall and grabbed up my own humming cock, stroked in rhythm to Dexter's pumping. My hand was slippery, my cock ultra-stiff, and I really didn't have to pump at all, the big man's brutal pounding rocking me to and fro, doing the erotic job for me.

He flung himself at my bent-forward body, driving my ass, holding nothing back now. My butt was on fire, anus burning. I cried, "Yes!" then blasted, my cock going off in my hand without notice. Just as Dexter hammered his last loving stroke home, and shouted, and jerked. Hot semen sprayed my chute, jetted out of my cock. My head spun and body floated, getting fucked full of cum, emptying a gallon out the other end.

Dexter held me in his big, strong arms afterwards, the pair of us trembling, despite the hot water and steam. I apologized for jerking him around, and he apologized for acting like such a jerk.

Gym harmony was restored. Workouts never went so well.

PWT

By Roscoe Hudson

Drew's grandfather had been eyeing the activity across the street all weekend, evaluating the various pieces of furniture movers carted into the Jenkins' old house. All of it was high end and in much better condition than the worn out, aged furniture and bric-a-brac that took up space in the Palmer's house like wild animals felled by a hunter's bullet. The old man did his best to glean something about the new neighbors from their belongings, anxious to know whether the new neighbors would be friend or foe.

"Ain't got no kiddie beds," he said. "Could be old folks, but ain't no old folks got no metal refrigerator like that one."

"Probably stainless steel," Drew said. He lay on the couch flipping channels on the plasma television his grandfather bought with last year's settlement check. It rested atop the busted floor model with dials and faux wood panels his grandparents bought years ago when his mother was a little girl.

Drew's grandfather stood at the living room window wearing only dingy socks and sagging underwear and continued to spy through the dusty half-closed blinds. "Big bed, though. And a flat screen TV." He scratched his privates while he chewed Skoal and spit murky fluid into a plastic Fred Flintstone cup clutched in his bony hand. "Gotta be young folks. Foreclosure always gets 'em in. Hope they ain't loud."

An hour later when the movers left and Granddad cried, "Goddamn shit!" Drew joined him at the window. Across the street, a black man moved boxes out of a nacreous white SUV parked in the Jenkins' driveway and into the old two-story house. Aside from his dark skin, the first thing Drew noticed about his new neighbor was his muscular arms. When he lifted them, his biceps looked like mountains. The taut definition of his muscles and the darkness of his skin made his whole body appear sleek and elegant. He took long imperious strides across the Jenkins' lawn – now his lawn – and Drew watched the

motion of his calves and quads and his ample round butt, enamored of
the symphonic play of the man's muscles, tendons, and flesh. This,
Drew believed, must be what kings looked like when they walked
through the grand halls of their palaces – lofty, graceful, and
magisterial. The man had a frosty goatee that glared against his ebony
skin, bee-stung lips and a broad nose with large round nostrils. He wore
carpenter shorts, a sleeveless blue T-shirt and a black trilby, looking as
cool and sophisticated as some of the musicians in the pictures his
mother used to send from Chicago. After he carried the last cardboard
box out of his SUV and he closed his front door with his foot, Drew
and his grandfather heard the wheep-wheep of his car alarm.

"Neighborhood just went to shit," Drew's grandfather
mumbled before he spit into the cup.

# # # # #

Drew spent most of the next two weeks in his bedroom trying
to his ignore his grandfather's endless rants against affirmative action,
civil rights, rap music and Barack Obama. Drew graduated from high
school one month earlier, turned eighteen two months earlier, and aside
from his part-time job doing light custodial work at a local gym, he had
little else to keep him occupied. When he wasn't at work, he spent most
of his time in his room jacking off to muscle magazines. He kept a two
foot high stack of them on the floor beside his bed along with a bottle
of body lotion and a box of Kleenex. His house didn't have Internet
access; even if it did, Drew couldn't afford to buy a laptop, and his
grandfather certainly wouldn't buy one for him. He couldn't get his
hands on a gay porn magazine, but the muscle and fitness magazines he
bought at the grocery store or swiped from the gym provided him more
than enough masturbation material. The only men who aroused him
were bodybuilders so pumped full of steroids they resembled comic
book superheroes. The more muscle a man had the harder Drew's cock
got, especially if he was black, especially if his skin was a dark as
chocolate and his crotch bulged with a horse hung dick and nuts the
size of billiard balls.

Drew stretched out on his unmade bed one muggy night after
work and flipped through the glossy pages of the current issue of *Flex*.
Darrem Charles posed on the cover. A pecan brown juggernaut,
hairless and shiny, his Adonis physique was a harmonious symmetry of

engorged spherical muscles. Only a snug blue Speedo guarded him from complete nudity. The bodybuilders inside the magazine, oversized and half naked, were just as sexy as Darrem Charles and no less imposing. Their vascular, swollen bodies shined like the polished armor of gladiators. Each of them appealed to Drew, but the African American musclemen stirred a throbbing lust within him that others couldn't. Since he started working at the gym four months ago he had become enamored of a group of black bodybuilders who worked out there almost every day. All three – two with dark skin, the other with mocha skin – were lively and gregarious when they dressed and undressed in the locker room, but once they stepped onto the gym floor they communicated through a caveman's vocabulary of grunts and bellows as they hoisted the heaviest weights they could and slammed them on the rubberized floor so hard the entire building quaked. They performed incline dumbbell bench presses with one-hundred-twenty-pound weights, loaded eight forty-five-pound plates on the bar for squats, swung fifty pound dumbbells when they performed side lateral raises. Drew silently referred to them as The Warriors because he once overheard them discuss playing football a decade ago for the same high school where he had just graduated. The Marshall High School Warriors had a reputation for being a scrubby team, but Drew recalled hearing several teachers and coaches comment that years ago their football team ranked among the best in the state. As he ogled the formidable trio of hulking bodybuilders, Drew believed those claims.

Whenever they plodded into the men's locker room after a workout, toting plastic gallon jugs of water, distressed tan weight belts and dingy white lifting straps, he busied himself with some menial task that would allow him to spy on them as they stripped off their sweat-soaked gear and showered. When The Warriors ambled to the showers, Drew's heart beat faster and his chest warmed as if he had just swallowed a scalding cup of cocoa. He followed them, pretending to refill liquid soap dispensers and wipe down the tiles of the shower area with sanitizer while he took lustful sidelong glances at them. The Warriors, oblivious to his presence, lumbered ahead of him, talking about sports and laughing at crude jokes. Drew could smell the stench of their bodies: the sweat and funk accumulated from hours of persistent, strenuous weightlifting and rigorous cardiovascular exercise. He wondered if they smelled the same way after they fucked their girlfriends (from the bits of conversation he overheard they each seemed to have multiple girlfriends). When The Warriors walked to the showers, they sometimes wrapped short white towels around their waists; other times they carried the towel in hand and walked to the showers completely naked, unembarrassed to let the other men see their enlarged sculpted physiques, proud to exhibit their herculean bodies. The gym was so old the locker rooms still had communal showers. Warm sudsy water sluiced over their burly bodies, and Drew's cock stiffened when he saw The Warriors gathered around one of the old fashioned shower columns lathering and scrubbing from head to foot, pecs to lats, dick to ass. When they stroked their long dark cocks, Drew's eyes grew wide as each man's plump dick knocked against one husky thigh then struck the other thigh with a heavy pendulous movement like the clapper of a bell. Flaccid, their penises were longer and thicker than his penis when it was erect.

The Warriors populated many of Drew's raunchy fantasies, and as he lay in bed briskly stroking his six inch hard-on with a lotion-slick palm, he imagined himself on his knees in the locker room showers as The Warriors surrounded him and took turns shoving their dicks into his mouth. One prodigious black dick after another battled to fuck his boyish face, and when they tired of his moist pouty lips and wet tongue they pushed him to his hands and knees and gangbanged his virgin ass while they smacked his rump and called him their sweet little white boy. Drew tightened his grip on his cock, stroked faster and probed his anus with the middle finger of his left hand. He rocked and writhed in the bed, making the box springs yawn from exhaustion. He already shot three loads that day, but the wad building in his nuts as he fantasized about The Warriors felt just as potent as if he hadn't ejaculated in weeks. In Drew's mind, one of The Warriors slammed his stiff fat cock up his chute while he sucked off the other two, alternating from one cock to the other. Their muscles flexed and striated as they struggled not to splash his face with streams of molten cum before they each had a chance to stretch his apple shaped white boy ass. Suddenly, the two Warriors in front of him vanished. He felt another smack on his ass and turned to find the new neighbor from across the street rutting inside of him. Spasms of ecstasy seized his face as he packed Drew's ass with dick until he spattered the walls of Drew's rectum with cum. The thought of it brought Drew to the edge of his own convulsive orgasm, but he was forced to stop masturbating and put his shorts back on when his grandfather pounded on the bedroom door. He could smell Wild Turkey even before he opened the door.

"Slow as snails, boy."

"What, Granddad?"

The old man chucked a lightweight brown parcel into Drew's palm. "Run that across the street."

Drew read the address then lowered to box to his crotch, afraid his grandfather would see his erect penis though his boxers. "It's almost eleven."

"It's that colored guy's. No telling what kind of drugs or shit is in there. Get it out the house."

"You've been home all day? Why ain't you took it over?"

Drew watched his grandfather's hands and jowls jitter as he puffed on a stubby Pall Mall Red. He usually got the shakes whenever he drank too much. He slouched against the door frame and tried to give the old man back the box.

"I'll take it tomorrow."

"Hell you will. Ain't gonna have no more drug shit in my house. One nigger already got your ma on that shit. Get it out of here and tell him his shit better not turn up on my doorstep again."

Drew sniffed the package then shook it. It didn't make a sound. "Ain't no drugs in here, Granddad. It's late. Take this."

The old man pointed his cigarette at the nape of Drew's neck and began to gesture with it. Drew feared another burn. He had acquired several of them over the years, some from his grandfather's drunken stumbling, others the result of hastily plotted malice. Drew's elfin shape – he stood five-feet-six and weighed a scant one hundred thirty pounds – made him vulnerable to multiple injuries and abuses at the hands of not only his grandfather, but also a number of school bullies. Although he feigned a plucky assertiveness whenever an aggressor confronted him, they always seemed to see past the façade. He just wasn't good at defending himself.

His grandfather barked, "Do what the hell I tell you, boy!"

13

Arguing with the old man, particularly when booze and anger had gotten hold of him, was pointless. Resisting him would mean more shouting, more busted furniture, more flashing blue and red lights and conveniently explained bruises. Drew slipped on a pair of cargo shorts, a T-shirt and his Nikes and stepped across the street with the parcel in hand.

The new neighbor had already made improvements to the Jenkins' house. The lawn had been mowed, the hedges trimmed, and the porch railing painted light gray. The white SUV gleamed as it stood parked in the driveway, and a light shone in the living room. Drew stepped onto the porch, pushed the doorbell and nearly forgot why he came to the house when the new neighbor, the king, answered the door dressed only in a frayed pair of white boxer shorts. His nude torso, robust, sinewy and hairless, appeared much bigger than Drew had previously thought. His pecs, convex and thick, resembled large black concrete slabs, each dotted with a gumdrop size nipple. His shoulders were like boulders. With a flat, smooth stomach and the narrow waist of a pubescent boy, he was everything Drew fantasized about.

He stood in the doorway drinking a vanilla shake from a blender. As he lifted the blender to his mouth, Drew's eyes settled on a tattoo wrapped around his neighbor's arm: the equation $P=W/T$ in thick block letters. Drew watched him with his mouth agape, fumbling at the parcel. His palms had begun to sweat and stain the brown wrapping on the box.

"You the welcoming committee?"

"Um, are you Nelson Laramie?"

The man nodded and kept drinking from the blender.

"Hey, I live across the street, and we got this in the mail by mistake."

He handed Nelson the parcel and wiped his palms on his shorts.

Nelson read the return address on the parcel, stared at it curiously for a moment then extended his arm, holding the blender just inches from Drew's chest. "You mind?"

"Um, sure."

Drew took the blender and held it in both hands as if it were a bejeweled goblet. He smelled the vanilla, bananas and strawberries from the protein shake inside and scanned the length of Nelson's towering beefy physique.

When Nelson ripped open the package, he poured its contents into his large palm: a woman's gold watch, three rings and a pair of silver earrings. Drew noticed his eyes soften and glow. He thought Nelson might begin to cry, but instead his mouth formed a half-smile, as if giving a sarcastic reply to an off-color joke, and he scratched the side his goatee with his index finger. Almost unnaturally white, Drew thought Nelson's goatee made him look regal yet enigmatic. It matured his face and seemed wholly at odds with the rest of his strong athletic body, which exuded youth and virility. He wondered just how old Nelson was. "Nice jewelry."

"Nice, but not what I was looking for."

"eBay messed up?"

"Nah, my mother just passed away, and my sister sent me part of her jewelry collection. Well, everything except the one damn thing I asked for." Nelson sighed and put the jewelry back into the package.

"Sorry. About your mom and all." He quickly let his eyes travel up and down Nelson body again, committing as much of him to memory as he could, especially the bulge in Nelson's crotch. The action took less than a second and when he lifted his eyes Nelson was staring at him and grinning as if he knew Drew was cruising him. Drew's skin flushed, and he began to sweat more.

Nelson said, "Hot night, huh?"

Drew gripped the handle of the blender. "We ain't got air conditioning at home. Gotta use window fans."

"In this heat? Damn near eighty degrees tonight. That's messed up. Beat you get all hot and sticky, huh?"

Drew nodded. "I hate it."

"Really? I love it like this. The hotter the better. The heat just gets into your skin, man. Into your whole body. People walk around half naked and restless. I get horny as a motherfucker in summer."

15

Nelson tugged on his cock. Drew could see that it had gotten considerably larger. His own erection had sprung to life inside his jeans.

"Yep," Nelson continued, "nothing better on a night like this than some deep, hard fucking. Just getting your dick all the way up in somebody's guts, bouncing on the mattress, just slamming down on somebody; know what I mean?"

Drew's mouth went dry. His pellucid blue eyes widened for a brief moment before he turned his attention to the door frame, then the porch, then his Nikes. He scratched the back of his left calf with the top of his right Nike, and his eyes continued to rove self-consciously. He was unsure of where he should look, and as much as he wanted to he couldn't look at Nelson's body again. He felt rooted to the spot.

After a prolonged silence Nelson said, "So you live across the street?"

"Yeah. Me and my granddad." He pointed to the house and immediately felt embarrassed by the weeds that had overtaken the small garden his grandmother had planted before her death three years ago. Large random patches of dirt looked like spots where landmines had exploded in the overgrown lawn. Shingles dangled from the weather-beaten roof, and the entire façade of the house needed a fresh coat of paint. Nelson had barely lived in his house two weeks and it already been transformed into one of the best looking houses on the block. Nelson told Drew the house looked nice, but Drew felt he only said that to be nice. Their house was had always been little more than a junkyard and much less than a home.

"I've seen you riding your bike through the neighborhood," Nelson said. "Headed to your girl's house?"

"Me? No, I ride it to work."

"Looks like all that bike riding has been good to you. Got some damn nice calves, man."

Dimples punctuated each side of Drew's mouth. "They're not as big as yours."

"Seriously, man. You lift, too, don't you?"

"Well, I work at 24 Hour Fitness. I get a free membership, so I work out when I find time. Not regular."

"It shows. Nice calves, thighs." Nelson lightly placed a hand on Drew's shoulder and motioned for him to turn sideways.

Nelson chuckled and said, "You do lots of squats, too, I see."

A bead of sweat ran down Drew's temple. He wiped it with the back of his hand and shifted his weight from one foot to the other. He could have sworn Nelson groped his ass, but he hadn't touched him at all. The boy felt Nelson's hand gently stroke his upper back, a feeling that made him tingle and chill. His grandmother was the last person he had any physical contact with, and Nelson's touch, both comforting and sensuous, made him shiver despite the July swelter. He shut his eyes and enjoyed the feeling the way a hungry man savors his first taste of food. When he opened his eyes, he saw past Nelson through the open front door and into Nelson's living room. The blond hardwood floors glowed in the soft light, and the few pieces of furniture he glimpsed looked like they belonged in a magazine. The cool air drifting out beckoned to him. He didn't want to go home, but when he heard his grandfather yell, "Boy! Hey, boy! Get home now!" from across the street he knew he had to leave quickly. If he didn't, his grandfather would stagger over and make a scene.

"Gotta take off," Drew said.

"Thanks for bringing this over." Nelson gestured at the opened parcel still in his hand. "Come by one afternoon to cool off, Drew. Anytime."

"Get home now, boy!" With a cigarette in one hand and a bottle in the other, Drew's grandfather stumbled toward the curb.

"Yeah, I mean, thanks. I will."

"I'll make you a protein shake."

"Cool."

"But first, I need my blender back."

Drew was nearly at the bottom of the porch steps when he realized he was still holding Nelson's blender. He trotted back up the steps and handed it to Nelson before he sprinted across the street and ran past his grandfather so fast the old man may as well have been invisible.

# # # # #

The Warriors had spent the last hour in the gym working out their chests and triceps, lying and sitting on various benches and Nautilus machines. They never wiped down the equipment after they used it, but Drew liked that they didn't. He had just finished his shift and was working out on the same machines. He enjoyed being in the same space they had occupied only moments earlier. The dull gray upholstered benches and seats had absorbed The Warriors' sweat and body heat. Drew delighted in mingling his perspiration with theirs as he struggled and strained to hoist extremely heavy weights. Nelson's compliments the other night protracted his muscle lust and renewed his interest in building his own body. He thought gaining strength, mass and definition, in a way, helped bring him closer to The Warriors and Nelson as well. If he couldn't be a part of them sexually, he could enter their world in another way; eventually, he could substitute his own beefed up body for theirs and use it to satisfy his lust.

He lay on a flat bench beneath a barbell loaded with the maximum weight he could bench press, one hundred pounds. Ordinarily he would barely have been able to perform four reps with this much weight on the bar, but with The Warriors huddled around a peck deck nearby and Nelson's words solidifying in his mind, he was able to lift the barbell for ten easy reps. When he re-racked the barbell and sat up, his breaths heavy, his face red and sweaty, one of The Warriors nodded at him. Drew nodded back. A smile, both from self-satisfaction and gladness over finally being acknowledged by one of The Warriors, curled the corners of his mouth, but he quickly let it fade, remembering that hardcore lifters, the kind he wanted to be, never smiled. He got up, and feeling ambitious, added twenty more pounds to the bar. He lay on the bench again, determined to match his previous efforts, but when he lifted the barbell, his arms failed him, and the barbell descended. It would have destroyed his windpipe and may very well have killed him if someone hadn't quickly grasped the bar, helped Drew lift it and placed it back on the rack.

"You okay, man?"

Drew looked up and saw Nelson looking down at him. He sat up on the bench and caught his breath.

"Going kind of heavy, huh?" Nelson asked.

"That's what I get for not using a spotter." His face was bright red, as much from embarrassment as the strain of trying to hoist the barbell. He wondered if The Warriors had seen, but none of them was around. The rest of the semi-crowded gym members, oblivious to what nearly happened, continued with their own workouts.

"Gotta remember to get a spot, man." Nelson patted him on the shoulder and smiled. He wore white workout shorts and a sleeveless white T-shirt, looking more like an overdeveloped tennis player than a bodybuilder.

"When'd you start working out here?" Drew asked.

"Just yesterday. Missed seeing you."

"Yeah, I was off. Anyway I'm just a janitor. I'm not supposed to be seen."

Nelson scanned Drew's whole body and, smirking, bit his lower lip. "You can't hide what the Lord provides. Hitting chest, huh?"

Drew nodded. "Gotta hit my quads, too."

"Lots of squats, I hope."

Drew broke his rule against smiling and took another look at Nelson's tattoo. "P=W/T? What's that?"

"Physics equation. Power equals work over time. Got it in the army years ago."

"Why that?"

"I teach physics. Just got hired at UMKC. And I like the reminder, what power really means."

"I wasn't never good at science."

"I think you may have other talents." Nelson stroked his snowy goatee and gave him a soft, playful punch in the arm before he went to the preacher curl machine and started curling the heaviest weight on the stack.

An hour later, Drew decided to shower and bike home. He was disappointed that The Warriors had already left. He hoped instead that he would find Nelson in the showers, but he wasn't in the locker room either. It was nearly closing time, and the locker room was practically empty except for him and two other men, both of them old enough to be his grandfather. He took a quick shower and decided to sit in the steam room for a few moments. Every muscle of his body was sore and pumped from his long workout, and he wanted to loosen them and relax a little before he went home to confront the squalid house and his grandfather's latest drunken tirade. Whenever Drew stepped into the steam room, he always imagined he was walking into a cloud. He was blinded by whiteness, and after the cool shower, the heat felt good on his body. He groped around for the bench and when he took a seat he heard a deep voice say, "Been waiting for you, baby."

Nelson's body, magnificent, dark and naked, emerged from the smoke on the opposite bench. He sat on a white towel and stroked his huge hard dick while he leered at Drew with a half-smile.

"You want some Daddy cock, don't you boy?"

Drew's mouth dried. In spite of the steam room's blistering heat cold tremors went through him. He fixed his gaze on Nelson's coal black dick poking through the dense steam like a tower emerging from the fog of a great city. His own erect penis twitched beneath his towel, and he squeezed it, desiring Nelson's body as he had desired nothing else. Yet something in his mind, a particle of fear or self-consciousness or propriety, paralyzed him on his side of the steam room. The distance between his impish white body and Nelson's titanic black body seemed impassable even though only five feet separated them.

Nelson continued to stroke and squeeze his long, swollen dick. "Scared?"

Drew rested the chuff of his hands on the edge of the wooden bench and gripped it firmly. "I've cleaned up cum in here before."

"Yours?"

"Only at home. In bed."

"No one else's?"

"Ain't never had the chance with nobody else."

"Nobody? As much as these cats be checking you out? Damn! Come on, baby, let me hit that."

Drew looked at the door then looked back at Nelson. "I need my job. You want me; you take me home ... to your bed."

# # # # #

Thirty minutes later, they were kissing and rolling around naked in Nelson's king size bed. Nelson's goatee wasn't coarse and bristly as Drew imagined it might be; its softness made him kiss Nelson more passionately. Nelson ran the tip of his finger inside Drew's mouth. The boy sucked it for a moment then plunged his tongue into Nelson's mouth. As he lay on top of Nelson, Drew felt Nelson's hard dick press against his stomach, the mushroom head jabbing at his rib cage. Nelson's tongue fluttered in Drew's mouth, and he winced when Nelson's index finger penetrated his asshole. "So fucking tight," Nelson whispered.

Drew raised and lowered his hips, allowing Nelson's plump finger to probe deeper and deeper until Drew felt it stroke his prostrate, making the boy shudder and groan.

"You like that, boy?"

"Mmm hmm."

"Never had a cock up there?" Nelson kissed the boy's chin.

"No." Drew reached behind and began to jerk Nelson's wide dick. Nelson took his finger out of Drew's ass and dry humped him for a few minutes while they kissed, then he whispered, "Go down." Drew lowered himself to Nelson's enormous tool and took the head into his mouth. He opened his mouth wide, so he could cram in as much of Nelson's cock as he could, but he could only manage four or five inches before he gagged. He had never taken a man's penis into his mouth before, and Nelson's silence made him doubt his skill, but when Nelson put his hand on the back of Drew's head and began to moan Drew knew he was pleasing him. Saliva collected just under the boy's tongue, and he stopped sucking long enough to let the spit seep out of his mouth and trail down every stiff inch of Nelson's enlarged dick. Once he had gotten it slick, he took the member in his hand and gave it several swift, hard jerks, squeezing it at the tip and swirling his tongue

21

around the head. He was both fascinated and intimidated by the size of Nelson's penis, its immense girth and heft.

Nelson collected Drew in his bulky arms and with the quick agility of a seasoned wrestler flipped him over and pinned him to the mattress. Drew wrapped his slender arms and legs around Nelson as he slid his dick between the boy's butt cheeks. Nelson hoisted Drew's ass in the air and plunged his tongue into his hole, flicking and swirling while Drew jerked off with his eyes closed. Nelson put two fingers inside the boy and stretched; Drew winced again.

"Goddamn," Nelson said, "I can't wait anymore."

He got up on his knees, squeezed a generous amount of lube from the bottle on the nightstand onto Drew's hole and his dick, grabbed his cock at the base, and pressed the head against Drew's tightly coiled anus until Drew cried out and told him to stop.

"Come on, baby. I'll go slow."

"You' re so big, man. I can't take all that."

"Just relax."

"I want to but, hell, I ain't ... I ain't never been fucked before." He fought back tears. "I want to, Nelson, but ..."

Nelson gently placed a hand on the side of Drew's face then lowered his head and kissed him. He moved his dick back and forth in the boy's ass crack, slowly at first then so fast the mattress squeaked. The walls absorbed their manic panting, huffing and grunting. Drew held on to Nelson's hard ass as it rose and fell between his splayed legs with the intense unremitting rhythm of a locomotive. Nelson shouted, "Shit! Uhhh!" and dug his hips down deep. Drew felt Nelson's hot cum fill his anal cleft.

# # # # #

They spent the next two weeks having sex once or twice a day at Nelson's house, usually at night after they both left the gym. Each time, Nelson fingered Drew's anus until he got used to the feeling. Drew lay on his back with his heels in the air and listened as Nelson spoke soothing words of encouragement: "You're doing good, boy. Let yourself feel good. Breathe and relax. You can take it." Their sex was rigorous and prolonged and left them both more tired and sore than their workouts at the gym. Nelson always asked Drew to spend the night, but he never did. His grandfather had begun to question him about why he arrived home from work later and later each night, and although the old man spent most of his waking hours staggering around drunk, he was a nosy, shrewd old buzzard who not only caused trouble but knew how to work it to his advantage, evidenced by the settlement checks he had scammed over the years. So after spending hours kissing, sucking, jerking off and dry humping with Nelson, Drew dressed and crept out of his bedroom once he had fallen asleep, then crossed the empty, dark street and silently entered his grandfather's house with the stealth of a career burglar. He snuck upstairs to his bedroom, undressed and got into bed. A box fan whirred in the window, but his bedroom felt as hot and sticky as his Daddy's cum still coating his lips and tongue. He savored its salty goodness as he fell to sleep.

It was on one of these nights, just as Drew lay down and began to dream about Nelson, that his grandfather kicked in his bedroom door and screamed, "You goddamn faggot!"

Drew got up so fast he nearly fell out of bed. "What the hell?"

"Seen you in that bastard's car tonight. I seen you. Kissing on that black son of a bitch."

The old man rushed into the room. Drew braced himself against the wooden headboard just before his grandfather balled his hand into a fist and punched him in his left eye. He reeled back and scrambled to the foot of the bed while his grandfather punched him again and again and again, landing blows all over his head, neck, back and chest.

"You little faggot bitch! Sucking nigger dick! I'll kill you! Kill both of you!"

This beating had been like nothing his grandfather had ever given him. Usually it was just a slap, at most a few lashes with a thick leather belt. But the old man found strength Drew never knew he had. He had gone mad with rage. Drew wailed, "Stop! Get off me!" and tried to stand, but the torrent of violence his grandfather unleashed on him was unrelenting. Tired of using his fists, the old man began taking objects from the nightstand and throwing them at Drew: first a lamp, then the digital alarm clock, the framed photographs of his mother and grandmother. Drew cowered in a corner covering his head with his arms. Blood splattered the walls as if they were crying for him.

"Nigger lovin' faggot!"

"Stop, Granddad!"

"Faggot!"

He kicked the boy in the back twice.

"Whore for niggers, just like your mama! Faggot whore!"

Another kick.

"I'll show you what you are, boy," he grunted. "I'll show you, all right."

The old man unbuckled his belt and began to undo his pants. Drew lowered his arms and his head and saw his grandfather stuff in hands inside of his underwear. Drew's muscles tensed and enflamed. He leapt out of the corner and tackled his grandfather to the floor. They struggled for a several minutes before Drew pinned him to the ground.

Nose to nose, Drew blared in the old man's face. "Fuck you, asshole! You ain't shit! Old drunk asshole! You ain't hittin' me NO MORE!"

He spotted the alarm clock beside them on the floor, snatched it up and held it in the air, ready to bring it down on the old man's head.

"You better kill me, boy. Rather be dead than have a faggot grandson. Go on and do it. Kill me."

Drew breathed through clenched teeth. He straddled his grandfather's chest, keeping one hand on the old man's shoulder. The other hand gripped the alarm clock only inches from his grandfather's temple. Drew's arms shook, and his eyes welled with tears. His grandfather stopped squirming and lay beneath him silent and defeated, ready to let Drew bash his brains in. Drew threw the alarm clock against the wall; it shattered into uncountable pieces. He rose and dressed, ignoring the pain that cried out from every part of his battered body and went back to Nelson's house.

# # # # #

24

He spent an hour talking Nelson out of going across the street to beat up his grandfather. They went to the emergency room, and after the doctor treated him, they returned to Nelson's house. Drew slept for most of the day. He woke around six the next evening and found all of his belongings in Nelson's bedroom. Nelson sat beside him with a tray of food. "How'd you get my stuff?"

"Me and your granddad had a talk. I didn't kill him ... unfortunately."

Drew sat up. "What did he say?"

"Not a damn thing. I walked in, told him you were coming to live with me, and if he tried to cause trouble, I'd break my foot off in his ass. I got as much of your stuff as I could. We'll replace anything you're missing. Eat some soup while it's hot."

Drew leaned forward and kissed Nelson's thick soft lips. "Daddy, I love you."

Nelson put the tray aside and lay with Drew in bed. They took off their clothes, lay side by side facing each other, holding, kissing and fondling, each inhaling the breath the other exhaled. Nelson softly rested his hand on Drew's bruised hip, but Drew took it and moved it to his ass.

"It's time, Daddy."

"You've had enough pain. I don't want to give you more."

"You could never hurt me. I know that. I need you inside of me."

Drew grasped Nelson's throbbing hard cock and slowly pulled on it. Nelson took a bottle of lube from a drawer in the nightstand and applied some to his cock and Drew's anus; he fingered Drew carefully and deep, just as he had been doing for the last two weeks, first one finger, then another until Drew felt all four of Nelson's fingers filling and stretching his ass. He groaned and panted, "Now, Daddy. I need you in me now."

Nelson rolled onto his back and told Drew to get on top of him. "It'll be easier this way, baby."

25

Drew lay on top of Nelson and slowly lowered himself onto Nelson's rock hard dick. He breathed deeply, relaxed his sphincter, pressed down. After a few minutes of squirming, he eventually took his Daddy's massive cock inside of his virgin hole. They moaned simultaneously once their bodies finally merged and quickly found their rhythm. For Drew, the feeling of being filled with a man's dick for the very first time sent tremors through him. It was like taking a dumbbell into his body. Although he and Nelson had been preparing for this moment, Drew still experienced a little bit of pain and discomfort. He remembered Nelson's instructions: he breathed deeply and press down like he had to empty his bowels. Drew's plump ass rose and fell on Nelson's stiff dark dick at a slow pace, but once he had become accustomed to the feeling and the pain subsided, he began to ride Nelson's cock faster. Nelson countered Drew's quick movements and thrust his cock deeper into Drew's rectum. Soon the aggressive slapping of their bodies filled the room. Drew's fingers clenched the fleshy mounds of Nelson's pectorals as he gnashed his teeth and grunted.

"Get on your knees, boy."

Nelson maneuvered him to his knees. Drew arched his back as much as he could. Once Nelson mounted him, sliding his wide dick into Drew's slick asshole, he placed his hands on Drew's ass, bent down and whispered in his ear, "You're ass is smooth as a pearl."

"I love you, Daddy."

"I love you too, son."

Nelson spread his cheeks wide, so he could penetrate him as deep as possible. Before long, Drew could feel the head of Nelson's cock bumping against his prostate; the pleasure became so intense that he took his right hand and began to masturbate.

"Yeah, boy," Nelson said, "Jack your dick hard."

"Feels so damn good, Daddy."

"Yeah?"

"Uh huh."

"Daddy's getting close, son. Oh, shit!"

Drew felt Nelson's strong hands grab his shoulder just before cum flooded his ass and dripped down his hairy balls. Nelson grunted and kept pushing his semen into Drew.

"Aw, yeah, Daddy!"

Still on his knees, Drew's cum shot out of him in explosive bursts. He heaved and convulsed before he felt his body tingle and warm all over. Nelson stippled his spine with soft wet kisses all the way up his neck. Drew continued to tighten his anus around Nelson's hard dick. They collapsed on the sodden bed as limp and speechless as newborns.

# # # # #

It was a tough lift. The bar was loaded with four forty-five-pound plates and ten-pound plates, over two-hundred pounds in all. Nelson stood at the head of the bench as proud and cautious as a father. His legs bent slightly, he held his palms face up beneath the bar, ready to catch it if Drew reached failure too early. Even The Warriors crowded around to watch and offer encouragement. Drew lay on the bench, counted to three and hefted the bar off the rack. To everyone's surprise, he forced out more than the four reps he had planned to lift. He was going for a seventh rep when his arms began to shake and his face turned red.

"You got it," Nelson said. "Come on, Drew, lift it. Lift it!"

Drew's body absorbed the pain, used it, converted it into power. "Arrrrrrrgggggghhhhh!"

THE BOXER AND THE BANKER

By Jay Starre

Kevin would never look at a gym the same after that afternoon.

Sparkling clean or grubby, full of high-tech machines or merely barbells and dumbbells, full of preening muscle-bound gym gods or empty save one lean, whirling kick-boxer – it wouldn't matter for him. Because he knew what could happen.

Unexpected stuff, hot and nasty stuff.

The stocky red-head peered through a dust-grimed window as he hesitated at the door of the building at the end of the quiet street. Inside, a figure moved, arms flailing, feet flying, fists punching.

He looked closer, his heart beating faster. Dressed in boxer trunks, but otherwise naked, the figure inside faced a dangling body bag. Bare fists clenched, lean body poised, he danced on naked feet for a moment before launching into another series of punches and kicks that pummeled the bag in front of him.

Kevin's cock soared, stretching the front of his hiking shorts. The guy was a whirling blur of taut muscle, amber-smooth and tight-waisted. A solid butt filled the green silk shorts.

Should he go in? He was definitely enjoying the show, and would enjoy more ... as much more as he could get! He hesitated. He was a little intimidated by the lean and mean boxer and honestly not impressed by the run-down look of the place. He almost turned away. But, his stiff cock throbbed against his belly, and he gave in.

He pulled open the door, setting off a jingling bell that had the kick-boxer whirling to face him. His heart pounded as he blurted out his reason for interrupting. "Hi. I'm Kevin. The dude at my motel told me I could work out here. Are you the manager?"

Sweat dripped down a strong nose and over pursed, red lips. Dark eyes stared at Kevin from under darker brows. Raven-black hair, buzzed up around his ears, turned thick and wavy on top.

"Yep. I'm Bruno. Five bucks gets you weights and a shower room. Make yourself at home."

With that said, he whirled around and returned to his intense workout. Kevin's hard-on hadn't subsided, and he was acutely aware of the bulge in his shorts as he fished out his five bucks and deposited it on a bare counter just inside the door.

The young banker had escaped a sweltering summer and his downtown Chicago office job for a week in the Michigan lake country. After a little exploring, he ended up at a quaint motel on the shores of an inland lake. The hiking had been great, but he'd missed his regular weight-training. So, here he was.

The room was large with a high ceiling and a pair of fans whirling, weights and workout benches scattered along walls covered in either cracked mirrors or peeling paint. In the far corner, a roped-off boxing ring perched above the floor.

Not too inviting, but his hard-on insisted it was just fine, for five bucks at least. He peeled off his T-shirt and left it with his backpack on a rickety chair. The bench press looked serviceable and surprisingly clean. He plopped down on it and began to warm-up with just the bar.

No respectable gym would let you work out shirt-less, and he was enjoying the sensual feel of the smooth vinyl under him as he raised and lowered the bar, breathing rhythmically and getting his blood pumping. His stiff cock twitched when he glanced to the side and watched Bruno gyrate in a blur of semi-nude athleticism.

That boxer's ass was amazing. It swelled out from his lean waist, a pair of compact melons just crying out to be squeezed, spread, and explored. All that leaping had the round can clenching and jiggling.

That incredible show went on as Kevin slowly warmed up on the bench with the bar, then wasted more time adding a few plates at a time and trying not to gawk too blatantly. He was unsuccessful in that, unable to tear his eyes away from that gorgeous body on display.

It seemed as if the tireless boxer was working himself up to a climax as he increased the speed and intricacy of his punches. Flying feet slammed the body bag, then all at once in an astounding display, whirled through the air and sent Bruno landing in a crouch facing Kevin.

Their eyes met across the dozen paces that separated them.

"If you want a piece of this ass, you gotta give up yours first. I can throw a real mean fuck. Can you take it?"

He gasped, totally caught off-guard. Of course he realized where that sudden proposition came from. He was flat on his back. His boner jerked against the fly of his baggy shorts, obvious as hell. He'd been staring conspicuously at the lean boxer and hadn't even bothered to press the weights on the bar now idle on the rack above his head. Bruno would have been an idiot not to notice.

The boxer offered a crooked grin, jet-black eyes hooded under the thin brows. His body was poised, as if ready to attack – or fuck like hell.

The blue-eyed banker was momentarily speechless. He remained a little intimidated by the boxer and perhaps a little frightened. Besides, he wasn't one to make rash decisions. But, he also knew that about himself and more than once had vowed to become more adventurous.

And, the dude was absolutely fucking gorgeous! He'd be a fool to pass up the opportunity to find out what the boxer was made of.

"Uh, OK. Why not? Let's see if you can deliver on that promise."

Even as the words came out of his mouth, Kevin wondered if he'd regret them. Bruno was across the floor and hovering over him in a split second, sweat coating his clenched muscles, hooded eyes roaming over his prone body,

The boxer exuded power and energy. Kevin knew he was going to get fucked but had no idea how fucked he was about to get. Those

31

flying fists lashed out in a blur and attacked the waist of his shorts, unbuttoning and yanking so fast he let out a little yelp as his ass was lifted, and he was stripped right there on the bench in the blink of an eye.

Shorts and underwear flew off his feet and landed on the wooden floor. His rearing cock jerked on his belly, and his asshole twitched as the boxer grasped both his ankles and pushed them back against his chest. Just like that, he was naked and pinned against the workout bench.

Ass wide open.

"What if someone comes in and sees us?" He blurted out, all too aware of his nasty position and the unlocked door across the room. He might have decided to become more adventurous, but he was still fairly conservative at heart.

Bruno leaned over him, straddling the bench, fingers clasped tightly around his ankles. Sweat dripped down to land on his gaping mouth, and he found himself licking it off his lips. Bold dark eyes bored into his bright blue ones, slightly menacing, then the wide mouth grinned and the boxer let out a little chuckle.

"You're the only one to come in here since yesterday. But I'll lock the door if it makes you feel any better."

Bruno didn't wait for an answer. Whirling around, he abandoned Kevin there on the bench to trot over to the door and latch it shut. Blinds snapped closed over the dusty window before the boxer was trotting back to a trembling Kevin still sprawled on the workout bench.

On his way, the Italian snatched up a pair of wrist bands from a big tin bucket along the wall. Kevin realized what they were for when the boxer straddled him again and seized his left hand first, attaching it to the weight bar above his head with the Velcro straps. The right was attached immediately afterwards.

He straddled the bench, silken shorts pressing against Kevin's bent-back thighs. His fingers, sweaty and powerful, grasped an ankle in each hand pushing back so that Kevin's feet and hands touched.

He grinned down at the prostrate Chicago banker and began to thrust his crotch against his naked, wide-open crack. The sensual feel of silk shorts against his bare flesh was punctuated by the firm column of meat beneath, throbbing with a rapid beat as it thrust up down against his spread crack and twitching asshole.

Kevin tried to smile back up at that hovering face, but it was difficult. He felt totally overpowered, and it had happened so quickly! He was actually much bigger than the lean boxer. Although not much taller, regular weight-training had bulked up his naturally stocky body. He outweighed Bruno by at least twenty-five pounds.

"How's that cock feel? You want it up your butt?"

He nodded rapidly, unable to speak with those dark eyes boring into his, that moist mouth hovering just above and that stiff meat thrusting up and down between his spread ass-cheeks.

Bruno winked and chuckled again as he released one ankle and reached down to fish out his cock.

The heated spear rubbed directly against Kevin's naked crack! Up and down along the sweaty crevice, it probed across pouting ass-lips and banged against dangling nads.

He tore his eyes from the boxer's and peered down toward their mashed crotches. He just got a glimpse of that tantalizing cock as it pumped along his crack. Uncut, the hood slid back to expose the dribbling slit and tapered crown with every upward shove. Not so fat, but long. Very long!

Not only a red-head, but a real carrot-top, Kevin's pinkish-pale skin was dotted with tons of freckles from the summer sun. Bruno's amber flesh was dark against it, his cock even darker with the flush of lust turning it deep crimson.

Not only their bodies and coloring were different, their features and expressions were, too. Kevin had an oval, slightly chubby face with a button nose and a round pink mouth emphasized by a trimmed red goatee. His red-orange hair was fine and fuzzy and neat against his skull. He usually smiled easily, an aid to his job serving the public at the bank.

Bruno seemed the typical loner. His bold features were almost menacing. He'd only smiled twice briefly, yet hadn't been frowning or scowling either. His expression was sort of neutral. He appeared focused, self-contained.

Until now, at least. Lust brightened that dark complexion and set the black eyes glittering. The red mouth was pursed and slightly wet. Still focused, all right, but far from self-contained. He looked like he was about to explode – or fuck like hell!

Kevin groaned as the slippery crown of Bruno's cock thrust across and massaged his exposed asshole. The red mouth came down to crush his, tongue stabbing inside. Cock-head rubbed against his hole. Was the kick-boxer going to dry-fuck him?

A brief moment of intense tongue-drilling left him gasping before Bruno abruptly pulled up and slithered downwards. His mouth clamped over Kevin's twitching hard-on. Lips and tongue attacked, slurping and swallowing. A fingertip rubbed against the entrance to his asshole, roughly stretching the pouting port.

The mouth came up off his cock with a nasty slurp. A wink from his assailant, followed by a fleeting grin that totally altered his appearance, was again followed by that mouth descending to clamp over his throbbing asshole. Tongue stabbed while lips sucked furiously.

He shook from head to toe as he perched on the bench, his feet up in the air, his wrists attached to the weight bar. Bruno's wet mouth had assaulted his own mouth, his cock and now his asshole in rapid succession. What next?

The kick-boxer answered his silent question. "Time for cock!"

He bounded up and away, a seemingly tireless bundle of energy. His taut body glistened with sweat, every muscle etched in amber. His snug silk shorts were pulled down in front where his stiff cock reared out and upward, but his sexy butt-cheeks were still hidden behind the bright emerald. He was at a sink against the wall in a flash and snatching up a bottle of hand cream, turning and trotting back, and once more straddling Kevin in mere moments.

Now, he actually laughed out loud, and Kevin flushed brightly as he attempted to smile up at the bundle of lean muscle poised to fuck him. Still, no less menacing and no less alluring!

He squirted out a stream of white cream over the red-head's pale butt-crack. Hairless and smooth and devoid of the freckles that dotted the rest of his body, the spread cheeks quivered and the pink hole pouted. Already wet from the lips and tongue that recently attacked it, the slot now drooled hand cream.

Kevin groaned as he saw the look in Bruno's dark eyes. Intense! Hungry!

He returned to the attack just like that. Dropping the bottle of cream to the floor, he grabbed the backs of Kevin's knees, and thrust against him with his lean hips. That rearing dark cock slammed into cream-lubed hole, the tapered crown dividing ass-lips as it burrowed deep in a gut-churning punch of pulsing flesh.

"I'm so fucked," he blurted out as that cock began to drive in and out in a furious pummeling.

Bent backwards in half, held in place by wrist-straps and powerful hands on his legs, split in two by a pounding cock, buried in lean, sweaty muscle, he could barely catch his breath as Bruno laid into him with grunting enthusiasm.

He was certainly delivering on his promise to throw a real mean fuck – and little did Kevin know, he was just getting started.

Every slam forward had that lengthy bone driving deeper into his gut, causing his own cock to jerk and leak on his belly. He moaned and tossed his head, gripping the bar above with his fingers, wrists attached. Cock rammed deeper and deeper. Sweat flew from Bruno's dark brows and splattered him from head to crotch.

A seemingly endless succession of those wild gut-punches had the red-headed banker slobbering and grunting helplessly before all at once the boxer decided to change it up.

"Get on your belly. I want to see that white ass while I fuck it."

The demand was followed by a flurry of activity. The kick-boxer released his wrists, yanking his cock from Kevin's aching hole at the same time. He stood up, practically leapt out of his shorts to finally reveal his compact waist and rounded amber butt, then immediately grabbed hold of the red-head's knees and twisted, flipping him over onto his stomach.

Kevin was on his belly straddling the bench, flushed white butt rising and falling as he gasped for air and trembled all over awaiting the kick-boxer's next attack. It came quickly.

Hands seized his solid ass-cheeks, spreading them wide over the bench. The sound of more squirting hand cream barely preceded the ramming thrust of cock.

"Oh yeah. Take it to the balls."

That lengthy rod rammed home in one aching lunge. He grunted, blue eyes bulging, ass on fire. The sudden, deep penetration had him gripping the bench with clenched fingers, mouth open and asshole throbbing.

That cock was yanked right back out, leaving him gaping and empty. More cream landed on his battered hole as powerful fingers held his ass-cheeks apart. Cock slammed home again.

"Uhhhnnnnnn ... how long is that thing?" he blurted out as the head burrowed somewhere way up inside him.

"One fucking foot long," Bruno grunted out.

He knew it couldn't be true, but it was easy to imagine a foot of cock slamming into him. The kick-boxer continued to thrust balls-deep, pull all the way out, then jab home again. Kevin rocked on the bench under the anal assault with every lunge, now dripping as much sweat as the Italian.

His cock slithered under his belly, rubbing against the vinyl in a rough rhythm. The ache of stiff meat slamming into him combined with that slippery massage of his cock. He began to feel as if he just might blow a load at any moment.

But, the kick-boxer was far from finished with him. The hands on his ass slid up to his waist and pulled, yanking him up off the bench and onto shaky feet. "Get over there against the boxing ring. I want you standing up."

Kevin stumbled over to the ring, his cock lurching ahead of him, his battered butt-hole aching. Bruno was right behind.

A palm gripped the back of his head and shoved him forward. He was bent over the waist-high floor of the ring, feet kicked apart, as cock once more slammed right up into his throbbing asshole.

Bruno drilled Kevin's ass, hand cream squishing and dripping down his inner thighs. His head was held down by a strong hand, his legs pushed wide by lean thighs, another hand around his waist pumping his cock and yanking on his nuts.

He grunted with every violent thrust as hips slammed his butt with loud smacks. Bruno fucked faster, and it seemed certain the kick-boxer was working himself up to a wild orgasm.

But no, not yet. "Get up in the ring. I want you on your hands and knees."

A pair of hands seized his butt-cheeks and heaved. He was shoved up under the ropes and dumped on the ring floor. He'd just managed to crawl up onto his hands and knees and glance back when he realized Bruno was already there, standing behind him.

A crooked smirk was followed by the sudden thrust of a foot in his raised ass. A big toe jabbed at his asshole as Bruno laughed out loud. Kevin groaned and flushed, unable to keep from wriggling his white butt around that toe and realizing how much he wanted more! More of the furious fuck the kick-boxer was delivering so savagely.

In an instant, the Italian was down on his knees, then sliding his lean arms up under Kevin's armpits to grip his freckled body in a close embrace, hands curling up to clasp each other behind the red-head's neck.

Knees slid between his and shoved them wide, cock found and penetrated his asshole as sweaty hips slammed forward to slap against his ass. Bruno went right back to pummeling ass, in and out, balls-deep.

Kevin heaved against that tight embrace, gasping for breath. The pounding of his prostate and constant rubbing of his asshole had him burning up all over. He knew if the boxer even touched his cock, he'd spew.

He felt himself being rolled over, groaning as he sprawled on his side, the boxer's arms still under his armpits and hands around the back of his neck. Cock rammed into him from behind as Bruno's powerful hips jack-hammered his butt from the side.

He lifted one knee himself to open up his crack as that insistent cock drove into him. The ache in his guts was constant now, a plateau of heated pleasure reached as the Italian again twisted and turned. Now, Kevin was on top, sprawled out over Bruno on his back as cock thrust up into him.

"Sit on it. Ride it. Show me how much you love that cock up your butt."

The hands around his neck loosened. He took a deep breath and struggled upright. He was now squatting over the prone kick-boxer, cock up his ass. He faced Bruno's feet as he began to follow his orders. Planting both hands on the ring floor, he raised and lowered himself over the Italian's cock.

"Damn! It's so fucking long," he grunted out as he fucked himself over the stiff thing.

But he seemed to have caught Bruno's furious fuck-fever. He spotted that bottle of hand cream to their right; apparently Bruno had brought it with them. He snatched it up with one hand and reached behind to squirt more down over his own ass and the cock buried up it.

The carrot-topped banker tossed back his head, closed his blue eyes and rode cock. He rose and fell over the kick-boxer's long shank in a gut-churning grind, slamming down to impale himself to the balls, lifting himself up so that the tapered head just stretched his aching sphincter, then driving back down to bang against Bruno's crotch.

"Now it's your turn," Bruno suddenly growled.

He barely had time to catch his breath before he was dumped onto his back, and Bruno was squatting over him. What now?

A brief glimpse of dark eyes, menacing grin, and then the Italian turned and squatted over Kevin. That gorgeous compact butt spread apart and a snug hole pouted as he reached back between his thighs and grabbed hold of Kevin's cock with one hand and groped for the nearby bottle of hand cream with the other. A hasty but generous squirt coated Kevin's rather blunt and fat hard-on.

With no preliminary, Bruno then shoved cock up his tight hole and sat down on it. Kevin actually squealed as steamy innards clamped around his bone. But, that was just the beginning. Bruno began to ride Kevin's cock at a furious pace. He put the red-head's own attempt to shame as his tight frame drove up and down, slamming Kevin's body into the ring floor, snug hole massaging his throbbing cock in a torrid embrace.

Bruno's awesome ass clenched and jiggled as he fucked himself, the prone red-head mesmerized by the hot sight. Those amber butt-cheeks were so damn firm, as was the rest of his sweat-soaked body. He was a lean work of art.

The kick-boxer abruptly twisted around, cock still up his ass, and faced him.

"Here it comes. Here's my load."

That impossibly long purple bone erupted, untouched, as Bruno slammed his body down over Kevin's. A spray of cum splattered Kevin, coating his heaving torso in gooey nut-juice.

The kick-boxer's asshole squeezed the hell out of Kevin's cock as he unloaded, and that sensation along with the exciting vision of Bruno's taut body quivering in orgasm triggered his own release.

He let loose, grunting as he unloaded far up the kick-boxer's convulsing hole.

Barely coherent, Kevin sprawled out on the floor of the boxing ring. He'd been fucked every which way possible, first by the crazed boxer's cock, then by his impossibly tight asshole.

Bruno's dark eyes stared down at him. Somehow, the well-fucked banker knew there would be more.

He'd vowed to become more adventurous. So, why not?

"I've never been fucked upside down. Have you?"

Bruno's laughter echoed in the empty gym. Kevin knew he'd recall that laughter for years to come.

And never, ever see a gym in the same way.

MARATHON SESSION
By HL Champa

The sky filled with angry black clouds, as we circled the three-mile long gray path. I could hear Pete's heavy breathing next to me, see his firm, muscled legs flexing with each step. Training for the marathon was his idea, of course. I rued the day he became a personal trainer. Not that all that working out didn't have its benefits. His ass never looked better, and it was pretty good before. Watching him try out new squat techniques and finish every day with crunches was doing wonders for our sex life. Now, Pete was hell-bent on whipping me into shape, unfortunately for me, with actual exercise. While working out together sounded fun in theory, the practice was anything but. In the nine months since he started torturing me, I exercised more than I had in my whole life. Free weights and cardio at the gym, yoga on Thursdays, even Pilates sometimes. I started to look damn good, but still not as good as Pete.

The marathon, well, that was more of a dare than anything else. He said I couldn't do it. I ignored him at first, not taking the bait. He kept pushing me, wearing me down until in a weak moment, with his cock buried deep in my ass, I relented and agreed to run his stupid marathon. I regretted calling his bluff a little bit more with each lap I had to do. We ran every day, and while it had gotten easier, Pete could still run circles around me if he wanted to. He stuck with me, most of the time because he knew it was the only way to get me to keep running. After all this time, I was still struggling to keep up with the training routine he had set up for us. He kept telling me if I stuck with the workouts, I would be able to run twenty-six miles on the big day. I looked over at him, barely a drop of sweat on his forehead. He turned and managed a quick smile as he picked up speed and took off. He called after me, trying to egg me on.

"Come on, you pansy. Pick up the pace. You'll die by the fifth mile if you don't start working harder."

His steps were getting larger as the space between us increased. His ass flexed with each stride, his ease of motion making me feel like a clod. Every time my foot fell on the path, it felt as if I was hitting the ground like a ton of bricks. Pete seemed to glide, like one of those animals you see on television, running from a lion. Soon, he was further away, finding his own rhythm and leaving me in the dust. I kept running, refusing to give up just because he was trying to make me feel stupid. I pushed harder, willing myself to go faster and try to prove Pete wrong. My feet started to hurt a bit, but I was undeterred. This marathon may have started out as a joke, but now I was serious. I had never let anything get the better of me before, and I certainly wasn't going to start now. Pete turned and looked at me again, his stride staying full and confident even as he taunted me. I redoubled my efforts but still seemed to gain no ground on him. Reluctantly, I slowed a bit, my side starting to hurt as Pete faded into the distance.

I rounded the last turn, and I couldn't even see Pete anymore. Moreover, my right hamstring was really starting to hurt, each step sending a shooting pain into my muscle. I slowed down even more, but the pain continued. I was starting to falter, my willpower weakening with each stride. To make matters worse, a fat raindrop hit my nose. I looked up just in time to see a huge bolt of lightning on the horizon, the black clouds thickening and swirling in the distance. The thunder soon followed crackling and booming, as I got closer to the pavilion where Pete and I had left our things. It was pouring down rain in just a few seconds, the cool drops hitting me as I struggled to get to the shelter as quickly as I could. I looked around the path, trying to see Pete, but the wind and rain were making it hard to see.

By the time I got to the tables, I damn near collapsed; my right leg tight and painful. I grabbed at the cramped and sore muscle and stared out into the downpour. Pete was coming around the last turn, his clothes soaked completely as he ran toward me at full speed. When he emerged from the rain, he was sodden, his face red and blotchy from exertion. He leaned on the brick wall that closed in one side of the building, trying to catch his breath. He finally noticed me wincing, and came over and sat down next to me.

"What happened, Murph? I lost you."

"You think? You took off, and I fucked up my hamstring trying to catch up with you."

"Well, what the hell did you do that for, Murph?"

"Let me think. I seem to remember you calling me a pansy, Pete. Then you deserted me."

He leaned in and kissed me, his wet hand running over my cheek to try and placate me. The raindrops, hitting the ground fat and heavy were already making puddles, their rhythmic cadence filling the air. He pulled back just for a moment and smiled, his hands dropping, rubbing my tired shoulders as he went back to nibbling my lips. I squirmed away, trying to hold onto my anger at him, but he was making it difficult.

"Come on, Murph. I just wanted us to get a good run in before the storm. I didn't mean for you to hurt yourself trying to outpace me. If I didn't know any better, I'd think you were trying to get out of the marathon all together."

"You caught me. I purposefully pulled my hamstring, so I could get out of a race that is months away. Right, Pete. Makes perfect sense."

"Alright, well then, let me take a look at it. Maybe you just need a good stretch. Lie back on the bench."

He dropped to his knees next to me, my eyes wary; as I knew whatever he had in mind was probably going to hurt like hell. Ominously, the sky picked that moment to put on another light show, the thunder rattling the tables as it exploded over us. I let Pete push me back against the old wood of the picnic bench, his hand dropping to my knotted hamstring muscle. At first, I flinched and yelled as his fingers dug into me, trying to find the source of the pain. My hand flew to my chest involuntarily as his thumb hit the tender spot of the muscle.

"Shit, Pete. That fucking hurts. Do you even know what you're doing?"

"Sure I do. You know I do. Now quit whining and let me help you, Murph. I'm going to straighten your leg to stretch it. Just try and relax."

He pushed my leg back toward my head, one hand on my ankle, the other on my knee. I hadn't meant to yell, but I did, the pain so sharp it made me lightheaded. He backed off a bit, but didn't let go. I grabbed him by the wrist and looked into his eyes.

"Pete, if you do that again, I swear I'll kill you."

Instead of firing back at my threat, he leaned down and kissed me, his soft lips tasting both salty and sweet. As his tongue swept over mine, he pressed my leg back again, the muscle still screaming out even though I couldn't. This time, the stretch seemed to help, the muscle finally relenting a bit as Pete pushed my leg a little further. I wrapped my hand around his neck and deepened the kiss, my cock starting to stir despite the residual pain in my hamstring. Finally, Pete let go of my leg and eased away from me, staring down into my eyes as he spoke. The rain seemed to be slowing down a bit, but the thunder rolled again, sounding like breaking rocks in the distance.

"See, now isn't that better, Murph?"

"Yeah, it is. Can I sit up now?"

I tried to move, but he kept me lying down. His fingers went to the waistband of my rain-soaked shorts and started pulling them down.

"Pete, what are you doing? We're in public."

"You really think anyone else is crazy enough to be out here in a storm, Murph? Now there's one other thing I want to do for your leg, to help you relax?"

I opened my mouth to protest, but his lips on the head of my cock stopped the words from getting out. I could hear the blood rushing in my ears, my heartbeat once again racing, just as it was on the track. His nose nudged my stomach; the heat of his mouth enveloped the full length of my cock. My hands moved to his head, his wet hair slipping easily through my fingers. Even through the noise of the rain, I could hear him hungrily slurping on my cock. My hamstring was the last thing on my mind as his hand cupped my balls, gently stroking and tugging as he sucked my cock.

The smell of wet earth filled my nose as I felt my impending orgasm getting dangerously close. I tightened my fingers on his head, my voice getting lost in the pounding rain and thunder. Pete seemed to sense my urgency and backed off, returning to teasing strokes of his tongue on the underside of my dick.

"Damn it, Pete. I'm close. Don't stop now."

I groaned as he released me completely, pausing to pull down his own shorts, his hard cock springing free from the wet cloth.

"Sorry, Murph. Just needed a minute. Now, where was I?"

He smiled at me for a second, before leaning forward to take my cock in his mouth once again. This time, I didn't let him set the pace; I pushed my hips up into his mouth, ignoring the slight tweak in my hamstring every time I bottomed out in his throat. I looked over and watched him stroke his cock, the tip flushing a deeper read with each twist of his fist. I could have stayed all day in his talented mouth, letting him slide that fat tongue all over me. Watching him deep throat my cock, his wet hair clinging to his forehead, was one of the sexiest things I had ever seen. The rain was heavy again, and the thunder and lightning seemed closer than ever. And, so was I; Pete's mouth putting me right back on the edge. This time, there was no way to stop myself from coming, his relentless mouth leaving me no choice. I felt no pain as all my muscles tensed at once, fucking Pete's mouth with abandon, my hand keeping him from getting away until I was done. I listened to Pete swallow my cum, my eyes pinched shut as the last shudders of pleasure moved through my body.

As much as I wanted to rest, to relax, I let Pete pull me up to sitting position, until I was face to face with his dick, which was hard and waiting. I could smell his musky scent, thick and pungent after his run. He guided me down onto his cock, a firm hand on the back of my neck, pulling my wet hair. I let him fuck my face, too tired and satisfied to put up much resistance to his thrusting hips. I could hear the thunder receding, the rain diminishing as Pete started to moan louder. I no longer cared about being in public or who might see us under that roof. All I wanted was to taste him. I tilted my head back and looked up at him, focusing my sucking lips on his velvety cock head. His eyes were glassy, his voice rusty as he stoked my fire with his words.

"Oh, God Murph. You look so hot sucking my cock. I can't wait to get you home and give that ass a workout."

My tongue moved slowly over every bump and ridge, finding his sweet spots easily as I squeezed his tightly muscled ass. I couldn't resist slipping a finger between his cheeks, I pressed into his puckered hole, gently rimming the tight bud as I sucked him back down into my throat. Hard. The tip of my finger slipped inside him, and he gasped, a mix of shock and lust in his voice. It was as if he couldn't decide between my mouth and my hand, his hips moving frantically back and forth between them.

I gave him every trick I knew he liked, until he was slamming into my mouth, sending hot cum deep into my throat, his strong grip forcing me to take every drop. He made me look in his eyes again, his cock still moving in my mouth as he softened. Grabbing the base of his cock, he ran the head over my lips, and I gave his spent cock a soft kiss. He staggered back when he was finished, yanking up his shorts before slumping onto the bench next to me. I stood up and straightened myself out before testing my tender hamstring. I had a slight limp as we walked out into the gently falling rain, the storm now over the horizon. Pete kissed me before we got into the car, giving me a light slap on the ass.

"Hey Murph, how's the hamstring?"

"I don't know, Pete. I think I might need a little more help with my recovery. Know any good trainers?"

CLEAN SWEAT
By Fox Lee

When I first became a personal trainer, my friends congratulated me and said I was going to get more ass than I would know what to do with. Reality was a bit different. Despite the fact that the gym was gay-owned, and popular with men who dug men, we got just as many straight customers. Most of my clients were women and guys who thought that the name Max Chan meant I could teach them mixed martial arts.

Another reason I didn't combine business with pleasure was that I liked my job more than I wanted to screw anyone I worked with. Other than Terry the owner, who hit it off with Carl, the kick-boxing instructor, there were plenty of cautionary tales. And, once an in-house relationship turned sour, someone always got fired. I decided that unless I met someone that knocked my socks off I would keep my personal and professional life separate.

It wasn't always easy. The guys I worked with were good-looking, and most were available. The worst was when the gym closed for the day, and we got the place to ourselves for three hours. After the workouts were over, I would be in a dressing room with half a dozen sweaty, naked men. Mostly, we joked around and did the usual immature guy stuff. Of course, there were always exceptions. Like the guys who went to use the steam room and came back looking a little too relaxed.

I had been at the gym a few years, when Terry announced that he was going to Italy for his niece's wedding. Since it would be a shame to go all that way and miss out on the sights, he was going to turn it into a summer holiday. Of course, Carl was going with him. That meant a substitute kick-boxing instructor would be coming in, an old student of Carl's named Tommy.

I got my first look at Tommy the next day. Carl was showing him around the gym, and I happened to cross paths with them on my way to the bathroom.

"Max!" Carl called out. "Come meet Tommy. He was my student, back when I was your age!"

For a kick-boxing enthusiast, Tommy was incredibly shy. His eyes were hidden behind a head of shaggy, dirty-blond hair, and he barely looked at me when we shook hands. Though he seemed like a nice person, he didn't make much of an impression. I almost forgot I met him at all, until I ran into him in the dressing room. This time, it was just the two of us.

Tommy was stripped down to the waist, when I arrived. I noticed we had similar bodies, with long tight frames rather than bulging muscles. Tommy's skin was darker, a tan I could tell came from being outdoors, as opposed to inside a tanning bed. My eyes lingered on his happy trail, which ran along a flat, defined abdomen before disappearing behind loose-fitting workout pants.

With the lower view obscured, I roamed upwards to Tommy's smooth chest and broad shoulders. He spoke up, as I was contemplating what his nipples would feel like against my tongue.

"You're Max, right?"

I nodded and hoped he didn't suspect I had been about to mount him with my eyes.

"You're filling in for Carl," I said, as if he didn't already know why he was there.

Tommy put his shirt on and fidgeted with the hem.

"Are you one of the trainers?" He asked.

"Yeah. For about three years. Do you live around here?"

"I just moved. I used to live with my brother, but he got a job in Ohio. I thought as long as I had to get a new apartment, I would try someplace I had never been before."

"What about your old job?"

"That gym closed down. The owner got divorced, and his wife is turning it into a daycare center for dogs."

"Oh." I paused. "Do dogs need daycare?"

"I don't know."

The conversation dried up after that. It was just as well. I was out of segues, and my first appointment of the day was due soon. As I took off my street clothes, including my underwear, I turned to the side. Tommy was on the bench tying his shoelaces. In that position his hair obscured most of his face, but I could tell he paused when he happened to glance up. My cock was a good six inches, eight if it decided to misbehave, and thick. I wished I had gotten a look at Tommy's earlier. With a body like his I could forgive a less than stellar package, but I was curious nonetheless.

I snuck peaks at him the rest of the day. The kick-boxing studio had glass walls on three sides, which made it easy to see Tommy from almost anywhere in the gym. I was fascinated by the change that came over him. In front of the class, Tommy was confident and assertive. It was slightly eerie, but mostly I was incredibly turned on.

It was an unexpected reaction. When it came to sex, I was a fairly dominant guy. The more I thought about Tommy; however, the more I wanted him to use that "take charge" attitude on me, which meant I had to make my move while he was still in the zone. Once Tommy left the studio, he would go back to being sweet and subdued. All well and good, if his Jean-Claude Van Damme routine hadn't given me a raging hard-on.

As luck would have it, the last kick-boxing class ended right before the gym got ready to close. While the other trainers went home or started their own workouts, I made a beeline for the kick-boxing studio. Tommy was practicing but stopped when he saw me come in.

"It's OK," I said. "You can keep going."

"Do you need anything?"

"I want to watch you."

"You do?"

Tommy's brow furrowed, and I knew I had to do something. I crossed the room, until we were close enough to touch.

"How do you do it?" I asked. "How do you flip the switch, just by walking into a room?"

He looked confused at first, but after a moment, his expression cleared.

"It's not the room. It's knowing that I'm doing something I was meant to do. I can feel it in my whole body."

Tommy pressed his palm against his chest, and I swallowed hard. Sweat had dampened the ends of his hair, and made his shirt cling to his upper body.

"Show me." I said.

"You want to learn how to kick-box?"

"No," I told him. "Show me what I saw in here." My hand cupped his cock and balls through his pants. Tommy was already hard. "You really do feel it in your whole body, don't you?" I asked.

Tommy stared at me, and for a second I thought I went too far. He could have a boyfriend, or worse a girlfriend, and be offended that I waltzed in and commanded him to play naked kick-boxer with me.

"I don't want to be on display." Tommy touched the side of my face, and pressed his thumb against my lower lip. "Let's go up to Terry's office."

"He locks it."

I felt light headed. Tommy was willing to give me what I wanted, but had I really thought it through? What would he do to me, once we were alone?

"There's a spare key under the statue by the door. I saw it, when I accidentally knocked the statue over this morning."

"Ok, but we have to hurry. If anyone sees us ..."

"They won't," Tommy said. "Let's go."

Terry's office was on the second floor, past rows of stationary bikes, stair climbers, and treadmills. Tommy fished the key out from under the statue, and we slipped into the darkened room.

I always thought it was weird that Terry chose a space with no windows for his office. Today, I was thrilled about it. I turned the lights on, reassured that no one down on the first floor would notice. There wasn't much to see. The only office furniture Terry had was a giant desk and a leather sofa. I looked from one to the other, and wondered which I would end up on.

"Is this what you wanted?" Tommy asked.

I turned around to see him already naked and waiting.

"Hold your arms up," he said.

I obeyed immediately. Tommy eased my shirt up, and wound the fabric around my wrists. Next he made me walk backwards, until I was up against Terry's door. There was a heavy metal coat hook at the top, which Tommy slipped my shirt over. I had to hold myself up by the balls of my feet. Tommy pressed our bodies together and gyrated against me, his hard-on teasing the one trapped under my pants.

"If you keep doing that," I said, "I'm going to come."

Tommy kissed my neck, and sucked the spot behind my ear.

"If you do, I won't fuck you. Do you want me to fuck you?"

"Yes."

"Yes what?"

"I want you to fuck me."

I was familiar with the game Tommy was playing, yet I was also nervous. For one, I had always been the one giving orders with past lovers. Secondly, we never did anything elaborate. I told myself that, if Tommy did anything weird, I could scream like hell and someone outside would hear me.

Tommy hooked his thumbs into my waistband, and slowly pulled my pants down my legs. My briefs stayed put, much to my disappointment. I could feel the wet patch, where precum had soaked through the fabric. Tommy gripped my cock, and rubbed the wet spot with his fingers.

"I want to touch you," I told him.

Tommy shook his head. I was prepared to beg, but he kissed me before I got a word out. His tongue invaded my mouth, until my knees shook. My lips felt bruised by the time Tommy ripped my underwear past my hips and bent down to suck the tip of my cock into his mouth. He put a hand on each of my thighs to keep me upright as my full eight inches went down his throat. I remembered what he said about not coming and struggled to keep myself from getting too excited. In the back of my head, I could hear the theme song from *Mission Impossible*.

I was grateful yet extremely frustrated when Tommy got up and went to Terry's desk. He had to search a few drawers before he found what he wanted: lubricant and a box of condoms. I wasn't surprised. The way Terry and Carl carried on around each other, I knew Tommy and I weren't the first ones to use the office for recreational purposes.

Tommy returned to the door, his fingers coated in lube. His hand brushed my balls as it eased past to stroke my hole, and I squirmed at the contact. The lube was cold, and it had been a long time since I was at the receiving end of that kind of attention.

"You're really tight," Tommy said, as his finger gradually slid inside me. "Do you want me to stop?"

"No."

"No?"

Tommy retracted his finger almost all the way, then angled it back in again. He fingered me faster and added a second finger, then a third, after I began to thrust back.

"You make me want to touch myself," he said. "Look down."

I craned my neck and saw that Tommy was stroking his cock. He ran his hand along the underside of his shaft, down to his balls, and back to the tip.

"You can't make too much noise," he cautioned. "No matter how hard I fuck you."

"I won't," I promised.

With the condom on and slick with lube, Tommy put an arm under each of my legs and lifted me up on one smooth motion. He locked eyes with me, his cock brushing my asshole, but made no move to enter.

"When do you get to come?" He asked.

"I don't know."

Tommy leaned in to kiss me. It was gentle, little pecks and nibbles. He used them as punctuation, for what he said next.

"How about this? You can come, as hard as you want. But not until I'm done fucking you. Can you do that?"

Tommy lowered me down, enough to bring about half of his cock inside me. I gasped, and sank my teeth into my lower lip.

"Say yes, and you get the whole thing," he said.

I barely managed the yes. The next thing I knew, Tommy's balls were smacking against my ass, and I was trying to brace myself against the door for leverage. As hard as he fucked me, I knew he would stop dead in his tracks if I broke the rules. Part of me didn't want him to stop. Tommy felt amazing, but it was torture to hold myself back. I was going to come soon, whether I wanted to or not. I moaned, terrified that it was too late, and I was going to ruin everything.

It must have been what he was waiting for. Tommy's movements abruptly became erratic. A few seconds later, I felt him throb inside me.

"Come for me," he gasped. "Now."

Tommy's face was flushed, and I could feel his hold on my legs weaken from the sweat between us. At his command, my cock jerked and shot cum across his chest. I whimpered from the force of it, and gripped the shirt tethered around my wrists for dear life. Had Terry chosen a cheaper door for his office, the entire gym would have known what was going on upstairs. I didn't let go until Tommy carefully pulled out, and eased me into a standing position.

"Hold on to me," he said, his own legs shaking.

With our arms around each other's shoulders like drunken sailors, we hobbled to the couch and collapsed in a two man dog-pile. As our wits returned, we sorted our bodies out: Tommy on the outside, me on the inside. He was hiding behind his hair again, but he was smiling, too.

"Was it OK?" He asked.

"Aren't you supposed to tell me that I'm a bad boy, and I got what I deserved?"

I couldn't keep a straight face while I said it, and started to laugh.

"I don't know," Tommy said. "It didn't seem like you were suffering."

"Bullshit! I thought my balls were going to fall off."

We were both laughing then, and I pulled Tommy closer, so he wouldn't fall off the couch. Our noses bumped, which only made us laugh harder. Somehow it turned to kissing, until we were both hard again and Tommy was underneath me. He looked up, with big brown eyes.

"So, have I been a bad boy?" He asked.

"Yes," I smirked. "And if my legs hold up, you're going to get everything you deserve."

NEW TRAINER'S BOLD BALL WORKOUT
By Jay Starre

The pair were an unlikely match. And, what happened between them was just as unlikely.

Michael, the new trainer at the upscale gym, was easy going and sociable, while the hefty bodybuilder, Duncan, was painfully shy. Michael was keen to make a good impression on his employers and would never have risked his job for the sake of an inappropriate liaison with a member, especially right there in the gym. Duncan would never have dreamed of having sex in a public place, or in his own gym where he worked out nearly every day.

Yet, those stark differences in their personalities, and their own sense of what they were willing to risk, meant absolutely nothing when they finally met face-to-face. In the end, it was because of the quirks in their personalities that they did it. And, did they ever do it.

Michael was the new star in the gym. Practically every guy in the place had a hard-on for him. With a sexy gap between his front teeth, his easy grin made him a favorite right away. Not tall at five-ten, but with broad shoulders and impossibly muscular thighs, his slim waist and sexy ass made him the envy of all.

He wore neat little glasses that framed a perfect-featured face, and with his light brown hair recently buzzed short he managed to look both intellectual and military. Helpful, courteous, and knowledgeable. What more could one want?

There was more. Members who caught the hot new trainer changing in the dressing room had to bite back gasps of admiration. His dick was a monster!

Duncan heard the gossip and naturally was intrigued. A handsome stud in his own right, he was quite a bit heftier than Michael. Taller, too, he had the softest blue eyes under startling dark brows. He was shy and soft-spoken to Michael's genial friendliness, but it wasn't long before the two ran into each other and sparks flew. The result was an inferno neither could have anticipated.

"Hi. You're Michael the new trainer, aren't you? Everyone says you're real helpful and real hot," Duncan blurted out when he ran into Michael in the narrow stairway leading to the stretch room. He was like that, not saying anything at all or blurting out something embarrassing or even inappropriate. That's why he usually said little or nothing.

Michael beamed. "I like to be helpful, and hot is good, too," he replied with an easy chuckle.

Their bodies were close, and they made eye contact briefly. Duncan had just been lifting, and a sheen of sweat covered his bare arms and thighs. Pumped from exercise, breathing a little heavily from the stairs, and suddenly excited to be standing close to the new trainer, he exuded a distinctly sexy stink.

The moment would have passed and an opportunity for something more if the new trainer had been less engaging. But, it was his job to help out the clients and to be friendly. Besides, Duncan was cute as hell with his wavy black hair and button nose.

Michael's dick stirred, and he glanced down to notice a similar bulge growing under Duncan's skimpy workout shorts. The trainer decided to take a chance and see what developed. "Would you like me to give you some stretching tips?"

Duncan's breathing quickened. Here, too, the moment might have been lost except for the nature of the hefty bodybuilder's own reserved personality. He would never be the aggressor, but he was also often too painfully polite to outright refuse someone else's advances. "Sure. If you've got time. If you don't, that's OK, too."

"We're just about to close, but we can do a bit upstairs before everyone gets kicked out."

Duncan nodded his agreement, his dick stiffening as he contemplated what little bit they could do together. A little bit of fucking? A little bit of sucking? Hardly! Sex in the gym he worked out at every day would be hot, but hardly likely.

A few moments later, they were upstairs in the small stretch room, deserted so near to closing time.

"Why don't we try the ball? You can lie over it and relax your muscles first off," Michael began in his professional voice.

Duncan accepted the big blue exercise ball rolled over to him and followed the trainer's instructions. He found himself suddenly face down and spread-eagled over a ball with a sexy stud right behind him. His dick swelled against the rubbery resistance under his crotch. He was acutely aware of his naked thighs and the tight workout shorts he knew were riding up his asscrack.

"Just relax. Especially here in the lower back just above your butt."

Michael's hand was on his back, hot and firm. That hand slipped down so that it rested on the upper area of his ass-cheek. He was trying hard to relax, but all he could think of was his stiff dick and that hand on his butt!

"You've got an awesome body, Duncan. With all that muscle, you have to take extra time to stretch. Otherwise you might run into problems, like strained tendons or torn muscles." He spoke in a chatty tone rather than offering a rote lecture, which soothed Duncan's nerves just a little. His next words undid all that. "You've got a great butt, too," he added with a small chuckle.

The trainer couldn't help but feel the trembling in Duncan's body. He found that very exciting, all that muscle quivering. His dick, which had stiffened in the hallway and hadn't really softened, now stretched out in front of him to create a wicked tent in his sweat pants. Duncan's big round butt-cheeks, encased in tight khaki brown shorts, were right below him.

The intercom crackled out. "Closing time. Please vacate the training areas."

Duncan sighed and started to rise. The hand on his upper butt cheek was firm. "Don't worry about it. I'll lock up a little later after we've stretched you out properly."

His ass-cheek twitched under the trainer's hand as the words sunk in. Stretch him out? Stretch out his asshole maybe? His imagination ran riot, picturing the dick he'd heard about from other admiring members, long and fat and hopefully stiff now. He imagined it probing and then penetrating his quivering butt-hole. His own dick jerked and leaked precum into his shorts against the rubbery ball under him.

Michael smiled. He had the muscle-bound hunk right where he wanted him. He could feel the tension in his body. He could smell the sexual reek emanating from Duncan's pores as sweat trickled down his massive arms and glistened on his pale, muscular thighs. The stragglers in the gym would take a few more minutes to leave, so he'd content himself with teasing Duncan a bit before chancing any bolder moves. He knew he shouldn't be taking chances, with his new job and all, but that quaking butt-cheek under his palm was damn near irresistible.

And, the thrill of the risk itself was making him even harder.

"Raise your left arm and point your hand while you raise your right leg and point your toe."

As Duncan followed his instructions, he moved his hand lower so that it rested directly on the tensed mound of his right butt-cheek. "Hold your leg up with your gluteus muscles while you reach out with fingers and toes. Hold. Hold it. Keep holding it. Feel the stretch?"

He grinned as Duncan obeyed, reaching forward and stretching backward with opposite limbs, the ball under him moving slightly as he worked to maintain his equilibrium. His gluteus, that big globe of butt muscles, clenched and quivered with the strain. Michael went a little further in his baiting, raising his palm and slapping the cheek lightly. "Keep it tensed and really stretch out before we try the other side. Yeah. Like that. Hold it as long as possible."

He bit back laughter as the straining stud rocked over the ball and gasped. He placed his hand back over the hefty mound and squeezed it. "Good! Now we'll alternate."

The brown-haired trainer was really enjoying himself at the shy stud's expense, especially since it wasn't really appropriate, this being an expensive private club with a lot of wealthy members. Even though a large percentage of those members were openly gay, it was far from a sex pit of nasty goings-on.

He wouldn't have teased Duncan or been so forward if he hadn't overheard him talking with another member the previous day. Carrying fresh towels for the change rooms, he'd hesitated at the door as he heard his own name bandied about.

"Have you seen that new trainer Michael's dick? Donkey-sized! I bet you'd love having that fuck-pipe drill its way up your big sweet ass, Duncan!"

"You like a big dick as much as me, Terry!" Duncan had protested, sounding embarrassed. With a grin, Michael had turned around and headed back to the desk upstairs. He didn't want to embarrass the gossiping pair by appearing while they were talking about him.

As soon as he ran into Duncan on the stairs, he'd recognized his voice. Assessing that hint of a boner in Duncan's workout shorts, his smell of sweaty lust, and the stunning body he possessed, Michael decided he'd do his best to get a piece of him – or at least have some fun teasing.

Duncan lowered one set of limbs and raised the opposing ones, huffing with the effort. How much effort it took to stretch as far as he could was surprising, and just as demanding was attempting to hold up his arm and leg for as long as Michael asked. Trembling all over, he was acutely aware of the trainer's hand on his ass and back.

Compounding that struggle, his throbbing dick mashed against the rubbery surface of the ball under him. And, his imagination wouldn't stop playing games with him. As Michael switched hands so that now his left cheek was being squeezed, he fantasized about the size and shape of the dude's dick, which he'd been told was fat as hell and long, too.

"Hold ... good ... hold ... very nice!" Michael said as he laid on a second light slap, this time to the tensed left butt-cheek. He couldn't help himself and actually chuckled this time.

"What's so funny?" Duncan blurted out, red-faced from his struggles.

"Nothing, nothing. I'm just teasing. I admire your effort. One more time on each side."

Not only was he taking his time so that the last few members would be out of there and they'd be alone in the gym, but also he was getting off on the spectacle of the beefy gym stud straining to stretch over that ball.

While copping a good feel of his awesome ass at the same time.

Duncan did as he was told, left arm up and right leg raised, right ass-cheek tensed. His huge shoulder and powerful biceps bulged on the raised arm, his baggy grey tank top damp with sweat and revealing more than it concealed of the broad back, while his beefy hamstrings quivered and his muscular calf bulged.

This time Michael really squeezed the massive butt mound, barely able to keep from laughing. "That's right! Good! Hold it ... tense those gluteus muscles ... hold ... great job!"

He wouldn't have gotten away with it if Duncan wasn't so bashful. The big stud wasn't clueless and had some idea he was being played but didn't know for sure. He hoped the new trainer was gay and coming on to him, but he wasn't prepared to confront him about it or make any move of his own. He'd just have to go along with it and not make a fuss.

Anyway, he wasn't about to complain. His hard dick was getting massaged as he struggled to maintain his equilibrium and the ball jiggled back and forth. His ass-cheeks were heated up nicely from all that squeezing – and the playful slaps.

"One more time, Duncan. Let's see how long you can hold it. That's it. Go for it ... hold ... very good ... hold it ... more ... I can feel those muscles work ... hold ... you can do it!"

He grinned wickedly as he gripped that left butt mound with the palm of his hand and squeezed. Poor Duncan shook all over, his raised arm wobbling, his left leg twitching. His face was beet-red. All trainers had a bit of the sadist in them, and Michael was not above subjecting this beefy gym rat to a good tormenting.

But, now it was time for more. Regardless of any qualms about his job, he was going for it. His dick hard and his heart beating rapidly, he made his move.

"Roll a little forward and relax your back. Put your hands down on the floor," he ordered in his most soothing trainer voice.

As Duncan obeyed, his ass quaking under Michael's palm, the trainer placed both hands on the waistband of his khaki brown shorts. He yanked down just as Duncan rolled forward.

"What are you doing!" the beefy gym rat gasped out, his hands firmly on the mat to hold himself from rolling forward onto his head. His shorts were suddenly down around his ankles.

He was butt-naked!

"Getting you all nice and relaxed. This will really help, I'm sure," Michael said, then laughed out loud.

First, he quickly pushed his glasses tight against the bridge of his nose, then seized one of Duncan's solid cheeks in each hand. Bending over at the waist, he buried his face in the stud's creamy crack.

When wet lips and tongue mashed against tender butt flesh, Duncan grunted with heated disbelief. The trainer had his tongue in his crack!

The sound of lapping tongue and smacking lips had the sprawled gym stud quivering from head to toe. He could do nothing but hang there, his cock driving into the ball under him and his ass quaking as he felt that tongue snake closer to his hole.

The bold trainer inhaled sweaty crack. He loved a gym stud's smell, frothy sweat from good hard exercise – excellent! His nose rooted around in the smooth valley, his tongue and lips roaming up and down as he pulled the crevice wide open with strong hands. He tasted the salty sweat.

He couldn't have cared less about the risks to his job now that he had his face buried in that awesome butt.

He was amazed at how silky smooth that crack was. He dug into the crevice in search for the hole and found it. With a juicy smack, he kissed it and then began to tickle it with his swabbing tongue.

"Fuck! You're licking my asshole," Duncan panted, trying to keep his voice down. He prayed everyone had obeyed that intercom order and left, so they wouldn't be discovered. His shorts were around his ankles and a tongue twirling over his asshole, and although it was nastily awesome, he was far, far too timid to want any witnesses.

Michael squeezed Duncan's massive cheeks with his fingers, kneading them while spreading them farther apart as he began to work on the stud's pucker hole. He fully intended on opening up that hole for his dick, which lurched under his shorts eager for action.

Duncan's face flushed pink. Panting, his tongue came out of his open mouth to lick nervously at his full lips. He squirmed over the ball as Michael's tongue lapped at his asshole, teasing the lips and stabbing at the sensitive center. It dug into him, probing deep as the trainer pulled his crack wider open. He twirled that wet tongue like a moist drill.

Draped over the ball, Duncan was practically helpless. His hands and feet were busy preventing him from rolling off, while his will power was shattered by the effort he'd exerted moments earlier. Now with that tongue assaulting his asshole, he was too weak to make even a token effort at resistance.

If he'd actually wanted to resist.

Michael abruptly drove a hand down to reach under his belly. He found and seized stiff dick, pulling it down and backwards. The assaulted gym stud's blue eyes went wide when hot tongue abandoned his asshole and slid downwards, over his perineum, over his balls and then finally over his leaking dick.

"Nice hole and nice dick," Michael murmured between licks and sucks as he attacked that boner.

The meat was thick and juicy and straining against the rubber ball. Michael nursed the head and teased precum from the slit as his victim squirmed helplessly beneath him while moaning incoherently.

Michael's quick mind had already formed a plan of action. While he sucked Duncan's hard dick, he eased a hand into the stud's crack and began teasing his wet asshole with a pair of fingers. The juicy hole convulsed and then gaped as he tickled the rim and spit-oozing entrance.

"Ohhhh ... yeah ... don't stop, uhhhn," Duncan moaned as those fingers stroked and teased his steamed-up ass entrance. He was helpless under the trainer's sexy assault, the tongue and hands on him driving him crazy. At this point, all his inhibitions were pretty well abandoned, and he admitted to himself he'd probably take whatever the trainer was going to give him.

Half the lights went out, the signal Michael anticipated. The girl at the front desk was always anxious to lock up and go home, which she'd do as soon as she cashed out. Often she would leave Michael or the other trainers to scare out the last member, in this case Duncan. Her final act before leaving was to turn down the lights.

Now, he was alone with Duncan.

He rose up with a wet grin. "Stay put. I'll be right back with lube and a condom. You're about to get some dick up that sweet ass."

Offering a quick smack to the spread ass-cheeks, he whirled away without waiting for the sprawled stud's response. A good judge of people, he figured Duncan wasn't going anywhere. His day locker was right next door in the staff lunch room, and it took less than two minutes to race in there, grab what he needed out of his locker and race back.

With half the lights out in the stretch room, there were deep shadows in the corners, but right in the center, one of the remaining lit ones glared directly down on Duncan. Michael grinned. What a sight! He pushed back his glasses against his nose, prepared for action. He could have taken them off, but then he wouldn't have been able to get such a crystal-clear look at all that awesome muscle and smooth flesh.

Still draped over that large blue exercise ball, his shorts were down around his ankles and his big pale butt exposed. His pink cock stretched down between his thighs, pressed against the blue rubber. His toes and palms were planted on the floor mat while his broad shoulders and hefty thighs bunched with the effort to hold him in place.

He hadn't moved.

Michael tore down his black sweat pants and hopped out of them as he approached that ball and butt. Just when he was almost there, he pulled down and discarded his underwear, too. Now he was dressed in only black sneakers and black tank top.

Duncan turned his head and watched him approach. His blue eyes widened and his full lips pursed with appreciation as he got his first look at the new trainer's dick.

"It's a fucking battering ram!"

Michael laughed, stroking the rearing pipe with one hand and holding the lube and condom in the other. Then, he abruptly leaned down to yank off Duncan's shorts and toss them aside.

"You better spread those legs wider if you're going to take all of this."

He obeyed with a little moan as he bit his plump lower lip and prepared for the inevitable. He fully expected the hot trainer to rubber up quickly, lube up and then ram that fucker home, but he should have known better by now.

Michael was a born tease. He laughed as he knelt down between Duncan's splayed thighs and tore open a packaged condom, then rolled it down over his big fuck-pipe. He flipped open and aimed the tip of the lube at the gym stud's flushed asshole. He crammed that tip right into it and squirted.

Duncan grunted and pushed back against that gooey flood. It was over almost immediately as the tube of lube was discarded and a finger replaced it. Before he knew it, Michael had his face back down in his crotch and his wet mouth attacking his stretched-back dick.

The trainer licked downwards on his dick, sucking on it with wet slurps as he slowly pushed his finger deep into his steamy asshole. The anal flesh gave way, opening around and throbbing over that invading digit. He added a second finger, the hole squishing with all that lube, spit and sweat. He twisted both fingers around, digging and stabbing.

Duncan really began to squirm now, the ball going back and forth under his jerking crotch. Michael held him in place firmly with one hand on a big butt-cheek, the other crammed in his spread crack and up his hole. His knees pressed outward against the stud's sprawled thighs. Adept at ball work, he knew what he was doing – although this was his first try at this particular kind of ball work!

He tickled the head of Duncan's cock with his tongue, getting the ball all wet with his drool. He ran his tongue up and down the length of his engorged pink shank, slobbering loudly, nipping at the hot tube and then gulping in his plump balls both at once. His hot mouth worked all over dick and balls while he continued to abuse the stud's asshole with a pair of prodding fingers.

Duncan's cock twitched wildly under his mouth and fingers, leaking copiously all over the rubber ball. His asshole yawned open to the pair of thrusting fingers. Now, it finally seemed the muscle bound stud was primed enough to take his monster meat.

With a noisy smack, he raised his head. "Time to drill your sweet ass," he panted out.

With a pair of fingers still working Duncan's butt-hole, he scooted right up and aimed his dick at that smooth white ass.

"Are you ready for this?" he teased. His cock arched out in front of him, purple and drooling.

Duncan craned his head around to see an amazingly lengthy fuck pole aiming at his butt. It was so fucking long! It jerked and leaked, eager for action. His own dick twitched along the ball, all wet and hot. His asshole ached as the trainer continued to root around with his fingers. He gawked a little fearfully at that stiff donkey-dick.

But, he wanted it so bad he could taste it. "Fuck me!"

"I'll do my best," Michael replied cheerfully.

His glasses were askew, his lips and chin wet with drool as he grinned devilishly. He stared down at the spread-eagled stud, wearing only that skimpy tank top and his sneakers, sweat-soaked muscles quivering over the big blue ball. Dick strained against the blue rubber, wet and leaking. His fat balls mashed against the rubber. His massive ass quaked, the hole pink around his buried fingers.

Awesome!

After a final savage twist and with a noisy plop, he pulled out his fingers. He immediately dropped down to drape himself over the sprawled gym stud. His dick slid into place as he covered Duncan with his own body. He probed with his hips, his blunt dick head searching and finding the stretched ass slot. They both grunted when the gaping lips captured and held it. He dropped his head down beside Duncan's and whispered in his ear.

"Here comes dick. Relax and let it in. You want it, don't you?"

Duncan trembled all over as he felt the knob begin to ease past his butt-lips. His body was trapped under lean, firm muscle. The rubbery ball was a spongy springboard that gave and resisted at the same time beneath him. Dick began to invade him.

"I want it. Uhhnnnnnggg … yeah … ohhhhh … give me that big fat dick," he admitted with a loud groan.

Michael fed the groaning stud dick, inch by fat inch. Half way in, he pulled out, then began the slow insertion again. Their bodies bounced slightly over the rubber ball. Duncan strained to hold them in place with his hands and feet, his entire focus on that long shank sinking into him, maddening inch by maddening inch. How fucking long was it?

His asshole surrendered. It yawned open to caress Michael's probing pole with quivering kisses. As he began to fuck in and out, the steamy insides yielded even more, allowing him deeper and deeper access. Soon, he was driving balls-deep into the gym stud's gut.

He grunted at each deep probe. He'd never been fucked so deep. The long rod sank into him with slippery ease, his ass-lips reveling in the massaging friction. His insides were stuffed and probed like never before. They began to rock and dip as Michael established a pounding rhythm. Duncan's own dick drooled as it rubbed back and forth under him against the slick rubber ball.

"I want you to come. Spooge all over the ball while I fuck you up the ass," Michael whispered nastily in Duncan's ear.

The raunchy order had Duncan shaking all over. His dick was hard and slippery. He'd been close to orgasm since the moment his shorts had been ripped down! Now, he let go. Relaxing his anal muscles, he allowed that hard dick to slide in and out and in and out. His banged prostate ached, his mashed balls ached, his own dick rubbed and rubbed against the spongy ball under him-

"Oh god! I'm coming! Oh god … oh god … oh god!"

His dick spewed. Pressed backwards below his balls, the fat tool erupted goo all over the rubber ball. His guts churned as dick continued driving into him while waves of rapture rocked his massive body. He unloaded like a burst pipe, cum spurting with every thrust of dick up his asshole.

"Nice load, buddy. Let it all out while I fuck a big load of my own up your sweet ass."

Impossibly long dick drilled Duncan as he floated in a moaning orgasm. The ball supported him beneath Michael's taut body as the trainer began to fuck really hard, slamming into him from above, whispering moans in his ear, sliding his hands all over Duncan's sweaty sides and ass. He'd never felt so possessed and so fucked. With his dick dribbling out its last droplets, his attention reverted back to that one area of intense sensation … his fucked asshole.

Michael didn't hold back. With powerful thrusts of his muscular hips, he slammed his donkey-dick home. The moaning gym stud's asshole was all his, slippery, wide open and willing. The ass lips yielded wetly, the fleshy butt cheeks were slick under him with both their sweat. The stench of spooge lingered in the air, reminding them both that the hefty gym stud just had the cum fucked out of him.

"I'm blowing up your sweet, sweet ass," he crooned in Duncan's ear as he let it loose.

That piston-prick kept on pounding, the ball bouncing under them as Michael unloaded up Duncan's ass. With a final thrust, he rolled them off the ball to tumble onto the mat in a tangle of sweaty, jizzed limbs.

Duncan stared up into Michael's blue eyes. The glasses were steamy. The gap-toothed grin made Duncan laugh out loud. "Thanks for the excellent stretch session. Do you think I could schedule another?"

"Sure," Michael chuckled, returning the gaze. "One of us has to clean up that ball, first though."

They both burst out laughing. The blue ball rolled away, slippery and scummed.

What happened afterward was probably inevitable. They'd both enjoyed the dangerous thrill of that nasty workout so much it became a regular practice. Duncan came in late to exercise, and Michael asked for the evening shifts. They both waited anxiously for that final lights out and then went at it with a vengeance. The blue exercise ball was their favorite and got scummed regularly. But, they made inventive use of other equipment, workout benches, barbells, rubber exercise bands, even skip ropes!

A month of hot and heavy ass-fucking, dick-sucking and butt-munching kept them both in nasty paradise until it all came to a crashing halt. The manager of the gym forgot something and returned to discover Duncan tied up with a pair of skip ropes on a workout bench with his hefty white ass spread and roped back. Michael was busy cramming the lubed end of a barbell deep into the gym stud's puckered pink hole. The trainer was wearing only his black uniform shirt and his huge donkey dick reared straight up from his crotch, drooling precum.

Michael was fired, and Duncan's membership was revoked. But, neither cared. Michael started up his own personal training business, and they moved in together and saved a bundle on rent.

They had their own equipment at home, too. Their big blue exercise ball required regular cleaning.

THE THIRD MAN
By Landon Dixon

I was curious about my new next-door neighbor from the get-go. And when the parade of beautiful boys began almost immediately after the guy moved in, my interest, along with other things, really piqued.

Scott moved in on a Saturday, driving up in a rented van with him and another guy unloading a minimum of furnishings and appliances. I watched from my bathroom window that overlooked his driveway.

Scott was absolutely gorgeous, clad that day in a striped orange and blue T-shirt and pair of tight white shorts. His arms and legs were the color of bronze – molten bronze – smooth and flowing, and his body was lean, long and luscious, blond hair cut short, blue eyes shining bright. My hand trembled on the cracked-open curtain as I watched the man climb in and out of the van, carrying his belongings into his new home. The sun beamed down happily on his sweat-dewed body, as I beamed happily out the window and dewed sweat.

The guy with him was anything but beautiful, on the other hand, a ponytailed, beer-gutted type who seemed to be hauling more electronic gear than a Bon Jovi roadie. But after he drove off in the van, more beautiful boys started showing up, adding to the contingent of one already in attendance.

On the Sunday: a muscle-ripped redhead wearing jeans and a tee and a heart and dick-warming grin. On the Monday: two boys, one blond and one brunette, each buff and sun browned, young and eager. The guys stayed maybe a couple of hours, by my log, and then departed the quiet residential neighborhood.

Being the neighborly type, I felt it my responsibility to check out the new arrival a little more intimately than from my bathroom window. So, on the Tuesday night, I crept through my backyard and down the lane and through the gate and into my neighbor's backyard, to see if he needed anything; to see what I could see.

I'd been at work all day, but when I'd gotten home and been tea bagging a sack of pasta in a pot of boiling water, I heard a car pull up in the driveway next door. I just made it to the bathroom without scalding myself in time to see a tall, muscular guy with long, dark hair go in through the backdoor of the house. Then I scarfed down pasta and tomato sauce and made tracks.

It was already dark out, and the lights were shining bright in the back windows of the house. I skulked across the yard and cozied up to the wall, peeked in the kitchen window. Didn't see eye candy of any variety. I Spidermanned along the wall to the bedroom window, poked my nose past the frame and spotted a bed and some sticks of well-appointed furniture, but nobody using the articles of good housekeeping.

I moved over to the garage, keeping to the shadows, avoiding the light casting out from the house windows. I wasn't nosy or anything; I just didn't want to bother my new neighbor if he was busy with something.

The garage had three windows, two on the sides and one at the back. There was a sliver of light leaking out under the closed overhead door, but the two side windows were done over with black paper from the inside. I balled my hands into fists of frustration and slithered around to the back of the garage, careful not to crunch too much of the overgrown vegetation and strewn debris back there.

My heart pounded in my chest with cardiac intensity, as I noticed that this window was black-papered, as well, except for a small triangle at the bottom. Either someone had done a poor tape job, or simply run out of the Ozzy Osbourne home décor, because I could actually peer into the garage from the peep opening.

And what I saw made my hair stand on end, at the back of my neck and all over my balls. The interior of the car-park was lit up like the Late Show set, two particular spotlights aimed at and illuminating my next-door neighbor and tall, dark and handsome, making out in the scantiest of gym togs.

"Hi neighbor!" I breathed, gaping at the stunning scene.

The garage was decorated like a small gym, blond beauty stretched out on a weight bench, dark-haired dude on top of him, their arms around one another, their mouths locked together, tongues bulging each other's cheeks. There was a pair of cameras set up on either side of them, catching the glorious erotic action from the look of their blinking red lights. Either my new neighbor was a raging videophile, intent on taping all of his conquests, or he was producing his latest batch of steaming hot homemade pornography for fun and profit.

Either way, I was getting an eye and pants-full. The crotch of my jeans surged with excitement, and my feverish body tingled all over, as I ogled those two gym buddies kissing and Frenching and fondling one another. Their tongues shot out of their mouths and into the open, entwining together, the dark-haired hunk feeling up Scott's chest, Scott clutching the guy's gym-shorted butt, working the hard, mounded cheeks with his hands.

I dove one of my own shaking mitts down and rubbed my fully-engorged cock, the boys grinding their cocks together on the bench, along with everything else. There was no one manning the rolling cameras, just me manning the window, fogging the pane with my appreciation of the men's fine acting – if it was acting.

Scott pushed the hunky brunette off his chest, and the two guys climbed to their feet, their lush lips hardly ever breaking contact. Scott shoved up his friend's mesh workout shirt, pulled it over the guy's head then went to work on his nipples.

The bare-chested man tilted his head back and groaned, the pleasurable sound waves seeping through to my other hand pressing against the side of the building. His chest was smooth and muscle-plated, tan nipples pointing the way to Scott's mouth, Scott licking, swirling his tongue all around them, taking them into his mouth and sucking and biting and pulling.

I rubbed my expanded jeans even faster, really getting into the message the beautiful boys were conveying in this scene of their film. Then I gulped, when Scott trailed his wet, pink tongue down his friend's muscle-ribbed torso to the top of the man's tiny blue shorts, let the slippery slurper dabble there for a moment. Scott bit into the waistband and really chewed up the scenery, pulling the shorts down with his teeth, releasing his photogenic lover's long, hard cock into his face, right before my wondering eyes.

The blond-haired, bronze-dipped god gripped the clean-cut erection at its base and breathed hot, humid worship onto its crown, staring up at his companion. Dark-hair laced his long fingers into Scott's hair, staring down at his handheld dick; then jerking with joy, when Scott slid his plush lips over the hood and tugged.

I jumped right along with the lucky knob-gobblee, banging my nose against the window, my body against the stuccoed wall of the garage.

Scott twisted his handsome head to the side and spotted my eyes in the spy hole. I froze, fearing the worst. And getting the best – Scott crooking a finger at me, beckoning me to come on in, his other fingers otherwise occupied sliding up and down the smooth shaft of his friend's granite cock.

I didn't stop to think, just ran. Around the two sides of the garage and up to the overhead door just as Scott was hoisting it. I slid under like Charley Hustle into home plate.

The dark-haired stud's name was Dirk, so he said. And, yup, they were making a porno for distribution to homoerotic horn dogs everywhere. Dirk's handshake was firm and warm, his cock firm and bobbing.

"How'd you like a part in this one?" Scott asked.

I tore my orbs off Dirk's dong and stared into Scott's sky-blue eyes. "Uh …"

"I'd pay you. Two hundred dollars?"

I could've used the money, but not the publicity. "Uh, no, thanks. I don't, uh, think I quite … measure up."

I'm not a bad-looking guy – kind of short, sort of stocky, with brown hair and eyes and a round, boyish face – but I wasn't built along the camera-ready lines of Dirk and Scott.

"You sure? Okay, no problem. Do you mind if Dirk and I use you to warm up a bit, get the juices really flowing."

They needed heating up like the Devil needs oven mitts. But I nodded up top and bulged down below, eagerly accepting their offer.

Scott turned off the two cameras and then took me in his strong arms, pressed his wet, full lips against my gaping mouth. I quivered with erotic electricity, a live wire in the man's hands. Dirk crowded in behind, pressing his hard body into mine.

Scott shot his tongue into my mouth, up against my tongue, and I responded in kind. We Frenched with on-set precision, but in-camera passion. And then Scott and Dirk kissed and Frenched over my shoulder, our hot bodies sandwiching together.

I'd never been in a threesome before, let alone with two beautiful boys trained in the fine, fine art of man-loving. I praised the Lord for the local housing bubble burst that had left the home next to mine vacant, a bargain for a man like Scott to move into.

The two guys began pulling at my clothes, Dirk stripping off my shirt from behind, Scott my jeans and underwear from the front. I felt like a rag doll in a sexual spin cycle. And when it was all over, I was naked from tip to toes, my cock poling out unselfconsciously before the men's appreciative eyes.

"You sure you're not in the business?" Scott joked.

I was about to answer with a modest chuckle, when the guy grabbed onto my dick, lacing his slender brown fingers around my pink, pulsating shaft. I shuddered like I'd hit the jackpot. Cushioned somewhat by Dirk from behind, his own hard-on getting intimate with my bare butt cheeks.

Scott stroked my cock, gazing warmly at me. I went five-alarm red in the face, gaping back, feeling his hot, sensuous hand on my sensitive prick all through my body and soul. Dirk gripped my chest and pinched and rolled my nipples, undulating his cock back and forth in my butt cleavage.

Scott released my cock, leaving me hanging. He proceeded to do a slow striptease, pulling off his skimpy muscle shirt and tossing it aside, shaking out his blond hair and his bronze pecs. The guy's chest was clean enough to eat off of, and he let me have a taste, gripping his pecs and feeding his jutting nipples into my hungry mouth. I licked at the rubbery buds, sucked on them, thrilling at the taste and texture, the man's moaning reaction to my mouth work.

Dirk took my cock in hand and stretched it out with long, slow pulls, as I tugged on Scott's nipples. I burned red-hot, the fondling and frotting and feeding turning me almost molten liquid.

Scott pulled back, his nipples glistening with my spit. He turned around and slid his red shorts off his mounded buttocks. He did it nice and easy and awesome, the garment molding to his taut, round, sun kissed cheeks, before sliding down his long legs. Then he turned back around and showed off his arrow-straight erection. His balls were shaven as smooth as the rest of him, his cock dwarfing them, filling my eyes.

"How 'bout we give this guy a real workout, Dirk?" Scott said to his buddy. "Since we've got the equipment all set up."

'The equipment' was a double-entendre as broad as the men's chests and shoulders. But they meant it both ways, getting me to kneel on all-fours on the weight bench, my ass sticking into the air at one end, my head at the other.

And then, they put their personal equipment to work. I jumped when Dirk greased my crack, his fingers scrubbing my grinning vertical smile; jumped again, when I felt the meaty tip of his prick press up against my manhole. He gripped my waist and pushed his hood right into my pucker, through my ring and into my ass, his cock gliding home smooth and sensuous, swelling me with pleasure.

I barely had time to bask in the anal glory, for Scott was wagging his lovely prick in my face, obviously wanting to be sucked. I opened my mouth up wide, and he plunged his cock inside, going almost as deep as Dirk at the other end.

I just about jimmied off the bench, I was shaking so hard, taking beautiful cock up the ass and in the mouth. I sealed my lips around Scott's pulsing shaft, and he gripped my head and gently pumped his hips, sliding his dick back and forth in my mouth. As Dirk pumped my ass, his cock stretching, sawing my chute. I burned with raw eroticism, receiving the casting call of my life.

I bobbed my head in rhythm to Scott's thrusting, sucking on his cock. Helped in my excited motions by Dirk rocking me from behind, deep-anus strokes that pushed Scott's cock almost right down my throat, then glided it out from between my lips dripping and shining. My head spun, and I saw stars other than the two men, breathing through my nose in gasps, chute and mouth getting righteously reamed.

The boys torqued up the pressure, skilled sexual artisans that they were. Dirk's fingernails bit into my waist and his muscled thighs thumped against my ass cheeks, cock pistoning my shimmering anus. Scott clutched my hair and donged my mouth at an accelerated pace, plumbing the depths of my throat and my oral depravity. I performed like a true porn superstar, I think, gagging only a little, moaning a lot, heartfully pushing my butt back to meet Dirk's headlong thrusts, sucking fiercely on Scott's delving pipe.

I was bathed in sweat, the temperature in the garage-cum-gym soaring to bathhouse levels. The men grunted, the smack of thighs against cheeks, balls against chin, filling the suffocating air. Risking it all, I tore a hand off the Naugahyde and grabbed onto my own flapping cock, pumped quick and hard like Scott fucking my mouth and Dirk fucking my ass.

My stamina wasn't up to the big boys, of course. My hand flew up and down the humming length of my prick only ten or twelve times, before I jerked, spasmed. Semen jetted out of my dick and sprayed the weight bench, orgasm ripping through me like a firestorm.

The two men hit their cue, Scott clawing at my scalp and bucking, blasting hot, salty jizz into my mouth and down my throat. As the man holding up my other end pumped me in a frenzy and then pumped me full. He growled and spurted, heated semen flooding my chute. I rode out the storm on cloud nine, taking all they could give me.

"Well, thanks for the session," Scott said, as the pair of hung hunks helped me to my feet.

I stood, then staggered, drained to the bone. The men held me steady, until I finally regained some of my equilibrium. Then they each gave me a kiss and a slap on the ass and sent me on my way, Scott promising me a return engagement whenever I wanted.

It was later that wonderful night that I hit onto one of Scott's websites: 'Backyard Amateurs.' And there I was, my face blurred out, but everything else on display, right from the opening introductions to my awesome initiation. Judging from the camera angle, it looked like that roadie wannabe had shot me and the boys from the very window vantage point I'd initially exploited myself.

I went from stunned to mad to proud of my performance to turned-on, as I watched the footage. I saluted the beautiful boys and their cunning with another hand-cranked blast of exuberance. I could hardly wait for Act Two.

YOU CAN LEAD A HORSE TO WATER ...
By Mark Apoapsis

I wish all my clients would take off their shirts when I tell them to, I thought, watching Kevin valiantly straining under twenty pounds more weight on the barbells than he was used to. I studied the bulging muscles in his arms as he lifted the weight overhead and could tell at a glance that he was using the muscle groups I'd intended and not inadvertently cheating. I circled around behind him to check out his back muscles. He'd gotten noticeably bigger in the months I'd worked with him and had lost all traces of flab. He'd worked hard and made an obvious effort to do everything I told him. Today was typical; we were only halfway through the session, and already his normally curly chest hair was plastered against his now-well-defined pecs. I was proud of our results and pleased to be able to inspect them so easily. I wished they were all so cooperative.

"Two more," I said.

"Sorry, Tony, I can't," he gasped, setting the weights down.

I had a strong hunch that he had at least two more reps in him; for one thing, his muscles weren't visibly trembling, the way a man's body usually does when he wills it to do something it doesn't want to do. But, I had to take him at his word. While I know exactly how hard I can push my own body – just a little harder than it thinks it can go – when it comes to another man's body, I could stare at it all day long from the outside, looking for signs of muscle fatigue, but only the guy inside it could tell how much it was hurting. I wasn't convinced Kevin understood how much it was supposed to hurt, but I just had to trust him on that.

77

I had him do some leg presses, so he could rest his upper body. His hairy legs, which had been scrawny when he'd first come to me, were thick and strong and powerful now.

Soon it was time for my next appointment, another regular client. Marshall was an exercise in frustration and a frustration in exercise. He was making some modest progress in the amount of weight he could lift, but I could only guess whether that meant he was building up muscle or just trying harder. He'd gained five pounds this month, which I hoped was muscle, but I couldn't tell, not under the loose-fitting gray sweat shirt and sweat pants he always wore, even when I put him on the scale. He still weighed much less than I, despite being several inches taller, but I'm pretty much solid muscle, and for all I knew, he might need to burn off a few extra pounds.

I decided to have him warm up with some jump rope, just in case. It was hard to make him work up a good sweat when he kept tripping over the rope, though.

"Just don't think about it, and let your body get into its own rhythm," I advised. "You can't possibly think fast enough to see the rope coming and command your muscles to move. It's like walking. You don't think about lifting each foot before you take a step, you just tell yourself to walk."

Making him jump rope had another advantage: his shirt hiked up on each jump. From my vantage point seated on the linoleum floor in front of him, hugging my knees, I had periodic glimpses of his belly, which seemed to be nice and flat. He wasn't carrying any extra weight there, as far as I could tell. Just to be sure, I next made him do some sit-ups on an incline bench. Sure enough: pale but firm and flat, with a light trail of blond hair both above and below his navel. I decided to spend the rest of our session on strength training.

He was definitely lifting more than he had at first but was not progressing as rapidly as I'd have liked. I didn't know if he was giving up too easily, or using the wrong muscles. I'd have loved to wrap my hands around his biceps, both to reassure myself that there was now some solid muscle there and also to make sure the right muscles were bearing the weight. But the last time I'd tried to so much as press a palm against his lats, he'd recoiled and dropped the weights. Not free weights, fortunately for the innocent bystanders. We'd gotten enough dirty looks as it was, as the clatter echoed across the gym.

"Man, am I sore!" he said as we knocked off early.

"Where do you feel it, exactly?" I asked. That would tell me a lot.

"All over. A hot shower is gonna feel good."

"I'll bet just getting that sweaty shirt off is gonna feel good," I said hopefully, following him into the locker room.

"Yeah, you really worked me hard today, Tony," he said, making no move to open his locker or to peel off his gray sweat shirt, which was darkened with sweat around the neck and halfway down his chest.

"Have you thought about coming twice a week? I have an opening on Thursday nights now."

"At what you charge? Sorry, I can't afford that."

I engaged him in conversation for a few minutes more. Many guys would have stripped as we were talking, but not Marshall. He was going to wait me out before he so much as peeled off his shirt. I wished I could see for myself if he was improving and assess which muscles were still underdeveloped. Besides, isn't it only fair that I get to admire the results of my work? It's like an artist not being allowed to see his finished paintings on display before they're sold.

Well, if I couldn't use the time remaining before my next appointment to inspect Marshall's body, I'd use it to give my own a little extra exercise. Leaving Marshall to strip and shower in privacy, I headed outside for a quick jog through the woods behind the building before it got too dark.

The evening was pleasantly cool, and the fresh air was a nice change of pace after hours of being closed in with the familiar musky scent of sweaty men. But on my way past the loading dock in back of the building, I caught an unexpected whiff of beer. I turned and saw a supine figure sprawled in the doorway, a bottle in his hand. "Hey! Buddy! You can't hang around here."

Ignoring me, he took a long swig from the unlabeled bottle. "Did you hear me?" I demanded, squatting down to confront the drunk, who was younger than I expected.

"Want some beer, man?" Through the clear glass, I could see foam rising into the neck of the oddly shaped bottle, which was nearly filled with amber liquid.

"No, I don't want some beer! I'm working. I work here. Get up!" Grabbing him by the front of his T-shirt and the edge of his unbuttoned outer shirt, I hauled him halfway to his feet.

It was no use. It's true what they say: you can lead a horse to water, but you can't make him drink. I could haul the guy to his feet, but I couldn't force him to walk. I didn't have time to march him home. My next client was a lawyer who complained whenever I wasted one minute of his valuable time.

"I want you gone in five minutes, when I get back from my run. You hear me?"

But, he was still there when I got back. "Get up!" I snapped. He just took another swig from the still-full bottle. "Want some Scotch? It's good Scotch."

"I thought you said it was beer." It did smell like well-aged Scotch. "What did you do, go to the liquor store and come back? I told you to get out of here!" The new bottle, also an unlabeled clear bottle, looked identical to the first.

I would have kept haranguing him, but I saw headlights pulling in at the far corner of the parking lot and recognized Richard's broad-shouldered figure striding from his car toward the front door. It would take him less time to change from his lawyer garb into gym clothes than it would take me to budge the young drunk, so I headed back in, warning the kid that he'd better be long gone when I checked on him at closing time. I knew that what the drunk needed was someone to whip him into shape and force him to clean up his life, but I only do that sort of thing when they pay me.

# # # # #

Richard was frustrating to work with in his own way because the only way to work with him was to do it his own way. Nature had been kind to him and given him a big, beefy body that developed muscles with very little work – and very little work was all that he ever did. I wished I had a body like that; if he worked at it half as hard as I did, he'd soon be twice as hard and strong as I was. As it was, I could kick his ass if I wanted to, even though he was taller and heavier than I.

"You're probably overdeveloping your deltoids," I said resignedly. "It would be a better use of your time to work on your triceps. But what do I know? I'm just the guy you're paying obscene hourly rates."

"Which I can afford, since I make five times as much as you do. Anyway, you were just complaining that you can't tell which muscles I'm working."

"Well, it would be easier if you worked with your shirt off."

"Construction workers work with their shirts off. My gardener works with his shirt off. You're my employee, too, Tony. Maybe I should make you take your shirt off when you demonstrate how to do an exercise."

"I've given up on demonstrating anything to you. You know it all. I'll just stand here getting paid for nothing."

"I just like to be in control of my own workout."

Right. And everything else, I'll bet.

# # # # #

It was my turn to close, which included picking up the sweaty towels that Richard and other inconsiderate members had left on the floor. I was in a bad mood when I locked up for the night. When I found the drunken kid semiconscious in back of the building, clutching another unlabeled bottle, identical to the others but filled with clear liquid, I was furious.

"Why do you keep coming back here? Where are you getting all this booze? Are you even old enough to buy it?"

Over his languorous protests, I roughly rolled him over onto his belly and took his wallet out of his back pocket. "Ha! I thought so. That makes you 20 – no, 19. They raised the drinking age to 21, buddy. Who sold you the vodka?"

"It's gin," he said. "I like variety."

Well, maybe you can't make the horse drink, but you can sure prevent him from drinking. I snatched the bottle from his hand and hurled it into the darkened parking lot. It landed with a satisfying sound of broken glass and a surprisingly impressive gout of what I took to be beer foam, even if it was supposed to contain gin. In the shadows, it seemed to squirt up six or eight feet. Then, instead of falling back down or being wafted away, it vaporized. As it did, I noticed for the first time a very tall figure standing where it had landed: male, judging by the broad-shouldered outline, and impressively muscled to my professional eye, judging from the outline of his pecs, picked out by a lone streetlamp far off to his left. Funny, I could have sworn he was standing there shirtless in the cool evening. And, his pants were so tight, he might as well have been nude, for all I could tell in the dimness.

"Free!" he shouted in a deep voice that echoed off the wall behind me. "I have been the slave of that unworthy drunkard for fifteen months and a prisoner for untold ages before he found me in the forest."

"Whoa," said the kid softly. "Now, I know I'm plastered."

"As a token of my gratitude, I will grant you your heart's fondest desire. Choose carefully."

I recovered my wits enough to say, "This is some kind of joke, right? I get it. You're giving me one wish. Shouldn't you be wearing a turban or something?"

"Do not try my patience. Make your decision."

I supposed it couldn't hurt to play along, just in case. A lot of very shortsighted wishes came to mind, ranging from merely selfish to downright sordid, but then I thought of how much I loved my job and how frustrating it could be. "If this were real," I said, "all I would wish for would be to be able to help other guys get in shape. You know, really get inside their heads and feel what it's like for them, what they're not doing right in their workouts, and lead them through the right way of doing it. I know how to make my own body do it, but I can't explain it to them."

"So be it!" He clapped his hands together. I could feel the sound reverberating in my chest cavity, rattling my bones, jiggling my balls. "It would be fitting for you to use my erstwhile master for practice. You need only place your hand on any exposed part of his body."

I looked at the kid, who had staggered to his feet by this time. "Get away from me," he said nervously, edging away. Not wanting him to run away just yet, I grabbed his arm just below the sleeve of his outer shirt.

"Now say this word: 'Orthrocorporso.'"

"'Orthrocorporso'?" I repeated dubiously. And, a strange thing happened. I could feel a strong hand clamped around my biceps. But not really on my biceps; it was as if I'd grown an extra pair of arms somewhere nearby. The new pair felt much thinner than my own arms. Experimentally, I tightened my grip on the kid's biceps and felt the phantom grip on my extra arm instantly tighten. It was painful, in a distant sort of way. The kid grunted and started to reach over with his far hand, as if to try to pry my fingers loose. As he did, I felt my other new arm move. I willed it down again, and his arm fell to his side. Apparently, I could control him like a puppet.

"Say it again," the looming figure commanded.

"Orthrocorporso." The world flipped around, and I was no longer standing with my right hand clamped around the kid's left arm; my hands were at my side and a big guy on my left was loosely gripping my left arm, which ached. I did a double take and realized that I was literally beside myself. Glancing down, I saw I was dressed as the kid had been: ripped-up jeans, dirty sneakers, and a blue short-sleeved shirt hanging open to reveal a beer-stained white T-shirt. Just to make sure that I hadn't just been teleported into his clothes, I pulled up the T-shirt and saw a flat but completely unripped abdomen. And the thin trail of hair above my navel seemed to be missing; instead, thicker hairs began below the navel – which was now an outie – and disappeared into my pants.

"Please tell me this isn't permanent," I said desperately, and the words came out in the kid's voice. Although, come to think of it, getting a body ten years younger wasn't a bad trade, and I would enjoy whipping it into shape. I studied my old body, wondering if the kid was now occupying it, but it was staring ahead, blinking absently, as if lost in thought.

"Fear not. Say this word: 'Osroprocorthro.'"

"Osroprocorthro," I repeated with the kid's mouth, and instantly found myself back in my own body. The kid, wide-eyed, backed away, then took off running.

What he didn't know was that I could feel his legs moving as if I owned them. In a way, I did. I stopped him in his tracks and made him turn around and walk back to me. It felt as natural as commanding my own body; I just had to decide to make him walk, and each step took care of itself. His eye were wide with wonder. Or terror.

"Say 'osroprocorthro' one more time when you desire to relinquish control," the looming figure said. I turned to thank him, but without another word, he vanished in a second explosion of foam, or steam, or smoke. This time it did waft away, heading up over the trees.

"You want to run so bad? That might not be a bad idea. All this lying around drinking isn't good for you."

"Please, sir ..." he began, but he was already shrugging out of his outer shirt. "It's cold," he complained, but I made him toss it aside.

"Not for long," I said, and sent him running across the parking lot. "Orthrocorporso," I added before he got out of my sight, and my point of view jumped to the edge of the parking lot.

The guy was really out of shape. His lungs were burning after only two laps around my usual jogging path, and his legs felt like rubber. He was so overheated I peeled off his damp T-shirt as he ran. The cool evening air felt good against his bare chest.

I brought him trotting up to my body, still standing by the building. It had probably been risky to leave it undefended on a dark night like this. If someone mugged me, would I even feel it in time to transfer back and fight them off? Experimentally, I reached out with the kid's hand and slapped my own shoulder. I did feel it, in a distant sort of way. "Osroprocorthro," I said with my borrowed voice.

The kid groaned and tried to double over, but I forced him to remain upright. "Not used to a real workaround, are you?" I said. "No pain, no gain. Come on."

"Where are we going?" he asked, unwillingly following me to the front door, which I unlocked.

"You need to learn how to treat your body right, and I need someone to practice on before I try this on my paying customers."

# # # # #

I learned a lot in the next few hours. I learned how to use my new power more subtly. I experienced first-hand what it feels like to start a new exercise program with an out-of-shape body. And, I learned that some guys want to give up too easily.

"Please, no more," the kid moaned for the thousandth time as he lifted the lightly loaded barbells over his head, sweat running down his nearly hairless torso and soaking into the waistband of his white briefs. His dark armpit hair no longer stuck out, but was plastered against his pits. Normally at this point I would wonder if I were pushing a client too far and risking injury, but in this case, I could gage from the burn in his muscles just how much many reps he could do. "Three more," I said. Not a request, not an instruction, just information. He whimpered all the way through them, but really, it didn't hurt that bad.

The hot water, when I finally marched him into the shower, felt so good on his sore muscles that I couldn't resist entering his body all the way, so I could enjoy the sensation. I knew by now that he could feel it as well as I could, even when I transferred over completely. As I soaped up his body, using his own hands, I had to resist a perverse desire to let his hands linger on his hairy balls a little longer, to continue stroking his shaft longer than necessary to get even an uncut cock thoroughly clean. Would it feel to him like he was masturbating, since he could feel his cock in his own fist, or would it feel like another man was stroking him, since his hand was under my control? But, it wouldn't be right.

Back in my own body, I handed him a towel and let him dry himself off. "If I catch you drinking again, or if you tell anyone about my ability" I warned, "next time it'll be ten laps outside. And first, I'll make you take off more than your shirt."

He blushed, glancing down at his naked body. "No one would believe me anyway. They'll say it was the booze. And don't worry; you won't be seeing me again at all."

"Fine with me." And, I let him dress and walk himself out.

# # # # #

"Move your shoulders down just a little, and sort of shift your weight ... perfect!" I told Kevin during our next session.

"Feels heavier now," he grunted.

"That's because you're not cheating. Do you feel it here in your upper back?" I prodded his rhomboids, and he nodded. "Until now you were only using your lower back." I slid my hand down his sweaty back to his lats.

This was working really well. Whenever he repositioned his body trying to obey my vague instructions, I just had to nudge him a little and stop him at the right point, and he thought he was doing it himself.

"I've got muscles aching that I didn't even know I had," he complained cheerfully, less than halfway through his session. He flopped down onto a mat to rest.

"I know," I said. "That's a good sign. Say, as long as you're down there, let's have you do some sit-ups."

He groaned, but started to do them willingly enough.

"That's it."

Several moments passed. "Hard to stop once you get going, isn't it?" I remarked after he'd done twenty reps.

"Yeah," he panted, sounding surprised. "Hurts, though."

He was feeling it, but not that much worse than I would after twenty reps. He usually quit at ten, and I'd always suspected he could do a lot more. I decided to keep him going until it was physically impossible to continue. "Just don't think about it and kind of zone out," I advised.

He almost made it to fifty before his muscles gave out, and he fell back exhausted, his wet back slapping the mat.

"That was great!" I said. "I knew you could do it if you wanted to. And it'll be worth it. Before you know it, you'll be developing washboard abs." With my finger, I traced imaginary lines across his unresisting, heaving belly.

# # # # #

I normally don't do more than wave at my clients on their way in, until they're changed and ready. We have plenty of time to chat during the session. Today, though, I contrived to be in the locker room when Marshall came in, giving me an excuse to hang around while he changed. Normally, when I try that, he hangs up his jacket, takes off his shoes, and then stands around awkwardly until I leave. Maybe his outer shirt, if he's wearing a T-shirt underneath. Today, he was wearing a flannel shirt with nothing on underneath, but as soon as we shook hands, he found himself automatically starting to unbutton it as we talked. I kept talking and tried to act as if it were the most natural thing in the world, which, of course it was.

When his lanky body was bare to the waist, I was glad to see that he had more muscle definition than I had guessed. I could make out the curve of a deltoid and a hint of biceps. I wondered how much of that I could take credit for. His pecs, which were flat plates but reasonably well-defined, were dusted with blond hair. I was curious to see if it would look darker once his chest was bathed in sweat.

He looked nervous at my presence, despite my feigned disinterest, but he looked downright ashamed when an exhausted Kevin hobbled out of the shower wearing only a towel around his buff body. "You're well on your way," I whispered to Marshall encouragingly, "to looking at least that good".

"Aw, come on."

"No, really. You've got some muscles, I can tell. Try flexing them; you'll see."

Without any conscious intent, he glanced at the mirror and flexed his arm and chest muscles. Without any conscious intent on his part that is.

"Now finish changing and let's get started."

He had just pulled his sweat pants over his long, skinny legs and was snapping the lock shut and spinning the dial when he stopped himself. "What am I doing?" he muttered. "I left my sweat shirt in the locker." He dialed the combination, but somehow he kept fumbling it.

"We should get started," I said after several tries. "Think of how much you're paying me per minute."

"But ..."

"It's just as well. Like I told you a long time ago, I encourage all my clients to leave their shirts off, so I can see which muscle groups they're working. No one will think anything of it; in case you haven't noticed, half the guys here work out bare-chested."

He was going to protest, but I had turned my back on him to lead the way out of the locker room, and he was already following me out.

# # # # #

Marshall was really pumped up when we returned to the locker room at the end of our session. He was the opposite of Kevin: reluctant to get started, but willingly pushing his body almost to its limit once I'd adjusted its position from inside and forced him through the first few reps. I had briefly transferred over to his body just to feel what it was like to fill that scrawny chest with air and to see the world from that height, but otherwise had just stood back and nudged him from a distance.

Sweat was pouring down his lanky frame, soaking his waistband. I caught him glancing at himself in the mirror. "Don't expect these sore muscles to look bigger yet," I told him, squeezing a particularly tender trapezius next to his scrawny shoulder. "That will come with time."

He grinned and turned to go to his locker. I muttered "osroprocorthro" to release him. He strode to his locker, radiating confidence, but seemed to deflate when he saw Richard in the midst of changing out of his street clothes a few lockers away, the sleeves of his white T-shirt barely roomy enough to contain his biceps. The big man gave him a scornful look, as though he was thinking about stuffing him into a locker just for the fun of it. Just what the poor guy needed. What a jerk!

# # # # #

"Five more," I commanded. Richard looked as if he wanted nothing more than to let go of the chin-up bar and drop to the ground, but his hands wouldn't obey him. He looked exhausted, sweat slicking down his once bushy armpit hair as he hung there in front of me. He had surprisingly little chest hair, just a scraggly patch between his pecs and a wispy tuft near his sternum. Somehow I'd expected a big burly guy to have dense curly black hair all over his chest, something like the man who was currently working out across the room from us at the moment. Maybe that was the real reason Richard had never taken off his shirt until I made him.

"Come on," I said, and forced his lats and biceps to struggle to raise his hefty body one more time. Then again.

"How are you doing this?" he asked softly. No one was in earshot.

"What do you mean?"

"I'm trying to let go, but I keep doing pull-ups. Somehow you're forcing me into it like, like a puppet."

"Don't be ridiculous. You can let go anytime you want," I said, and loosened my mental grip on him. He dropped to his hands and knees, breathing hard.

I put him through a long series of punishing workouts, not caring that he was getting more and more convinced of the incredible truth, or that it was way past closing time.

"Now pull yourself up on that bar and get your knees over it and hang upside down. We're going to do an exercise that'll work your abs."

89

"No. It's some kind of spell, isn't it? When we started, I heard you mumble something that sounded like a cross between 'abracadabra' and a something in Latin about bodies."

"You know how crazy that sounds, right?" I forced him to turn to the bar and start raising his arm. Then something happened that I had no experience with: he managed to stop himself with his arm halfway raised, apparently by sheer force of will. I concentrated, and his arm trembled as we fought for control. After a moment, I won, and regained complete control over his body. But when I had him hanging upside down by his knees, I was unable to force him to curl his torso up. It felt like willpower at work, not exhaustion.

"You need to do this," I told him. "You're getting a little soft in the middle." I poked him in the belly and said "orthocorporso" softly.

I fought down a brief wave of vertigo as my perception instantly flipped over. I was looking at my own body upside down, and the blood had rushed to my borrowed head. Every muscle in my new body felt sore, in the familiar and not-unpleasant way that follows a good workout. I forced it through the abs exercises. Then, sore as I was, I made a circuit through half the weight machines and free weights in the room, just for the joy of being in a big, broad-shouldered body. Richard's body had a lot of muscle, even if he'd let it start to get soft. It was going to be a pleasure getting it into shape. In fact, it would be hard to give it back, although I supposed I would need to return to my own body, if only to eat and drink and pee. Speaking of which, Richard's bladder was getting pretty full. I walked into the men's room to relieve him, relishing the novelty of an unfamiliar dick in my hand. I was amused to find that the arrogant bastard's dick seemed to be a good bit smaller than my own. Alone in the men's room, I stroked it for a few minutes to work it into an erection. Yes, it was definitely at least an inch shorter than mine. I repeated that aloud, just so Richard, helpless in his own body, would hear.

About twenty minutes later, I froze in the act of walking from one weight machine to the next and couldn't get my feet to move. I started to tremble with the effort.

Then my borrowed mouth said on its own, "If I'm crazy, how do you explain the fact that you've been standing over there staring into space for the last hour? You're inside me, aren't you?"

I didn't respond. He wrested control of his legs back and walked us over to my body, which was still standing where I'd left it. "You're not in there anymore, are you?" he asked, poking my abandoned body in the chest and staring into its vacant eyes. "You're in here, aren't you?" he asked, slapping his own bare chest. I'd felt the poke, a little more distantly than I now felt the slap.

"I wonder," he said, "what would happen to you if I use your body as a punching bag?"

Enough of this! I could still kick his ass. "Osro …" I started to say with his mouth, but he clamped his jaw closed in mid-incantation. I was trapped! I watched helplessly through his eyes as he socked me in the stomach, just hard enough to hurt.

"Wow," he said, and yanked my shirt up. "Nice abs." He jabbed my exposed belly with his fist a few more times, then began pummeling my chest. With nobody home, my body seemed to automatically keep its balance up to a point, but it was rocked back on its heels by the blows and eventually fell sprawling, grunting as the wind was knocked out of it. I would have cried out myself, through Richard's mouth, if he hadn't had his jaw clenched so tightly.

Silently, he threw my unattended body over his back. It felt heavy; we really needed to work on his lats. Grunting, he trudged toward the locker room.

# # # # #

His hands trembled as he wrung out the towel he had just soaked under cold running water. I was fighting him with all my might, but all I accomplished was the tremor, which slowed him down not one bit. He turned around on shaky legs and walked back to my limp, defenseless body, which he had stripped of its shirt and laid out on its belly along a bench. "All the times you badgered me about taking care of my body, and now you leave your own body lying around unprotected for anyone to mess with! This is gonna hurt when I finally let you back in your body with your back red and raw."

Of course it actually hurt the instant the towel snapped across my bare flesh, and he found out when my scream was forced out of his mouth. "Oh," he said in delight, "so you can still feel your body?

91

That'll be even more fun. This is great! My big tough know-it-all trainer lying there helpless." He spat at my prone body. I felt the wetness hit my bare back as the same instant I saw it land through his eyes. He raised the towel for another lash, and this time I found myself able to stop it, to freeze his arm in mid-air. His mouth opened, and I tried to force out of it the word I had been trying over and over to say: "Osro ...". He clamped his mouth shut again, but I forced it open by an act of will. "Osroproc ..."

" ...tology", he finished for me sarcastically, regaining control. He hooked his free hand under the waistbands of my gym shorts and the boxers underneath and yanked them down to my ankles. Then, with a trembling arm, he slapped the wet towel against my bare ass again and again, laughing at the cries coming out of his own mouth. To my surprise, I could feel that this was giving him a hard-on.

When he stopped, there were rosy welts crossing my back, and both my ass cheeks were pink. Then, to my horror, he pulled down his own gym shorts and underwear and bent over my body, grabbing it under the armpits to reposition it on the bench. It was an odd sensation, simultaneously feeling his thumbs digging into my armpits and my armpit hair against the pads of his thumbs, his smooth chest plastered against my sore back and my damp back against his chest, our sweat freely mingling. And then, the most novel and disturbing sensation of all, the head of his dick probing between my ass cheeks, and the feel of my cheeks giving way to his dick.

"A lot of good these big muscles are doing you now, when you're not in there to resist," he growled, gripping my limp biceps painfully.

Somehow, I regained partial control – of his body; my own was still lying there helpless – just as he was about to enter me. I forced him to stagger back a step. Then I grabbed his dick in his fist. I could tell that he was so close that a few quick strokes would deprive him of his weapon, so I began using his own hand to jerk him off.

As I saw a rope of white fluid splatter across my sweaty back and felt its sticky warmth, I felt my control over his body strengthen. "Osroprocorthro," I said quickly through his mouth.

Finally, I had control of my own body again. I rolled over onto my back, just in time for another spurt to hit me square in the chest. Neither of us had any control over his dick at the moment. But the warm white fluid brought with it with another surge of control over the body it had come from. I was able to halt his attempt to lunge at me. It was as though by mingling his semen with my sweat, he'd given me more of a handle on him. I did something I'd never have thought I would do: I scraped some of his cum off my chest and put it in my mouth. Sure enough, I felt it: his body was mine, firmly and finally.

"This is good stuff," I said. "You should try some. Come here and lick the rest of it off my chest."

Trembling, he approached me.

# # # # #

Marshall waved at his former trainer, Tony, on his way into the gym. Tony was about to replace a burned-out tube in one of the light fixtures in the low ceiling, riding on the broad shoulders of his new assistant, Richard. Back when they'd both had regular sessions with Tony, Richard had routinely arrived at about the same time Marshall was leaving, and Marshall had raced to be fully dressed by the time the beefy lawyer came in. That was back when he'd been ashamed of his body. He was in much better shape now, thanks to Tony.

Tony waved back. Richard kept his eyes downcast, but turned slightly, so Tony could see Marshall better. The two men made a good team, working together silently as Richard positioned Tony at just the right spot to unscrew the tube, as gracefully as if he were an extension of the other man's body.

Tony was with a new client when Marshall came out of the locker room in his gym shorts. Taking a nearby machine, Marshall overhead him say, "Any of my clients will tell you that I've helped them to work harder than they ever thought they could, and the results are worth it. Richard here used to be a client, and look at him now. Take off your shirt, Richard."

Instantly, Richard peeled off his T-shirt. All the time he spent here now working for Tony had left him in even better shape than Marshall remembered from glimpses in the locker room. His arms, even relaxed, bulged with muscles, his chest was chiseled perfection, and he had six-pack abs without the slightest trace of fat. He stood there for inspection, blushing slightly, and shivering even though the air didn't feel chilly against Marshall's own bare chest.

"See? That's what a thousand sit-ups and two hundred pushups a day can do for a man. Show our new client how to do sit-ups, Richard."

Richard obediently lay down on his back and started doing sit-ups, breathing hard and whimpering slightly as if he'd been doing them all day and it hurt. Yet, he kept going.

# # # # #

Later, passing Tony's office on his way to the showers, Marshall saw Richard giving Tony a massage. Tony had lately become a great masseur himself and charged even more per hour for massages than he got as a trainer. All the guys said he had an uncanny sense for zeroing in on just the right sore muscles to knead, just hard enough, with his strong hands. From the blissful look on Tony's face now, his assistant had a similar skill, but if so, Tony wasn't sharing him with anyone.

Emerging from the hot shower with a towel around his waist, Marshall was surprised to find Richard in the locker room, picking up towels, still shirtless. "Is that part of your job, too?" Marshall asked him.

"Yeah."

"I heard you were some kind of high-powered lawyer."

"I took a leave of absence to spend more time working out. Money isn't everything."

There was one other guy in the locker room, just putting on his shirt and zipping up his gym bag. When he was gone, Richard commented, "The last hour on Friday night is always pretty dead. We've got the place to ourselves."

"Um, I'll be out of your way soon, if that's a hint."

"Th-that's a hint, all r-right," Richard said. Marshall hadn't ever heard him stutter before. "But n-not that you should leave."

Marshall stood there in his towel, not sure he understood what was going on. Could it be that this hunky jock – who could still wipe up the floor with him, despite Marshall's new muscles – was actually offering to pleasure him instead?

"May I t-take your towel, sir?" Richard asked, kneeling at Marshall's feet. His eyes pleaded with Marshall to give him the answer Richard hoped for.

"What if Tony comes in?"

"He fell asleep during the massage. Trust me, he's out cold until ... until w-we're d-d-done." He bowed his head deferentially and fixed his gaze on Marshall's bare feet.

Marshall rested his hands on Richard's meaty shoulders, which were trembling. "Is this your first time, too?" Marshall asked gently.

"N-no, I do this a lot," the big man stammered, and unknotted Marshall's towel with trembling fingers.

CUSTOMER LOVE
By Derrick Della Giorgia

Before concretely seeing it about an inch away from my face, I recognized in my nostrils the dense, sharp and sweet fragrance of fucked asshole mixed with lube. I opened my eyes and was suddenly assaulted by three horrid interrogations: to whose face did that ass belong? Was it right after lunch time or right before dinner time? What alcohol had provided me with such a painful hang over? I wasn't ready for any of those answers, so I shut my eyes and thought of him. I was one of those who didn't believe in love at first sight, and maybe that is why cupid had punished me so cruelly.

My heart had flown away from my chest and liquefied over his shirtless body when I first saw him at Mena & Craft on Fifth Avenue. The store had immediately become an attraction for girls and gay guys since it had opened, mainly due to its policy of having their sales people – who were surely picked by modeling agencies – walking shirtless and dancing to the blasting club music pumped on every floor at every hour. A whole year of unconditional love, and I didn't even know his name. Three-hundred-sixty-five days of thick infatuation burning on my face when I saw him, making me happy when I thought of him, keeping me company when I fantasized about the first words we would tell each other on our first date. When anyone asked, it was the hardest thing to describe him physically. It was much easier to just tell people to go online and Google Leandro Okabe, the half Japanese, half Brazilian model who was making the news. They looked so alike that they could switch jobs and nobody would notice. Maybe my husband was a little shorter and younger, but that was it. He must have been twenty-one or twenty-two and about five-nine. But, that was perfect because I was twenty-three and five-eight. Nobody would have flinched looking at us walking down the aisle.

The brown bubble butt in front of me changed position and in doing so let two big balls slide down on the right thigh of the nameless guy I'd fucked only hours before. Unfortunately, that sight didn't work for me anymore. I looked in the direction of the only window that my studio apartment on 23rd Street had, and in the little corner of glass my golden curtains lazily missed, I saw countless snowflakes coming down silently. It was Sunday, March 17. An exact year had passed since my heart had been occupied by that beautiful nameless tenant. I had to go see him. But before, I had to find a nice way to get rid of "bubble butt." Now, I was starting to remember the pleasure it had given me on the edge of the bath tub, and I felt bad. I slowly crawled out of my queen size bed and walked barefoot to the bathroom, checking one last time on him before shutting the door.

I was surprised to see that my face in the mirror looked much better than it felt on my cheek bones. I had to thank my French mother for my delicate features, and my job as assistant editor for the non-significant amount of physical stress I was subjected to. It was 5:00 pm, and the store closed at 9:00! I jumped into the shower and went on with my toxic desiring the naked oriental model/clerk by my side, underneath millions of soap bubbles, caressing his smooth skin underwater until the snow got tired of falling on the Big Apple. I passed the lavender-body-wash-soaked sponge on my chest and my modest but defined pectorals contracted as if he was there to look at me. Then, I hugged my lathered up torso and with the shower head aiming at my forehead, I imagined him blocking me in his strong embrace from behind, softly kissing my neck with his story-teller lips and warming my back with the fruit of his crunches and sit-ups. After the shower, we could get dressed – him with a dark collar shirt that would enhance his penetrating gaze and his silky black hair – and jump into a cab for a romantic candlelight dinner Downtown. I was dying to learn about his ethnic background, the percentage of Asian he had in his blood, the second language he spoke, the culture he would integrate in my French-American environment.

The piping made an awkward noise when I stopped the water, and the silence of my studio brought me back to reality. I needed to apply some anti-aging cream around my eyes before meeting bubble butt. My complexion was very light, and the gelid winter of Manhattan dug its way into my skin if I didn't take care of it.

With my hand on the door knob, I inhaled deeply and walked into the kitchen/living-room/bedroom. He was awake and still completely naked. As he heard my steps, he turned toward me and smiled.

"Good morning!" A young voice came out of his smile. Bubble butt was Latin, a cute, young, probably eighteen-year-old, smooth boy.

"Good morning to you!" I sat on the bed and kissed him to make the whole situation more comfortable and less surreal.

"I missed you."

"I was freshening up."

"I loved last night, Arthur." He remembered my name, and I didn't remember his. It was going to be harder than I'd thought to let him down softly.

"It was amazing." My comment was more referred to the athletic sex he'd been able to perform in the bathroom than any sentiment of love or tenderness, but he couldn't know it because he ignored the fact that I was in love with my husband.

"What time is it?" He asked, finding it intriguing that we had shared the bed for so long.

"It's 5:00 pm. Do you have to go?" I attempted a half preoccupied, half sad expression.

"No. No. I was just wondering. Do you have something to do?" He politely returned the question.

"Unfortunately, I do. I have to be somewhere very soon." I caressed his brown hair and rested my hand on his neck.

"It's ok. Don't worry." He kissed me on my lips. It was awful. I had a nice cute boy, caring for me instead of running away before getting too involved as often happened, and I sat there by him unmoved, yearning to get dressed and run to Fifth Avenue until I hit the tall metal door that protected my man's naked chest from the cold wind of March.

"I'll call you later, and we'll get some dinner. How's that sound?" Damn! The lie I hated the most. The one lie that only the cheapest sluts in the city had the balls to come up with.

"Sounds perfect ..." He tried to make a sexy voice, but he was too young to go down that path. He stared at me for a second and then slid his hand under my robe and grabbed my balls. He was still naked, and he was getting an erection.

"I'm sor ..."

"Just wanna say goodbye to him, too ..." His face reached his hand, and he started kissing my dick.

" ... Hmm ... really ..."

"Yeaaah ..."

" ... I really have to ..." He put it in his mouth and with his tongue played with my half erection.

"OK! I'll finish that later. Aaall riiight?" He talked to my cock, shaking his head like nannies did in Central Park to toddlers when they tried to explain something in the easiest possible way.

"I'm sorry, but I really need to be at this place in an hour."

"No problem. We have all the time in the world." He stood up and started gathering his clothes from all the different places where we'd thrown them in the heat of the alcoholic sex.

When I turned on Fifth from 23rd, a tank of wind and snow hit me in the face so hard that I couldn't breathe and tried to hide behind my scarf. Around me, everybody ran from store to store and from store to cab, trying to minimize the time spent in that weather. Instead, I needed to get to him. In a year, I had bought about fifteen T-shirts and four polo shirts – five of which I had also exchanged to increase the number of times I could see him in a short period of time – but I had never ventured into anything past store-talk. Too scared of saying the wrong thing. "What size are you looking for there? Let me help you." Or, "You're pretty tight there, you must be a medium." A collection of question marks, adjectives and pauses in which I detected a little sparkle of interest, a feeling of familiarity and vicinity that went beyond customer care. I couldn't see my face, but I felt the warm smile of pleasure forming on my eyes remembering his words. I kept my face skywards, and people probably thought my awe was due to the big Macy's sign you could see on the Broadway side of the store.

After he moved to the second floor, where his job was mainly to spray the new fragrance on his naked chest – which turned shiny and even more perfect after that – and on the thin white strips he handed out from the back pocket of his cargo pants, I started to buy underwear. Briefs, boxers, tank tops and everything that was sold on the shelves that decorated the room he was in. In July, I got a nice longer than five seconds look, and in December, right before Christmas when he had to wear a red bow on his chest, he gave me his first smile – a sincere luminous delicate smile that exploded on his face just for me. Hidden under his thick eyebrows and below his eyes, the little black pearls strategically placed on his high cheek bones. Next to his nose that widened a little at the bottom making him more masculine than all the other perfect faces working there, and on his lips, the puffy sashimi pieces ready to be licked and sucked.

I ran into the deli across the street from the store to grab a hot coffee, and I stared at the tall door, studying the situation and planning my excursion. The banana muffins smelled so good now that my nostrils had defrosted and suddenly reminded me of bubble butt. His skin smelled a little like that, too, sweet and creamy. I had his number saved on my cell phone, but with the only secret hope that my exotic prince would find it later – when we went out on our first date – and get jealous. He would grab my arm right above the elbow and pressing his strong fingers into my white tensed biceps, he would tell me to immediately delete that number because I was his and his only. In the pocket mirror my friend Carolina had given me, my skin had reddened a bit from the wet cold and my blue eyes were shiny, giving me a cute twelve-year-old boy look. I bent my hair a little more to the left to enhance the spikes, and I ate a piece of gum to get ready for a kiss.

Madonna's "Hung Up" was bouncing off the walls, the volume so high that you would imagine all the clothes hanging would vibrate. It didn't feel good in my head. I was still digesting my hangover, and the low lighting reminded me of the club in the East Village where I'd picked up bubble butt.

"Hi. How are you?" The first model saluted me by the black velvet stairs that separated me from my love. "Are you looking for something in particular?"

Yes, the hot guy that works upstairs. I would like to marry him! "No, thank you. Just browsing."

"Enjoy!"

Halfway up the stairs, I took my coat off and fixed my collar shirt, exposing only enough chest to show my Polynesian tattoo. Next, I lowered my jeans making sure they were wrapped around my ass and shook the biggest snowflakes off my hair with my hat.

I never really understood the order in which they happened every time, but in about thirty seconds of exposure to his person, I got scolding hot cheeks, an erection and tachycardia. He was there, only thirty feet away from me, but holding no cologne in his hands. Instead, he was engaged in the launch of a new product. The effect was so powerful that I felt as if someone had literally kicked me in my throat. He was literally suffocating me with his body – Hybriefs, the briefs he was promoting with only the help of his naked body. He was swaying that mighty weapon to the notes of "Hung Up" as he turned on himself, so customers could appreciate the perfection of the design. A white tiny bandage that lifted his bulge and followed his ass on every curve his muscles created. I got dizzy. His eyes or his thighs? His mouth or his bare feet? His nipples or his square knees? Calves, talons, back, ass, elbows, belly button, neck ... I could have spent hours looking at all that. My blood pressure went up, and my heart kept hammering huge nails into my rib cage with every single beat. I walked toward him, automatically, unconsciously.

"Hello. Welcome back!" He said to me. He knew I was a customer; he remembered my face.

"Hi." To extract that little word, was so painful.

"Do you care to see Hybriefs?" He pointed with both his index fingers at his butt and his bulge in the front, and blinked at me.

"Hmm ... hot ... I mean they're hot ... I-I like them ... I mean the briefs."

"They feel very good, too." He stretched the elastic a little with his thumb.

"I'll check what colors they come in ..." I stepped closer to him to get to the shelf and ... my ankle got trapped in the table leg he stood by, bringing the weight of my twenty-three-year-old body on the verge of disaster. My hips moved backwards to recuperate balance, but my arms went miserably down with the coat, the scarf and the hat.

"Watch out!"

I landed face first into his stomach, plunging my nose and my forehead into his muscles, which defensively contracted and parted my lips leaving me on him as if I was wildly kissing him before a royal blow job.

"Here you are ..:" He picked me up, one hand on my chest, the other on my back, gently fixing me back in a standing position.

"I am so sorry ..." I might as well have told him 'I love you, I wanna spend the rest of my life with you' because my eyes turned into hearts, and my brain acted like milk shake.

"It's ok. I am sure you wanted to check Hybriefs from very near before purchasing them!"

"Sorry" I said again while he laughed. I had never been so close to him. I could smell the cologne on his skin, even the warmth of his body under the lights.

"Are you buying them for your boyfriend?" He nonchalantly asked with a smirk on his face.

"My boyfriend?" I stepped back, underlying my disapproval for the use of that word referred to me. "I don't have a boyfriend."

"Hmm, so are you gonna buy them for yourself?"

"I'll get a pair."

"Ok, 'cause I want you to check them out in blue. They match your eyes." He grabbed my wrist and pulled me. "Look, they come in night blue. How do you like them?"

"Very nice." My brain was still a milk shake, and he was the straw stirring my thoughts. No control.

"Good. I know a place where you can wear them, too." He whispered to me, putting the box in my hands and laying his on top. "Dinner at nine thirty."

"Nine thirty." I repeated mechanically.

"Would you like to keep me company for dinner?" He was as elegant as I had imagined for the past year. I just couldn't believe it was really happening, and I was scared I was going to wake up any second, in my bath tub, in my bed, a deli or somewhere far from him. "I know you are a guy to marry." He looked around and swiftly kissed me on my lips.

PUBLIC DISPLAYS OF AFFECTION
By Logan Zachary

"Quentin, we have a problem."

"Casey, you know I hate when you say that." Quentin walked down the long marble hallway of the Minneapolis Institute of Art, the MIA, which was hardly missing in action. The place was bustling with activity.

"I'm down at the new display, and you're really going to hate what I've found," Casey said into his cell phone.

"What? The jock straps on display exhibit?"

"The history of the uniform is far from jock straps on parade, but I think we ordered the mannequins from the wrong place."

Quentin ran up the marble staircase to the second floor, heading in Casey's direction. "Why? What's wrong? Did we get women? Children?"

"Worse." Casey said as he inserted the arm into the mannequin's body and stepped back.

"We're gay men, and I know all we wanted were men. What did we get? Dogs and cats?"

"You'll have to see it to believe it." Then he laughed.

Quentin passed the information desk and slipped under the rope with the sign, 'Exhibit Instillation in Progress.' "I'm almost to the display area. Which room are you in?"

"I'm in the locker room."

"Ooo, my favorite one."

"Mine, too."

As Quentin walked into the locker room display, a naked man's backside greeted him. His ass was a perfect bubble butt. His skin was tan and beautiful. "Casey, why are you naked?"

Casey's head popped up over the naked man's shoulder. "I'm not, but I'm admiring the artwork."

Quentin did a double take and noticed a seam above the man's ass and another one by each shoulder. "That's the mannequin? Wow! They're so realistic."

"You ain't seen nothing yet." Casey swiveled the male model around.

An enormous penis hung between his legs, thick and veined with a full bush of dark pubic hair. A mass of fur covered each pec and thinned as it lowered across his washboard abs.

"Impressive," Quentin said. "He's almost as big as you are."

"Thanks for the compliment, but I think you're missing something."

"Doesn't look like he's missing anything at all."

"Exactly."

"What? Oh. OH! Now I see. Are they all like that?"

Casey nodded his head. "Oh yeah. Some even better than him."

"The exhibit opens in two days." Quentin ran his hand over the chest of the mannequin. His fingers combed through real hair and the skin felt warm and realistic to the touch. He pulled his hand away as if burned.

"I know. It's creepy. It's almost like that movie *House of Wax*."

"What are we going to do?"

"I've called Sportin' Men, and they don't have any other models in stock."

"We've always ordered from Sporting Men before, they're great."

"I know, but these are from Sportin' Men." He stressed the 'N.' "There is no G, and that's how they keep the two separate."

"I don't understand," Quentin walked around the man and felt his cock swell in his pants.

"Sporting Men have athletic bodies, Sportin' Men are anatomically correct, and they're all sportin' wood, or some form of arousal."

"Some of these are fully erect?"

"Oh yeah."

"Wonderful," Quentin said, sarcastically.

"They are," Casey said as he pretended to smoke a cigarette. "So fine. I've been sportin' wood since I opened the first crate."

Quentin lowered his hand to hide his arousal.

"I can see it from here dear. Nothing I haven't seen before." Casey walked over to Quentin and kissed him.

Quentin gave him a quick peck and stepped back. "No PDAs, you know, at work."

Casey pointed down at Quentin's groin. "Tell your big buddy that."

Quentin looked around the locker room, wishing the showers really worked to take a cool shower.

Casey picked up a towel and wrapped it around the mannequin's waist. "He's shy."

As they entered the main office, his secretary, Roberta Schwartz, said, "Quentin, Mr. Rothenberg called to confirm his meeting with you tomorrow afternoon. He said he should arrive about one. Did you want me to contact you as soon as he arrives or should I show him around, and then let you know?" She leaned forward behind her desk waiting for his answer.

Quentin rushed passed her and into his office, followed closely by Casey.

"Call me as soon as he arrives, and I'll meet him on the tour."

"Okay, hi Casey. How are you doing?" She waved as he passed by.

Casey rolled his eyes and smiled. "We're trying to put out a possible fire in the new uniforms display."

Roberta looked shocked.

"Oh, no. Not a literal fire, just a small problem arose, I mean came up." His face burned red.

"Stop making jokes at a time like this," Quentin said. "Rothenberg is a huge contributor to the MIA. The last thing we need is a sex scandal to happen when he arrives. He hasn't written his check to us this year. He wants to inspect the new display and make sure it's worth his money."

"I'd pay to see it," Casey said, "and I get in free."

"You're not helping."

"I wanted to open the crates last week when they arrived, but someone wouldn't let me inspect them."

"So this is my fault?" Quentin said.

"I'm not blamin' no one." He stressed the N's.

Quentin flopped down into his chair and pulled out a folder on his desk. He flipped through a few invoices and found one. He picked up the phone and dialed.

"Could I speak to someone in the service department?"

Casey watched as he nodded his head.

"They've all left for the day?"

"I told you ..." he started, but Quentin held up his hand, stopping him.

"Will anyone be in tomorrow? I see." He hung up the phone. "Shit."

"I told you," Casey said.

Quentin grabbed his arm. "Come on. We'll see what we can do."

Roberta watched as the two stormed out of the office. "Lovers shouldn't work in the same place," she said and returned to her work.

"What are we going to do?" Quentin walked over to an open crate and saw a ten inch cock sticking straight up. It was thick and uncut, a foreskin hung off the tip. His hand involuntarily reached forward and retracted the skin. A dark pink mushroom tip slipped out of the sheath. "Are these for medical students?"

Casey pulled out a sheet of paper from another crate and started to read it. "No. You're going to laugh when you hear this."

"I doubt that." Quentin continued to stroke the cock and worked his way down the shaft to the balls. The balls swung free as the fine hair tickled his fingers.

"They're used with sex workers for therapy."

"What?" Quentin's finger trailed underneath the testicles, which swung out of the way, and he slipped along the butt crease. His finger found the anus. He circled the spot and felt it give under his pressure. He probed harder, and his fingertip inserted itself into a smooth canal. Pushing deeper, his whole finger entered. "Now I see," he said.

Casey stepped next to him and saw what he was doing. "Did you ask him for his permission?"

Quentin pulled his finger out and waved it at Casey. "Do I need to ask you for your permission?" He approached Casey; his finger still extended and grabbed him. He waved the finger under his nose.

Casey pulled his head back and laughed. "You're naughty."

Quentin hugged him close and said, "Well, should we get started?"

"Doing what?"

"Let's put them together and see what we have to work with. We'll try and dress them in the uniforms that fit and see if we can somehow tone down their assets."

Casey's hand caressed the front of Quentin's pants. "You're hard."

"Aren't you?" His hand explored Casey's inseam and found the same aroused flesh. "I think we need to get to work, before we get sidetracked."

Casey broke the embrace and started to assemble the man in the crate closest to them. This man was a leather bear-type if he ever saw one. Thick furry chest and muscular hairy legs. His huge uncut cock stood out proud. "I wonder if we could mold them into any position we want."

"That will help, but can we pad the uniforms?"

"They aren't big enough?" Casey smiled.

"Oh yes," Quentin said, rolling his eyes. "I wanted to pad their shorts to cover up their bulges."

"These men are hung."

"Well, get tucking."

"I love when you talk dirty to me."

"Tuck you."

All the men were assembled and stood in the shower room. "I've died and gone to heaven," Casey said.

"I hope this is what heaven is like." Quentin looked at the bear. "So, what do you see him as? The football player?"

"That's what I was thinking." Casey picked up the duffle bag with the word football printed on the side. He unzipped the bag and pulled out the uniform. "Do we need the shoulder pads?" he asked as he dropped them on the floor. "His body looks big enough without them."

Quentin picked up the jock and stretched it out. "Do you think this will hide that?"

Casey laughed. "No."

"Could we cut it off?" Quentin asked, holding the man's cock.

"You can't. That's just wrong."

"Let's see if this works." Quentin picked up the mannequin and waited as Casey slipped the jock over his feet. His fingers slid between his butt cheeks and entered his hole. Quentin's erection sprang to full length in his shorts.

Casey pulled the white elastic strap up the model's hairy legs as Quentin set him down. He pulled the pouch over his dick and straightened his butt straps. The mesh stretched to its limit.

"Huge," was all Quentin said. They slipped on the white football pants and inserted the pads. Casey tied the laces at the waistband. The pants tented in front of the man, but it looked as if it would work.

"Do we have to put his shirt on?" Casey asked. "I've always had a football fantasy."

"You want to be the tight end?"

"I already am." He slapped his butt. Casey pulled out a Speedo and dangled it from his finger. "Who gets to wear this?"

Quentin searched for a swimmer's body and found a perfect one. He picked him up, as Casey looped the leg holes over its feet. As Quentin set him down, Casey worked the Speedo into place.

"There isn't enough material."

"Leave it, what a great fantasy and look."

For the next few hours, Quentin and Casey dressed the mannequins with the perfect uniform, deciding who would get the chainmail, and which one looked like a hockey player, a runner, or a knight, and which model would play cricket, basketball, or soccer.

Quentin's phone rang, but he ignored it. They were having too much fun playing dress up and finding the perfect uniform for the right mannequin.

Finally, all but one mannequin was dressed.

"So what should we do with him?" Quentin asked. He took the man into his arms and danced around the other men.

Casey took Speedo man and joined in the dance. "Trying to make me jealous?"

Quentin caressed the mannequin's body, he cupped his buttocks and dug his fingers into the bubble butt. His finger explored the opening. "How do suppose the sex workers use these?"

Casey spun around and slipped his hand into the blue Speedo. "I would guess that they'd use them to help their clients try all the things they're afraid to try with another person."

"Do you think these openings are usable?"

"Only one way to find out." He set Mr. Speedo down and took Quentin's partner. "You've always enjoyed a bubble butt, and this one's perfect."

"I wouldn't say that. Your ass is perfection." Quentin kissed Casey.

"PDA at work. PDA anywhere. What gives?" Casey started to unbutton Quentin's shirt. He rubbed his hands over the thick mat of hair that covered his chest. He pinched his nipples and felt them rise up into points under his touch.

"I've been hard since we started this."

"Me, too."

Casey's hands unbuckled Quentin's belt and unzipped his fly. He reached in to pull out his uncut cock.

Quentin's erection sprang free of his pants.

Casey caressed down the shaft and felt precum ooze from the tip. It slid along his palm as Quentin threw his head back and moaned. His hands found Casey's T-shirt and pulled it over his head.

"You always wanted a three-way," Quentin said. "This could be our first."

"Fooling around at work is a first, too."

112

"Stop talking," Quentin's mouth descended on Casey's and quieted him. His tongue explored and tasted his lover, as his hands undid Casey's jeans.

He kicked off his shoes and let his jeans slide to the floor. His Calvins clung to his body like a second skin. A wet spot formed at the tip of his dick in the sheer cotton. The outline of his mushroom head showed through the fabric. A dark shadow of pubic hair contrasted with the pale skin below.

Casey looked around and saw all the men staring at him in his underwear. He covered himself as he felt his arousal start to shrink.

"What's wrong?" Quentin asked.

"I've never been the center of attention before."

"It's kind of creepy, but it's also kind of hot and sexy." Quentin slipped his pants and underwear off. His erection bounced up and down with each beat of his heart. His foreskin was wet and a small drop of precum clung to the flap.

Casey licked his lips, but didn't move.

Quentin knelt down and pulled his briefs off. He leaned forward and ran his tongue around the tip and kissed it. His lips puckered and drew Casey's semi-hard-on into his mouth.

Casey threw his head back as the warm wetness took him and sucked his shaft. Blood raced to re-fill his shaft, and his erection stretched to its painful maximum length. It felt as if would burst as Quentin pulled back.

Quentin grabbed his low hanging balls and rolled them between his fingers.

Casey moaned in pleasure. His hand reached over to Mr. Speedo and rubbed his bulge. His fingers pulled the fabric down and removed the cock from its restraint. He milked it as Quentin milked his dick with his mouth.

Quentin freed Casey's cock and said, "Don't come too fast, I have plans for you."

"Anything you want," Casey exhaled, as a shudder washed over his body. He almost pulled Mr. Speedo off of his feet.

A footfall echoed down the hallway display, but neither man cared.

Quentin worked Casey's arousal and felt his balls start to rise. "Take his Speedo off," he commanded.

"Why?'

"I want him to join in. I want to rim his ass and lube up his tight hole." Quentin wagged his tongue at Casey and smiled. "You're the one who wanted to try a threesome. This is perfect and no guilt."

Casey pulled the Speedo off, bent the mannequin over, and held his cheeks open for Quentin.

Quentin's cock dripped with precum, lubing the opening. He pulled back his foreskin, allowing more clear fluid to escape. He painted it on the opening and pressed forward. The hole was tight and his girth was massive. He knelt and stuck his tongue between the fleshy orbs. He tasted his own juices and added saliva to the opening.

Casey knew what the mannequin was feeling, if rubber and plastic could feel. He twisted the model's head back and slid his cock into its mouth. The fleshy lips and tight tunnel formed a suction on his engorged dick.

"You always wanted a spit roast." Quentin stood and drove his cock deep into the mannequin. His hips drilled his erection in deeper and deeper. The narrow passageway was also airtight and formed a vacuum around his dick.

The men slid the doll back and forth on their cocks. The pressure that drew down on them grew and grew, adding to their pleasure and sensation.

"I'm going to come," Quentin said, as he grabbed the man's hips and slammed back into him.

Casey pulled on his ears and increased his speed. "Me … me … me, too."

114

Quentin dove into him one more time as his balls slammed into the bubble butt. They released their load, and it shot out of his cock and filled the tunnel.

Casey's dick rolled across the mannequin's tongue and that extra wave was all it took. Cum burst out as he pulled back, the suction increased and pulled more out of his balls. He pushed in one more time and pulled back. A wet pop echoed in the room as his cock escaped from the lips.

The model snapped in half, as each man took his piece with him to the floor. Their fleshy asses hit the tile and both sweaty men clung to their half as if it were a life jacket.

Quentin withdrew from the perfect ass and lay back waiting for his breathing to return to normal. "Wow. That was hot."

"Yeah," was all Casey said.

Quentin crawled over to Casey and pulled him close. He kissed him deeply and whispered in his ear, "Do you know what I want?"

"Like that wasn't enough?" Casey laughed.

"I want to see him do you. Fuck you, fill you up."

"What?"

"I want to use his dick in your ass." Quentin turned his half of Mr. Speedo around and stroked his cock. "Look how long and thick this is. You and I have never had anyone like that before …"

"And you think that will fit in me?"

"I would love to try." Quentin kissed him again.

"What's all of this? One of your secret fantasies you want to live out?"

Quentin's face reddened and he nodded. "Yes, is that so bad?"

"No," Casey agreed.

"We know he's clean and safe, and won't tell anyone."

"He's the perfect man."

"No, you are."

"You're just saying that to get …"

Quentin cut him off. "No, you are the perfect man for me, but this is something else."

Casey sat up and stared at the enormous cock. "I did feel sorry for the Speedo."

"Let's lube him up and see how it goes." Quentin milked his cock for what was left of his load and smeared it down the mannequin's shaft.

Casey pulled out a small bottle of lube. "Don't ask, but it's not for men, it's for some of the tight spots these pieces of art need to be slipped into."

Quentin nodded and took the bottle. "Let me apply it to you." He poured some on his hand and worked it around his fingers. "Bend over, baby."

Casey didn't look sure, but slowly he turned his butt to him.

"Beautiful." Quentin's hand slipped between the cheeks and greased his crease. His fingers ran over his opening, but teased it as they passed back and forth over it.

Casey moaned. "Do it, please." He widened his legs, opening wider to allow easier access.

Quentin slipped his index finger to the hole and circled it, probed, circled and probed.

"Deeper."

His finger pressed down harder.

"Deeper."

His finger slipped into the first joint.

Casey rocked back on his knees and forced his ass onto Quentin's finger. It slipped in all the way to the knuckles. "Yesssssss."

Quentin tapped Casey's prostate and watched as his body rocked back and forth. Low animal moans escaped from him. Quentin used his other hand to stroke Casey's cock, which grew hard instantly.

"You're going to make me come again," he said.

"Is that a bad thing?" Quentin asked.

"No," was all he said.

Quentin withdrew from his butt and moved Speedo man's lower half into position. "Sit on him."

Casey moved over the erection and paused. "I need the upper half, too. This way is too strange."

Quentin added the top half and secured it into place. "Ready?"

Casey lowered his bottom, as Quentin aimed the mannequin's cock to the tender spot. Slowly, Casey descended on the ten inches. He felt the firm tip seek entry, and he pressed down.

Quentin firmly grasped the mannequin's cock as he stroked Casey's butt cheek. "Relax," he soothed.

"Relax? With ten inches trying to rip you open?"

"Breathe out."

Casey exhaled and his sphincter relaxed. He felt the cock slid in. The mushroom head stopped were the girth prevented further entrance, but he sat down harder and stretched his muscle around and over it. Once inside, the rest was thinner, and it glided deeper inside him.

"Good job," Quentin said.

Casey grasped the mannequin's shoulders and rode up and down on his cock. He threw his head back as he slid down the pole. Its pubic hair tickled his ass cheeks as pure bliss entered him.

Quentin's erection returned and so did his desire to join in. "Get onto your hands and knees."

"Doggie style?"

"Please."

"Why?" Casey's rhythm increased, and he didn't want to switch positions.

"Mannequin in the middle."

"You want to tap his ass?"

"Oh yes."

Casey stood up, and Mr. Speedo's cock popped out of his butt. Quentin pulled the model back as Casey got down onto his hands and knees on the floor.

Casey spread his legs apart, as Quentin moved Mr. Speedo between his cheeks and slid the giant cock in. Casey was relaxed and lubed, so it entered easily.

Quentin jumped behind the mannequin and pressed his erection into the groove. He entered with one swift movement. His hands clasped the model's hips and pulled him onto his dick. He pushed it away and drove it further into Casey's ass.

Casey moaned as he backed up onto it. His butt pushed Mr. Speedo onto Quentin's cock.

Quentin guided him off his dick, and Mr. Speedo entered Casey to the hilt. Its balls swung freely between its legs.

"Faster, harder," Casey urged.

Sandwiched between the two men, the mannequin bounced back and forth, gaining speed and depth.

"I'm getting close," Casey warned.

That was all the encouragement Quentin needed. He plowed into Mr. Speedo and doubled his speed. "Me, too."

Casey jacked his cock faster and faster. His balls rose and shot another huge load.

Mr. Speedo continued to hump his butt and forced wave after wave of cum out and onto the floor.

Hearing the wet splat, Quentin's cock released and filled the mannequin's tunnel.

Casey's legs gave out, and he landed in his pool of spunk.

Mr. Speedo toppled and landed on top of him, followed by Quentin, cock still buried to its root.

They lay in a pile for several minutes, unable to move.

Quentin pushed up and pulled out. He lifted Mr. Speedo off and set him down. He savored the view of his partner's ass. As he bent over to caress it, Quentin's cell phone rang. He looked around and saw it on the floor. It rang again. Dripping from his cock and balls, he walked over to it and said, "Hello."

"Did Mr. Rothenberg find you?" Roberta's breathless voice asked.

"He wasn't coming until tomorrow."

"He's early. He came in today. He likes to make surprise visits before he writes a check."

"Where is he?"

"We sent him down to you a half hour ago. He said he'd find you in the new display."

"Shit," Quentin scrambled, picking up his clothing. "Get dressed now," he ordered Casey. "He's not here, are you sure you sent him to the right display?"

"He hasn't found you yet? He left here about thirty minutes ago. I called to warn you, but you didn't pick up."

"Oh fuck," Quentin looked down the hallway. He flipped his phone shut and slowly started to walk out of the locker room. "Mr. Rothenberg? Are you there?"

Casey gasped as he pulled his briefs over his ass.

The mannequin lay on its side. Cum seeped out of its mouth and its bubble butt. Small semen pools covered the tiled floor.

Mr. Rothenberg stepped out from around the corner. He struggled to zip up his fly.

Quentin relaxed as he spotted a creamy white spot on the floor behind him. "Did you enjoy your sneak attack?"

Mr. Rothenberg's face flushed and said, "So, is this the display that you are planning on installing?"

119

Quentin froze. Maybe he misread Mr. Rothenberg. "I … we got carried away for the moment. It won't happen again."

"So, your performance won't be repeated?"

At home, hell yeah, but at work … Quentin thought. "I'm sorry," was all he said.

"Don't be. Do you know how many boring displays I've seen? Do you know how many I've even paid for? I want this one to be hot, controversial, banned from children."

"But sir, this is a public building."

"I don't care. I'm paying for this display, and I want it NC-17."

Casey adjusted his clothing and joined them. He handed Quentin his shirt and pants. He stepped in front of his partner and asked, "How would you like to see this display?"

Mr. Rothenberg walked into the shower room and untied the football player's laces on his pants. He reached into the jock and pulled it down, freeing the mannequin's cock. He pulled it out and let it dangle. He re-positioned the arm as if he was jacking off.

"I see what you're going for, and I know we can do that." Casey smiled.

Quentin finished dressing behind him and stepped forward. "We can do that." His face still flushed red.

Mr. Rothenberg stepped over to the naked mannequin standing in the corner. "What will he be wearing?"

Casey shrugged his shoulders. "We ran out of uniforms."

"Maybe he can be naked in the shower?"

"Great idea," Casey said.

"But before you do that …" his voice trailed off.

"Yes?" Quentin asked.

"I would like to borrow him for the night."

"Borrow him? Oh, yeah, sure. Why don't we bring him to your car through the delivery door?"

"Perfect. I'll send my driver around in ten minutes." He extended his hand to Casey. "Thank you." He turned to Quentin and shook his hand also. "I'll be in tomorrow at one, and the check and new contract will be signed." Mr. Rothenberg turned his back to the men, adjusted his fly one more time and pointed to the floor. "You may want to clean that up." And he walked away.

Quentin walked over to the naked mannequin and picked him up. Casey grabbed the towel and wrapped it around his waist. "Makes it more fun to unwrap him." Casey smiled as he helped Quentin carry the model down the hallway. "I have one question for you."

Quentin switched his hand position and asked, "What?"

"Why did you give him this one to take to his hotel?"

"He wasn't being used in the display."

"I know, but maybe we could've taken him home with us ..."

Quentin stopped and set the model down. He waved his hand back at the display. "We have all of these to pick from, who needs this one tonight?"

Casey kissed him. "I love the way you think, and I hope this display is here for a very long time."

"Maybe we'll have to make this a permanent display."

"Maybe, maybe."

BEND FOR A FRIEND
By R. W. Clinger

Can Ty Masters see the outline of wood in my thigh-tight chinos while keeping his eyes on my prize? Or, is he a gentleman like the one perceived on the six o'clock news covering sports, concentrating on my blond hair, dimpled cheeks and deep-green eyes? There is no way in hell he's a gentleman. Ty is a dog, just like all the other guys in this city. He wants to strip me out of my casuals, touch every part of my twenty-six-year-old body, my five-nine frame and reddish Robert Pattinson lips. The dude definitely wants to carry out some naughty jock-lust with my cock and ass, among other various places of deep interest on my ripped body.

I move my eight inches of stem from the right side of my chinos to the left. This action processes a few bubbles of man-spew to leak out of the joint and stick to my skin. In doing so, I provide a cough, showing how uncomfortable (and nervously excited for Ty) I am at the moment.

"What's going on, Chip?" Ty's deep-dark brown eyes take in my middle while licking his lips.

I ignore his question. What the hell else am I supposed to do? I can't possibly drop my chinos to the future gym's floor, turn around, bend over, and let him have his way with my adorable and bulbous ass? This isn't going to happen, of course. Instead, I rattle off, "Stand right there," and swing my right palm forward and press it against his hulking, tee-covered chest. As I accidentally rub one of his firm pecs, I add, "Let me visualize you in your own private gym."

I carry this out with all of my clients before their ordered equipment from Daily Works arrives: Tell them what they want to hear. Point out all of their physical attributes. Heighten their greed for the best personal gym they can possibly buy from me. Will them to feel eager about purchasing a multi-station, bench and rack, elliptical trainer, free weights, or other extras for their room. In most cases, I have to stretch the truth a little about how pumped a client looks in their future gym. But, Ty Masters is in a different category altogether, already drop-dead muscular and gorgeous, built like a rock wall.

What I visualize is simple: Ty ripping his bulging canary-yellow tee from his Sioux Indian skin, allowing me to pinch one of his stern nipples with two fingertips, and begin something erotically strong between us … something unyielding and potent as our torsos and cocks meld together in fag-bliss. Instead, what I really see, and share, is quite dull, but honest, "Your triceps will bulge with a weight bench to the far right. Your tree trunk-like thighs will enjoy a treadmill to the left. And, don't forget a single strength machine for the middle of your ripped core."

He is not falling for my gig. The deep cleft in his rigid chin slowly moves as he says, "Listen, Chip. You had me sold the first time I laid eyes on your rocking body. No need to try and flatter me with more bullshit. Honestly, I'm going to be very pleased with your system … and with you."

He catches me off guard by this last comment. I bat a smile, play dumb, and inquire, "How do you intend to enjoy me?"

Let this whimsical game of sexual tension between us continue. Ty lights up with a dashing smile, reaches for my right bicep with one of his hands, provides it with a manly squeeze, and replies, "Do you stand behind your product, Chip?"

"I do. One hundred percent."

He massages my bicep with a firm grip and rolls fingers into my flesh. "Do you use the equipment you sell?"

"All the time," I say, knowing exactly where this is going, and loving every minute of it.

"Then take your shirt and chinos off and show me what your equipment can design."

I've done worse things to land a sale. Once, I had to sleep with a guy twice my age, then his lover. Another time, I had to jack off in front of two brothers in their thirties. Ty's request is nothing. In fact, I'm kind of thrilled that the celebrity sportscaster wants to see me out of my clothes.

I take off my shirt and drop it to the cement floor. He checks out my clean-shaven and glowing torso: mounds of abs, cliff-like shoulders and pecs, and nipples the size of cock rings.

"Damn," he whispers and shakes his head with satisfaction. "That is irresistible."

To my liking, he presents his right palm to my stomach, rolls it along my abs and up to my left pec and solid nipple. Ty gives the nipple a little pinch, twist and release.

What I see between his legs, underneath his shorts, is a solid outline of penis: ten inches of veined and throbbing meat. The guy is obviously turned on by my magazine-perfect chest.

"There's more," I admit, teasing him. I unbutton my chinos, pull their zipper down, drop the material to my ankles and ...

"No underwear," he whispers, open-mouthed and wide-eyed. He consumes my eight inches of flag, its curly pubic triangle, and hairless man-sack of swinging balls between my legs.

I'm a little disappointed he doesn't take in my toned thighs, but whatever, I'll get over it. I stand with my arms at my sides, showcase my fully inflated stick, and smile like the top salesman of the year. "So, Ty, what do you think about my equipment?"

He doesn't know if I'm talking about Daily Works or my championship-toned body. Ty seems dumbstruck by my beauty, lost somewhere in a personal state of bliss.

Under my skin's spell, he says, "You got some amazing shit going on."

"What do you think of the back?" I spin around clumsily, show off my ass, and tighten my gluteus muscles.

To my amazement, he inquires, "Would you bend for a friend, Chip?"

"Fuck yeah," I chant, find my ankles with my palms, and show him a view of my tight asshole.

Not even two minutes later, fingertips pull open my rump and he rolls his tongue around the smoothness of my core, tempting me with his heightened desire. Although I'm ready for some heavy-duty licks and laps with his mouth, connecting our muscular bodies together, he holds his desire back. Instead, he toys with the circumference of my hole, applying the area with a tongue-bath.

Steel-hard between my legs, knowing I can bust a load without having my cock touched, I moan and groan with pleasure. An escalating vibration sweeps throughout my being, waving to and fro. I become dizzy while bent over, misplaced for a few seconds. My ball sack is caressed and licked with Ty's diligent labor. My bulbous ass is pulled open and ... investigated by his mouth: the tip of his soothing tongue enters my middle and causes me to burn with developed contentment. I grunt helplessly in front of him, bedazzled and misplaced, unaware of my whereabouts. Another shiver of ecstasy works its way through my center, which causes me to gasp and lose oxygen.

He murmurs with gratification on his knees. His face is nuzzled firmly against and inside my behind. He continues prosaically to dab the tip of his slippery and warm tongue to my epicenter. When he takes a break, searching for air, heavily inhaling, he ruggedly warns, "I'm going to make you shoot, Chip. You up for it?"

I'm up for many things with the Sioux Indian, feel easy in his presence, uninhabited and rather keen for his unstoppable lust. Hyperventilating, overwhelmingly woozy, I groan, "Get me off ... please."

He reaches between my legs as he continues to use his straying mouth on my firm ass. One of his palms finds the eight inches of rock between my thighs and grasps it, pulling it down. Stroke after meticulous stroke to my shaft ensues. Slurps and heavy moans are heard as he fulfills his hunger. These unstoppable actions continue for the next ten minutes ... twelve minutes ... sixteen minutes.

Elation is found as my stick is being yanked on in hyper motion. Ty's mouth and handy work send me into a state of contentment. Shivers of ecstasy sweep throughout my system. No longer can I hold my load in, wanting to spray it all over the cement floor, ready to fire it out of my rod. Helplessly, I warn the sportscaster, "Blowing, Ty ... Shooting now ... Here it comes."

White arcs of sap fly out of my cock and splat against the floor, missing my feet by just a few millimeters.

Our naughty connection is not over yet. Ty kicks my feet apart and informs rather diligently, "I can't wait to shove my rod into your ass, Chip."

"Go for it, man. It's ready for you."

He loses his yellow T-shirt and shorts, instantly becoming naked except for his Nike running shoes and booty socks. A condom is found and rolled down and over his goods. The foil wrapper is dropped to the cement floor. A disposable packet of lube is found and dribbled on my hole. Seconds later, Ty directs his firm cock into my tight bottom with skill. One inch after the next is haphazardly shoved into my behind and causes tears to form in the corners of my eyes.

I waver in front of him, windblown, shocked and at a loss for breath by his sudden cargo ramming into my center. He prevents me from falling to the floor by grasping my sweaty hips with his palms. He digs his fingertips into my flesh and holds me up while directing his thumper into my compressed core.

"Jesus," I whimper, "you're fucking huge."

He brags, pushing all of his meat inside me, "I'm ten inches, pal. You'd better get used to it because it takes me forever to come."

It's true; he rams me for what feels like an eternity. Consecutive humps are carried out for eight minutes … twelve minutes … sixteen minutes, building a steady friction between us. He groans and murmurs behind me. He slaps my ass numerous times with a swift palm. He calls me the naughtiest names and …

Sweat drips from my body onto the cement floor. I heave to and fro against his ramming weight. Fingers dig into ankles as buck after sturdy buck occurs to my tight bottom. It feels as if a barbell slams into my ass. The empty room spins around and around, and I become weak by our connection, dizzy and inebriated by our sex. I gasp for air, winded and semiconscious. Joy is found from his roughness, elation … man-bliss.

"Coming, Chip," he moans, gritting his teeth. The guy's hip-thrusts become wicked, banging into my middle. His fingers burrow into my sides, almost breaking my skin open. Drooping balls consistently slap against my back side, rhythmically.

I pull off and away from his swollen shaft, spin around, and watch my client lose the rubber covering his spike. Helplessly, I study his hairy chest, inflated nipples and thatch of thick and curly pubic triangle above his erect knob. Face-to-face, cockheads only inches away from each other, he bolts his left fist up and down on his tool. Perspiration builds on his sculpted torso, flying off in swirls by his spasmodic motion. His jacking continues, becoming stronger and stronger. Ty's teeth clench, and he shares a monstrous noise, bucking his hips upwards, relishing his moment of gratification.

In a matter of seconds my torso is covered in his gooey spunk. My hard pecs and nipples glisten with the thick juice. The shit clings to my pumped abs and dented navel. Jiz flies against my cock and balls, decorating my equipment, glazing my flesh.

He drops his left hand from his huge wanker, finished with his speedy tugging. Half of me believes he's going to drop to his knees and lick my skin clean, swirling his tongue against my sticky torso, removing every last drop of his spent with utter delight.

This doesn't happen, though. Instead, he leans into me, strongly kisses my neck while holding one of my hips with a massive palm, pulls away, and whispers, "There's something about you I like, Chip."

I don't know what to say, bemused for a moment. I watch him find a few paper towels for a quick clean-up.

Ty's cell rings, which he finds on the floor and takes the call, finalizing our meeting. One minute I'm butt naked in his future gym, post-sexed and sticky. The next minute, I'm in my Ram truck, driving away with a greedy smile of contentment smeared across my chiseled face, maybe having a crush on the stranger/client.

Two days later, I do something crazy … something completely unacceptable as a salesman. I sort of stalk Ty Masters. I wait for his shift at WPXT to end and follow his Mustang to Pump's Gym. Here, I follow him into the gym with my own bag, weaseling my way inside with my Pattinson looks by flirting with a nineteen-year-old twink at the welcome desk, and …

The place buzzes with jockish hunks of every size and color. The variety of straight men are scattered here and there, busy with their individual workouts, sweating, flexing, and showing off. Treadmills line the left wall. The Olympic-sized pool area sits in the rear. Elliptical trainers are centered next to a mass of multi-stations. Cycles form an area to the left of the treadmills. A track circles the perimeter of the gym, sporting bare-chested muscle heads with fake tans and Gatorade bottles.

Ty sits on a weight bench, lifting a heavy looking hand weight in his right palm, pumping his right bicep and arm, popping his triceps muscle. Before he makes eye contact with me, I stare at his sculpted bod: broad shoulders slick with sweat, hairy torso lined with pulsing abs, loose running shorts covering his muscled thighs. My stare concentrates on the ideal area between his legs. His shorts gape against his right thigh and … low and behold, I see no underwear inside. Instead, his limp snake with its single eye is at sleep, flush against his skin, dormant for the time being, but just as striking as when it is completely firm and alive with much male-action.

He finally spots me. He stops lifting his hand weight, broadly smiles, and says, "Chip, what are you doing here?"

I step up to his Native Indian-sculpted body. "I was in the neighborhood and thought I would stop by to see where you work out."

"Home away from home. I can't wait for my own personal gym to be done, though."

"Soon enough, pal. You're equipment should be delivered by the end of the week. My men will even set it up for you. You'll be using your gym by Friday evening."

He smiles. His eyes light with intoxicating fire, obviously happy with my news, and to see me. "Sounds great, man. You and I can have some one-on-one workouts together." I swear he winks at me, hitting on me in front of a dozen or more straight dudes in Pump's. Ty adds, "Your guys installed the lighting, flooring and mirrors today in my gym. It's coming along great. You should stop by and check it out."

"I might just do that."

He wants to know if I will lift weights with him, which I accept. In the next hour, we accidentally/purposely/discreetly brush fingertips along each other's rounded shoulders, hard chests, pulsing thighs and Rufskin-covered cocks. By the end of the workout, I'm eight-inches hard and ready to burst my churn all over the gym, spraying it down with my seed. To top it off, Ty insists we take a shower together, enjoying some water-play with soap, shampoo and ...

"Buddy, although a shower sounds great with you ... I have to go," I say.

He stands next to the bench and rack with beads of sweat clinging to his hairy torso. A white cotton towel hangs around his bulky shoulders. The man is ripped to the core, a Colt model if I've ever seen one, massive in size, fully toned, and one-hundred-percent all beef. He provides a cheerful smile with a hint of seduction and charm, and whispers his response, "My cock misses your ass, Chip. It wants you to bend for a friend again ... sometime soon."

I clear my throat, nervous that some straight bully will hear us. I look to my left and right, spot a dozen or more muscle heads doing their workouts, and reply, "I'll see if I can fit you into my schedule, Ty."

Passing me, his right hand cups my goods and provides it with a hefty squeeze, gaining my full attention. He discreetly mumbles, "You'd better. I can't wait to fuck you again."

The moment ends quite abruptly. He heads to the showers, and I stand with a hard tool in my shorts. Thank God for my white towel, which I hold in front of my excited middle, escaping the den of delicious looking straighties and the sportscaster I have a crush on.

I am certainly not a man to pry into a client's life. Something draws me to Ty though, which I really can't justify. Maybe it's the way his cocoa-brown eyes twinkle or how he snuggles his erect beef inside my bottom. Truth is, I find out where he grocery shops for his protein bars, where he goes for his caramel lattes (Cannondale Coffee), and what bars he likes to frequent on the weekend (Low Boys and The Splentini Club). I learn that he doesn't have any siblings; he likes to read the morning newspaper opposed to novels; and his favorite color is green. By the time I'm finished spying on Ty Masters, I have over forty pages of hand-written notes, with topics ranging from enjoyed restaurants to favorite porn stars.

We meet again, our fourth and final encounter to wrap up business. Ty invites me into his home, down a flight of black and silver aluminum stainless steel stairs, and into his newly furnished personal gym. The place is absolutely fresh looking with modern gym equipment by Daily Works. Everything gleams a white, silver and black hue, spanking new and shiny-perfect. I study the elliptical machine, cycle and multi-station. Ty shows me a fruit and vegetable bar, a two-person sauna and a hot tub. There's even a tiny area for back massages by a hired professional or a touchy-feely boyfriend.

"I don't want to sound arrogant, but this place looks amazing," I study the area, blown away by its masculine beauty.

"Sharp and crisp, and exactly how I wanted it to look. You know we have to celebrate now." He turns to me and leashes his right palm to my hip. He draws me toward him and meets his mouth to my mouth, exploring my insides with his tongue.

When he releases his mouth from my mouth, he says, "I know you've been watching me. I'm kind of flattered by it, if you want to know the truth."

"You can't prove it," I play, caught off guard by his accusation.

"I like that you're seeking out a boyfriend. Do I fit the bill, Chip?"

He does, in more ways than one. Ty nods his head and smiles from ear to ear. He steps a foot back from me, rips off his shirt, and exposes his hairy chest with its steel-plated abs and firm nipples. He flexes his biceps, one after the other, and asks, "Tell me you don't like to watch this body in motion?"

I'm numb, durably silent. My middle comes alive, and a bolt of energy shifts through my tight torso and cock with high-spirited excitement. I keep my stare on the sportscaster, eyeing him up and down in a sexual frenzy, hungry for his hot flesh to indubitably mix with my own.

"Is this the boyfriend material you want?" he inquires, unbuttoning his jeans and pushing them down to his ankles. He manhandles his floppy beef while facing me. One hand jerks on the protein between his sculpted legs in an up and down motion, bringing it to life. His balls flop back and forth between his stern and veined thighs.

Helplessly, I lick my lips. My eyes consume his goods with utter pleasure, wanting nothing less than to have his tube inside my mouth and pressed down the back of my throat. Unconditionally, I say, "It is what I want. Can I help you make it hard?"

"Trust me, pal, you don't even have to ask." He kicks off his leather dress shoes and jeans. He pushes me down to my knees, gently positions me in front of his limp dick, and coaches, "Do your thing … I'm ready for it."

"Woof!" exits my lips without a single thought.

Above me, Ty laughs, already growing firm with the mere thought of my mouth cradling his rod. With a driving passion, he grabs his tool with both hands and directs it between my lips. Again, he coaches me and utters, "Suck just the tip. That's the way I like it."

Like a good salesman, I listen to his demands and follow his instructions. My tongue rolls around the dick's cut cap, which causes a groan to escape his towering frame. Slowly, with a prized surety, I provide suction to his cock's head.

"Take two more inches into your mouth," he utters above me.

Fuck his instructions. And fuck him. I take four; one inch after the next, coveting the beef as if it is my last meal. Happily, I plug my face with his rod, jabbing my throat with his weight numerous times, disinclined to listen to him anymore, obviously making up my own rules.

Ty is not at all disappointed with me taking control of the moment. In fact, I think he gets off on it, desiring nothing less. He definitely doesn't complain when I take another two inches of his stem into my system, attempting to blow him with the finest homoerotic connection and skill. "Chomp on it, pal," he mumbles, into our gig, satisfied with our flesh connecting.

I tease him until I believe he's going to shoot his load inside my mouth, drowning my interior with his ooze. One suck turns into thirty, consecutively, without stopping. All of his inches pump my throat, quickly pull out, and pump it again. Ty is definitely ready to burst, swaying above me, losing his balance and ready to fall to the gym's Astroturf floor.

Truth is I have to pull off him or he'll come in my mouth, which I really don't want. Keeping safe, I remove my face from his dog, stand up, provide both of his nipples with a kiss, and now his mouth, and whisper, "I want to rim your ass. Bend over your brand new bench and let's break it in."

Finding elation, Ty smiles in a greedy manner, and responds, "Only if you shove it all into me."

"Hell yeah," I reply with a smile of my own, spin him around, drop to my knees again, and go to work on his rear.

With one foot planted on his weight bench and his tight ass ready for my mouthy work, he begs, "I'm bending for you, bro ... Show me what you've got."

It's an invitation of a lifetime to tell you the truth. In fact, I want nothing more than to shove my slippery tongue into his ready-to-hump rump.

"Lube it," he groans, balancing himself on the weight bench, obviously horny for more action and ready to churn out a load of his gooey goods.

My tongue-tour doesn't really last as long as I want it to. In fact, my mouth is only connected to his bottom for a mere two minutes because he is far too greedy and needy to have my rod jammed into his center. What little time I do share my lips and tongue with his rump is fully enjoyable. Chaotically, I dab and lap at his tight and hairy hole, probing his center with skill. Fingers pull his core apart, and I proceed to go deep into his system, enlightening his world and causing the sportscaster to grunt and growl like an animal.

During this short period of time, Ty cranks his own beef with his right palm. His meat is tugged on with a fierce speed and jostled with a fineness that prompts him to become bliss-filled while carrying out. The local celebrity cannot keep his load in any longer, manipulating his ten-incher. Gasps of excitement fill the gym and ...

white jiz blows out of his joint and decorates the turf. String after string of his load ornaments the floor between his foot and my knees.

To no avail, though, our gig is far from over. Ty immediately pulls away from me, lies down on the bench, spreads his legs, stares up at me with affection in his eyes, and demands, "Fuck me, Chip. There's a condom and lube in my jeans. I want it hard and fast … and don't hold back."

I become submissive and listen to him again. After finding the square of plastic from his jeans and applying it to my wanker, I climb between his legs, touch the tip of my pole to his now-lubed opening, and whisper, "Get ready for it, here it comes."

"Nail me! Pump it into me!" he abruptly demands inside the home gym, his voice echoing off the walls. "Fuck me hard!" he blares, beating my solid chest with one of his fists, attempting to intensify our shared moment.

My palms clamp to his ankles and pull his legs apart for easy access. Two … four … six inches of my dong press into his center, release, and press into it again. Bolt after steady bolt thumps his bottom. I ride his ass like he rides one of the machines in his new gym. Helplessly, I become like a prize-winning athlete inside him, banging his taut bottom, working it over, unable to stop.

As sweat reflects on my torso, he groans with absolute delight, lost in his sexual world, enjoying my stick inside his middle. Thump after continuous thump sends the man into overdrive, prompting him to call me the nastiest names, which I crave, and want to hear more of because they make my tool hard as steel, plowing his bottom with unstoppable man-action. Again and again, I pound him, banging his core, using his skin for my personal pleasure, building up a fine orgasm within my system. Sweat flies off of my body and stings his furry chest. A snivel of excitement exits my mouth. I am overjoyed with our man-bond, dizzy inside him, proficient with my movement, and utterly unyielding.

"Hit it," Ty begs, whining. "Don't stop. Make it last."

Unfortunately, I am not the porn star I wish to be. I am only mortal, a gym equipment salesman, and seem to find my orgasm rather quickly. A sweeping vibration swirls within my axis. A warning surfaces and I announce, "Ty, I can't hold it in any longer ... I'm shooting."

"Do it, guy ... Don't hold back."

As if on cue, I huff and puff, pull my shaft out of his hub, rip off its plastic coating, and toss the condom to the gym's floor. Feebly, I stroke myself off once ... twice ... three times and feel a flood of thick emulsion dribble over his ripped torso. Globs of the blend cling to his chiseled stomach and pecs, decorating the Sioux's dark skin.

"That's what I needed, Chip," he whispers, into my show.

"It's not over yet," I reply, dying to eat up my own goop.

"Bring it on," he challenges, grinning from ear to ear.

Lap by lap, I lick up my junk from his sculpted torso, sucking the seed into my system. The taste is bittersweet and exactly what I desire. Like a skilled boyfriend, I bend over his hairy chest with my lips and tongue, making sure that every drop of my spent is cleaned away.

On his back, Ty watches and feels my motion. He says, "You're pretty good at that, pal."

"I've had some practice."

"Is this how you make your monthly sales?"

"Trust me; I don't give out that secret."

Honestly, Ty doesn't care how I make my sales. He's into my body, which seems to be the most important fact at the moment. With one powerful push by his hulking arm applied to my chest, I'm on my feet in a matter of seconds. Ty stands up, still sticky and covered in my spew-residue. He reaches for my right hand, pulls me toward his two-person shower, and announces, "I have some secrets of my own, Chip. Let me apply a few of the naughty ones to your skin in my shower."

"I'm all for that," I reply, smiling and feeling greedy for more of his affection, becoming his boyfriend for the next six months, or longer – however long he wants to keep me around for his cock's appetite and satisfaction.

PAIN IS WEAKNESS LEAVING THE BODY
By Conrad James

Aspen is like a mini-Paris where it's hard to tell the metrosexuals from the homosexuals. Not at the Brownlee Street Gym though. Billed as "the bodybuilder's gym," the guys here are working to build serious muscle. The atmosphere here provides a lot of inspiration with pictures of bodybuilding greats lining the walls, punctuated with encouraging slogans like "Pain Is Weakness Leaving the Body" or "Shut Up and Train." Shelves lined with trophies of local champs and pictures of proud and smiling iron-jocks are everywhere. The ceiling is a labyrinth of duct pipes and circuitry, giving the place an industrial-strength feel. There aren't a lot of fancy machines like at the posh resort-like fitness center across town, but everything a guy needs to build muscle is here. The gym is always on the warm-side. The sounds of clanking weights, the grunts and groans of exertion, the smell of man sweat, all set to the backdrop of boom-bam tunes, create a sense of tribalness.

The Gym is located in a trendy complex of shops, restaurants, and multistory condos. Gazing out the floor-to-ceiling windows toward the condos, I wonder what it would be like to look across or down from those balconies at night when the muscle-heads are going at it. I do love coming here. It's such a contrast to the rule-ridden generic gym I use back home. Maybe a guy could even go shirtless. Just as that thought was trailing through my mind and I'm finishing my last set of lat raises, Steve comes in, reaches me a knuckle punch and says "Hey Bro."

I met Steve at Booksellers earlier in the day when I stopped in to ask about the availability of Internet connections for travelers such as I. I spend about a week here every year for the Music Festival, but the nearby campgrounds don't offer luxuries like Wi-Fi. Steve is a blond stud, pure and simple. Best way to put it. Maybe early- to mid-twenties, tanned, dressed in cargo shorts and a gray tee that drapes over his muscular body, showcasing his hulking delts, traps and thick pecs. Great physique, but his face and demeanor are what captivate me. Handsome angular features, broad smile, sea-blue eyes, and blond hair with some kind of funky highlights that make him look so athletically appealing. A California surfer type transplanted somehow here in the Rockies, Steve exudes a masculine persona that is amplified by his deep baritone voice. A maturity you wouldn't expect from a guy his age, if I'm at all right about his age.

Need to tell you that I'm a shrink here on vacation, but vacation or not, I study human behavior constantly. It just comes naturally for me, and I think that I've become a pretty good judge of people. Me, I'm five-ten, late thirties with salt and pepper hair. Gym-toned body yes, but these muscles were also earned from hours of cycling, hiking, and construction tasks that I enjoy and pursue to manage the stresses of my work. Not that I need to escape the college classroom or my consulting room because I really love doing what I do, but dealing with the problems of others or coping with a gaggle of reluctant learners can become challenging at times.

Back to Steve. Turns out he is a graduate student at CU in Boulder and spends his summers here in Aspen working at Booksellers. He told me right off that his job is really a front for his real summer occupation here as a gigolo. A job he claims to thoroughly enjoy. I surmise that he must be very successful at it because of his good looks and charm. I admire his honesty and openness, but then I guess that's what makes him successful. Wish my clients could be that transparent.

I think Steve knew from the onset that I wasn't going to purchase his time and services, not that I wasn't tempted. We chatted for a bit, but not for long. Most serious iron-guys, me included, come to the gym to work out, not socialize. But, catching me totally off guard midway in an ab-crunch, Steve jams a fist gently into my gut and says, "Hey Sigmund, how about joining me for a little dinner tonight?" Pointing across the way to a second story condo he continues, "I live up there in that condo just across the way."

Flashing on my earlier speculation I quickly replied, "Absolutely, name's Bart by the way."

"Yeah, I know," Steve reminded me.

Couple of hours later, Steve buzzes me in and meets me at the top of the stairs. Dressed in a loose fitting tank top and some worn/torn board shorts, he waves me inside. Padding around barefoot, he says, "Make yourself comfortable Bart." After shucking my shoes and opening my shirt, I grab hold of his bubble ass with one hand, reach through the armholes of his tank with the other and run my hands across his chest, brushing my fingers over his hardening nipples. "This too comfy?" I query.

Steve jams his hand between us to get at the bulge in my jeans while I continue to explore his muscled body. All the while I'm thinking to myself, maybe he is more used to giving than getting. Too bad, but hey, maybe I can change that, at least for an evening. Or not.

The upper level patio doors are open, and I can hear the clanking of weights and the grunts of the bodybuilders down below and across the walkway. Can they see us I wonder? Excited by that possibility I spin Steve around, thrusting my tongue deep into his throat. Steve pushes my shirt down off my shoulders and begins to emit moans of pleasure as his hands grip my upper arms and roam my back. He reaches down inside my jeans, grabs my ass-cheeks and pulls me against him, hard.

"So, what's for dinner, Steve?" I whisper.

"You, Sigmund, er I mean Bart," he replies.

We break away as Steve asks me to join him for a cocktail on the balcony. He has things all set up, a pillar candle on a little bistro table, place-mats, tableware, a bottle of wine. We sit side-by-side shirtless, sipping our drinks, ogling the muscle guys below, all the while fondling each other, casually exploring one another's bodies. A little like watching a porno flick and being in one at the same time, or like being both an exhibitionist and a voyeur all at once.

"So, Steve, what is your going rate?" I ask.

"Depends" he replies. "I like to make guys' fantasies become realities. Having the power to pull that kinda shit off turns me on, big time. Sometimes I discount my rates if I'm really into a scene and really having fun. Not gonna quote you rates, Bart, but let's just say I make enough dough in summer and winter break here to fund my entire education at CU and then some."

"What would be some of your fantasies, Steve?" I query trying not to sound too professional. After all, it's not as if I'm doing an intake interview here.

"Just going to ask you that, Bart. I may not look the type, but I gotta admit I get off on some BDSM and leather shit. In fact, I have a whole closet full of gear. Wanna see?"

"Cool, giving or taking? And yes, I definitely wanna see," I quickly answer.

Steve whips the heavy cord out from the waistband of his board shorts and wraps it around my neck forming a collar/leash and says, "Both, Bart, but I'm thinkin tonight is your night to be taken."

I swear I see a couple of bodybuilders looking directly up at us with a what-the-fuck look on their faces. The little balcony is softy lit, and it would be pretty easy for anyone looking up one story to see exactly what is going on.

Using my cord-leash, Steve pulls me close and mashes his lips against mine in a grinding, passionate kiss. I'm wondering is he gonna fuckin take me over this table, or is he gonna have my ass out here on the balcony with me leaning against that iron rail?

We finish our drinks then stand face to face, chest to chest, cock to cock. Hell, isn't this what man-sex is all about? Simultaneously, we divert our eyes to the guys in the gym below. Most of the guys have removed their shirts or tanks, their built bodies glistening with sweat, their manly voices emanating grunts of exertion shouting, words of encouragement and praise to one another.

Stepping back, Steve leads me over to the rail and barks, "Stand with your butt against that rail and grab it with your hands directly behind you. Now." Removing my rope leash/collar he ties my wrists to the railing and adds, "And don't move till get back."

What the fuck am I doing? I think to myself. Here I am standing half naked, tied to a balcony rail, my cock sticking straight out from my jeans, all in full view of a bunch of gym rats below. With all the courage and bravado I can muster, I forcefully shove my fearful, anxious thoughts aside and nod, "Yes, Sir."

Excitement and terror are an odd mix. I know it's an endorphin thing, but knowing that doesn't change how I feel. Doesn't mean diddly shit. This scene is a unlike any other I have experienced. There is an amorphous sense on anonymity, but probably a false one at best. Is this at all safe I wonder, or am I being all-out recklessly nuts? What the fuck is going to come of this? Turning my head, I look below and observe that the muscle guys I was observing only moments ago are now observing us. I'm freaked. I've treated exhibitionists and voyeurs in my practice, and now I'm acting out features that fit the diagnostic criteria for both for God's sake!

I freeze when I see a uniformed Aspen cop enter the gym through the side door. He doesn't see me – yet. God only knows what will happen if he does. Hell not if, WHEN! Muscular cops with hand cuffs and night sticks have always been a draw for me, one that I have acted out several times with a colleague in forensic psych, But, this looks and feels way too public for comfort. Or does it? When the cop emerges from the locker room, he's wearing only some cut-offs, but his handcuffs dangle from his belt along with his phone and badge. Guy is built like a brick shit house.

My thoughts come to an abrupt halt when Steve reappears at the patio door wearing a top harness, wrist cuffs, and studded arm bands that swell his triceps and biceps. God what a site of male power and raw sexuality! The board shorts are gone, and his massive cock juts up against his eight-pack, like a missile poised for launching. He carries a black leather bag that when dropped to the floor of the deck makes a loud thud, startling me and doubtlessly garnering even more attention from below.

He's gonna fuckin do me right out here in the open I'm thinking to myself. I'm gonna wind up in jail on charges of lewd and lascivious behavior or worse. My license to practice! My academic career!

Removing the rope, Steve cuffs my wrists to the rail. My jeans are completely unbuttoned now, and he is fingering my leaking piss slit, grinding against me forcefully. Steve mauls my pecs and nips. Roughly, he traces my jaw line and grabs my throat making it difficult to breathe. After a drilling tongue-fuck of my mouth, he whispers, "You afraid, Sig?"

How the fuck am I gonna answer that? Afraid is a gross understatement. I've got a lot at stake here. Playing in private is one thing, but this public performance? I'm fucking terrified! Nevertheless I shake my head and answer "No, Sir, not with you, Sir," though clearly I am scared beyond shitless.

Steve reaches into his bag and brings out a riding crop that I immediately feel warming my pecs, abs, arms, and finally my thighs. His strikes on my flesh make a snapping sound that can't help but be heard below. Gritting my teeth, I mumble a string of "Thank you, Sirs," as he continues to pummel my body with that biting leather pad. I wince and almost yell out loud when he puts nipple clamps on my reddened tits, then watch with amazement when he attaches clamps to his own nipples, tethering our nips, criss-crossing them with a steel chain.

Helplessly, I watch him as he uses me for his pleasure. Sort of. This is the beauty of bottoming. Surrendering to a top is a gift willingly given that blesses both. I see Steve look down to the windows of the gym, and I swear he makes eye contact with the cop who seems to give him a thumbs up in acknowledgment of his apparent dominance and my obvious submission. Sweat pours from my trembling body. My mind is a mass of conflicted thoughts and feelings. And yet, the continuing pain reminds me that I am a man, giving myself to another man in some crazy symbiotic way that unites us both in a sacred act.

My churning balls signal that I'm prime and ready to shoot my load at any second. I clench my Kegel muscles hard, trying to delay the inevitable. Steve moves tight against my body and holds me in his strong arms, mashing our nipple hardware together causing it to come loose and fall to the balcony floor. But now, the studded hardware on his harness and arm bands dig into my raw flesh as he holds me in a bear-hug.

Backing away, Steve jams his fist into my stomach and says, "You are NOT gonna come without my permission, Bart. Trust me, you'll regret it." Then, he lands a dozen blows up and down my gut with his fists Tensing my abs, I take it like a man because I fuckin know how to take it like a man. Still, I wonder how Steve knows that getting gut punched is pure erotic pain and pleasure for me, one of my favorite scenes. Maybe a favorite scene for others, too, I realize when I glance below and see the hunky cop flanked by two other bodybuilders looking straight up at us, nodding and giving a thumbs-up approval of my abuse.

"Performance time, Bart-buddy." In a flash, Steve clears off the little bistro table with one sweep of his arm, barely salvaging the bottle of Merlot. Releasing the cuffs that held me to the rail, Steve throws me across table so that I'm spread-eagle on my belly, ready for his taking. Gobbing his fingers with lube, he quickly opens me. I can feel his hard prick running up and down my ass crack. His iron rod pushes through my sphincter, then inches its way slowly into my clenching ass. His thrusts increase in intensity and frequency, smashing my body hard against the latticework of the little iron table. Our mutual sex-heat builds to a sweaty and guttural crescendo until we both moan in unison as we shoot our loads, his deep inside my battered ass and mine splattering the balcony floor.

For a very long moment – total silence, except for our heavy breathing. Suddenly, reality kicks in, and I'm thinking my god what the fuck have I done?

I'm startled when I hear an applause from below, along with a few catcalls and whistles from the Brownlee Street Gym muscle boys, now standing in the courtyard below looking straight up at us.

Slowly withdrawing his prick from my hole, Steve whispers, "Let me introduce you to a few of my friends, Bart. I know a cop who wants to meet you."

TESTOSTERONE FUELED JUNKIES
By Donald Webb

It's Friday afternoon, and I'm loaded down with a laptop and textbooks, heading for the college parking lot.

"Hey, Matt ... wait up," a loud masculine voice calls out.

I stop and look toward the sound. Zach and Billy, two wrestling jocks in my second year psych class, are jogging in my direction. I'm surprised they know my name. They've been ignoring me for two years – probably because they don't want to be seen talking to an openly gay man, so what's with their sudden acknowledgement of me?

They come to a halt in front of me. Zach, a tall brunette with a punk hairstyle, wearing a loose fitting sleeveless sweatshirt, tight faded Levis, and black boots, seems to be the spokesperson. I glance at his basket. I can't help myself. He always shows a hefty bulge – that's why I first noticed him, and today's no exception. The ridge of his dickhead is clearly visible over his left groin. Biceps balloon when he raises a hand and places it on my shoulder as if I'm a long lost friend.

When I look back at his face, he smiles and says, "How you doing, bro?"

He must have me confused with someone else. Why the sudden familiarity?

"I'm good," I say.

"Say, bro," he says. "Did you hear about the gym?"

"You mean that it's going to be closed for a couple of weeks?"

"Yeah, that's it." He looks at Billy.

Billy, who's a couple of inches shorter then Zach, is bouncing from one white sneaker encased foot to the other as if he's high on energy – or something else, runs a hand through his long dirty-blond hair. His prominent nipples are the only things that disrupt the smooth surface of his tight white tee. He hoists up his baggy cargo pants – which sag below his buns, and then gives me a high five like we're best friends.

"We hear you got a gym in your basement, dude," Billy says. "We's wondering if we can use it while the gym's closed?"

Ah ha. So that's what it's about. I feel like telling them to get lost, but that would be ridiculous considering I've been lusting after them for years. This would give me the opportunity to observe them up close, and maybe – if I'm lucky, I'll get more than just a look.

Billy continues to bounce as he awaits my response.

I'm getting hard just thinking about it. "Sure ... why not," I say.

"That's great, bro," Zach says, giving my shoulder a squeeze. "Can we do it tonight?"

"Sure, I'll be home if you wanna drop round."

We arrange a time, and I give them the address. My parents are on a cruise, so I've got the place to myself. I watch them depart fantasizing about making it with them. On the way home, I stop off at the Red Hot video store and pick up a couple of straight porno videos – ones featuring two guys and one woman, and then I pick up twenty-four cans of Bud, lube, and a package of condoms.

When I arrive home, I take a shower, slip on a jock, a pair of silk running shorts, and white socks and sneakers. I leave my chest bare because I'm hoping they'll do the same. We have a great gym in the basement. It contains a rack with a set of barbells, a bench for chest presses, an inverted leg press, and a ten-by-ten exercise mat stored on one of the walls. The other end of the room has a fridge, loveseat, recliner, coffee table, and fifty-three-inch flat screen TV.

After stocking the fridge, I drop my gym bag containing the safes and lube next to the love seat.

I'm pacing the floor when the doorbell rings. They're dressed in the same clothes they had on earlier, but now they carry gym bags.

"Great place, bro," Zach says looking around the basement. "You gonna join us?"

I nod, then watch as they strip.

Zach stands naked in front of me. His big dick flops around when he nonchalantly scratches his low hanging nuts. Dark hair abounds on his chest and trails down to his pubic bush. He stands with his hands on his hips and stares at me. "Well?" he asks. "Is it everything you imagined?"

My face flushes, but I don't care what he thinks, they're in my territory.

He looks even sexier when he pulls on a tight white singlet and adjusts his dick.

Billy is more reserved. He turns his back to us when he lowers his briefs. I'm glad because I get a good look at his buns. They're big and muscular. Kaiser buns would best describe them. When he bends over to step into his red singlet, I get a tantalizing glimpse of his tight pucker. His upper body is hairless, but his legs are covered in downy blond hair.

Luckily, I'm wearing a jock, because I'm already hard and leaking. It's going to be tough controlling myself.

We start rotating through the equipment. Zach lies on his back doing chest presses while Billy does the spotting. I'm using the barbells, but my eyes are focused on Zach's dick, which seems to grow with each press. Billy's dick, positioned above Zach's face, is tenting out his singlet. I'm on the inverted leg press when they switch positions.

The torture continues for over an hour, and the aroma of the testosterone fueled junkies permeates the humid room. I think about turning on the air, but I don't want to dilute the odor. Zach spreads the mat on the floor, and they start wrestling. Sweat dampened singlets cling to their bodies, showing every bulge and crevice. When Zach's hand slides through Billy's thighs and grips Billy's butt, I wish for a video camera, so I can memorialize the session. This is fodder for later jerk-off sessions.

Eventually, Zach pins Billy, and they decide they've had enough.

I throw some towels to them and hand out the beers. Zach reclines on the loveseat and Billy relaxes in the recliner. I join Zach.

"Fuck, you guys are good," I say. "You're gonna make state champions."

"You think so?" Zach says flexing his biceps.

His pheromone output extinguishes my inhibitions. Unable to control myself I say, "God, your muscles are big! Can I feel 'em?"

He smiles and flexes some more. "Sure, go ahead."

I reach over and feel his biceps. They're pumped and hard, but the skin covering them is as smooth as satin. I run my hand over his hairy chest and feel his pecs. He sighs, lifts his arm, and takes a swig of beer. The raunchy aroma emanating from his pits sends me into orbit. I lean forward and take a deep breath. I'm just about to lick a pit when I come to my senses and back off. That was close.

Billy is watching us through lowered lids.

My beer is finished, so I bring three more out of the fridge. We guzzle them down. When we're on our forth beer I decide it's time to bring out the big guns.

"You guys into porno?" I ask.

"Fuck, bring it on, bro," Zach says.

After loading one of the rented DVDs, I sit back and watch the action on, and off, the screen. It's not long before Zach's dick starts twisting around in his tight singlet as if it's looking for an escape route. A wet spot forms at the head.

"I can't believe how big your cock is," I say to him.

He grips his boner and gives it a shake. "That's ten inches of solid muscle, bro."

"I don't believe you," I say. "Everybody says that."

"Well, dude. I've measured it, and it's a true ten incher."

"Can I check it out?"

He doesn't hesitate. He's probably been in this position before. "Why not? You've been wanting to do it ever since we arrived."

And, you've been wanting me to do it, I feel like saying. But I keep silent, reach over, and grip his shaft. He pushes against my hand and precum seeps through his silky singlet. I slip the straps off his shoulders and lower the singlet. He lifts his backside, so I can strip him. His released cock jerks up and rests on his six-pack abdomen. When I run my hand up the thick-veined shaft, semen lubricates my fist.

Billy's watching us, and his hand is covering his hard on.

"What about you, Billy?" I ask as my hand works its magic on Zach's dick. "You got a big one?"

His face flushes, and he doesn't say anything.

"He's got a biggie, but it's not as big as mine," Zach says.

"Sure it is," Billy says.

"Come over here and prove it," Zach says.

Billy thinks it over, then stands up and lowers his singlet.

Zach's right. It is a biggie. I'm wondering how Zach knew.

His horizontal dick leading the way, Billy walks over to us.

I kneel on the floor, and he sits next to Zach. What a sight. Two beautiful dicks throbbing between muscular thighs.

Billy gasps when I take hold of his boner. The mushroom head pops out of its protective covering. I've got a dick in each of my fists, and I can't decide who to do first.

"Zach's a little longer than you, Billy," I say. "But you've got a bigger head. Let's see if I can get it in my mouth."

It's not difficult for an old pro like me. I've never met a cock I couldn't handle. Before he knows what's happening, I'm deep throating him, and his silky pubes are pressing against my lips.

"Oh, fuck, dude," Billy says, "no one's ever done that to me."

I'm pumping his shaft with my throat and playing with his nuts, when Zach says, "What about me? I could do with some of that."

After a few deep breaths, I sink Zach's dick down my throat.

"Fuck, you're good," Zach says as he places his hands on my head and fucks my mouth.

I suck on Zach for a while, but I don't want him to come – so I sit back and admire the scenery. I've got other things planned.

Billy spreads his legs. He wants more. But, I want something different. I remove his sneakers and socks, and then lift one of his feet to my face. I lick the arch of his foot then suck his perfectly formed toes.

"Fuck, dude," Billy says squirming around on the seat. "They's all sweaty."

"That's how I like them," I say switching to the other foot.

When I've had my fill of Billy's feet, I move over to Zach and push his legs up to his chest.

"Whoa, bro," Zach says. "What're you doing?"

"I wanna taste your butt," I say.

His eyes open wide. "You want to lick my ass?"

His masculine aroma wafts up into my face as I slip his nuts into my mouth. They're big and hard, full of creamy juice waiting to gush into a receptive channel. I pull his ass-cheeks to the edge of the seat. His pink pucker peeps through the luscious bush between his cheeks. He groans when I lean forward and lap his sweaty hole.

"What's it taste like?" Billy asks after I've been at it for a few minutes.

"Come down here and see," I say.

Billy kneels next to me. I push his face toward Zach's crack. His tongue gently laps Zach's hole.

"Fuck, good buddy," Zach says hooking his legs behind his arms. "That's awesome."

I remove my shorts and jock to free my aching boner, move the coffee table out of the way, lie on my back, and push my head between Billy's thighs. He lets out a long groan when I lick his smooth pucker. He nearly suffocates me when he sits back on my face and spreads his cheeks.

I'm probing his chute with my tongue when I hear Zach say, "Suck my dick, bro."

This I have to witness, so I come to my feet and watch Billy doing his gym buddy. For a beginner, he's pretty good. He's able to go halfway down Zach's shaft before he gags.

Zach's watching me stroking my rod. He licks his lips, so I climb onto the loveseat and rub my dickhead against his mouth, wondering how he'll handle it, but he's cool. He opens up, and my rod slips into his mouth. He grabs my butt and pulls me into him. I can't believe that the butch number I've been lusting after appears to be enjoying the taste of my dick.

He sucks me for a few minutes then I withdraw my rod and ask, "You guys ever fuck?"

Billy sits back on his haunches, and they both look at me as if I've lost my mind.

"You mean up the ass?" Zach says with an incredulous look on his face.

"Yeah, it's great. You should try it."

They don't object, so I pull the safes and lube out of my bag and roll a safe down Zach's towering pole. I lube him and my chute and then lower myself, engulfing his dick with my craving hole.

"Oh, fuck, dude," Billy says as I ride Zach's dick. "I can't believe you've got his cock inside you. Doesn't it hurt?"

"Am I complaining?" I say as I pick up speed.

Billy places a hand around the root of Zach's dick, so he can feel it sliding in and out of me.

"You wanna try it?" I ask.

"Go ahead, good buddy," Zach says. "It'll feel great."

"You'll take it easy?" Billy asks.

"Would I hurt my good buddy?"

I raise myself and cover Zach's dick with a fresh safe.

"Get up here, Billy," Zach says.

Billy straddles Zach's thighs. I lubricate Zach's dick, then I use a couple of lubed fingers to open Billy's chute. He's tight, real tight. It's been a long time since I've had a finger in a virgin hole. I hold Zach's dick in place as Billy slowly lowers his butt.

"Oh, God, it hurts," Billy says in a whining voice as his sphincter slowly stretches to accommodate the girth Zach's cock head.

My ass twitches when I remember the pain of my own deflowering. "Take some deep breaths and push down as if you're taking a dump," I say.

He does as I say. I watch in awe as Zach's dick slowly disappears up Billy's chute. He takes a breather when Zach is fully embedded, and then he slowly starts riding the mammoth cock up his virgin ass.

"I want your cock back in my ass, Zack," I say after they've been at it for a while. "Let me fuck Billy, and you can fuck me at the same time."

Billy eases himself off Zack. I roll a safe down my dick, position Billy on his back, and my rod slides into his well primed hole. Zach puts a new safe on his rod and throws it into me. I'm in heaven and can't believe I'm sandwiched between them.

Zach's pounding me like a jackhammer, and I'm throwing it into Billy. I lower my head and lock my lips on Billy's gasping mouth. His tongue duels with mine. I'm getting close. Zach's hot breath in my ear is sending shivers down my spine. I turn my head and lick his lips. He opens his mouth, and we suck face.

"Ah, ah," Billy groans as he spontaneously erupts, spreading loads of cum between our bodies.

I'm shooting my load when I feel Zach erupt in my clinging channel.

Later, when they're getting ready to leave, Zach asks, "Are we cool for tomorrow, Matt?"

"I'll be waiting," I say.

TINY
By Diesel King

Little Dude let me dig up in that bitch.

I guess that ain't quite the way I want to put it. So let me rephrase it this way:

Little Dude let me tap that ass and dig out that inner bitch we both knew was living deep inside of his sweet little cunt hole.

The way I see it that shit was funny as fuck, listening to that bitch boy yelp in his high-pitch squeal, reminding me of a long-winded Chihuahua in heat. 'Stop it Fatin, you're killing me with that thing!'

Well, isn't that what good pipe suppose to do? Slay the insatiable pussy from the hunger pangs of dick withdrawals. Quiet the stomach rumblings. Stretch out the intestines like a thorough colonoscopy.

I mean, what exactly did Little Dude think was going to happen when I stuck my jimmy up his tiny little poop chute? That I was going to take it easy on his ass like we were Driving Miss Daisy? Hell naw! Doesn't he fucking know already that a big dick plus a tight hole equals piston-like strokes into submission with a smooth silky finish of a fiery hot nutt?

Dumb ass motherfucker!

I probably should've known he was fresh virgin ass the first time he stepped up in our gym. Now, I know I'm hood, but there isn't a black guy in this world that I know that walks that upright! I'm not talking about military straight because even a guy that has no real rhythm is issued some kind of swag or style when he is taught how to march. Little Dude was just a cornball with it. A pure cornball. Hole and ass cheeks so tight loose shit would have a time making a run for it.

Still though, we thought Little Dude was cool. He may have had the face of a mutt hit by a pile-on with his low-Caesar fade and thick flavor savor running off his bottom lip, but Little Dude got that our gym was a gym to pump iron. Not some seedy little spot to shuck the corn with a well greased hand. That was important to me and my three buff dudes (Tim, T-Bone, and Tyrone) before we gave the little bastard clearance to work out at our gym.

We don't exactly have papers on the place per se, but we take a considerable amount of pride in running it as unofficial ambassadors, as it relates to keeping out the riff-raff and the queers. Particularly those fucking queers! They are out of fucking control! It's like a faggot plague! Now before you go out and start drawing up protest signs and prancing around in your little tutus and vogue-ing down the avenue, I am not a homophobe. Like any other red-blooded man that fears the Blue Balls epidemic, I love a good cocksucker or a skilled butt boy when the regular bitch is out of commission with her monthly friend. But when it comes to the fairies and the locker rooms, one too many do-it-yourself stories told all of you that it's one big sexual playground to explore. It wouldn't be so fucking bad if so many of them didn't look like Shrek or Fiona, hiding out in some obscure corner or trying to convert the whole thing into one big glory hole: The stalls, the saunas. There's a real fucking reason there are hollowed out video booths in those X-rated video stores other than to preview your neighbor's flick. It's a bad economy. Keep them those motherfuckers in business, too! Even the pretty fucks work a nerve sometimes, acting all prissy like running on the treadmill at 3.5 incline thinking that sweating and smelling like a real man is a terrible sin all the while posting a hard-on in their shorts while a real dude hits the weights. Sometimes I want to scream at every one of those motherfuckers 'You like ball juice doncha? So it's going to smell like balls in this bitch, you dimwitted motherfucker!'

Where was I? Oh, yeah. Little Dude. Little Dude came off as something new though, standing about five-six, somewhere over two hundred pounds boasting an incredible physique. His well-developed delts and serratus brought forth a pair of high-sitting, countrywide pecs that were almost surreal; shoulders well rounded, with his triceps competing with his biceps and massive forearm to create limbs that appeared to be carved from Herculean stone. And his thighs and glutes were just as equally impressive instead of the usual afterthought of most modern-day bodybuilders.

Before I found myself deep in another bromance, I took a step back and regrouped. I've been psyched out before. Riff raffs had their stunts just like the queers. Their way of sneaking into our gym is either by being an ex-con straight off the yard with nothing else better to do or flex around muscles made from human growth hormones. While the ex-cons annoyed me by playing hard to avoid being bitched, I had a special hatred brewing for those fucking chemies that gave the rest of us natural dudes a bad name.

Little Dude had it together though. He knew his body type. He knew all about the different philosophies of the different bodybuilding magazines and books out there, from the old school to new. He knew his supplements like the back of his hand, the purpose of each, and which ones was pure garbage for the yuppies that needed more junk to put in their bodies to feel like they were doing something big. More importantly, he knew the difference between sets and reps. He knew which combination of which offered growth or strength depending on the amount of weights he used and the conversion he needed to get the desired results.

So from a distance, Little Dude was quite cool, giving his usual nod when he saw us. And, from time to time, he would spot us with our weights when we were a couple of men down, and we would do the same for him since he was forever riding solo.

Tim, our black built titan, was the friendliest out of the four of us. So, it was only natural that he reached out to Little Dude first and introduce the rest of us. Little Dude was quickly impressed with T-Bone. T-Bone was closest to him in height, standing about a couple of inches taller than him at five-eight. T-Bone was diesel-cut like a motherfucker, boasting a 50-inch chest, 21-inch guns, and a 29-inch waist that made competitive athletes everywhere froth at the mouth. Whereas Tim had an imposing superhero's super body, my skull-cap wearing four-eyed friend Tyrone didn't come off as a much of a bone crusher as he bragged. At best, he was just a corporate thug that looks like he got carried away with the dumbbells for his weekend motorcycle club.

"This here is Fatin," Tim introduced me last. "But everybody calls him Tiny."

Little Dude chuckled, knowing that my six-foot-four, nearly three hundred solid pound frame disqualified me from being teeny in any sort of way.

While it would be easy for me to say that I had the best body out of my crew, I don't. I don't look like a freakazoid bodybuilder like Tim or T-Bone, but my immense muscular cuts only enhanced my great looks and supported my health nut ways like my boy Tyrone.

"And, as you can see I ain't tiny down there either." I bragged to Little Dude just days after our official meeting, stripping out of my jockstrap to jump into the steaming shower. "I can charge a lot more than $5 for this good-ass foot long!"

I should've known by the way his eyes nearly popped out of their sockets as I playfully grabbed the dickie that dude was really jonesing for it. He was probably going home and rubbing one out just thinking about the white syrupy taste. If not then, especially the way Little Dude always "accidentally" brushed up against me at the gym whenever he could score an unquestionable freebie. I mean damn, I know I'm as big as he is short, but I was starting to think that I was becoming some sort of cuddle post for the naïve kitten. But, I was still green to him throughout all those months, and then California happened.

California was the jump off point for me dissecting Little Dude when we went down to Venice Beach for this fitness and charity thing Labor Day Weekend. Everything was going good the first night we shared a motel room. The night after that, after I sifted through those bodybuilder brochures and saw the chat line numbers for buff men looking for buff men, I tried to push that fucked-up shit out of my mind. I was desperate not to believe that I left another queer slip into the gym. The proof proved to be in the pudding when I came back to my room early from a seminar only for a chair to be posted up against the door. And when Little Dude came to remove it, he was escorting this tall ugly dude with an incredible body and a cheesy smile out of the room. When I took the mature route and asked what was up their goofy grins, Little Dude decided that he had a case of Alzheimer's followed by a bad pack of lies.

This was totally new to me. Usually when we had a queer in the mix, it was nothing to smoke him out. Flash him the baby maker, and he's getting whiplash to fall to his knees. Little Dude was giving lingering glances in, but he wasn't biting, obviously fighting the urge to see it through.

I was just about to give up on Little Dude when my three road dawgs started swapping notes in the locker room about Little Dude giving everybody head. That is, everybody except me. I didn't know how to take it until they said that he was unbending about not letting them bust in his mouth and was giving them hell about them trying to get in that booty.

"I bet he's saving that for Tiny." Tyrone boasted throwing on a pair of boxer briefs to show off his bulky bulge.

"Why you say that?"

"You blind? Little Dude is stuck to you like a Velcro condom."

"Yeah, right," I said, pulling a well-fitted T-shirt over my formed body. "I've tried to get him to take care of the stick for awhile. He acts like he's scared of it."

"No, homo," Tim said, "I'm scared of that elephant trunk, too, and I got its twin right here!"

I burst out laughing as Tim grabbed himself through his briefs. Tim had a monster dick, but he was just extremely chunkier than it was long. I had a well rounded double-digit donkey dick.

"That's because he wants you to put a ring on it before he gives up the cakes." Tyrone said through my laughter.

"Just like a bitch." T-Bone, our recently engaged comrade, beamed.

"Yeah, just like a bitch!" Tyrone laughed.

"Once he get it from you, he'll probably become an unfaithful wifey and spread the love to the rest of the hood. Give the rest of us a wink of that brown eye pie." Tim smirked.

There was a brief silence between us, as the same thought seemed to pop up in our heads.

"You're thinking what I'm thinking, folk?" I asked.

"Hell yeah," Tyrone said. "It would be a nice way to send our boy T-Bone off into that dark night."

"…without worrying about getting another bachelor party stripper pregnant," Tim said, looking over at Tyrone.

"Again," T-Bone chuckled.

"A good old-fashioned Chattanooga choo-choo," I hollered, pulling the imaginary chain with my muscled arm, "is definitely in order for that bodybuilding trick!"

# # # # #

"You sure we're cool doing this?" Little Dude worriedly inquired.

"Stop acting like such a scared little pussy and man up!" I barked in a friendly manner leaving him unsuspecting of my real intent as I fumbled with the key in the lock.

It was precisely ten minutes after midnight, and I had went from zero to hero with Little Dude over the passing weeks. I struck out a time or two trying to find my in. I found a crack by helping him change his tire on his Hummer. But I finally broke ground around Christmastime when I thought to include Little Dude in my gift-giving rounds. It wasn't anything spectacular – just some heavy duty hand grips with 300 lbs resistance – but it touched him enough to put me and the crew on the VIP list of some trendy club he was DJ-ing on New Year's Eve. So by the time T-Bone's Super Bowl Party came about, I pulled Little Dude to the side as one self-scheduling businessman to another about asking him to join me in a late night workout after we spent most of the afternoon gorging on everything in sight.

In the moment, I lied and said it was somehow good for the muscles. Later, I left him guilt-ridden about his ravenous appetite with the desperate need to exercise some of it off before we hit the hay for the night. He agreed.

"I wouldn't have my own key if it wasn't cool for me to work out after hours." I said, watching Little Dude take a water bottle to the head, rehydrating after the liquor we poured during the party.

After we got in and locked the doors behind us, I started out doing my thing with the cables to work out on my broad shoulders and he went in to do some lying triceps extensions. As we worked our respective body parts, we met back in the middle when I needed a spotter for the bench press. I returned the favor in kind by standing on the calf machine when the given load wasn't heavy enough.

Little Dude always had an incredible pair of legs in a muscled up masculine way, so it should've came as no surprise that his head was elsewhere not to hear the Three Musketeers come in with their own set of keys.

"Looking good back there," Tim mouthed off, startling Little Dude. I knew this by the way he jerked the shoulder pads I was standing on. Tim wasn't giving a fuck about me about to lose my balance subtly looking at the sculpted ass coming through the form-fitting Under Armour before him.

"No doubt," Tyrone said less subtly, leaning back to get the same view of the perfect fleshly round ass.

"I see you got away from the future wifey." Little Dude said specifically to T-Bone, looking down at the machine, oblivious to everything going on behind him.

"Yeah," T-Bone said. "She wasn't in the mood to give up the goodies tonight after her team went down with the ship. So, I figured I could stay at home and beat my meat or make sweet love to the bells. Strangely enough, they never say no."

"I feel you on that one." Little Dude ended it there.

"I know you do."

The three of them stood behind Little Dude for a few minutes more admiring the view and making animated plays around his booty.

I jumped down from the machine after Little Dude had finished up his sets. He was obviously stunned to find the same three men in the same place they were when he was working out.

"What?" Little Dude asked looking out at the three of them.

"I was thinking that you got some nice-ass glutes." T-Bone smiled, stroking his hairy chin like he was seriously thinking.

"Thanks ... I guess." Little Dude said cautiously.

"Watching the game tonight, I don't think there was a player on the field with an end as tight as yours." Tim added straight with T-Bone and Tyrone chuckling in the back.

"You know," Tyrone said starting on his rehearsed spill. "Me and the boyz were talking, and we were saying how much we admired that nice muscled butt every time you walked away after giving us some head."

From where I stood next to Little Dude I couldn't make out his face without being so apparent, but I could make out the cold fear that must've been running through his veins.

"Hold up," I injected on cue. "You need to quit all that shit! My man here ain't gay." I said, slapping Little Dude on his hard shoulder.

"I ain't say all of that. All I said was Little Dude gave good face." Tyrone said.

I acted as if I was sincerely shocked, "To the three of you?"

The three of them answered in there melody of nods and personalized statements.

"Tell me that ain't true folk. You like a hard dick in your mouth like you like Jolly Rodgers?" I asked, trying not to laugh.

If it was just one of them Little Dude could've bucked and flat out denied it, but with three of this accusers standing there in front of him like that the only thing he could do was turn red, storm out of the gym and into the locker room, leaving the three of them to laugh and me to call Little Dude back.

By the time I got back into the locker room, Little Dude had his stuff and was ready to go. He said he didn't want to talk about it. I said that I did, wanting to know where his head was to serve up the crew with throat jobs. He said he didn't have to answer to me and that he was going home. I told him that was fine by me, if he could find a way there as I gently reminded him that I was his ride to the party and to the gym. And, it wasn't like he wasn't going to get a cab to come on that side of town that hour of the night. Then, he threatened to walk it out, before I told him that even with all his muscles he couldn't stop a round of stray bullets.

He started off saying that he liked dudes but didn't see himself as being a faggot. That he liked me, but when he saw me flirting with some random broad that he thought it gave him the license to suck off Tim. After I dropped the bitch and was going about business as usual, Tim threatened to tell if he didn't continue to suck him off only for Tyrone to catch them in the act just to turn around and get T-Bone on the act, too.

"So it sounded to me like you've been busy bobbing your head left and right on some dick next to working out."

"Not the three of them at the same time." Little Dude said softly in defense.

"Not the three of them at the same time." I mocked from my seated position on the bench. "Like that makes it sound a lot less whorish."

"You mad at me? I know how you feel about the queers."

"I ain't the one that gave head to three motherfucking dudes that can bash my skull in! The question is how come you hadn't tried to slob on my knob? I'm like the three of them combined!" I laughed.

"Yeah, you working with a trouser snake of the likes I've never seen before." Little Dude said coyly.

"Thanks. That's saying a lot coming from the mouth of a dude that took care of three friends with it ... and probably a lot more to do something that slutty. Three dudes that is thick as thieves? Really?"

"I know. I know. Stupid." Little Dude shook his head.

"You know the way they were talking about your butt they want a crack at it."

Little Dude shook.

"What's that about?"

"I've never been fucked a day in my life."

"You're a virgin?"

"Back there. I know this is a lot to ask, seeing that they're your peeps, but you think you can help me out of this?"

"No." I said flat out.

Little Dude was surprised.

"I thought we were cool." Little Dude cried.

"I thought so, too. But I guess my dick ain't where it's at."

"It ain't like that, man."

"Then tell me what it's like then."

Little Dude paused. "You ain't going to make me say it are you?"

"Say what?" I asked, still pretending to be naïve.

"Say that I was feeling you more than I was feeling the others."

"Man, that don't even make sense!" I said sincerely. "You like me so much you gave my peeps a constellation prize of blowing them off and leaving me curbside. But even if I could help you out of this situation, there are three dudes we would have to battle to get you out of here safely. They got motivation to come after you. All I have is a dis to ignore you and get back to my workout while they hem you up."

I was off of the bench heading back into the gym when I heard Little Dude plea, "Please, man," with his strong hand reaching out for my awakening dick.

"Ain't that what got your weak ass in trouble in the first place?" I said coolly removing his hand.

Little Dude looked like he was going to bust out crying, but mannish pride was keeping him from shedding a tear with this sort of puppy face hopelessness that was tugging at heart strings.

"I'll tell you what. I'll get you out of this situation."

"Really," he said with a Kool-Aid smile.

"I wouldn't be too excited because it's going to cost you your ass."

164

"What is it? Whatever it is, I'll pay." Little Dude rattled off, not listening to what I said, but I was game to play along.

"The down payment consists of some of that mouth-to-lip service you seemed to be passing out like Halloween candy."

"Okay," Little Dude said jumpily.

"I said that was the down payment, something that you can easily come off of. Paid in full, like I said, is your ass. Sacrifice that virgin booty to my dick."

I would've laughed at the way Little Dude turned ghost white.

"Hell naw! I've seen what porn stars look like going through it taking regular size dick, and you're easily twice as big as them!"

"Hey, that's the cost for putting yourself out there like a ho when you're not broken in to play the game." I said coldly.

"There's got to be another way."

"No, there isn't."

"I can give you money."

"From spinning tables? We're not even in the same league of dollars, partna." I paused, and then made my way to the door leading out to the gym. "Fuck it then! Let them run a train on your punk ass. I was going to take my time with it, and at least make your first dick sweet on you. With three dudes taking it like it's their last good fuck before death row, don't be surprised if your farts come out muffled like the dad from *Family Guy*."

"Wait!"

"What?" I stopped.

"So you want to lead me out and take me back to your spot, and do the damn thing there?" Little Dude said concededly.

"My thing is right here and now. Suck and fuck."

"And what'll stop them from coming back here?"

"Absolutely fucking nothing ... which is why if you let me fuck you we might be good."

165

"How you figure?"

"I can go the distance. They're like rapid fire little boys that just discovered themselves. I know I can outlast them! So by the time they rub out one or two good ones, I'm still going up in you like the Energizer bunny, and they're too tired to come at you. Now, it doesn't keep them off your ass, but at least it makes your first time not so traumatic."

Little Dude was slow to come up with some kind of answer and my dick was growing in my jockstrap by the second that I just whipped it on out in front of him. He had seen it countless times since we met, but his eyes popped like he finally got his hands on the golden ticket to touch it.

"Don't be afraid to grab the handlebar. I know you're not a virgin to that." I said.

He reached out and wrapped his callus hands around the semi-hard thing, and slowly pumped it in his fist.

"Feel good, don't it? So why don't we take it around the corner where we have some privacy just in case they want to rain on our parade earlier than expected."

We moved over to the last hole of lockers in the far back. I posted up against the wall, and Little Dude fell to his knees. He was strangely delicate in stroking me hard, and when he was ready the center of his tongue slapped the tip like a sloppy wet kiss. The cold sopping felt good, but felt even better when his warm mouth gave me the deal that it gave three of my fellas. He was quiet, putting that tongue to work over my most sensitive parts. Loud and slurping when he needed me to know how much he was enjoying servicing me. And, he didn't even have to do all that with the ease he deep-throated me. Even the size queen queers had a time doing that. I guess it was the sheer sight of that alone, that was about to make me bust a nutt right then and there.

"Cool it, man," I said, trying to maneuver my dick from between his tonsils. "You got a good mouth, but I want to crack open that ass-safe."

Little Dude was praying that I forgot and tried to get in a few quick strokes to make me come before I guess he remembered that there were three dudes out in the gym that I was protecting him from.

After retrieving some fire and ice lube, I put Little Dude doggie-style over the bench, so that he kneed the wood, and so that he could use his hands to brace the locker. "Man, you're freaking short," I stated facts, awkwardly squatting down in the tight space so that I could guide my dick down through his sweaty crack.

The tip of my dick was perfectly aligned with his hole when I grabbed his shoulders and let myself in between those rigid glutes.

"Stop it Fatin, you're killing me with it!" Little Dude screamed in pain.

"Let me push that flared head all the way in that wet pussy, midget. I promise you it'll make you feel real good in a minute." I assured him.

He was tighter than a motherfucker, and I probably could've enjoyed opening up his virgin hole more if it wasn't for the lube doing a number on my dick with the fluctuating sensations that was trying to force me to come mid-stroke.

"That's it, baby boy ... let me iron out those guts ... and make myself right at home here," I breathed, sinking it further in the clenched channel drilling for rock bottom.

It took putting Little Dude on his back and about twenty-five minutes before I got any sort of enjoyable rhythm out of mounting the dude. It was like his hole was so closed up and came with so much friction that it was trying to rip the foreskin off my jimmy. But with a constant supply of lube and sweat, Little Dude went from squealing in pain to becoming a nympho in heat, eventually throwing his ass back and letting me dig out his inner bitch.

"All those blowjobs you were doling out and all you really wanted was some dude to take care of that ass for you, huh?" I huffed after some time, whipping away pouring sweat from my forehead and feeling good about stretching out his dripping wet asshole.

I caught a second or third wind and started pounding him out for about fifteen minutes more, listening to him whimper about being split in two with my balls slamming up against him.

"I got to bounce." I said looking at the hour and a half I spent up in his hole. "I got to let go of this nutt! I ... got to ... let it ... gooooo!"

I fucked that ass harder than hard, his hole was shivering and quivering wet around my dick, and before I knew it, it clenched down hard on my dick and forced me to shoot like a broken hydrant deep inside of him, screaming and hollering all the way.

"Damn, motherfucker! You got some of that good pussy!" I puffed out, catching my breath, looking at the load that painted his abdomen. I almost broke into laughter the way his used hole farted like well-fucked coochie as I pulled out. "So good in fact that 'it ain't no fun unless the homies have some!'"

I got up and was quickly replaced by my good gym buddies. Minutes turned into hours watching everybody get some of that sweet ass. It was like our dicks refused to die out that night. It was like the more ass we got, the more we wanted. Even after his butthole started kicking out every load we ever put up in him, which made the ride even smoother and sweeter. And when that wasn't enough, we got Little Dude to lick off our scummy dicks, seeing that we had girlfriends and future wives to get back home to.

After we left Little Dude to lie there on the bench with his sloppy hole to recuperate, the four of us jumped into the shower and saw each other off. But, I couldn't let things go without letting T-Bone know that that counted as his wedding gift from the crew. "So if you're wifey starts bitching out the side of her neck about us not getting her a gift, tell her we don't mind parking the train into her station anytime. Tell her your boy Tiny says so!"

MEETING BLACK ZEUS
By Diesel King

Five foot freaking six!

Excuse me if I laughed at that too heartily. It isn't that I have anything against short people. I don't. It's just that for a towering football player from the small town of Old Texas Alabama who spent most of his closeted teen years jacking off to this black god, I honestly thought he was much taller than that! At least I always pegged him for being a smidge taller than five-eight, which later I learned seemed to be the threshold for most competitive bodybuilders. But, of course, Romulus Cornell was no ordinary man winning over several dozen muscleman awards and, of course, the coveted Mr. Zeus title, a poster of which I once owned that spent most of the 80s hanging just above my dumbbells and jump rope.

I had nearly forgotten all about my longstanding crush from over twenty years back when I happened to be down in Cuba on vacation visiting a dear friend. My friend also had an aged picture of the Black Zeus from the same time period hanging ceremoniously in his beachside gym. The only difference between my picture and his was that his picture was a lot less formal and looked to be on the same beach just decades earlier. So when my friend asked me to fly with him back to Miami for this fitness symposium, I think we were both surprised to find our bodybuilder hero at the same event discussing his lengthy career and his recently earned lifetime achievement award.

As he stood up at the podium talking, a lot of those old memories came flooding back. In particular, those cold lonely nights when I wanted nothing more than to caress the hard oiled muscles of another black man, to work my way up from those delectable calves to those incredible deltoids that needed man-hands to massage them right. In a few cases, his image in Joe Weider's magazine collection was the only motivation I had to stay hard in the back of my pickup truck when I was bordering on "stage fright" with a handful of my loose girlfriends. And while the man was never a bad-looking guy, age somehow made his angular lines more becoming, and his light plain suit just offered a maturity that he failed to achieve in his earlier years pronouncing his alpha masculinity even more.

While my friend was eager to get to another class featuring another relevant body sculptor, I patiently stuck around through the madness that was the Meet & Greet just to be awestruck to have a few moments of his time and the fine penmanship of his autograph. There was so much I wanted to say without plenty of time to say it, wanting to tell him how he changed the life of a rural black boy just a few miles away from his hometown. That he was the reason that I had a body that made most men leave wet spots in their drawers. But, I didn't, fearing that I might embarrass myself by accidentally revealing my truth to him, telling him that I knew I was gay when I imagined my legs wrapped around his narrow waist using my hole at his will.

It wouldn't come until later on that night that instead of being frightened by my confession that he might've been flattered by it when I learned that the silver-headed muscle tank proved to be a silver-headed muscle brick shithouse dad eyeing a demonstration at the local leather club. I guess it was well-known to the known world that he was gay except me. And not just gay, but openly gay, to the point that he never hid it during his entire career as it was just assumed that he was unquestionably hetero with his deep voice and ripped physique.

"I knew something about you told me you were family," Black Zeus spoke to me, bringing his heavy hand down on my broad shoulder.

With a boner proudly streaming down my thighs, I turned to look down at him looking up at me beaming, showing me his perfectly lined white teeth before turning to watch a submissive in a spreader taking a paddle to his reddening backside. When I turned to steal a second look at him, Black Zeus had quietly disappeared out of sight.

Left there turned on by him and raw red ass being beaten before me, I scoured the club looking for a nice ethnic boy that I could handle drive during my layover. And just when I was about to close the deal with one boy, this other boy came to me with a note in tow, asking me to follow him for a good time.

I honestly didn't know what to make of it, the unusual request, so I tried brushing the kid off. So when he refused, I walked away with my original boy, only to be stopped on my way out to the parking lot by him and another boy flanking my bodybuilding idol.

"I must be slipping." He bemoaned jokingly. "I thought I sent my finest boy to lead you astray."

I was looking for the other boy next to him to react as he was just as equally attractive, but he didn't, like he knew his place.

"No, sir," I retorted respectfully. "It's just that I usually don't have a strange boy come up to me with a note asking me to follow him without knowing why."

"Am I a good enough reason?"

"Of course," I smiled more than I wanted to.

I was so charmed by Black Zeus and his entourage that I foolishly left my friend back at the club, forcing him to find a way to make other plans back to the hotel as I followed Black Zeus blindly into an elevator up to some obscene floor level of some luxury high-rise on South Beach.

"How do you like the place?" He asked.

"Great," I smiled nervously, watching the two young men scurry across the room through what I thought was a bedroom door.

"I have a mansion with a well-equipped dungeon in West Palm Beach that's undergoing renovation right now. Next time you make your way back to Florida, I'll definitely have to give you a tour of it."

"Okay," I agreed.

"Have a seat," he offered, leading me into this spacious living room with two leather recliners facing the television and the dark ocean behind it.

I sat, waiting for him to say something else. But, he refused, choosing only to after one of the young men presented himself in the doorway butt-naked and only then to ask me if I wanted something to drink.

I gave my drink order after he ordered his 'usual' and then ordered me to undo my pants as he was doing. That was unless I liked the arduous ceremony of one of the boys doing it for me.

I got what he said technically but couldn't actually connect it in my mind. Then, as the two boys practically ran over to us, throwing our drinks on the table next to us, and proceeding to suck us off, it was very much easier to get what he was saying.

Even without my hero saying anything else, it was obvious that this was his lifestyle. Getting sucked off like this, in front of another man, was just as customary to him as lazily watching late night television. Given as many blowjobs where I had been on the receiving end, I probably could have easily done the same. But, the boy between my legs didn't just suck dick, he had mastered the art of fellatio beautifully.

"How're you doing over there?" Black Zeus asked.

I was breathing harder than I wanted to, but he was such a natural with using his skilled tongue that it was hard to hold back and talk at the same time.

"Don't feel embarrassed if you let go in his mouth so soon. They've been trained relentlessly everyday for the past two years to extract warm jizz juice straight from the source. So if you must, feel free to take control of your boy."

I did, grabbing his head and ramming my dick in and out of his mouth like a favored sex toy.

"Damn, you were born to suck some dick!" I encouraged, feeling the head of my dick punch the back of his throat. Though, the way he looked into my eyes we both know that my roughhousing failed to give the same sensation when I let him go at it on autopilot.

After I saw that my host wasn't nearly as interested in my antics as that, I set the pace even slower, restoring the balance and enjoying the ride. Before long, his nose was buried in my pubes and his forehead was hard-pressed against my abs.

"Keep it up. I'm going to shoot!" I warned.

"Go ahead," Black Zeus warned. "It's like a yummy protein shake to them."

I was a bit startled when the boy started to pull halfway off my dick before I had to hold him still, thrusting my hips into his mouth.

"That's the stuff." Black Zeus said licking his lips.

I had a few good lunges in me before I felt the back of the boy's mouth lock around my head, and with such a vice grip and a hard tug I felt my load run out of me and into his mouth.

"Drink up boy, and swallow it up!"

I was squirting jets, and he was gulping it up like he was thirsty, stroking every little drop that he could get out of me, licking me clean and letting me go when he was sure that I had nothing else left to give.

"So how was it?" Black Zeus asked.

"Needed," I answered.

"I'm glad you liked him." Black Zeus said, looking at my dick not going soft for one second and then snapped his finger. "I would keep him around for another round, but you seem like the kind of man that can go for some ass after someone sucks you off."

"You know me so well," I said, feeling the slight need to want to cover up. But as I watched my boy with his juicy booty rush out into the other room, I felt less self-conscious about it and mildly regretful that I didn't get a chance to fuck such a beautiful ass.

"Don't worry about that," Black Zeus said sensing my concern with his own boy eagerly working between his legs. "This boy here loves it on both ends."

I took my time getting from where I was to behind his boy.

I was amazed that his crack was already well lubed and ready for me to slide in. I thought I was doing him a favor teasing his back entry way, only to prematurely push the head of my dick in when the other boy startled me running out the door.

I made the boy that I was fucking scream into the lap of Black Zeus. It could have been the sudden surprise or the fact that he was quite tight for my blunt object shoving its way through his back door.

"As much as I fuck him, his hole always seems to snap back to when it was a brand new cherry." Black Zeus seemed to apologize.

I tried easing the boy's pain by sliding up his body to twist his nipples. He seemed to moan in pleasure instead of pain this time, letting me work my way from gentle strokes to brutish pound with sweat rolling off of my face as Black Zeus sat there calmly unfazed by the action going on in front of him.

His boy, however, was feeling every pump, with grunt coming from his diaphragm every time I pushed in. Sometimes letting it out on the dick in his mouth or altogether taking his mouth off to have his scream.

"You need to quit all that hollering up there." I warned, being mindful of the neighbors. "You got some nice tight ass, but it isn't like it's the first time it's been poked."

I grabbed the boy's shoulder, holding him steady as to fuck him without ramming his straightened throat into the lap of the dick he was sucking.

"That's it. Let it out nice and gently. Give me that hole. There you go. That's how you give it up to a real man."

There was no doubt that the boy was in pure bliss the way he let out his pleasurable moans every time I scraped by his prostate with every stroke. After he reached down and jerked off, I sank my dick deep into him and shot off another powerful load.

Unlike the other boy, this boy just pulled his ass off my dick with a fuck fart and gave Black Zeus a few soulful licks of the pipe and got up and went back into the other room.

I was still catching my breath when he got dressed and immediately left the condo.

My mind must have been elsewhere because when I looked over at Zeus, his dick was standing hard and arrogant double-coated in saliva. I mean, I knew Romulus Cornell was Mr. Zeus, but I had no idea that Zeus the man was Zeus in the pants. Never in my life would I have suspected that a man that I looked at for almost a decade on my wall that packed so much incredible muscle and spent most of his career parading around in low cut trunks was just that hung. And, it wasn't because he was much shorter that made him look so much bigger either. He was big period.

"It took us a while, but we finally got to the main course." Black Zeus said boastfully.

"Yeah," I said, licking my lips and nervously looking on. I was best at being on the receiving end of getting head, so giving it wasn't my forte. And, this was a man that I wanted to please.

"Suck me off, son," he said authoritatively, almost militarily, taking off his suit to reveal a smooth freckled chest.

I put my mouth around his dick, popping the head and working along the long thick shaft. This seemed to stir some delight from his lips as I felt confident enough to take it as best I could into my mouth, fighting my gag reflexes and all.

"You look good on your knees, son," he encouraged me with a big silky ball sac in my mouth. "You would look better with my ass on your lips."

My tongue slipped behind his balls and into his ass crack. He had to adjust the way he sat a couple of times before he granted me full access to his hole. I licked it very slowly waiting for his reaction, feeling more in my zone putting his charming hole through some changes, like swirling it around in circular strokes to broad swiping it tongue fucking it insanely, all the while taking from grabbing the back of his chair and grunting it out to twisting his hard pump ass across my ass with his dick straining hard against my forehead.

"That's it! I can't take it anymore. I need to be inside of you." He sighed.

Like a well choreographed dance, I ended up kneeing his leather chair bracing myself as my bodybuilder hero took the precaution of lubricating up my ass. Much like the boy I had just fucked, I wasn't a virgin either. But got fucked so far and few in between time that for the few older men that ever had the pleasure of using me, it felt like they were the first to pop my cherry. As I felt like I was being slowly invaded by an army, I moaned in appreciation for that pimple-faced teenage boy that had a great love for this man and then cried out as he mounted me and then penetrated me, like I was some whore that was built to take it. Even though my hole conceded as if I could, the throbbing inside my ass let me know that it wasn't so.

"You worthless piece of shit!" I bawled without control.

"Push out," Black Zeus instructed. "Just push out and just give me your hole."

I tried, but the initial pain was just too damn much. But after a few minutes, my body trembled, my hole gave in effortlessly.

"Just relax, I know boys like you like your hole packed in."

He fucked me like this for a long time, occasionally slapping me on my cheeks before moving our show into his bedroom, with him telling me that he liked fucking my ass and that he knew he could get in it the way I was looking at him earlier. He pegged me perfectly as being one of those horny boys that used to get off on his picture. There were many of them, he informed me, ranging from the she-males to the queers to the controlling down low men that wanted nothing more than to be conquered by his formidable muscled body.

I thought something was wrong when he stopped our doggie-style marathon, but he simply wiped his sweaty hands on my oblique and pulled out. "I want to watch your face when I pump you full of cum."

As we got into this new position, I was thrown that as short as he was, our torsos and face lined perfectly. He didn't miss a beat battering my guts, stretching hole at a different angle. I tried throwing my ass back at him hoping that he would come sooner. But, the former Mr. Zeus was having none of that, putting me through the ropes using my ass for his pleasure.

"I got some jizz dreams I want to share with you!" He huffed, slamming hard into my pitiful ass. "I got your ass moaning, huh?"

I let out some sort of sound that I wasn't sure belonged to me.

"Watch this!" He said, as I felt him reach over and give my hard dick a half a dozen good tugs before I screamed out my nutt. "Oh shit. Oh shit! I'm going to … ahhh! Ahhh! Ahhh! Sheeeettttttttttt!"

I was too engrossed in my own orgasm to feel his fingers dig into me, holding me in place as he filled me up with cum like a car at a gas station, shoving whatever excess there could be further up my hole.

"So was I as good as you thought I was jacking off to my muscles all those years ago?"

"Better." I said, quite satisfied, "though your shorter in stature than I suspected … but not where it counts!"

A DIFFERENT KIND OF KNOT
By Rawiya

"I bet ..." I was saying to Andrew as he walked out the door. The short man really thought that he had met the crème de le crème' with his last fuck, oh pardon me, client. Little did he know this heiress was a married woman with three little brats?

'Doesn't he read the gossip papers?'

Yes, everyday this pricey private gym to the wealthy and snooty, Belvidere Wellness & Spa was where I made my living. Although I wanted to be a free agent to gain my own clientele, the money that they offered here along with all the perks, was too hard to ignore.

I mean, yes, I hate working for the man, too, but he was giving me too many reasons to hop onboard.

Still thinking of my fellow therapist, Andrew, I shook my head when the phone rang with a number I did not notice. "Yes, this is Roberto speaking."

There was no answer at first, then, "Um, are you the massage therapist, Roberto Castellano?"

I smiled wryly, "I am, the best in the business to those with knots in their bodies, and how may I help you?"

"Well, see, I've been having problems with my back, and well, my body really. It just aches all the time. A lot of tightness, it seems as though I am just tied up in some ropes or something. A friend of mine recommended you."

I leaned forward in my chair, "I see, and who would this friend be?"

"Oh it's um …" he chuckled softly, "Wes Martin?"

'Wow, who is this?'

"Oh yeah, good ol' Wes," I grinned like a Cheshire cat. "Yeah, I've been working with him for quite some time. Wes is erm … a lot better now that I've been gettin' those kinks out of his back …" *'side …'*

The sensation in my groin, thinking about my last fuck session with Wes Martin was very intense. He was a musician on the down low, who really liked to take it up the arse; and I, being a massage therapist, was the perfect person to give it to him. Wes had paid me nicely not to tell anyone.

"Yeah, he mentioned that you were really good with your hands. I was wondering how much you would charge for your services?"

I sat up in my chair, looking over my own price list. "Okay, well let me see. My scale is as follows: a full body with oils two-seventy-five, but if you wish me to work out the knots by the hour, that will be seventy-five per. If I may make a suggestion though, if you are having pains all over your body, then I would say a complete treatment would be in order."

The gentleman on the other end sighed, "Well, if you insist …"

I smiled, "I do indeed, sir, any questions before we make the appointment?"

"Well, actually, yeah, just one …"

"Hmm?"

"I'm wonderin' if you are one of those masseuses that really, erm well, touches evverrrryyy part. I'm just concerned …"

"About …"

"Well, that you might try going for my …"

I knew exactly what he was thinking because I had tried it. "Cock …"

The man paused, "Yeah, well, it's just that I'd heard a lot of male massage therapists are ..."

"What?" I picked up my pen, twirling it with my fingers. I was aware of what the next sentence was, but I wanted him to complete it.

"Gay ... some of my friends said so."

Rolling my eyes, I leaned back once more in my seat. "If that were true, would it be an issue?"

"Well ... I mean ..." he was now stuttering.

"Answer me, it's only a question."

"Well, are you?"

"If I were that would be none of your business. I am a professional masseuse. You don't have the right to ask me that question."

"Hmph ..." I heard that through the handset. "You're gettin' so riled up; I guess it's true then ..."

My brows furrowed, I threw the writing utensil against the wall. "Listen sir, do you want your kinks worked out or not?"

"Yeah, yeah, but no touchin' my dick, yeah? I'm no Nancy boy ..."

"Too bad for you that you're not ..." I muttered.

"I beg your pardon ..."

"Nothin', now what will it be, the hourly since you are afraid I'll handle your jewels?"

He laughed, "Nope, I'll take the plunge and have the full body please. Like I said, my pecker is off limits ..."

Just wanting to get him off the phone, I took another pen from the cup. "Your name please?"

"Darren Sterling ..."

When I realized that Wes and Darren were in the same band, I said, "The, Darren Sterling from Hearts Afire ... the bassist?"

The grin came through the phone. "Yes sir, I am indeed. Wes says you are really, good at getting him loose."

'Oh if you only knew ...'

"Uh huh, so what day, time, and place would you want me to do this. Wes usually flies me in on a private jet if he is in need of some help ..." Immediately, my mind drifted to our last rendezvous. Wes and I had been doing the horizontal tango for over two hours, incredible stamina that man has.

Sterling was quiet a minute. "Well, this is kind of urgent. I thought if you had an appointment with Wes, then you can see me as well."

I glanced at my book on my desk. "I do see Wes again in another two weeks, my friend."

'Formally anyway ...'

"Hmm ... pity ... well, I guess I will go on and get you out here, too. About how much does it cost for you to leave Los Angeles and come out to London on short notice, round trip?"

"Well, without hotel, about fifteen hundred ..."

Darren paused a moment, "Damn, I wish that Frederic did not take the jet ... okay fine. Well, can I get you out here by Friday?"

"Sure, Friday, about what time?" I wrote down the date in my book.

"Ummm ..." I sensed he was having a hard time getting a date together. "How about one? We are in the midst of mixing the album now, so it would be good to have you here while I'm trying to get rid of some of the tension. Recording with these bums stresses me out ..."

"Fine ..."

"Good, so umm ... when you do this you will come to my home, yeah?"

"Yep, I have a mobile massage table."

"And uh ... remember my rule ..."

Again, I sighed, "Darren, what makes you think that I would want to touch you there?"

"Well, fuck ..." he ceased speaking again, "Why wouldn't you, I'm Darren Sterling ..."

"And so, you think just because you are big time rock star that someone wants to fondle your cock ..."

"Well, yeah, and um ..."

"Stroke it till it turns all those pretty colors like blue, pink, purple ... mmm, and the swelling ..." I took my own dick out of my shorts, thumbing the head, invoking precum from the slit. "Your pre-passion juice oozing from the tip ... mmm ..." My own manhood was hard as a rock.

"Uhhh ..." I heard the hesitation again, but something told me he liked what I was talking about.

"Fuck ..." I whispered, "So why wouldn't you want me to massage you there? Don't you know that the dick is a muscle, too?" Repeatedly, I pumped my shaft; I knew I was close to coming.

"Uhhh damn ... um ... Roberto ..." I heard him panting on the phone. "I, uh ... I ain't no bender, I uh ..."

I looked straight ahead, the vision of me plunging into Darren's band mate's tight ass in front of me, replaying as if it were a gay flick. "Of course you're not, silly, but every man likes a little action on their hardened flesh ... and I just bet that you are stiff as a board right now, aren't ya?"

"Uhhh ... fuck ... hell yeah I am ..."

"Well then, you want me to help get that knot out of your groin? The tightness, the feeling there means you need to release, like now ..."

"Uhh shiiittt ... Roberto, you got me ... fuck, where is my damn, girlfriend ..."

"She isn't there is she, so I guess you gotta take care of that problem on your own." I moistened my lips, trying to keep my composure. I really wanted him and me to climax together if possible.

"Dammit …" he muttered but loud enough for me to hear. "I don't do the five finger knuckle shuffle dude, that's for people that can't get none …"

"Well, my dear, Darren, that appears to be you, right? No one is with you … so again, I will help you come just so you can get some relief …"

Darren paused a moment, "Fuck, okay, fine …"

"Now, do exactly as I say. Take your cock out of your pants, stroke your shaft slowly with your fist encased around it while your thumb massages the head of your penis."

Darren was silent for about two minutes. "Shit, that feels good," he said through the phone. I could hear him breathing hard as I dreamt him taking all my eight or so into that puckered hole.

"Good right? Now, go just a tad faster." I lay back in my chair, my own midsection in pain as I tried my best to hold on. "Fuuuccckkk … fasterrrr …" I let my eyes roll in the back of my head.

"Shiiittt … Roberto, damn … man … oh my Godddd …"

"Come for me, Darren … c'mon, now …" As I spoke those words, I heard the loud cries on the other end.

"FUCCCCKKK … SHIIITTT …" he yelled at the top of his lungs. I bit my lip, trying not to do the same.

"Ooohh … Shiit …" I whispered, the ooze flowing from the mushroom head, the trembles were starting to take over.

While I was trying to regain my composure, I heard nothing but exhaling in the other end, then, "Shit … um, well, uh, okay. Friday, then."

Out of breath I simply nodded, "Yep …"

"Great … and er, Roberto …"

"Yeah?" I put my wet, flaccid cock back inside my boy shorts.

"If the massage is that good, you can touch my cock, but don't tell anyone okay? I got an image to protect, especially from Wes, that fucker is so homophobic …"

"Hmph, alright Mister Sterling, no worries, I won't tell anyone about our session."

"Good, then, erm, I'll see you on Friday, just uh, let me know of your flight plans and I'll ..."

"Yep ..." I licked my own wine off my fingertips. "This is your cell number; I can just text you, right?"

"Uh huh ... alright well, I'm goin' for a shower, I look forward to our, umm, appointment."

"You bet ..." I said before pressing the disconnect button.

'I'm looking forward to it as well; I have more knots to get out.'

PAHOKEE PETE:
A JOE MARTINEZ STORY
By Jesse Monteagudo

In 1973, gyms were not the lavish community centers that we know today. Outside of the big cities, most gyms were small storefronts owned and operated by retired boxers or bodybuilders. One of those gyms was Pahokee Pete, a storefront in downtown Pahokee, Florida. Located on the shore of Lake Okeechobee, Pahokee means "grassy waters" in the Creek language. Once the "Winter Vegetable Capital of the World," by 1973 Pahokee was long past its heyday, which gave a small business owner like Pahokee Pete Turner the opportunity to rent main street space at a back street price. Even so, Pahokee Pete struggled through its first year and was barely surviving the day that I first entered the premises.

Pahokee, Florida, is the last place on earth that one would expect to find a nineteen-year-old, Cuban-American, Miami College student on his spring break. But, I needed the money; and part-time job openings were few and far between in Miami in the recession spring of 1973. Through a friend of a friend, I found a part-time job working as a delivery boy for a Lake Okeechobee construction company, which meant that I would have to spend spring break out of town and away from my Miami College gym. Not wanting to spend a whole week without my daily work outs, I searched for a suitable gym and discovered that the only gym east of Clewiston and west of West Palm Beach was Pahokee Pete. I called for an appointment and found out that Pahokee Pete was open for business but usually closed by 5:00 pm on weekdays. However, since I would only be around for a few days anyway, Pahokee Pete promised to stay open just for me, "since business is slow around here."

I spent my first day in Pahokee learning the ropes, driving the company truck around the Lake Okeechobee area and making deliveries. When I arrived at Pahokee Pete at 5:30 pm, with my gym clothes in a carrying case, the gym appeared to be completely empty. Pahokee Pete was your typical, small-town, storefront gym. It had all of the standard gym equipment, mostly free weights and benches but also a few Universal weight machines. The gym also had a treadmill, a stationary bike, parallel bars and even a pommel horse. There were also doors in the back that led to a storage room, a locker room, a steam room and showers. Off to one side of the room, I saw a file cabinet, a desk and chair and there, sitting on the chair, was Pahokee Pete himself, who stood up to greet me.

"You must be Joe Martinez. I have been expecting you." Pahokee Pete Turner was forty years of age, with a rugged but handsome face and salt-and-pepper hair, mustache and goatee. Though Pete was not a tall man (he was about my height, five-six) he had a powerful build, and a no nonsense approach that would put many a bigger man to shame. He wore a Pahokee Pete T-shirt that covered his muscular torso, workout shorts, socks and sneakers. This was a man who had experienced much, and it made me wonder what he was doing running a gym in a one horse town like Pahokee.

We shook hands. "Thank you for keeping your gym open for me, Mr. Turner. I would have had to drive over to Clewiston if not for you."

"Think nothing of it. And, please call me Pete. The gym is closed to the public now, but business is slow, and I have nothing else to do, so it was no problem to keep it open just for you."

"How long have you had this gym?"

"For a couple of months. Business is slow, and I don't know if I can keep it open. But, Pahokee is my home, and I'm glad to do something for the folks who live here. I got some locals who come over for workouts during the day and on weekends, and they keep me in business. And, I'm glad to keep the gym open for you, a hard-working boy who is not out partying like the other spring breakers. How old are you?"

"I am nineteen and a freshman at Miami College."

"I remember when I was nineteen, myself," Pete smiled, as he led me to his desk. "But, things have changed a lot since then." As I

188

filled out some necessary paperwork and paid my fee, I noticed a bodybuilding trophy on top of the file cabinet. Next to the trophy was a photo of a young Pahokee Pete, in posing briefs, in all his glory. Things have changed a lot, I thought.

"That was taken the year that I won my first bodybuilding competition. I was twenty, just a bit older than you are now, and a native Floridian, which you don't meet too often these days. I was set to become Mr. Universe," he paused. "But then I joined the Marines, eventually ending in Vietnam. It was the Marines who called me Pahokee Pete," he noted. "Though I tried my best to keep up with my workout regimen, it was hard to stay focused when you are out in the jungle fighting the Vietcong."

"You are still in good shape." In fact, Pete Turner was in excellent shape, with a body that put someone like me, who was more than twenty years younger, to shame. Though I did not serve in the military – I lucked out in the draft lottery, since my birthday got a high number. I knew the Marines valued tight, muscular bodies. It was obvious that Pete continued to work out, even in 'Nam. "I am sure you had plenty of opportunity when you came back to the States."

"Not really. When I returned to civilian life last year, I was forty years old and too old to be a competitive bodybuilder. I looked for something else to do and found there was an old gym for sale in downtown Pahokee, my hometown. That is how I ended back here. But enough of me. Tell me about yourself."

"As I said before, I am a student at Miami College. I have been living in Miami for most of my life, though I was born in Havana, Cuba. I have been working out since I was in high school and though I do not expect to make a career out of bodybuilding, I hope to enter some competitions. In fact, later this year, I plan to enter the Latin Teen Bodybuilding Competition in Miami. That is why I want to keep up my daily workouts, even during spring break."

Joe smiled. "You remind me of me, back when I was your age. But, let me see what you have. Take your shirt off." As I removed my shirt, I nervously awaited Pete's reaction as he checked out my naked torso. Though I had a pretty good body for a nineteen-year-old, I could not compete with Pete who, at forty, still had a competitive physique.

"You are quite muscular for a boy your age," Pete said, as he examined the muscles in my arms, shoulders, chest, back and washboard stomach. "But I have seen better. And if you want to compete, you are going to have to really work out."

"I do my best."

"Sometimes your best is not enough. But I'm going to help you. Since there is no one else here to distract us, I'm going to train you myself all week long. I'm going to put you through a workout that you will never get in a big city gym. Are you ready for this?"

"I guess I am."

"Good. Now go back to the locker room and change into your gym clothes. And, don't think about anything else. I'm going to give you the workout of your life. Now go!"

"Yes, Sir!" I shouted. Once a Marine, always a Marine, I smiled to myself. But, Pete was right. I needed to really workout, if I was going to enter a bodybuilding competition in the fall. So, I did what I was told. I spent the next two hours in agony as Pete worked me through almost every muscle of my body, including my legs and my gluteus maximus. By the time we finished the regimen, it was late in the evening, and I was dead tired.

"You did great tonight, Joe. And, you look great! Most guys don't work out their legs and their buns, but you do and it shows. If you keep this up, you are going to win the Latin Teen title and any other title that you choose to go for," he smiled. "We will have our next workout at the same time tomorrow. But now, go ahead and take a shower. I have to do some paperwork around here." As Pete went over some of his paperwork, I went over to the locker room, where I removed my sweaty gym clothes before heading to the showers.

As I began to scrub myself clean, I thought about Pahokee Pete and wondered what he looked like naked. My question was immediately answered when Pete himself entered the shower room, proudly nude and ready for action. It was obvious that Pete sold himself short, for at forty, his muscular body was still quite competitive. Though Pete had aged a bit, and the fur on his chest was now mostly gray, he was as fit and muscular as he was twenty years earlier, when he won his first title. Completely naked, Pete was even more amazing, with a thick, uncut cock and a pair of low-hanging balls that emerged from a thick forest of black pubic hair.

"You like what you see?" Pete asked, as he pinched my nipples with his strong hands. A wave of electricity shot through my body. Though I tried my best to resist, my cock immediately hardened as I stared at this specimen of manhood. "We worked out most of your muscles; now we are going to work this one," he added, as he took my hand and placed it on his own cock, now fully hard.

"But, Pete."

"Pete nothing," he snapped, as he took hold of my own restless cock. "I knew you were queer for dick the moment we met. And, I wanted you right then and there. There are not too many boys your age around here who are uncut, but when you told me you were born in Havana, I knew there was going to be some uncut *pinga* waiting for me. And, I was right." As the shower continued to pour water on us, we began to work each other's thick, uncut cocks, low-hanging balls and sensitive tits. There was no danger of anyone walking into the gym, which was closed for hours. It was just the two of us, two muscle men hot for the pleasure of each other's bodies.

"Come over here, Joe," Pete said, as he turned off the shower. "Stand against the wall." As I stood against the wall, Pete got down on his knees, taking my hard cock in his mouth. I sighed with pleasure as Pete began to work on my *pinga*, pushing the foreskin back to reveal the tender head within. Like the experienced cocksucker that he was, Pete took my eight inches deep inside his mouth and throat, while at the same time licking the hard shaft with his eager tongue. Here was a man who knew how to treat a cock! After a few minutes of cocksucking bliss, Pete began to work on my low-hangers, taking each tender ball in his mouth and driving me out of my mind.

"Take it easy, Pete," I pleaded. "I don't want to come yet."

"Don't worry, Joe, there's more to come," Pete promised, as he got up and led me out of the shower room to the locker room. "I want to eat your ass," he said, as he threw me on a bench, face down. "I heard Cuban boys have hot bubble butts, and I'm going to find out for sure. Now spread your legs!" As I obediently spread my legs, Pete got down behind me, reaching inside my muscular glutes to reveal the tender hole within. I sighed with pleasure as Pete fingered the rim of my asshole before sticking his tongue inside it. As Pete ate out my asshole, a wave of erotic energy filled my body. Only a man knows how to work another man's ass and give him the pleasure that he deserves.

"You like that, don't you, Joe?" Pete asked, as he continued his experienced rim job.

"You know it!" I cried. "But, I need more than your tongue inside me. I want you to fuck me!" Since the day I lost my virginity, on my eighteenth birthday, I became a total cockhound, addicted to the power of an older man's experienced cock inside my young ass. As Pete continued his expert rim job, I hungered for the feeling of this forty-year-old ex-Marine and muscleman's hard cock up my ass. "Please fuck me, Pete!" I begged. "I need it!"

"My cock is all yours, Joe," Pete replied, as he lubricated my asshole with massage oil, he just happened to have handy. "Now take it like a man!" I screamed with surprise as Pete thrust his thick, ten-inch, ex-Marine's cock into my tender rectum. With the savage fury of an animal, Pete held my legs apart as his cock impaled my sensitive boy hole. Soon the pain turned to pleasure, as my muscular lover massaged and energized my prostate with his rock-hard prick.

"You have a hot asshole, boy," Pete shouted, as he continued to plow my tender *culo*. "Hot Cuban boys like you need to get fucked, again and again! And I'm the man who's going to do it, again and again!" Pete was right. Since I came out at eighteen, I have heard from others that Marines and bodybuilders are uniquely experienced cocksuckers and ass fuckers. And, here was Pete, an ex-Marine and bodybuilder, fucking my brains out like I had never been fucked before. After he spent a few minutes fucking me doggie style, Pete changed positions, throwing me on my back with my legs up in the air while he continued to shove his ten-inch man-muscle inside me. As Pete continued to fuck me, I played with myself, stroking my restless cock to keep up with my lover's savage fuck. We were two sex-hungry males, hot for each other's bodies, and the fact that one was a forty-year old Anglo and the other a nineteen-year-old Cubano did not matter at all. All that mattered was the force of Pete's cock up my ass and the thrust of my own cock in my hand. It wasn't long before the two of us reached the point of no return.

"I'm coming Joe!" Pete screamed. "I'm gonna shoot my cum inside your beautiful Cuban ass!" As Pete shot his load inside me, I reached my own savage orgasm, shooting cum all over Pete's chest, the bench, and elsewhere in the locker room. Now totally spent, Pete and I held tight to each other, kissing passionately.

"That was quite a workout," Pete said, as we held on to each other. "Now I expect you back here at 5:30 pm tomorrow. For both of your workouts." For the rest of spring break week, I continued my sessions at Pahokee Pete, where I worked out all of my muscles. And though I never saw Pete again after I left Pahokee, I never forgot this ex-Marine and bodybuilder, who taught me the pleasures that masculine muscle men can get from each other.

A REAL GYM
By Milton Stern

Michael spent more time than he wanted on the road. When he accepted the job as a consultant for the Department of Homeland Security, he thought he would be spending his time in Washington, New York, Los Angeles and Chicago, but that was not the case. Michael found himself waking up in sleepy little towns that cartographers did not take the time to notice. Towns with names like Pungo, Kincaid, Swelterville and Destination, a town so small it was named for being a stop on a long abandoned railroad.

In an effort to ensure that the government would function in the event of a national emergency, Michael's job was to negotiate contracts for bunkers and other sites to house the country's leaders. Uncharted towns made the perfect locations for these future government facilities. The secret was negotiating a deal that did not bring attention to the sleepy hamlets. Many of the civic leaders wanted the attention and hoped to boost their economies with the government contracts. Michael, however, managed to quiet their aspirations with promises of infrastructure improvements, new schools and other necessary projects.

One Monday, Michael arrived in Erlach, Virginia, a town, located southwest of Richmond, but so small, that even the citizens of Virginia's capital had never heard of it. He was pleasantly surprised to find a motel off the main highway through town. At sixty miles per hour, one blink and the motel would have been missed; two blinks and the town would have disappeared.

Michael grabbed his bag from the trunk of his car and knocked on the office door to the Erlach Motel, which was attached to the Erlach Diner, a converted railroad dining car that held the promise of good Southern cooking that Michael always craved. No one answered the door, so Michael walked over to the diner and entered.

It was three-thirty in the afternoon, and only a couple of patrons, mostly elderly gentlemen who looked as if they had retired from a lifetime of dairy farming, were sitting at the counter. Michael sat on a stool and removed his jacket.

At forty-one, Michael looked to be in his prime. He was wearing a dark blue T-shirt and jeans. Michael loved working out, and it showed. He was six-foot-two and weighed 240 pounds. Although on the road, Michael managed to find a gym most every place he went, and when none was available, he would work out with the sixty-pound dumbbells and the push-up bars he picked up in a fitness store he stumbled upon in Swelterville. Michael's favorite exercise was push-ups. He would do a set between every exercise even when working out in a gym. If he had a couple of hours free, he would spend them doing set after set of push-ups. Michael lived for the feeling of his chest getting pumped with every rep.

He would often be in a motel room in some hick town, stripped to his briefs, sweaty and pumped from hours of push-ups. Michael would then flex in the mirror and finish his routine by rubbing out a big load from his thick cock.

One of the retired farmers took notice of Michael and stared at him. He was used to being ogled for he was a fine looking man with his olive skin, dark curly hair, thick eyebrows and lashes and dark bedroom eyes. His body was big, hairy and muscular, and Michael was often asked if he took steroids. One look at Michael's large, full balls confirmed that his physique was all natural. Michael liked to eat, and fortunately for him, everything that went into his mouth turned to muscle – everything.

The cook stepped out from the back and walked over to Michael. Michael liked what he saw. The cook was not quite as tall as Michael, but his white T-shirt and stained apron barely contained his powerful form. There was no hint of hair under his hat, and he had the face of a professional wrestler. Michael noticed the scarred forehead, which was a sure sign of self-inflicted, razor wounds to give a paying crowd the blood they craved. He judged the chef to about fifty or fifty-five, and Michael considered inviting him to his room later that night to see who could do the most push-ups for the longest time. The thought made his cock leak.

"Can I get you anything?" the cook asked.

"Actually, I wanted to get a room for few nights at the motel next door, but no one answered when I knocked," Michael said.

"That's because I'm standing right here," the cook said with a smile. He was missing at least three teeth, probably knocked out by a metal chair in some noisy arena, Michael thought.

"OK, how much is a room?" Michael asked.

"Fifty dollars a night," the cook answered, "paid in advance."

Michael leaned forward and removed his wallet, noticing the cook staring at his flexed triceps. Michael looked at the retired farmer and noticed the man had also never taken his eyes off him. He pulled $150 from his wallet and handed it to the cook while rolling his eyes in the farmer's direction.

The cook looked over at the retired farmer and back at Michael and said, "Don't mind Smitty. Every time a big, good looking guy comes into town, he wonders if he is another of my old buddies."

"From wrestling?" Michael asked.

"Yeah, how did you know?" the cook asked.

Michael motioned to his forehead and said, "You have the battle scars. I follow professional wrestling, but I cannot place you."

The cook put Michael's money in the cash register and reached under the counter, plucking out one of the keys, hooked below. He handed Michael the key and smiled.

"Remember the asshole that always wore an orange mask, wrestled dirty, and was hated by the crowd?" the cook asked.

"You're the Southern Terror?" Michael asked, and he almost shot a load in his briefs.

"The one and only," the cook said. "So, you want anything to eat before you check in?"

Michael was usually hungry, but he only ordered coffee, explaining, "I really want to work out before dinner. There wouldn't happen to be a gym in this town, would there be?"

The cook poured him a cup of coffee and said, "Believe it or not there is. It is located in the building behind the motel."

Michael put cream and sugar in his coffee, stirred it and said, "Let me guess. You own that, too."

The cook smiled again and told Michael, "As a guest in my motel, you can work out there for free. I warn you, it's just a gym, no fancy machines or prancing personal trainers, or spandexed pretty boys."

The thought of the cook's gym made Michael's cock leak again, and he said, "That's perfect. I haven't seen a real gym in years. Tell me you don't play loud bar music, and I may buy a house in this town."

"Well, you know that house across the street with a for sale sign in front?" the cook asked.

Michael laughed, wondering just how much of Erlach, Virginia, this hot, retired wrestler owned.

Michael checked into Room 24 and put his bag on the bed. He checked his messages, of which there were three from the DHS, one of which confirmed his meeting with the Mayor of Erlach the following morning at ten.

He opened his bag and pulled out his black sweat pants and an old, gray tank top. Michael was never a slave to health club fashion, so he was sure he would blend in at the cook's gym just fine.

He decided to change his underwear, since the pair he was wearing was stained with precum, not an uncommon occurrence for Michael. He never wore a jock strap, preferring the security of tight, form-fitting briefs. He slipped on his sweat pants and tank top and laced up his black Converse hi-tops. He was looking forward to walking to the building behind the motel and having a real workout. It had warmed up a bit, so Michael figured he would not need a jacket for the short walk to the gym. He also didn't bother to take a lock or gym bag, reasoning he would shower in the motel room before going to the diner for supper.

Michael stepped out of his room and made his way around back. The gym was just fifty or so feet from the motel and looked to be an old converted warehouse. Painted on the door was "S-T's Gym." Michael opened the door, and to his surprise, there were quite a few men working out. There was no foyer, only a small office to the left of the door, and two paces in, Michael found himself in the middle of a large weight room. The place was mainly lit by fluorescent light bulbs, the walls were all mirrored, and any surface that was not covered by mirrors was painted a charcoal gray.

Michael first noticed the lack of music; the only sound that could be heard was the clanking of weights and the grunting of men as they struggled against the iron. He also took in a deep breath, savoring the smell of chalk, sweat and testosterone.

As he looked around, he also noticed that most of the men were working out shirtless. No rules about decorum here. This was a real gym. His cock leaked again.

The door to the office opened, and the cook stepped out and put a hand on Michael's shoulder.

"Just like I told you, nothing fancy, but it's mine," the cook said.

Michael turned to look at him and saw that he had also changed his clothes, wearing a pair of gray sweat pants and no shirt. Even past fifty, the man was powerfully built. His shoulders were like cannonballs, and his pecs were two giant plates of muscle. Michael was jealous of the old guy's enormous traps.

"Hey, this is perfect," Michael said.

"Have a good workout," the cook said as he slapped Michael's large, round, muscular ass. It wasn't a playful slap; it was the slap of an athlete, masculine in its intent.

Michael felt his muscles pumping with blood just from standing in this gym, but he came to work out, and he was going to have a workout reminiscent of the first gym he ever joined. It was similar to this one, and he could have sworn the same shirtless muscle gods were also working out there a long time ago.

The gym was hot and humid inside with the only ventilation coming from the narrow rectangular windows located between the mirrors and the ceiling. Michael decided to forego stretching and work out like a man.

No need to warm up, he thought. If I pull a muscle, I'll just grunt and bear it.

His only worry was that he would come during his first set. Michael was glad he was wearing tight briefs and baggy sweat pants for his dick was already getting hard.

He walked over to the bench where a couple of obvious steroid users were working out together, and before he could ask, they offered to let him work in with them.

Wow, Michael thought. No attitude. Just work in with us.

This place was heaven. The guys were not only big, muscular, hot and half naked, but also they were gentlemen. But of course, they were all gentlemen; they were all between forty and sixty – that perfect generation between attitude and troll.

Michael worked out harder than he had in years, working in a set with this pair of partners and that pair of partners. He benched, he pulled, he curled, he rowed, he squatted, and he lifted. A couple of the guys kidded him about how he did a set of push-ups after each exercise, but when Michael decided to remove his loose tank top before a set of dumbbell flyes, the men took notice, and a couple of them also dropped and did twenty. His hairy chest was so pumped and his big round nipples so hard that Michael could not even see his large feet when he looked down.

As it turned out, most of the guys were old friends of the cook's and retired wrestlers, too, many of them from the days of local circuits before the extreme professional wrestling of today. Although in the ring he was the Southern Terror, the cook was popular in the arena locker rooms, and when he retired to Erlach and opened the diner, the motel, and the gym, many of his former colleagues soon followed, taking up farming or just retiring and enjoying the simple life.

The weight room started to thin out after an hour, but Michael was enjoying the place so much that he decided to keep working out. Before long, the only two guys left in the weight room were Michael and the cook.

"Don't you have to go back to the diner," Michael asked him.

"We don't get busy until about seven, so my two waitresses handle the kitchen and the floor until then," the cook said. "The gym closes at six-thirty, so if you want to get in a shower, you will need to now."

"Oh, I was hoping to work out some more," Michael said.

The cook furrowed his brow and pounded Michael's pumped chest with his fist and said, "If you do another set, you are going to bust an artery. Hit the showers, we open at eleven tomorrow. You can come in then and work out for seven hours if you want."

"That's OK, I was going to shower in my room, thanks," Michael said.

The cook grabbed Michael's shoulder and said, "You will be better off showering here. The showers in the motel will barely hold you, and besides the pressure sucks. It's a dump, but it's my dump, and I wouldn't lie to you."

Michael told the cook he didn't bring a lock or a change of clothes, but the cook would have none of it. He told Michael that these guys could be trusted and just to go commando when he walked back to his room. Michael worried that if he showered with these guys, going commando in his loose sweats would cause him a great deal of embarrassment.

The cook kept his hand on his shoulder and guided him back to the locker room. Michael had no choice.

The locker room was steamier than the weight room, and Michael could hear four or five guys in the shower laughing and talking. He located an empty locker and started to untie his hi-tops. The cook stood next to him and did the same. Michael tried thinking of dead kittens and fat women with hairy vaginas in an effort to keep from getting hard, but it only semi-worked. He hoped that straight guys did not look at another guy's dick, and when he stripped off his sweats and briefs, he took a deep breath. The cook was naked at this point and grabbed two towels, throwing one to Michael.

He looked at Michael's large endowment, including his huge, hairy balls and smiled.

"Damn kid, was your father a buffalo?" the cook said. "Is there anything small on you?"

Michael blushed and wrapped the towel around his waist catching a glimpse of the cook's ample manhood in the process. He was happy the man was circumcised as he was not a fan of foreskin. Michael figured if he was going to look, he might as well enjoy the view.

He walked toward the shower, following the cook. The shower room was as old fashioned as the weight room – just a big, open, tiled room with ten shower heads. Five of the big guys, including two of the men who let Michael work in with them on the bench were showering and talking. To Michael's surprise, one of them was soaping up the other's back, and the one getting lathered was sporting a raging hard on.

Michael averted his eyes and turned on the shower next to the cook. Showering was the only thing Michael enjoyed more than push-ups, and he stood with his hands on the tiles and let the water cascade from his head down his back. He enjoyed the feeling for quite a while. Lost in the warmth of the spray, Michael closed his eyes and turned around to let the water hit directly on his back. He then reached behind himself and spread his butt cheeks to let the warmth hit every crevice. As he turned his head and opened his eyes to locate a bar of soap, he didn't see one in the dish under his shower head, so he looked across the room. The two guys who were enjoying each other's company were now soaping up with the other three guys. Hands were everywhere. Michael's dick started getting hard, but at this point, he didn't care.

The cook grabbed Michael's arm and placed a bar of soap in his hand.

"Is this what you're looking for?" he asked Michael.

Michael thanked him and started lathering up his hair and then his face. He rinsed the soap from his head, and then he started with his shoulders and worked the lather slowly down his big, pumped, hairy, muscular body. He enjoyed every inch of himself. He slowly soaped his raging nine-by-seven-inch boner and lathered his hairy, buffalo balls. The guys were watching him and from the looks of their own boners were enjoying the show. That didn't stop Michael.

He bent over to soap up his legs, and when he did, he felt a hand on his back. The cook, with his own bar of soap, proceeded to lather up Michael's back, and when Michael stood up, the cook put one hand on Michael's shoulder, and with the other, he lathered Michael's large, round, muscular ass. He was gentle in his touch. The cook squatted down and lathered Michael's legs, slowly with up and down strokes. Michael resumed lathering his chest, stomach, arms, shoulders, and neck. Then, the cook rose and lathered Michael's ass and back again. With his other hand, the cook reached around and put his meaty paw on Michael's aching cock. The huge, mushroom head was swollen, and his balls were ready for release.

Michael continued to lather his chest, shoulders, biceps, triceps, and forearms, and he reached around to lather his own huge lats.

The cook firmly but slowly stroked Michael's hard soapy cock, and after just a few seconds, Michael shuttered and blew a load into the center of the shower room. The sight of Michael coming sent the other five muscle-heads over the edge, and each of them spunked the shower room floor, too. The cook's own large dick creamed Michael's hip, and he continued to stroke Michael's cock until he was sure those big balls were empty.

With everyone's needs fulfilled, the men in the shower finished rinsing themselves off and left the shower room without saying a word, the cook and Michael included.

Michael pulled on his sweats and slipped into his hi-tops, carrying his briefs, tank top and socks back to his room.

He then changed into a fresh pair of white briefs, jeans and an orange T-shirt and walked over to the diner. Michael took a seat at the counter, and the cook came out in the same outfit he was wearing when Michael first met him. Nothing was said of what just took place in the shower.

Michael understood that it was just men, big muscular men, bonding after a good, healthy workout.

The cook smiled at Michael and recommended the fried chicken, mashed potatoes, green beans and cornbread. Michael didn't argue. He trusted the cook's judgment, and with the first bite, he knew the cook was right.

While he was enjoying a cup of coffee and fresh apple pie, the cook came over to Michael and leaned on the counter in front of him.

"So, what's your business in town," the cook asked.

"I am here to meet with the Mayor about some government business," Michael said.

"At ten tomorrow morning?" the cook asked.

Michael looked at him and asked, "Are you the Mayor, too?"

"And your last name must be Greenberg," the cook said.

They both laughed.

"Good," the cook said, "Tomorrow, after our meeting, you can come back over to the gym, and I will put you through a real work out."

And Michael asked, "How many push-ups can you do?"

Two years later, Michael bought the house across the street, and he always showered at the gym after his workouts.

THERAPY
By Ron Radle

Landon had his reservations about physical therapy – chiefly its ultimate efficacy and the fact he would have to take time off from work three times a week – but after his knee surgery, his doctor said it was mandatory, or Landon, only thirty years old, would hobble around like an octogenarian the rest of his life.

The knee replacement came as a result of his years as a high school and college basketball player. The problem began with shooting pains similar to sciatica, but when he collapsed that morning in his shower and had a hell of time getting himself upright again, he knew he was in trouble.

After the surgery, his doctor made the arrangements for his rehabilitation. On the first day, Landon drove himself to the rehab center, got out of his car on crutches, and swung himself into the quaint brick and glass facility. In the lobby, he was greeted by the center's co-owner and head therapist, Les, a short, middle-aged man who maintained a good, solid build. He led Landon into the gym, and right away Landon's eyes began a quick hunt for eye candy, or mandy, as it had now been dubbed, a visual diversion to make the whole process easier to take.

At first, he was disappointed. The preponderance of the clientele were elderly men and women who were nevertheless making great goes of the treadmills and lateral pull-down and rowing machines. Most of the therapists appeared to be young women, shapely and attractive young women, but not at all what Landon hoped to find.

Les took Landon the greater length of the gym to a raised mat, where Landon sat and across from which Les sat in a swivel chair to chat with him about the surgery and about a therapeutic regimen. There would be some low impact stretching each time to help him limber up, some time spent on the Biodex machine, some exercises in the parallel bars, a few minutes on the NuStep bicycle, and finally an ice pack. Les must have been a used car salesman in a previous life. He made it all sound so peachy keen and fun, just like summer camp or something.

"And no reason we shouldn't get started right away!" he concluded with a good-natured slap on Landon's shoulder. "Stacy," he called to one of the girl therapists, a young woman with her dark hair in a ponytail who was presently occupied with an elderly gentleman in a shoulder sling. "Have you seen Corey? I want him to get Mr. Burgess here started with some stretching."

"He's in the laundry room folding towels," Stacy reported.

Les raised his index finger to Landon. "I'll be right back."

And he was, accompanied by Corey. *Bingo!* Landon thought, feeling better already. Corey stood five-foot-eight, had thick, dark brown hair worn rather indifferently, and beautiful brown eyes. His body, with the thick, rounded, muscular arms and pectorals conspicuous beneath his white pullover shirt, showed signs of a serious gym rat. And his smile, displayed at once upon their formal introduction to each other and a handshake, was framed by a pair of irresistible dimples.

Corey was much more than eye candy; he was a whole dish of boyish bon bons.

Les laid out Landon's situation for Corey and explained the exercise routine he wanted to follow. Corey nodded as each item was ticked off a white sheet secured to a wooden clipboard. Then the two of them looked up at Landon together.

"You ready to get to work, Landon?" Les asked with a wide grin. "You'll be in good hands. Corey's smart. He just graduated from Wofford." Wofford was one of the most prestigious private schools not only in South Carolina, but also the whole Southeast.

Just graduated from Wofford. That would put him at twenty-two years old or thereabouts. Landon nearly swooned to consider this combination of youth and beauty. Yes, he was ready to get to work. Oh yes he was!

Les departed the scene, and Corey told Landon to lie back for his stretch.

"This'll help keep the good knee limber," he explained as Landon reclined on the mat. Corey took the knee in question in hand and lifted the entire leg onto his broad left shoulder. Landon could not help himself but picture the scene: the handsome young man lifting his leg and taking it upon himself. It looked like ... well ... as though Corey were about to enter and fuck him. Landon could not help the erection he got as a result of the fantasy.

Corey looked down at him. Their eyes locked. Corey smiled a lovely smile and awoke those dimples on either side of his mouth. Did he like what he saw – what he held in his hand? If he indeed were gay, he more than likely did. Landon was handsome in a boy next door way. He had sandy blond hair and frank blue eyes and a frame that was well-muscled but not bulky. He had been, even after high school and college, a devotee of the gym and was proud that at thirty he maintained a body of compact and defined muscles that a man ten years younger would have envied. He had always concentrated more on his upper body working out than his lower, and he realized, too late, that if he had spent more time working on his legs he may not have experienced this particular problem. He also had one thing many if most boys next door don't have: an enormous prick, which when hard rose to a nine-inch length and a six-inch circumference. Did Corey realize Landon had a hard-on right then? Why sure he did. He was right there in the center of action. And, Landon's cock made a more than perceptible outline in his blue sweat pants. It curved banana-wise and bulged. More than that, Landon read the message in Corey's baby browns. They were kindred spirits. Landon wanted to verbalize so much what he was feeling, but there were too many other people around at the moment. He would have to wait.

Done with the stretch, they removed themselves to a different side of the gym where three massage tables stood against the wall and were, of necessity, blocked off by curtains for privacy's sake. Corey informed Landon that they would be using e-stim, electric stimulation, to help stir feeling and reaction in the operated knee. The procedure necessitated that Landon remove his pants for full effect. Corey drew the curtains around the table and disappeared. Landon shucked his sweat pants and lay down upon the table. His hard-on had not yet deflated but stood out against his jockey briefs. It might not be a good thing to sport such a woody right then, in the case Les or someone else from the rehab center were to show up. He tried to think of decidedly non-erotic things to get it down – car wrecks, poverty stricken villages in the third world, his great aunt Susie with her blue-rinse dye job – but all to no effect. He mashed the erection and gave it a couple of reprimanding slaps, but that only made things worse. If anything, his cock got bigger and stiffer.

Corey returned with the e-stim device, a bulky battery on the flat surface of which rested various knobs and buttons and to the side of which was attached a long wand secured by a black cord. The machine could be turned up to succeeding volumes to allow greater stimulation. Corey saw Landon's problem outlined against his briefs and smiled.

"Well, there's one part of you at least that doesn't need stimulation."

Landon grinned. "No, but it sure could use some release right now."

Corey remained calm and cool. "If Les poked his head in here and saw that kind of release going on, I'm afraid the both of us would be out on our asses."

"Hey, man, you got to live dangerously now and then. I think a few shakes of the fist would do it."

Corey pretended to ignore him. He activated the e-stim battery and slowly rolled the wand along Landon's affected knee. "Feel that?" he asked. Landon nodded. Corey went back across the knee then back up again. The e-stim produced the tiniest of noises. On the second trip back up, however, Corey did not stop at the knee. He went further, up the outer thigh, taking a sharp turn into Landon's crotch and the stubborn, irrepressible bulge of Landon's hardened dick. At the same time, he adjusted the knobs so that a higher stimulation could be produced. "How's that?" he asked, smiling down at Landon. "Feel it?"

"Not bad," Landon answered. Indeed the rolling wand mimicked the effect of little fingers dancing up and down the underside of his prick. The sensation caused him to wiggle his toes and squirm just a bit. "I'm not sure it'll get the job done, though, if you know what I mean."

Corey removed the wand from Landon's cock and returned it to his knee. At the same time, he allowed his free hand to wander over the crotch. He gave Landon's bulge a squeeze. Landon groaned softly. Corey shushed him. His fingers crept along the elastic band of the briefs slowly and ever so cautiously and folded them down far enough to expose the head of Landon's dick. A pearl drop of cum was already lodged in the piss-slit. With the last three fingers of that hand, Corey massaged the cockhead slowly, methodically bringing out the cum-pearl and turning it into a string of jism, which covered his fingers and made them sticky. The motion set off an explosion of tingles all over Landon's body. He wanted to weep with both his pleasure and his need to empty his nut sack into Corey's maddeningly marvelous hand.

"I'm about to die, man," he whispered. "Please get me off."

Corey worked at his own speed. He rolled down a bit more of the briefs, exposing more of Landon's cock. "You got a nice big piece of meat," he commented softly. He rubbed his whole palm over the head and that part of the stem, which had just been revealed. It felt like sandpaper on the dick's sensitive glands. Landon's feet jumped. His arms shivered.

"Please!" he whispered again, this time desperately.

Suddenly Corey grabbed the cockhead into his entire first and jerked with force. When Landon announced in a pained whisper that he was about to come, Corey plugged the tip of his prick with his thumb as though to impede the flow of cum. This only drove Landon to greater ecstasy, one he thought would detonate throughout his whole body. And the second Corey removed his thumb from the piss-slit, Landon's cum leapt out like foam from an uncorked champagne bottle. Landon shivered in the aftermath of his orgasm then went still. He had left a mess on his lap, on his shirt, and on Corey's hands.

"Let me get a towel," Corey said, grinningly, and stooped to the shelf beneath the table. He stood and dabbed Landon's crotch with the towel, rubbed his belly, and wiped his own hands. The ammoniac smell of sperm remained in the air.

"I want you," Landon whispered. "I want all of you. I want to make you come, too.

Almost as though on cue, Les stuck his head through the curtains.

"Well, Landon," he said. "Has Corey got you good and stimulated yet?"

Landon lifted his head from the table, his face all aglow. "Oh yes. You wouldn't believe how stimulated I am right now."

Landon invited Corey to his home after he got off work, but Corey refused, although with a gleam in his pretty brown eyes. He said he had a key to the rehab facility, and he had fantasized about fucking in the gym ever since he had gone to work there.

So that evening, with everything good and dark, Landon showed at the rehab center and on his crutches hobbled to the front door, which Corey had left unlocked for him. A single light showed in the foyer, but the gym itself was nearly pitch dark, save for touches of silver on the equipment courtesy of the full moon that poured through the plate glass window at the gym's rear. Landon stood trying his best to spot Corey in the shadows. He started to call out but didn't; noise would disrupt the mystery of the event. A wheelchair sat near the door. Corey had no doubt placed it there for him. He eased down into it and abandoned his crutches. He rolled over to the lateral pull down machine and waited. There! Movement. A figure in the dark picked out by the moon. Corey coming toward him, naked as the day he was born (but much better built).

Landon licked his lips and dug his hand into his sweat pants to massage his stiffening prick. Corey stood behind the machine in the crevice between the two standing panels that balanced the plates. He slid his own prick between the opening and wagged it in invitation. Landon lifted himself from the chair and landed carefully on the short leather bench, his face mere inches from Corey's dick. Corey moved closer. His dickhead touched Landon's lips. Landon's tongue crept out of his mouth and found the underside of the cock. It tickled the glands delicately, teasingly, until his tongue reached the head. It danced at the tip, poking at the piss-slit, entering it, wiggling. Then Landon flattened his tongue and lapped the entirety of the head before engulfing it in his whole mouth. Corey gasped softly. Landon reached behind the panels and gripped Corey's cool, smooth, muscled ass and pressed him closer as he sucked with increasing hunger and vehemence. Corey's dick hit

210

the back of his throat again and again, gagging him, but it didn't seem enough. Landon wanted more. He wanted tears and dripping saliva, so he pounded his face against Corey's crotch as though intending to devour him whole, dick, balls, soft brown bush. Finally, he let go. He needed air. His rasping was deep and heavy.

"Lick my nuts, man," Corey ordered.

When he regained sufficient breath, Landon did just that. His tongue traced the contours of the round balls, digging into the seam which divided the sack. He slipped one ball into his mouth, sucked it, let go, and did the same to the other. Like Corey's cock, the balls tasted delicious, firm and without scent. Landon dug down further back with his tongue, as though searching for Corey's asshole. Meanwhile his fingers found it, forcing their way into the tight ring, spreading it and fucking it with quick, jerking motions.

"Let's go to the goddamn mat," Corey whispered above Landon, his voice nearly breathless.

He rolled Landon in the chair over to the elevated mat where earlier that day he had stretched him. He helped him move to the mat, and once Landon lay back, Corey undressed him, yanking off his shirt, pulling his pants over his sneakers, knocking off the sneakers themselves. The nine inches of Landon's cock stood stiff and hard in the poor, silvery light. Corey wrapped both hands around it, kissing it reverently, nibbling at its head, finally plunging the length of it down his throat. He gagged right away but did not let that stop him. He quickly found his rhythm and had the fat prick sliding up and down his throat as smoothly as if it were moving through pure air. His hands moved to Landon's big, smooth balls; he fondled them, letting them roll through his fingers. His index finger toyed with Landon's ass crack. Landon lifted slightly, and the finger slid into Landon's hole. Corey finger fucked Landon, synchronizing the thrusting with his sucking. Landon shook and moaned. He rubbed the back of Corey's neck and slipped his hand down Corey's firm, broad, smooth back.

Suddenly, Corey ceased sucking. He looked up at Landon, his eyes shining in the dark. "I want you to fuck me with this monster."

"You got rubbers?" Landon asked, now propped on his elbows.

Corey disappeared in the shadows but returned promptly with a condom and lube. He dressed Landon's cock, rolling the condom slowly down to the base then slicking it up with the jelly. He straddled Landon's hips. Landon spread Corey's ass cheeks and rubbed the hole vigorously, sliding his middle finger in, stretching the hole. Corey couldn't wait. With Landon's cock in his hands, he sank slowly on the head, letting it penetrate him. He stalled a moment to allow the hole to absorb the cock-crown then descended another few inches until he just knew that Landon's cockhead reached the near vicinity of his intestines. He braced himself with his hands on Landon's sparsely hairy, square-cut chest and began a hesitant rocking on Landon's prick, increasing speed as he grew more comfortable, careful not to recline on Landon's troubled knee.

Meanwhile, Landon's hands traveled up Corey's furry, flat belly, counting each of the rungs in his chiseled abdomen, all eight of them, before settling on the twin, hard squares of Corey's pectorals. He squeezed them repeatedly and took the fat, protuberant nipples between his index fingers and thumbs, pinching them until Corey let out a cry he could not muffle. Landon pulled the nipples from Corey's chest, stretching them, twisting them, and rubbing the tips with the tops of his thumbs. He let the tits go and punched the pecs with his fists.

By this time, Corey was riding him like a wild steer, bouncing and trying to keep his balance. His cock and balls slapped Landon's crotch over and over. Landon cupped Corey's nuts in one hand and took the dick in the other. He jerked it to the rhythm of Corey's thrusts. It did not take long for Corey to announce he was coming. He shuddered and shot his wad into Landon's still-moving fist. Landon smeared the stuff onto Corey's stomach and chest and shoved his sperm-stained fingers into Corey's mouth to allow him to lick off the remains. Corey sucked Landon's fingers as though they were miniature versions of his prick.

"Turn on your side," Landon commanded. "I'm going to come in from the back." Corey dropped to the mat, his ass still clutching Landon's dick. Landon carefully turned on his left side, minding his right knee, and, gripping Corey's hip with one hand and his shoulder with the other; he pounded Corey's tight butt, feeling with each thrust that he was exploring some new vista of Corey's splendid body, indeed opening some passages up for the first time. He reached around

Corey's hip to find his sticky prick. He rolled it in his palm until it hardened again. Corey leaned into Landon's chest, and Landon was able to lick and suck the nipple he had tortured earlier. He bit at it, and to his amazement, Corey once again unleashed a flood of hot cum into his hand.

"I want to finish off standing up," he whispered into Corey's ear. The treadmill wouldn't do. They were after sex, not slapstick. "Let's go to the parallel bars."

The bars stood only a matter of four or five feet from the mat. They glinted faintly in the outside light. Corey rolled Landon over to them in the chair. Landon hopped up and entered the bars, turning to await Corey.

Corey entered backwards and bent over. Landon, careful not to put too much pressure on his right knee, grasped Corey's ass cheeks and opened them as wide as he could. He took his large cock and rubbed the head against the tightness of the hole. He teased the hole with several false thrusts then gave a sharp push that put the first several inches into Corey's rectum. Corey moaned. He did most of the work, allowing Landon to hold onto the bars and maintain his balance. He backed against Landon to meet Landon's thrusts, and just as Landon had expected, it did not take long for the first tingles of orgasm to go racing from the base of his shaft and expand into the head.

"I'm coming," he told Corey.

Corey suddenly freed himself from Landon's skewer and dropped to his knees. He pulled off the condom abruptly and milked Landon's cock close to the head. Soon jism flew into his face and hair. It covered his shoulders and chest like snail trails in the dismal light.

Landon had Corey by the underarms and pulled him to his feet. He licked the cum from Corey's shoulders and chest, taking time to suck the nipples again. He lathed Corey's wet face with his tongue, and that was when they embraced and kissed for the first time, tongues darting and stabbing, escaping and returning for more. They loved how their bodies stuck together, glued by cum. They did not even mind the slight pain that resulted when they broke their embrace and their chest hair caught and was reluctant to pull free.

Landon brushed his hands over Corey's beautiful face, feeling the dimples flare in the dark as Corey smiled. As his fingers slid down Corey's torso and found his semi-hardened dick, he thought how he could hardly wait for his second knee replacement and the therapy to follow and all the joy it would bring.

DISCO INFERNO
By Rob Rosen

"You one of those hippies?" the mountain of a guy asked, throbbing vein in his neck about ten seconds away from going boom!

"Nah," I replied, long hair sloshing from side to side, pink specs sliding down the bridge of my nose. "Summer of Love done faded to winter a good eight years ago. Funk is in; folk is out. It's disco, not Dylan, dude."

The slit that passed for his mouth barely moved a lick up or down. "Your hair," he made note of. "It's hippy hair."

I flicked said mop of a mane with the back of my hand for good measure. "I suppose. More feathers in it these days. Takes a good hour to get it to look this, um, natural." I pointed to his chrome-dome, and added, "Not that there's anything wrong with your, uh, look. Guess grass doesn't grow on concrete."

The complement went unnoticed. "You looking to join or what?" he grunted, arms now folded across his massive chest, blue peepers fading to gray with apparent disinterest.

"Guess so," I replied. "You ever tried dance-lifting your partner over your head, Donna Summer moaning something fierce in the background?" I didn't wait for a reply; it was, of course, a rhetorical question. "Gotta have some guns to get it just right." I raised my fist up and tried flexing my measly arm for him. The effect, needless to say, was less than stellar.

Again he grunted. "Twenty bucks a month. Locker included. Bring your own towel. Any questions?"

I looked past him – no easy feat, mind you – and asked, "That the gym back there?"

He turned around, scratching his shiny pink scalp. "Of course," he replied, before looking back my way. "Haven't you ever seen a gym before?"

"I skipped it in high school. Didn't see the point. One of those hindsight things, I guess. Go figure." Again I looked around him, squinting into the large room to his aft, at the metal and wood and cracked red vinyl, dumbbells and weights and all sorts of devices that looked more like they belonged in some sort of medieval torture chamber. "Those things come with instructions?"

"Trainer costs extra." He handed me the paperwork to sign. "Five more bucks a week."

"You the trainer?" I asked, a lemon-sized lump making its way up my throat.

He nodded, his tree-trunk-thick neck straining at the movement. "Lucky you."

I signed, despite my better judgment. "Yeah, lucky fucking me."

I returned the next night, pink raggedy towel in hand, matching pink headband atop my head. My cut-off jeans went knee length, sweat socks aiming up to their full height, bony knees the only swatch of flesh made visible. The 'I'm With Stupid' T-shirt I sported covered my upper regions. I prayed he wouldn't get the joke. As if. He grimaced when he saw me and showed me to the locker room.

"Um, I'm already dressed?" I tried, staring at the opened metal bins.

His eyes moved up and down, taking me in. Needless to say, it was a quick take. "Dressed for what?"

I grinned. "Duh, working out."

He sighed and went behind the long row of lockers, returning with a dismal looking lump of gray material. "Get changed," he commanded, tossing the shorts and tank my way before disappearing back inside the gym.

I sat on the bench, clutching the cotton. It was then I noticed all the other men, half-undressed or all-undressed, swaying cocks, sweaty dangling balls, hairy chests, skin stretched tight across acres and acres of finely worked muscle. The disco it wasn't. Not by a long shot. Still, a boy could grow to like such a place. Luckily, my jockstrap was tight enough to keep the old stiffening willy in place long enough for me to get dressed and beat a hasty retreat.

Iron-jaw was waiting for me up my arrival. That's what I called him, by the way. Not to his face, of course. Bert was his given name. "Ready, Bert," I said, all smiles.

And that's when, at last, he shot me one of his. And, boy, was it friggin' scary. "Yeah, that's what you think."

Two hours later, soaked to the bone, teensy muscles aching like they'd been run over by a steam engine, he freed me from my servitude. With cramped legs, I trudged my way back to the sweat-infused locker room, finding salvation on a wooden bench. It was way late now, only a handful of stragglers remaining, most of them in the showers, one long intoxicating stretch of them. Which, of course, put a spring into my now-crippled step.

"No pain, no gain," I whispered to myself, sliding out of my wet clothes and high-stepping it to the farthest showerhead, groin pointed to the corner tiles, cool spray quickly cascading over hot flesh.

Furtive glances over my shoulder revealed three buffed nude dudes, each one bigger than the next, two hairy, one smooth, all gorgeous enough to give Adonis an inferiority complex. My cock did a slow rise, arcing up and out, swelling with blood, my balls rising with my steely rod's exertion. I soaped it up, giving it a quick stroke, my back toward them, my ministrations going unnoticed.

Almost.

One of them left, then another, towels sadly covering their glorious pricks, both of them vanishing behind the row of lockers. I glanced over my shoulder. The third dude was bending down to wash his feet, alabaster cheeks spread wide, pink crinkled hole winking out at me. A jolt of lightening shot down my spine at the sight of it, goose bumps running like wildfire up both my arms, breath suddenly ragged.

His legs went farther apart, hanging nuts coming teasingly into view, causing an involuntary moan to escape from between my lips, drowned out, thankfully, by the two running showers. Not that it mattered, apparently. "Mirrors," he said, all of a sudden, his back still facing me.

I coughed. "'Scuse me?"

He stood and turned, pointing to his right. "Mirrors," he repeated.

It was then I understood what he was getting at. He'd seen my staring. Caught, like a bug in a rug, in a shower with a raging boner. A flush of red spread from cheek to scruffy cheek. "Um, sorry," I managed.

He turned to look at me, his index finger raised in the air, twirling around in a circle. Guy wanted me to rotate around. So I did, my cock pointing at him like a divining rod, his eyes now glued to my midsection, mouth agape. His twirling finger got pressed to full pink lips. "Wait," he mouthed.

"Okay," I mouthed back, boner still raging, his schlong doing a slow rise northward, thick like the rest of him, the fat head pulsing to plumb-sized.

A minute or so later, the other two gym bunnies left, leaving me and the other dude all by our lonesome. "Wanna fuck?" he asked, with a wicked leer.

The question, though lacking a certain amount of romanticism, didn't need to be asked twice. I turned off my shower, as did he, the gap between us closed in a heartbeat. "I break easy," I warned him, lips brushing lips, a deft tongue sliding in, gliding around its partner, his breath pushing down my throat and into my lungs.

"Don't worry," he said, his voice echoing off the blue tile. "I don't."

Which meant, little old me was gonna get to top big divine him. Gym membership, it seemed, had all sorts of hidden privileges.

He inched away, hands raised up, grabbing for the showerhead, legs spread wide, back against the slick wall. I gazed at the bronzed smooth flesh, muscle for days, veins jutting out like tree branches. Mine, all mine.

I moved in, hands up, index fingers and thumbs on either side of two pink nipples, thick as eraser tips, aching to be twisted and turned and pinched and pulled. Which is just what they got, in spades, his eyes rolling back in his head as I tortured them, my cock up against his, bush to bush, my teeth pulling down on his lower lip, the moan ricocheting around us. Bid dude, big pain threshold. Goody for me.

I pulled away, one nipple released, replaced by a smack to his chest. It was like hitting a fucking rock. "Owe," I grunted.

"Mmm," he groaned.

I balled my fist up and gave it another go. His cock bounced, a slick bead of precum oozing out, dripping down as the crimson flush spread across his wide expanse of pec. I backhanded his nipple, his legs buckling, his grip tighter on the showerhead. I moved south, a slap on each ab, a spank across a belly as flat as Kansas, his muscles quivering as I abused him, his head now tilted back, mouth in a pant.

I crouched down, stroking my throbbing prick as I took the head of his cock in my mouth, salty-sweet jizz hitting my throat like a bullet. He pushed his dick in, a happy gagging tear streaming down my face as my free hand grabbed his nut sac. He shoved as I yanked, his knees buckling again as I pulled and twisted, all while his massive prick filled my mouth. Round peg in a round hole. You gotta love the human body.

I extricated his dick from my face, spit dripping down off the tip, flinging off as I gave his shaft a smack, his meat swaying left then right. With his hairy nuts still in my grasp, I gave his cock another smack, sending it careening the other way, his face twisted in a look of both pain and pleasure, though I suspected mostly the latter.

"What's the B-side of this album sound like, dude?" I asked, still in a crouch as I released his balls.

He glanced down and smiled, blue eyes beaming at me as he briefly let go of the showerhead in order to turn around. "Have a listen, dude," he offered, voice raspy, sweat now trickling down his wide back and butt-crack.

His ass was perfect – pitch-perfect, that is – the sound of my spanks pinging all around us, playing out a syncopated rhythm worthy of any dance floor. Each time my hand made contact, he shuddered, moaned, tensed and then released, his ass jutting out to meet my palm, his flesh quickly turning beet-red.

I parted his cheeks and dove in, my tongue licking his hair-rimmed ring before shoving its way inside. He turned up the volume, his sighs rumbling through my body, his ass pushing into my face, rocking in and out. Meaning, it was time to take this baby for a spin.

I jumped up, spotting the soap dispenser on the wall. I chuckled, figuring he'd get good and fucked and clean, all at the same time. I pumped a few dabs into my palm and then slicked it around his twitching hole. He grunted and groaned, loudly, as I made my way inside, one finger replaced by two, both getting sucked in, vice-tight, his interior as well-muscled as his exterior.

I extricated my digits, lubed up my prick, and butted it up against his portal. "Ready?" I rasped.

"Set," he replied.

Then came the voice from behind us. "No go." It was Iron-jaw, tapping me on the shoulder, his breath hot on the nape of my neck.

I turned around, slowly, my rigid cock crashing into his leg. "Um, let me guess, no fucking in the showers?"

That shit-eating grin of his made the briefest of appearances. "Oh, you can fuck, all right," he replied, "but I get to watch."

"Deal," replied my beau-hunk, still hanging on to the showerhead, ass still primed and eager for a go. "Now hurry up and fuck me."

Iron-jaw winked. "You heard the man."

He moved to our side, both our heads turning his way as he removed his ultra-tight tank, his torso so rife with muscle it was a wonder his skin could hold it all in. His abs were as big as apples, pecs like melons, nipples like grapes. Dude was a veritable fruit salad, good enough to eat. He watched us watching him, his hand unbuttoning his shorts, the zipper sliding down, a blond bush poking out, the shaft of his cock evident. He kicked off his sneakers, rolled off his socks, the shorts sliding down and off, around legs as wide as both of mine put together. His dick sprang out, thick and short, a six inch slab of meat with blue veins running north to south, balls up tight to his groin, pink and hairy and creased. A spit into his mitt of a hand, his cock slicked up, he sunk to the floor and gave us the go ahead.

I smacked my palms on the other dude's back, grabbing on as I shoved my cock inside his ass, every nerve-ending in my body suddenly on fire, his asshole clenching around my shaft, pulling me in, deep, deep in.

"Fuck," he exhaled, head hung low, ass grinding into my crotch until all seven inches were fully embedded, my balls brushing up against his cheeks, my arms around his waist now, my fist pumping his gigantic prick.

"Let 'er rip," Iron-jaw grunted from the sidelines.

I turned my head his way. He was on all fours, one hand blissfully jacking away, the other behind his back, fingering his hole, his eyes glazed over, a trickle of drool dribbling down his chin. In other words, he was one hot mess of sweaty muscle.

"That cost extra, too, Bert?" I chided, pulling an inch out before shoving it on home again.

"On the house, boy," he replied, voice gravelly, sweat pouring down his hairless head, hands working in overdrive now.

Another inch out, another shove in, hard, deep, grinding my cock up his chute, moans and groans from all three of us at the same time. And then, as Iron-jaw had said, I let 'er rip, jack-hammering his ass while I pumped the come up from his balls.

"Oh, fuck," I yowled, yanking my cock out, legs nearly giving way as I shot and shot and shot, one steady steam after the next, white hot spunk streaming down his back and ass, his cock exploding in my hand a split second later.

"Oh, fuck," he yelled, body spasming, cum hitting the tiled wall, splat, splat, splat.

And, "Oh, fuck," it was thirded, my head again looking toward Iron-jaw, his muscles twitching, impossibly broad back arched, panting heavily as his Billy club spewed, shooting ounce after sticky white ounce onto the floor beneath him, etched belly wildly expanding and contracting all the while.

I turned my shower buddy around, holding his hands above his head with one fist, the other twisting his chaffed nipple. "Now that was a workout," I quipped, my mouth mashed into his, sweaty bodies pressed up flush together.

He hummed and ground into me, swapping some heavy spit before pulling a hair's breadth away. "You up for the disco now, sport?" he whispered into my mouth.

Music to my fucking ears. "What do you say, Bert?" I asked, neck turning toward my trainer again. "You up for it?"

He jumped back onto his feet, wiping the pool of sweat off his ample chest, his cock still steely, swaying. He shrugged. "Why the fuck not?"

I turned to my buddy again, a bite on his lip, then a suck. My hand went from his nipple to his bicep, barely encircling it by half. "More fun to be lifted than doing the lifting anyway, right?"

He grinned and flexed. "Amen," he replied, the smile rising high.

"Amen," I echoed, quickly adding, "Then let's go; Donna's calling."

Iron-jaw moved in tight to us, all three sets of lips up close, breath mixing with breath mixing with breath. "I thought Donna moaned," he said, his hand on my shoulder.

"You're learning, Bert," I replied, smacking his equally iron-ass for good measure. "Now you're fucking learning."

THE LAB RAT
By Milton Stern

Dr. Musclestein had a theory. Anyone could achieve the results of a steroid user, provided they had proper nutrition, access to the best weight training equipment available, unlimited time, and encouragement.

He had a state-of-the-art gym built in a wing of his home, complete with kitchenette, bedroom, full bath, and French doors leading to his backyard swimming pool. The subject of his experiment would be required to live in that wing of the house for thirty days. His waking hours would mostly be spent working out. He would also be eating quality proteins, fresh fruits and vegetables, and he would have daily, two-hour tanning privileges by the pool. However, no television would be allowed. When he was not eating or sleeping, he was to be working out. His muscles would be pumped during all his waking hours, forcing them to grow beyond anyone's expectations.

However, to test his theory, Dr. Musclestein needed a lab rat. He searched high and low across the local college campus, but there were no candidates who fit the bill. He visited all the local gyms, but no one was right for the job. He even scoured the beaches. There were those who were willing to be his subjects, but all had been on the 'juice.'

He needed a natural bodybuilder, and he was disappointed. All this expense to build the perfect lab, and he could not carry out his experiment. He was about to give up, when he noticed the man mowing his lawn. This was not his usual gardener. Bobby, his gardener, was in his sixties and although in good shape for his age, he was no muscle man. But Bobby's replacement was exactly what the Doctor had ordered.

Dr. Musclestein had an idea, but he would need to get dressed first. He usually walked around his home in nothing but black sweat pants. To look at him, one would have thought he had already tried out his theory on himself. He was six-foot-five and 260 pounds of smooth, rock-hard muscle. Everything about him rippled and bulged. But, if he was going to approach the gardener about his experiment, he needed to dress the part. He changed into gray slacks, a white shirt, striped tie, a lab coat and his black framed bifocals.

As he stepped out the back door, he spotted the gardener, who just at that moment was taking off his shirt. The man was five-foot-nine and looked to weigh around 190 pounds. He was hairy and thickly muscled. Dr. Musclestein guessed him to be Italian, and when the thirty-four-year-old man introduced himself as Scott Manicotti, his heritage was confirmed. Scott wore his black hair in a crew cut and also had a goatee. The doctor thought to himself, If this guy is not gay, he missed an excellent opportunity.

Dr. Musclestein explained his theory to Scott, who seemed more interested than any of the other potential subjects, and that afternoon, Scott moved into the lab wing of the house. Dr. Musclestein kept the door to the lab locked in the event that Scott might try to escape, which would cause him to have to start his experiment anew. However, since Scott had been there, he did not complain once. He enjoyed being able to work out all hours of the day and night.

Every day, Dr. Musclestein would unlock the door and enter the lab with two bags of fresh groceries – the highest quality proteins, fresh fruits and vegetables, and plenty of bottled water. After putting the groceries away, he would observe his lab rat, who could always be found working out. The lab rat, as per the doctor's instructions, wore minimal clothing, preferring only a jock strap, sweat socks and sneakers.

Dr. Musclestein would pull out his tape measure and chart the lab rat's progress. He would carefully measure his biceps, pecs, waist, glutes, thighs, and calves. The lab rat was doing well and had already put on ten pounds of solid muscle. His thick build had evolved into a ripped display of hairy, masculine strength.

Dr. Musclestein was pleased with the results, and every day, he would take the prior day's dirty jock straps and sweat socks and lock the door. After returning to his section of the home, he would strip off his lab coat, shirt, tie and slacks and stroke his thick, hard cock, while sniffing the lab rat's dirty jock, until he covered his smooth chest and belly in cum.

During the third week, Dr. Musclestein was so pleased with the lab rat's progress, he decided to give him a treat. He usually did not check in on his subject any time after the morning progress report, but he decided to surprise the lab rat this particular afternoon.

He unlocked the door, and he was surprised not to find his subject working out. However, he did hear the shower going. Dr. Musclestein placed the tray he was carrying on the kitchenette counter and sat down on one of the stools, waiting for the lab rat to finish scrubbing up.

He heard the squeaking sound of faucets being turned off and the shower door being opened. A few seconds later, the lab rat appeared. He was stark naked, pumped as usual and dripping wet. Dr. Musclestein was pleased with his progress scoping out the subject's beautiful muscles, especially the thick one that was hanging between his legs. The lab rat saw the tray and asked about it.

Dr. Musclestein pointed to the cake and ice cream on the tray and said, "I think you have worked very hard, and I brought you a reward." He then motioned for the lab rat to sit on the stool facing him and not bother putting on any clothes.

The Doctor looked him over admiring the results of his experiment. He then grabbed a spoon and proceeded to feed the lab rat. The more he fed him, the more he fell in love with him. The lab rat looked up at the doctor and opened his mouth invitingly with each spoonful of cake and ice cream.

The doctor scooted in closer and placed a hand on the lab rat's thigh while continuing to feed him his treat, spoonful by loving spoonful. His hand slid up the lab rat's thigh until he reached the prize. As he stroked the subject's hardening cock, he continued to spoon feed him. Precum was leaking heavily from the lab rat's dick, and he used the goo to slick it up and increase his stroke.

And, they never took their eyes off each other.

The doctor put down the spoon and leaned in, gently kissing his subject, tasting the cake and ice cream and exploring the lab rat's mouth with his tongue. His cock started to pulse as their lips moved across each other and their tongues intertwined.

Dr. Musclestein got up from the stool and leaned down in front of his subject. He removed his hand from the throbbing dick and with his mouth tasted a steady stream of sweet and salty precum, and as he cupped the large hairy balls that hung from the lab rat, he heard a quickening of breath, and felt the first shots of many of the subject's sweet, thick load hitting the back of his throat. He did not take his mouth off the cock until he knew it was completely drained.

Dr. Musclestein got up and sat back down on the stool, and the two of them kissed, tasting the load that was just released. They kissed for a long time, acknowledging their love for each other.

When they released their lips, the lab rat looked deeply into the eyes of the doctor.

"That was hot, really hot," Scott said.

"I couldn't help myself; you look incredible," Dr. Musclestein said. "Apparently, my theory works."

Scott looked down at himself, pleased with his progress. The doctor ran the back of his hand across the young man's hairy body.

"You know I have to be back to work tomorrow," Scott said.

"Yeah," the doctor acknowledged.

Scott stood up and put on a fresh jock. He looked over at the doctor and said, "Next month, I get to be Dr. Musclestein, OK?"

"Anything for you, baby," Dr. Musclestein answered and smiled as he realized how lucky he was that they still enjoyed these games eight years after they first met.

THE EX
By Milton Stern

I decided to go to the gym early that day, a Sunday, so I figured the place would be empty. I changed in the locker room, and when I emerged, who would be standing at the front desk but my ex.

We had not seen each other in over a year – since he moved to Minneapolis. What the hell was he doing here, now? Why was he back in town?

"Hey, sexy," he greeted me.

"What are you doing in town?" I asked.

"Here on business." Then, he leaned into me and said, "And, I am horny as hell."

"That's nice," I replied and went upstairs to the workout floor. I really was not in the mood for his bullshit.

I did my workout and spotted him on the treadmill for a second, but I was also proud of myself for not caring one bit that he was there. It took me a long time to get over him, and I finally was.

After an hour, I had lifted all I cared to lift, and I went back downstairs to the locker room to shower. I brushed my teeth (I don't know why working out gives me a bad taste in my mouth), stripped out of my sweaty gear, grabbed a towel and entered the shower room. Mine is an old fashioned gym with an open shower room. Being it was early Sunday morning, I and about two or three other people were actually in the gym, so the shower room was empty.

I was soaping up and had closed my eyes for a second when I heard, "Man, you are looking hot as ever."

There he was, under the shower head next to mine, in his hairy, muscular glory, with that thick cock just hanging there, as I fondly remembered it.

"Thanks," I muttered and proceeded to soap myself up.

"How's life?" he asked.

"Good," I answered as I was not really in the mood for conversation. I just wanted to clean up and get on with my day.

"Not much for talking today are you?" he said. Then he placed a soapy hand on my cock.

I didn't stop him, nor did I get hard.

"You usually harden up right away," he said as he used his other hand to cup my balls.

Then I started to get hard. Damn motherfucker, he knew how to get me up.

I pulled away.

"Really don't want to go there," I said. "It took me a long time to get over you, so let's not fuck things up, OK?"

He nodded. "No problem. I just like touching you and wouldn't mind having that up my ass right now." He winked.

I smiled at him as if he were a petulant child.

"I'm staying at the hotel next door. My flight leaves at noon, so I have an hour to kill."

"How long have you been in town?" I asked as if I cared.

"About a week."

Now, the old me would have said something to the effect of 'you've been here all week and you didn't call.' But, I was beyond that.

"I should have called."

"Why?" I asked.

He just looked at me then my dick, which had gone down a bit.

"Wow. You really do move on."

"Yep," I answered.

I finished my shower, grabbed my towel and exited the shower room.

He finished up then opened his locker, which turned out to be next to mine.

I dressed. He dressed. I said a quick goodbye and exited the gym. No sooner had the door closed behind me then it opened again.

"Fuck me now," he said to me from behind as I turned to walk down the street. "I am right next door, just take me and fuck me."

I turned and looked right at him. Should I fuck him? Would it bring back old feelings? Would this be a mistake? Could I do this and walk away again?

"What the hell," I said and followed him up to his hotel room.

No reason for pretense, we already saw each other naked in the shower room, we were together for over three years. No mystery there. We were naked in seconds.

I grabbed the bottle of lube that was on the night stand, greased up my hard pole pushed him back on the bed, lifted up his legs, aimed my dick, and entered swiftly.

He didn't even grimace, or yelp; he just smiled.

He put his hands behind his head and flexed his biceps. His dick was rock-hard and throbbing on his belly, and I was pounding him into the next time zone. He knew flexing his biceps would make me even harder. His kissed one then the other, while his hot, big, hairy ass swallowed my dick.

I fucked for points. I was determined to get off in him and fuck him until he begged me to stop. It takes me a long time to come, so he was in for a real long ride.

I leaned down and kissed him. Long and hard, we wrestled tongues, then he stuck his out, and I sucked on his tongue while I continued to drill him.

He was in heaven. What a bottom slut he was. His dick was dribbling all over his belly, and he was still flexing those baseball-sized biceps and smiling like a fat kid eating cake.

I don't know how long I fucked him. I just kept going and going. This was better than cardio. Finally, I knew I was going over the edge, and I looked right at him, right in the eyes.

"I am going to seed your guts," I said low and with a growl. And, I emptied my balls into him and continued to pound him until he let out a moan and came without touching himself.

I pulled out.

"I need a shower," I announced, then walked into the bathroom, turned on the water, and stepped in.

This is when he would usually join me. He didn't, and I was glad. I cleaned my dick, then took a long piss in the shower. I stepped out, grabbed a towel, and looked in the trash can. There were two empty Fleet Enema bottles. Miserable slut cleaned himself out, knowing he would get fucked this morning. Nothing changed. And, that is when I knew even fucking him wouldn't make me love him again.

I dressed and said goodbye.

I never gave him another thought. As a matter of fact, by lunchtime, I had forgotten I had even fucked him.

STEPBROTHERS
By Milton Stern

With spring semester over, Adam headed home for the summer before his senior year at State University. His mother had remarried in the last month, and she and her new husband were still on their honeymoon, so Adam knew he was coming home to an empty house.

After a three-hour drive, he was happy to be pulling up in front of the house, and he noticed the hatchback parked in the driveway and figured it must belong to one of his new stepfather's kids, probably checking on the house.

Adam pulled his suitcases out of the trunk and walked up the walkway, let himself in, and walked right up the stairs. After a long drive, he was in no mood to talk to anyone.

He put the suitcases in his room, and the first thing he noticed was how hot it was in the house. If one of his new step siblings was there, why didn't he turn on the AC? Adam shook his head and took off his shirt.

Adam had been lifting weights since he was sixteen. His body was perfectly proportioned and nicely muscled at five-foot-eleven and 185 pounds. He inherited his mother's smooth chocolate brown skin and his father's large round ass, among other large assets.

He walked downstairs to turn on the air conditioning. While adjusting the thermostat, he heard the front door open and someone saying goodbye, followed by a car speeding away. He remembered his stepbrother from the wedding. Louis was a little taller than Adam at six-foot-one, but he was leaner. His nineteen-year-old stepbrother had thick black curly hair and very dark features much like his father's, with black eyes and thick lips that begged to be kissed.

Adam remembered talking to him at the wedding and wondering if it would be incestuous to lay his new stepbrother.

"Hey, Adam," Louis said as he extended his hand. The two of them shook hands.

"Dude, what's with not turning on the AC? It's like a fucking oven in here," Adam said.

Louis shook his head and headed upstairs. That was when Adam remembered that Louis was not much of a talker, and from what he gathered from his mother and Louis's siblings, he was not always playing with a full deck either.

Nutty or not, Adam still wondered if the boy liked to play.

He headed back to his bedroom and unpacked his bags. After putting away the last of his clothes and putting the suitcases in the closet, he headed back downstairs to the kitchen for some water. His mother always kept a large jug of water in the refrigerator, and he decided to forgo a glass and drink it straight from the jug. As he was guzzling the water, Louis walked into the kitchen.

"Adam, the man," he said.

Adam quit guzzling for a second and looked at Louis who had stripped to his boxers. The boy was long and lean, built like a swimmer with broad shoulders and a six pack. This pissed Adam off because he knew Louis never worked out, but he did hold out hope that Louis would end up fat when he hit thirty!

"So, Louis, are you living here now, or are you house sitting?" Adam asked him.

"Wouldn't you like to know, bro," Louis said, and he grabbed a soda and headed back to his room.

Adam rolled his eyes and finished the jug. He filled it with tap water, put it back in the fridge and hoped it was full of bacteria for Louis to enjoy.

Adam headed upstairs, walked into the bathroom, stripped and stepped into the shower. While he was soaping up, he thought of Louis, the weirdo, standing in the kitchen wearing nothing but his boxers, and his dick started to grow. Adam had not come in a few days, so he took hold of his favorite toy and rubbed out a big load, barely taking a couple of minutes to do the deed, and hardly making a sound in the process as he learned to stay quiet while jerking off in the dorm.

He finished his shower and pulled the curtain back, grabbing a towel at the same time. Adam was startled to find Louis there flossing his teeth. The house had two full baths, why was he in this one?

Adam tried his best to conceal his cock, which was still half hard. It was difficult enough to hide when it was soft. However, Louis paid no attention to him, so Adam thought he would take one more stab at conversation.

"So, Louis, are you working or going to school?"

Louis stopped flossing and turned around to look at Adam, who had since wrapped the towel around his waist. Then he faced the mirror again.

"No," Louis said. He finished flossing and went into the guest room, shutting the door behind him.

"What a doofus," Adam said to himself. "I hope the little asshole isn't here all summer."

Adam brushed his teeth then crawled into bed.

At three in the morning, Adam was startled awake by some strange sounds. He thought there were cats fucking outside his window, but he soon realized the sounds were coming from the next room. He heard squeaking, then high pitched moaning, more squeaking, and then Louis's voice saying over and over again, "Good boy, good boy, good boy."

Adam never heard anyone come in. Who the hell was Louis talking to? Then he heard him yell, "AHHH AHHH AHHH," so loudly it shook the walls. Adam buried his head in his pillow to keep from laughing. Once the screaming stopped, he then heard Louis saying, "I am such a good boy, oh yeah, good boy, good boy." Then, there was silence.

Adam was still laughing as he thought about his strange stepbrother masturbating and congratulating himself. Then he got hard again, himself, but he was too tired to jerk off, so he rolled over and went back to sleep.

Adam woke up early the next morning and decided to make himself a pot of coffee and work out in the basement gym, provided it was still there. After locating his extra large mug, he filled it with the freshly brewed coffee and headed to the basement.

Since it was still pretty early, Adam decided to work out in just a black cotton jock strap, crew socks and cross trainers. The jock hugged his round butt and displayed his big basket perfectly, and he wished there were someone there to enjoy the view.

Once in the basement, he was happy to see that for the most part his equipment was still where he left it.

He loaded a couple of plates on the bar and secured them with collars. He decided to stretch a bit, and when he bent down to touch his toes he looked through his legs and saw Louis, stark naked and standing right behind him. Adam immediately stood up and turned around.

Louis was standing there with his dick hanging limp but low accompanied by two big, equally low hanging balls, and he was holding a cup of coffee.

"Adam, the man," Louis said. "I took some of your aromatic java." He then turned around and headed back upstairs.

Adam was only pissed because he would now have to brew more coffee.

He slid under the bar and pressed the weights for twelve reps, and he sat up after the set and admired himself in the mirror he had mounted across from the bench. Adam ran his hands over his chest and down his six pack abs. He then flexed both biceps, displaying the high peaks that always earned him attention in the gym at school.

He lay back down and did another twelve reps. With each set, he looked in the mirror and flexed his pecs, bouncing them before doing another double bicep pose.

Adam stood up and removed some of the plates and curled the barbell for ten reps very slowly, keeping his eyes on the vein that ran up his arm. Watching his biceps pump full of blood always turned him on, and his jock was beginning to get tighter.

He put the bar down, and flexed again, doing a crab pose, flaring out his lats and finishing off with another double bicep pose. Adam then did another set of curls.

During his third set, he heard Louis coming down the steps. Adam finished the set and put the bar back. This time Louis was sitting in front of the mirror drinking another cup of coffee, blocking Adam's view of himself. 'Fucking asshole,' he thought, 'Drinks my coffee and interrupts my workout.' However, Adam didn't confront him because Louis was still naked.

"Can I help you, Louis?" he asked.

Silence.

Louis just stared at Adam, studying every inch of him. Adam noticed how Louis was looking at him and didn't know what to make of it.

"Louis, you're sitting in front of the mirror, and I can't watch myself when I work out."

Louis turned and looked at the mirror as if he did not know it was there. He stood up and leaned on an old dresser that was placed in the basement a decade before.

"Louis, are you just going to stand there?" Adam asked him.

Again, silence.

Adam did another set of curls, watching himself in the mirror when he noticed Louis standing behind him. Louis reached around and felt Adam's biceps with each curl of the bar, running his hands over the pumped muscles. Adam continued his set, enjoying the feel of his stepbrother's hands on his muscles, and he started to get hard again.

Adam curled until he was exhausted, then he put the bar back on the rack. As he looked at himself in the mirror, Louis continued to explore his body with his hands.

Louis felt his stepbrother's lats, tracing his fingers up Adam's muscular back, then he squeezed Adam's softball sized shoulders, and as one hand made its way up Adam's neck the other reached around to feel Adam's pumped chest.

As Louis continued exploring his body, Adam's breathing became heavier. He let his stepbrother enjoy every sweaty, pumped inch of him and finally, Louis's hand was inside the black cotton jock strap and going for the prize.

As he released his stepbrother's enormous boner, Louis stepped around and brushed his lips against Adam's. Adam opened his mouth and reached around Louis's head drawing him in and kissing him deep, tasting the coffee the asshole had taken without permission. With his free hand, Adam reached down and grabbed the weirdo's hard dick and was impressed with its length and girth. Adam slid his hand up to the swollen head and slicked it with the precum Louis's big dick generously provided.

Louis had managed to get Adam's jock down around his ankles, and they continued to make out while stroking each other's dicks. Louis's free hand continued to explore Adam's pumped body and found a nipple, giving it a hard pull. Adam moaned, but he did not let go of Louis's mouth. Those full, soft lips were too good to let loose even for a second.

He let go of Louis's head and flexed his right bicep while his stepbrother felt it with his left hand, as they continued to kiss. Louis obviously liked the feel of flexed muscles because his dick would swell and pulse, emitting more precum whenever Adam flexed. This in turn made Adam's thick cock swell up, and he didn't know how much longer he could last.

Their breathing increased, and the stepbrothers were getting closer, but they never unlocked their lips.

Finally, Louis pulled away from Adam's lips and screamed, "AHHH AHHH AHHH," so loud it startled Adam. Then he shot his load covering Adam's belly and chest with pints of cum. The site of his stepbrother's load on his pumped chest made Adam shoot all over Louis, who groaned while Adam was shooting, "You are such a good boy, oh yeah, good boy, good boy." Then, there was silence.

They pulled away from each other, and Adam grabbed a towel to wipe himself off, but Louis stopped him. He bent down and licked his stepbrother's body clean. After he finished his breakfast of cum, he winked at Adam, turned and walked back upstairs without saying a word.

Adam stood there with his half-hard cock hanging out and his black cotton jock at his ankles and watched Louis's round butt bounce as he walked upstairs.

"What a fucking nut job," Adam thought. Then he smiled and hoped all his workouts would end like this one.

SCRUBBING UP
By Milton Stern

I had just come home from a business trip and was still wound up from days of meetings and travel. Normally, I would have had a martini then crashed for the night, but I hadn't worked out in a few days, so I decided to hit the gym. It was after 10:30, but they were open until midnight on Friday nights, so I had plenty of time.

After changing into my nondescript workout gear as I never really went for the Spandex/Lycra look, I walked upstairs to the free weight area, and to my surprise, no one else was working out. Usually this would bother me as seeing hot guys pumping up is inspirational, but I just wanted to get a good sweat going.

After an hour of working my chest until I swore my nipples would pop off from the pressure, I did some crunches and decided to call it a night and go downstairs to the locker room and shower. Interestingly, no one else came in to work out while I was there, and from what I could tell, only the night manager remained on duty.

As I undressed at my locker, the manager walked by and smiled. I am usually a talkative guy, but I noticed a while back, that although he was friendly and smiled a lot, this particular manager wasn't much of a talker, so I never initiated conversation. He was also the kind that never went for me – buzz cut, tattoos from neck to ankles, earrings, and from what I could tell through his tight shirt, nipple rings. He was also the bodybuilder type with big, thick muscles that were obviously enhanced through chemistry (and I'll leave it at that). He did have those dark features I find enormously attractive, but his look told me that I was not his type.

I bent down to slip off my jock, and I stood up to find him standing in front of me and checking me out.

"Pretty slow tonight," he said.

"Yeah, made my workout that much easier." I didn't bother covering myself up with a towel, as by then he had a full view and what was the point. I am also very well built with a naturally smooth physique and slabs of lean, hard muscle from years of working out, so I like the attention. My dick hangs nicely, too, with a pair of round full balls to support it. This would have been a good time to put on the moves, but as I said, this type never goes for me. My being blond doesn't help either.

"I still have time to shower before you lock up I hope."

"You have plenty of time," he said as he walked away then shouted over his shoulder, "I'm going to lock up early, but take your time."

We have open showers, which I like because there is nothing better than having a hot view of pumped up muscle-heads after a workout, and I had picked up my share of tricks after a shower in this gym as well.

I stepped up to the second shower head that I knew had the best pressure, turned it on and let the water cascade down my back as I faced the wall. I then shampooed my hair and turned around to rinse out the suds. I almost jumped when I felt a hand on my balls. I opened my eyes to see the night manager, naked and feeling me up while grinning at me.

"Mind if I soap you up?"

I just shrugged as if to say what the hell. He then squeezed some soap from the dispenser and proceeded to rub the soap on my chest, down my abs, back up my sides and indicated I should raise my arms as he scrubbed my pits. We didn't say a word as he continued to soap me up from head to toe while I drank in every tattooed inch of muscle on his beautiful body. Not only were his nipples pierced, but his belly button and big, thick cock were as well. I was intrigued by his body art, turned on by his beauty, and getting horny from his touch. My cock was standing straight up, thick and long, and the head was more swollen than usual.

He turned me around and worked my back, paying special attention to my hard, round glutes before he worked his hand between them and stuck a finger in my hole while he reached around with the other hand and stroked my now-aching cock.

Then he licked the back of my neck. That did it. About a quart of precum oozed from my cock, but the water and soap disguised it, although my moan was loud and clear.

I then felt his hard cock sliding up and down my crack and the smooth metal of the ring tracing its path. What a feeling, and I didn't want it to end.

I hardly ever bottom, but he was doing things with his hands on my body that had me almost begging out loud. I know he sensed my desire because he then let the head of his cock slide between my cheeks and without stumbling, fumbling or mumbling, he found the hole.

Yes, he was an expert top – a rare breed and a fantastic find. The few times I ever bottomed, I got annoyed when they would struggle to find the hole and get to work, always thinking, 'Find it already, fuck me and leave.'

He penetrated me ever so gently but with a steady movement, and before I knew it, that hard, thick pierced tool was all the way in, and I oozed another quart of precum. The metal ring just added to my pleasure as doing me from behind allowed it to rub my prostate just right. He continued to lick my neck and stroke my cock while he fucked me slowly never increasing nor decreasing his pace. I was in heaven. And, I was getting close.

Within a minute, I shot with a loud growl and painted the tiles with my thick load while he continued his steady fuck. Once he was sure I was drained, he withdrew his cock, and I ached for its return. It was over, and I wanted it to go on all night. I was embarrassed at my quick orgasm, but he seemed not to mind.

He turned me around and proceeded to soap me up again as he did before, but this time he leaned in and planted his full lips on mine. Not only was he a great fuck, but also the best kisser I have ever known. My cock, which I thought was through for the night, got hard again (his stroking it didn't hurt).

This time instead of turning me around, he turned around and rubbed his big hard muscular ass on my cock. I got the message. I found the hole with no problem and penetrated him with the same gentle but firm steady stroke he had shown me. I ran my tongue up his back and all over his neck, while I reached around and stroked his cock. He moaned with pleasure as I fucked him steadily, figuring he liked it as he gave it, slow, steady, firm and sensual. I have learned from years of casual encounters that if someone does something to you, they usually like it done to them.

He liked it.

Within a minute, he growled out his own thick load and painted the tile floor.

Strangely, we had only been at it for no more than ten or fifteen minutes, yet we had both come and fucked each other. I could have come again, but I withdrew. I also decided to return the favor and scrub him up.

His body felt fantastic; the more I felt of it, the more I wanted to go at it again.

"Come home with me," he said.

Those were the first words either of us had spoken since he entered the shower.

"OK."

We rinsed off, and as I walked toward his car, I wondered what a guy like him wanted with a guy like me.

That was more than twenty years ago, but I no longer wonder what he sees in me as long as he fucks me slow and steady and lets me return the favor every night.

HUMP HIS RUMP
By Logan Zachary
& R. W. Clinger

There he was again, working the Weider strength machine, exploding with muscle, ready to burst from his excessive workout. Jay Bison. My infatuation. I wanted to curl him over and ram my eight-incher into his hot bottom. All 230 pounds of him. Coveting his six-three frame of muscle and porn star good looks. The guy I wanted to explore with my straying fingertips and devour with my tongue. Mr. Perfect. Someone I desired to the fullest, unable to tamp my craving for the muscle god.

I stood half-hidden behind a pole and a Pro-Perspective cycle inside Man It Up Gym on Thyson Street. Again, I studied Jay's blond curls, fall-into emerald-colored eyes, gladiator-sized chest and muscled thighs. Fascination held me sternly within its untamable grip, and I longed to touch/lick/bite the pointed nipples under his tight tee, devouring his smooth and hairless torso. Elation curled itself inside my pretty boy stomach and begged me to caress his chiseled jaw, Swedish-sloped nose and bulging shoulders – whatever I could find the strength to reach out and stroke. And, there between his Rufskin-covered center – the place I wanted to keep for eternity and connect to with longing passion – the outline of his private part was limp at seven inches, but absurdly wide, just waiting for my mouthy care and concentration.

I knew him the way I shouldn't have known him: Facebook user, physical fitness teacher at Rossdale High, resident at 563 Merlot Drive, single for the past six months, twenty-six years old, son of Soozie and Brent Bison, Hummer driver, skydiver, runner, football player with his guy pals on Saturday mornings, Falcon movie watcher, John Patrick reader, morning masturbator, man-lover and …

Jay saw me behind my pole/cycle and waved to me. A smile beamed on his delicious looking face. So, I grew a pair, I manned it up, and I walked over to him on his strength machine and said the queerest thing: "You know you're on my machine, right?"

He gave me a look of confusion, with an exuberant smile, and said, "Dougie, you creep me out. How long have you been studying me now? Eight months? Nine?"

The pumped jock took in my black crew-cut, azure-colored eyes, fuzz on the bottom of my chin, boyish chest with its dime-sized nipples, smallish abs and five-eleven frame, charcoal-colored treasure trail beneath my navel, and five inches of deflated beef hidden under Diesel shorts. A twinkle in my eyes shined, and I replied, "You know you like it. Guys like you get off on the attention."

"Guys like me should kick your ass."

"Don't you mean lick my ass?" I answered, really stepping over a line, since we never talked before.

Jay chortled, beaming with an interested smile. The dude reached between his legs and gave his plump junk a quick jostle. His intoxicated stare never left mine and he said, "Truth is I wouldn't mind humping your rump ... even if you're stalking me."

"My rump is here for the hump," I played with him.

Jay looked to his left and right and saw that we were completely alone. Other hot guys were in the gym but mostly positioned on the opposite side near the Elliptical machines doing their own things, totally out of eye range. Jay knew this and took advantage of ... me. I was close enough to him, and he reached out with his left hand, gave the horny goods beneath my Diesel a light pet, and murmured, "Follow me into the equipment room, so I can have my way with your ass."

And, so it was done. Jay left for the equipment room first, and I followed behind him in a discreet manner approximately three minutes later. Once I opened the steel door, walked inside, locked it behind me ... Jay was all over me. The stranger pulled the white tee off my head, dropped it to the cement floor, and nuzzled his face to my chest. My slender neck and shoulders were absorbed by his straying tongue.

Fingertips discovered my ripe nipples, which Jay pinched and gently twisted. His right hand fell down and along my thin torso and discovered my shorts, which he pulled down to my ankles. Within seconds, he found the eight inches of stiff pole between my stern legs and started jostling it up and done, sending me into a breathless surge of man-with-man satisfaction.

"Play with it," I coached.

He had no qualms regarding satisfying me. Two strokes turned into a dozen strokes and catapulted me into a state of virtually blowing my load too soon. Noting my almost-explosion, the jock pulled away from me and instructed, "Turn around and bend over for my mouth."

Taking his instruction in heed, I absorbed the equipment room: two Weslo cycles, a treadmill with a sign on it that read BROKEN, excess barbells and weights, gymnast mats, and two mirrors. Now, with the teacher on his knees and my bulbous ass positioned in his face, I felt the tip of his tongue enter my bottom, swish around, pull out, and enter again. Helplessly, I moaned in front of him; an obvious mistake on my part. Truth is I couldn't help myself. Jay's roving tongue was perceptibly too much for me to handle. It kept sliding in and out, driving me mad.

His palms pulled my bottom apart, allowing more access for his tongue to delve into my system. Behind me, he ground his face against my core and grumbled with pleasure. The teacher became windswept by my rump, under its sexual spell. Over and over, his face jammed itself to my middle, quickly released, and jammed to it again.

I whimpered in bliss, overzealous for his mouth-play. I couldn't help it and backed into his face numerous times, enjoying our equipment room fun. Helplessly, a few drops of ooze dripped out of my firm shaft. Overjoyed with such an action, I stated in an irreversible whisper, "Yank me off, Jay … I want to feel your hand on my dick."

The steamy-hot gym monkey was happy to oblige. Left-hand fingers wrapped around my joint and began to stroke it off in a downward motion. Feisty milking continued for the next few minutes as he continued to toy with my man-split. Jay was consistent with his movement, unyielding and teasing. His hunger seemed relentless, gratifying my demands, perhaps pleasuring the both of us.

I exploded without notice; shame on me. A jolt of pent ecstasy shifted throughout my core like electric, and white cream fired out of my hose. Cement was decorated as well as my Reebok workout shoes and Diesel shorts. The sap splattered in every direction, unending. Liquid wouldn't stop shooting out of my rod in a porn star load, and I heaved for breath in chaotic motion, feeling as if I were going to faint. The smell of my own spunk was scathing but relished; a prize after Jay's hand-ride.

"Nice load," Jay said, holding me up.

"All for you," I replied, knowing my comment was true.

In truth, I had every intention of getting Jay off, replacing his tongue with his swollen nine-inch cock in my taut bottom. Selfishly, I wanted to wear his load over the splay of my back, sporting his masculine goo like a heartfelt lover/stalker. Instead, a rustling of sorts was heard outside the equipment room's steel door and ...

Shit! A key was turned in the door's lock, its knob was twisted, and in a matter of seconds, the door opened. Both of us saw Brick Tanner, the sexy-hot manager on duty, standing there with a surprised look on his Cuban-pretty face, who questioned, "What the fuck is going on in here?"

I grabbed my shorts and tried to cover my still-erect flesh. A thick blob of cum hung off the tip and dropped onto the floor with a splat.

"We couldn't resist a different kind of workout," Jay said, as he stroked his porn star cock at Brick.

Brick stood in the doorway and cocked his hips. "You can be kicked out of the gym for this."

"That is if someone turns us in ..." Jay continued working his tool.

"I ..."

"And, I'm sure we could work something out, don't you?" Jay stood up and walked to him.

Brick took a step back, but it appeared to be more to keep his eyes on the erection, than avoiding my buddy's touch.

246

I stood up and followed Jay, admiring his ass as it flexed with each step. How I longed to stick my tongue, my finger, and my cock inside. Despite my orgasm, I was ready for round two, and with Brick in the mix, which was going to be hot.

Brick brought his hands up and caressed Jay's pecs. He pinched the nipples and massaged the sweat over the well-defined muscle.

I spooned up behind him and my cock slid easily up his crease. Sweat dripped down his spine, and I rubbed my chest against his back. My cock burrowed deeper inside.

Jay squeezed them together and moaned as it rode up and wedged between the tight gluts.

I looked over his shoulder, and we stared at Brick, undressing him with our eyes.

Jay must have read my mind for he reached forward and started to unbutton Brick's shirt. A thick patch of hair filled the V-opening and trailed down his torso. His sculpted abs and bronze skin glistened in the light.

I slipped my arms around Jay's narrow waist and my fingers combed through his pubic bush. Electricity crackled as I found his thick shaft and stroked it.

Brick's shirt opened, and we moved forward. Precum from Jay's dick painted across his torso, and Brick pushed forward. His mouth opened slightly.

Jay took that as a sign and kissed him. His tongue entered Brick's mouth and sought his. His lips pulled hard on Brick's.

I guided Jay's cock up and along the furry abs. Brick's pants brushed against my hand, and I unbuttoned them. Unzipping the fly, I felt his cock swell and push against the newly found freedom.

"I can't, we can't ..." Brick tried, but couldn't pull his mouth away from Jay's.

I pushed his waistband down, and his underwear strained against his arousal. I rubbed along his shaft and felt his eight inches, thick and solid. His balls swelled and expanded, too. Heat radiated off his groin and the heavy, manly musk entered my nose.

Brick looked to the right and motioned to the door.

I read 'whirlpool' on the sign.

"In here." Brick pushed the door open. Behind the door, he pulled out a magnetic sign and stuck it to the outside surface: CLOSED FOR CLEANING. He locked the door.

Jay looked at the whirlpool and turned the dial to start the jets. Bubbles rose to the surface as the water swirled around in the kidney-shaped hot tub.

I walked to the edge of the tub and bent over as I looked into the water. I swiveled my butt at Brick and smiled as I felt the heat from his gaze. I flexed my gluts and heard him gasp.

Brick kicked off his shoes as he pulled his open shirt off his shoulders. He unzipped his pants and stepped out of them. His underwear clung to his body, leaving nothing to the imagination. His erection tented the sheer cotton. His dark hair pattern was easily seen against his bronze skin.

Jay moved over to my ass and spread my cheeks. "Brick, check this out. Wouldn't you like to tap this?"

Brick moved over and pinched Jay's butt cheek as he admired mine. He joined Jay in massaging me.

I spun around and faced Brick. "I've seen you walking these halls for months, and I've dreamt what is under there." I pointed to his briefs.

"Me, too. Do you know how many boners I've had to hide on the machines out there? And they all had your name on them."

"I thought my name was on your joint," I said.

"Both of your names are down there."

"But I want to see what's down there." I reached forward and pulled on Brick's waistband.

The tip of his cock sprang free from its confinement, and the uncut end waved at me like a Cuban cigar.

Jay reached forward and pulled on the other side of his underwear. They were off before I could blink. He slipped behind Brick and guided him to me.

My fingers wrapped around his cock and started to stroke it. The mushroom head peeked out as the foreskin retracted and disappeared as the hood worked its way down. Precum escaped out of the flesh capsule, and my hand spread the wetness down his shaft.

"We should get wet," Brick said. He jumped over the side of the whirlpool and waved for us to follow.

We didn't need any more encouragement. As I drew near, I took my hand and wiped it off on his hairy chest. "Here's a start."

Jay joined me and pulled on his cock. More clear fluid poured out into his palm, and Jay's cock wagged at him. He guided Brick's dick to his and retracted the foreskin. Tip to tip, he pulled the sheath over his tip and squeezed. Both men moaned with delight, caught up in their festive trio of lust.

I dropped to my knees in the water and opened my mouth. I licked over the double dick and wrapped my lips around the seam. Pure elation was found with a pint of naughtiness.

Jay and Brick moaned as they humped each other. They leaned forward and locked lips, sealed above and sealed below.

My mouth held them together. I reached up and stroked along both of their cocks at the same time. I slid down from one pubic bush to the other, back and forth.

Brick's foreskin swallowed Jay's head.

I could see both fat tips roll around each other in chaotic but pleasurable motion. The water swirled around me, and I sat down on the bench. I landed on a jet and felt the water pressure shoot up and stimulate my tight opening. I pushed down and spread my cheeks, enjoying the full blast as it tried to fill my ass.

Jay laughed. "He's riding the jet and loving it."

It was true. I couldn't get enough of the whirlpool's water pulsing against my puckered bottom. Defending my pleasure, I pulled my mouth away from their combined rods, looked up at the two handsome jocks, and suggested in a ballsy manner, "You two can replace the jet with both of your cocks. What do you think?"

"I'm game," Brick immediately said, glowing with a mischievous smile. "How about you, Jay?"

I knew Jay would be into humping my rump with our new friend Brick. Jay was a greedy bastard when it came to sex. He wanted it all the time, anywhere; another positive attribute about his personality that I was attracted to.

"There isn't anything like a threesome," Jay commented, overjoyed with the idea that my inflexible rump was going to be the center of their combined attention.

No, I had never been rammed by two guys at the same time. In truth, I was willing to try the duo out for size. Why not, right? Every queer wanted to ride two cocks … just for the experience; notches in their belts. Besides, I knew my ass could handle both of their hard and slick tools together. I was not an amateur regarding sexual gratification with gym buddies. Hell, I took pride in my stalking game, finding the biggest and best guys and their cocks … and prompting two of them to enter my behind. Honestly, two ramming poles inside my core seemed better than one, a frisky act that I wanted/needed/desired.

And, so it went down among us. Brick found two condoms and a bottle of lube inside a secret wall-compartment within the private room; he probably fucked a lot of guys in the whirlpool, but whatever. He passed one of the condoms to Jay and kept the other for himself and gave the lube to me to grease my asshole. Following that act, he instructed Jay to sit down in one of the whirlpool's jet-powered seats; Jay listened. Brick then said to me, "Jump on his lap, pal. Make sure you're facing him. And, make sure his dick finds your ass."

I followed Brick's placid order and climbed aboard Jay's submerged cock. In doing so, I groaned as his swollen inches entered me.

Jay said, "Pushing it all into you, man," and flooded my hole with his rock-solid pick. Gasping for breath, he jammed his beef into my opening, sneered with delight, and confessed, "Ride it all you want, guy."

My world had split into two pieces, one for each stranger. I pounced up and down on his veined meat, self-pleasuring my tight opening. Half of my body was in the jetting water and white bubbles while the upper half sweated from our combined bodies and fierce movement.

"He's a power bottom," Brick said from behind me. "I can't wait to get in on this action." As if on cue, Brick rolled the condom down and over his stern, eight inches, reached for my bottom with his palms, gave me a little push forward, and nuzzled his cock against my already-opened man-gap and Jay's working gym buddy-device.

Truth was I didn't know how Brick managed to balance himself behind me, sliding his condom-covered rod into my middle, snuggling the piece of timber against Jay's slick one, riding me from behind. As the old cliché went, if there was a will, there was a way, and Brick seemed to pull the sexual act off just fine, and with much skill.

I panted and cried out as the two jocks shifted in and out of my unyielding core. The pain was excruciating but pleasurable at the same time. Both cocks humped my rump in a consecutive manner. Anguish surfaced on every pore of my body, and I murmured, "Make it last."

Beneath me, Jay looked as if he were having the time of his queer life. One rise of his hips pressed into my opening, fell away, and rose again. His cement rock banged my bottom with boundless speed, and he was evidently unable to stop his diligent thrusts. Wide-eyed, sweating, heaving for air, he announced, "Two dicks are better than one … Ride them both."

Again, I obliged to his wish and rode the two poles inside my man-cavity. Gleefully, I chortled, "Brick, how are you doing back there?"

The gym manager was far too busy working in and out of my butt for a response. His ab-lined stomach and furry-wet torso pressed against my muscled back, pulled away, and grazed my skin again. The pipe between his legs, wedged itself inside my two-man tunnel, exited, and entered again. In my right ear, his tongue generously touched its earlobe, and he mumbled, "You like Brick's dick, don't you?"

I was sure that it was a line he used all the time, talking about himself in the third person, turning himself on as he hammered numerous jock-bottoms like my own. Replying to his question, I said, "Don't talk … just fuck," and meant every word of it.

"Suit yourself," Brick grunted, power-driving my outlet with all his weight, happy to get off with both Jay and me.

I was banged for no less than twenty minutes. The two erections worked together as a team inside my man-cave. Both seemed to bolt inside me at the same time, retreat, and push inside me again. The feeling of their combined wankers taking residence in my rump was nothing less than pure bliss. I could have had them plunge my system for the next two hours, if they were capable, but neither man was a porn star. To my utter surprise, both shared with me at the same exact time, as if they were twins or something: "I'm going to shoot."

Not even a minute later, I was positioned between both men in the whirlpool as they were seated side by side. Honestly, I was dazed and confused. Facing the windblown jocks on my knees, I wrapped my right palm on Jay's dick and my left palm on Brick's. Processing synchronized motion on the two men, I began to jack the athletes off. Promptly, I cranked their rods in a manipulative manner. Coaching them came easy, and I instructed, "Pump my fists. Release your loads."

Jay and Brick were on task. Both rose and fell in their seats as the whirlpool's pleasurable water-teasing continued. Each man bucked their goods into my palms, relishing their moments of pre-explosions, attempting to find their cream-flowing orgasms. To my surprise, the men kissed and groped each other's nipples; tiny twists and pulls ensued, causing my own pounder to bounce between my legs in the whirlpool's circular current.

"Come," I demanded in a brusque tone. "Shoot your loads."

"I'm almost ready," Jay replied to my insistence.

"I'm blowing now," Brick commented in a sex-driven pant.

Frankly, I could not see the men pop their velvety loads; the whirlpool's flow was far too strong and bubbly. Instead, I could only see the expression on their faces and realized they were coming at the same time: wide grins, semi-closed eyes, tight cords on their necks, untamed growls. Both of their torsos rose out of the pool of water and fell back inside. Their hips bucked one last time into my palms, and I listened to them moan in ecstasy.

Following their bursts, it was Jay who said, "It's your turn to fire off your load, Dougie."

"Yeah," Brick agreed.

Still hard between my thighs, horny as hell, devoted to their skin and pool friendships, I asked, "What exactly do you two have in mind?"

Jay looked at Brick and smiled.

Brick looked at Jay and smiled.

It was Jay who said, "Instead of telling you … we'll show you. So you'd better be ready for us."

I was ready; more so than they knew. Whatever they wanted from me, I was game, willing to provide my flesh for their needs, fag-fantasies, and whatnot. Ready or not, they were going to get me off, and my sap was going to fly out of my man-pick – no doubt.

So now it was my turn, and how did I want to get off? Two huge cocks plowed my ass and got my juices flowing, but what would see the climax explode out of me? A hot mouth on my dick? Or two? A perfect muscle ass as a target? Or two?

Jay and Brick guided me out of the hot tub and lead me over to a massage table. Brick threw a towel over the vinyl, and Jay patted where he wanted my ass.

I jumped up onto it and lay flat on my back.

Hands explored and caressed, prodded and probed my body. Nothing was left untouched. Pleasure soared over my skin and down to my toes. I curled them and Brick brought my foot to his mouth and sucked on each toe.

Jay's mouth found my own and kissed me deeply, his hands worked my nipples and pecs.

Brick took my other foot and sucked on each little pig. "This little pig went to market …"

Jay's tongue tasted mine, and he pulled hard on my lips.

Brick finished " … all the way home," and started up my leg. His tongue circled my knee and worked up my inner thigh.

I felt my balls rise up.

Brick licked my balls and worked up my shaft. He grabbed my legs and started to pull me.

Jay hung onto my shoulders and helped move me perpendicular on the massage table.

Brick opened the small drawer in the table and pulled out a condom. He sucked on my cock as he slipped it on. He pulled the lube out and applied some on his dick and then along my crack, slipping some into me.

Jay guided my head back and held it.

Brick moved into position between my legs and brought my ankles up to his neck. He spread my cheeks and inserted himself into my crease. He humped my rump and slowly entered me. As his pubic bush brushed my balls, he grabbed my dick.

Jay picked up his cock and rubbed it over my lips. "Suck it, baby."

I opened my mouth and swallowed his fat mushroom head. He pulled my head back further and surged deeper into my throat.

Both men drilled into me, making me their spit roast. Brick's hand worked my cock.

I rolled my tongue along his shaft and sucked hard on Jay's tool, pulling him deeper into my throat, loving every minute of our trio-time.

Brick increased his speed on my cock and in my ass.

My balls rose up, and I knew my sticky explosion wouldn't take long. I drew down harder on Jay, and he doubled his speed.

Brick and Jay slammed into me, pinning me there as their balls emptied again. Jay quickly pulled out of me and shot on my neck and on one of my nipples, letting out an exhilarating moan that only caused my beef to become harder. Then I felt the white heat explode from my balls and shoot out of my dick. Rope after rope of cum sprayed across my torso and Brick's.

He pulled out of my ass and rubbed his cock against mine. Another wave poured out of me and mixed with his.

Jay also added the rest of his fiery-hot load to ours, continuing to share that fun-filled moan. Three spent dicks still stood erect after the afternoon workout. Brick and Jay helped me sit up, and I felt the cum run down my belly and into my bush.

Their hands massaged the rest over my tan skin and sent shivers over my still sensitive penis.

"Wish all my customers worked out as well as you guys." Brick leaned forward and kissed me.

"Thanks for the great service," Jay said.

Brick walked over to a cabinet and returned with clean hand towels. He gave each of us one and wiped himself clean. "I can't wait to show you guys the sauna." He started to walk away from the massage table. "Coming?" He flexed his brown ass cheeks in invitation.

Jay and I followed, close behind.

THE AFTER-WORKOUT
By Milton Stern

Bobby always worked out at 5:00 am, walking from his home in Columbia Heights in Washington, DC, down 16th Street, to Results the Gym on U Street, in the dark, early morning hours six days a week. His friends worried that he would get mugged one day, but Bobby wasn't worried. Even though he was only five-foot-five, he weighed in at almost 170 pounds, and all of that was solid muscle. Some joked that at least twenty of it was cock as Bobby was known for his endowment, which would make a horse envious. This was another reason he chose to work out so early. Results had open showers, and Bobby grew tired of all the stares he would get while showering since his dick hung at least to mid-thigh even under the coldest spray. When he was done working out around 6:00 am, he was usually the only one in the shower, which suited him just fine.

This particular morning, Bobby was shampooing his hair after a grueling chest workout when he heard a showerhead being turned on, then another. Great, he thought to himself, more gawkers. Bobby turned around, so his back was to the wall as he rinsed the shampoo from his hair, and when he opened his eyes, he almost gasped at what he saw. He blinked twice to be sure he was not hallucinating. Standing across from him, using adjacent showers were identical twins, and these were no ordinary twins. They were blond, blue-eyed Adonises, over six-feet tall, with god-like physiques and hanging between their legs were the largest dicks Bobby had ever seen soft, with the exception of his own of course.

The twins pretty much ignored Bobby as they soaped up and rinsed off. Bobby decided to do the same, but he had to face the wall, for staring at the twins would surely cause his cock to swell, and there would be no hiding his hard-on. The three men finished showering at the same time, dried off and made their way to their lockers to get dressed. Bobby finished dressing first, and after deciding against introducing himself, he left the gym and proceeded to walk back home up 16th Street.

As he crossed Florida Avenue, Bobby noticed a car across the street that was moving in the same direction he was but rather slowly. He thought nothing of it, figuring it was probably one of the newspaper delivery drivers making his early rounds.

He walked just a few yards more when the car sped up, then made a sudden tire-squealing U-turn and stopped in front of Bobby. Before he could react, the passenger side door opened, and a man grabbed Bobby, placed a hand with a handkerchief over his mouth and threw him into the back seat of the car. Then, the car sped off.

Bobby blinked open his eyes and did not know where he was or how long he had been there. He tried to say something, but he had a ball gag in his mouth, and when he looked down, he saw that he was naked and strapped to a table on his back. He looked around the room and noticed it was a basement with little to no furniture that he could see from his vantage point. He started to panic and hyperventilate just as one of his captors entered the room.

It was one of the twins from the gym, and he was now standing over Bobby wearing nothing but a pair of lederhosen. The Adonis noticed Bobby was hyperventilating, so he removed the ball gag and put a paper bag over Bobby's mouth. Bobby breathed into the bag, and his captor kept the bag there until his breathing calmed down.

Once the bag was removed, Bobby started shouting, "Where am I? Who are you? What are you doing with me?"

The twin said nothing. He placed a finger over his mouth to indicate that Bobby should stop shouting. Bobby calmed down and waited for the blond to say something. But, nothing was said. Then, the other twin entered the room, dressed in identical lederhosen and stood on the other side of Bobby. The twins looked at each other then the twin to his right spoke.

"If you promise not to shout, we will make this as pleasant as possible, but if you do shout, you will regret the day you were born."

Quietly, Bobby asked, "Make what pleasant?"

"This experience, of course," the other twin said. "We just want to have a little fun with you, and if we enjoy ourselves, we will let you go when we are done, but if we find you tedious, we will torture you until you beg for your own death."

Bobby didn't have to think long about his options. He was apparently strapped tightly to the table, and even if he did manage to get loose, these guys were twice his size.

They looked at Bobby and smiled, then opened their lederhosen, pulled out their enormous dicks and proceeded to piss all over Bobby. The little muscleman was no stranger to water sports, so this did not bother him as long as they avoided his face, and fortunately they did even though they seemed to piss a gallon each. The stench of their urine permeated the room, and Bobby could only wonder what was yet to come as he had never before been in a situation such as this. Once their bladders were empty, they removed their lederhosen and ran their hands all over Bobby's thickly muscled body working the piss into every pore.

One grabbed his balls and gave them a good yank, causing Bobby to grunt, while the other squeezed his dick, which was now starting to fill even though he tried to keep it from getting hard. But, it was to no avail, as the hands torturing his cock and balls were doing more to turn him on than frighten him, and within a minute, his dick was at its full ten inches, which on his five-foot-five frame brought the mushroom head to right below his pecs.

The twin to his right hit a button under the table, and suddenly Bobby's legs were being pulled up and apart by some sort of pulley device he had not noticed before, and the contraption did not stop until Bobby was suspended by his ankles with only his shoulders on the table. Then the twin to his left hit a button, and the same thing happened to his wrists until he was suspended by his wrists and ankles, spreadeagled from both ends with no support for his back. He thought he was going to be quartered, when the twin to his right reached up and pulled down a leather strap, passed it under his back to the other twin, who then connected it to a hook in the ceiling, thus supporting Bobby's back. The table was then rolled away, and Bobby was lowered until he was just below waist level of his captors.

The twin on his right then moved down to his feet and positioned himself between his legs while the other one went to the other side of the room to get a cart and wheel it over to where his brother was standing. In spite of all this, Bobby's dick refused to go down. He wondered if he was suffering from Stockholm Syndrome. But, doesn't that take a few months or even years? He thought.

Bobby could not see what was on the table but guessed at least one of the items was grease or lard, as he felt his ass being slathered with something thick and gloppy. Then he felt the intruder – one, maybe two, maybe even three fingers being forced into his ass, twisting and probing with no finesse at all. Bobby gritted his teeth and took the intrusion like a man as the other twin walked over to his left and stood by his head.

Bobby looked over and saw that he now sported a huge hard-on that rivaled his in size, and it was sticking straight out at his face with precum practically pouring from the slit. Bobby involuntarily licked his lips, and this captor shoved his enormous meat into Bobby's mouth without ceremony. Bobby figured if they were going to kill him, he might as well go out with a smile, so he sucked hungrily on the huge cock in his mouth, which continued to leak pints of precum that tasted better than he would acknowledge to these two bastards.

As he was chowing down on the man meat, he felt the fingers exit his asshole, only to be rudely replaced by the other huge cock in the room, all greased up and practically up to his nipples within seconds. Then the pounding began – from both ends.

The twins showed no mercy as they used the little muscle man for their own pleasure as if he were just a hole to be plugged and filled with cock. No attention was given to Bobby's dick, which now ached it was so hard, while his huge balls drew up, ready to explode.

The twins had great staying power and pumped and pumped for quite a while, or at least it seemed quite a while, until the one in Bobby's mouth exploded with a yell, and shot pint after pint of his thick cum down Bobby's throat, which he didn't lose a drop of. Then, his brother yelled identically and left his own quart of milk in Bobby's ass, causing Bobby to shoot a load to be envied all over his torso with a few shots hitting his chin.

The twins exited their respective holes, and Bobby thought, That's it? And, with that, a hand with a handkerchief was placed over his face again.

Bobby opened his eyes, and after looking up, saw that a couple of people were staring down at him, including a police officer. He shook his head, and after looking around, realized he was in Meridian Hill Park.

The police officer helped him up and asked, "Are you OK? How long have you been lying there?"

"What time is it?" Bobby asked.

"Around 8:00 am," the officer answered, and Bobby took a good look at him. He was over six feet tall, blond and obviously built and hung. He then looked out to 16th Street at the patrol car and saw an identical officer waiting for his partner.

"Only two hours?" Bobby asked. "That's the best you could do?"

And, Bobby stood up and walked away with a smile.

THE WINDOW ESTIMATE
By Milton Stern

I hate being an apartment manager, and I only agreed to do it because my landlords promised me a fifty percent reduction in the rent for the four years they would be in Brazil. The worst part is that I have to listen to the constant complaining from the fat redneck, her drunk asshole of a husband and her future serial killer, slut daughter upstairs. I just wish the daughter would get it over with and kill them already, so I can clean up the mess and rent the place out to a couple of hotties. But, until then, I have to be the responsible one and that includes getting estimates for work that I would rather let go in the hopes the cast from Cops upstairs will leave in frustration.

Most of the time, these estimates are for things they have broken, and I know that the constant yelling and banging that goes on is the reason the frame of the large bay window in their master bedroom was cracked causing the glass to fall down into the wall, leaving a four-inch gap on the top.

I took my sweet time getting an estimate, but when the rain seeped in causing water to leak into my apartment, it became my personal problem, so I called a couple of window companies. I figured I would punish the landlords as well for sticking me with these assholes and get an estimate for all the windows.

Two salesmen had been here already, but they were so slick, I threw away their estimates before the door closed behind them.

On the day the third and final guy was to arrive, I pretty much didn't care anymore. I decided to work from home that day, so it was amazing I even bothered to shower, although I only wore a pair of gym shorts (actually cut-off sweat pants) and a wife-beater. I was totally engrossed in work when I heard a knock at the door.

I opened the door and standing there was what looked to be a teenager, wearing a loose fitting All-Weather Window Company polo shirt. He gave me the taillights to headlights three-second once over I tend to get from guys who see me for the first time, which doesn't even faze me anymore.

You see, I am an ex-professional football player (not that anyone remembers – third string center), and I am six-foot even, weighing in at around two-hundred-sixty pounds. At thirty-five, I still work out as if I am being paid to, and I won't deny I ever took a needle in the ass. We'll leave it at that. Now, I work as a bookkeeper for a nondescript company in a nondescript cubicle located in a nondescript building. I am one of the lucky few to have actually gotten paid to be a professional football player, but after almost five years on the bench, I got bored. I was told I was too nice, not aggressive enough, but the coach liked me, so I held onto my job.

Now, the kid in front of me may have played some sports. He had that college jock, too many frat parties body. You know the type – broad shoulders, decent arms, and remnants of the 'freshman forty' still around the middle. If they are straight, the paunch is there for life, and if they are gay, well, they wouldn't have taken on the freshman-forty in the first place. No gay boy in his twenties would allow such a thing to happen to him. This kid was definitely straight, which was fine with me as I don't like them young. I like them older, much older. I like being fucked silly by a big muscle bear with gray hair. If this kid had a twelve-inch dick, I couldn't have cared less.

"Mr. Kennedy?"

I let him in, and he introduced himself as Allan. I showed him all the windows upstairs and downstairs in all the apartments. Of course, the redneck had to butt in and say what she wanted in a window, but I shut her up immediately and continued to follow Allan from wall to wall while he measured and wrote on his legal pad.

When we were done, we returned to my apartment, and I had to ask him his age.

"I'm twenty-three. I couldn't find a job in my field, so I took this sales job, which has made my college education a waste … can I ask you a question, a personal question?"

I said sure.

"I can see you work out ..."

He could see I work out. He was brilliant. My arms relaxed are eighteen inches around. My pecs are so huge, I can't see my feet, and he can see I work out.

"I've been trying to lose this gut since I graduated, and nothing I do works. Should I do more cardio?"

"You should quit drinking so much beer," I said and raised my eyebrows. I may let a quack doc shoot what is probably horse piss into my ass to get huge and ripped, but I never drank or did drugs. Yeah, I know, what I do is just as bad. Whatever. You'd fuck me if you had a chance, especially if you saw my rock hard and huge bubble-butt.

"Yeah, I guess you're right."

"So, how long before I get an estimate?" I asked.

"Oh, I can have one for you this afternoon. I'll email it to you."

And with that, he was gone.

I went back to work and took a mid-day break to go to the gym because I have body dysmorphia or manorexia or some other psychological shit because I think I'm fat or skinny and have deep emotional issues. Please. I know what I look like. I look like a fucking freak, but I like the freak look, and the old muscle bear dads I let fuck me like it, too. Don't assume you know guys like me.

After I returned from the gym, I was mixing myself a protein shake when there was a knock at the door. I was back in my cut-off sweat shorts but not wearing a shirt anymore. I opened the door, and it was frat-boy window guy.

"I decided to hand deliver the estimate," he said as he handed me the envelope. "I can explain it to you if you like?"

I gave him my best you think I am a dunder-headed muscleboy with the IQ of a baboon look.

"Oh, I didn't mean it like that ... uh, I mean I like to explain why we may be higher than most anyone else," Allan recovered.

"I may look mean, but it takes a whole hell of a lot to offend me or piss me off … believe me, kid, I haven't lost my temper in years," I said with a smile as I motioned him inside.

What, you say? A juiced-up freak who hasn't had a roid induced hissy fit? See, you read too much. I have never been a hot head. That is why I sucked as a professional football player. I'm too easy going. The only side effect I ever got from the juice was shrunken balls, but I can still come a gallon of spunk.

I offered Allan a protein shake, and he accepted. As we sat there drinking our whey concoctions, he explained all the window crap, and I pretended to listen, but I couldn't get over how he was avoiding looking at me. I was shirtless, pumped from the gym and sitting no more than two feet away from him. Although I had showered at the gym, I hadn't bothered putting on deodorant, so I had a light musk about me, which some guys like.

When he finally looked up, I could tell he was enthralled by my pumped pecs and my nipples, which I pulled on constantly. They stick out a good inch even now.

"You want to touch them?" I asked.

His eyes bulged.

"Look, it won't make you gay. Straight guys always want to touch my muscles to see what they feel like. Are they hard, soft, will they vibrate?" I said with a chuckle and a smile.

"Sure," he said as he slowly reached over to kind of poke a finger at my bicep.

I flexed it for him, and he then caressed it a bit before taking his hand away. So, I was wrong about him. He was a big ole fag. I grabbed his hand and put it on my pec while I made it bounce.

"Damn, they are hard as a rock," he said.

I was not turned on by this. He just wasn't my type. Yeah, I know, get over it.

"Now, about this estimate. What can we do to get you to come down by at least ten percent?" I may have been pissed at the landlords, but I was still a tightwad at heart, and I wasn't going for the obvious scene you are expecting here.

"Become my personal trainer," he said.

I sat back and looked at him. He had potential and a good frame. And that gut he complained about wasn't really that bad, just a little soft.

"Take off your shirt," I said.

He stood up and without hesitation removed his shirt. His shoulders were broad, and his biceps a nice size, too. However, his chest was a surprise as it was huge, which made me make a mental note to suggest he wear a tighter company shirt, and it was covered with hair, curly blond hair that trailed down to his pants.

"You'll have to shave that," I said pointing to his chest.

"Really?" he said as he ran his hand seductively down his torso.

"But not until after you bend me over this table and fuck my brains out. The condoms and lube are in the drawer behind you. If you want me to train you, you better be ready to do what I say at the drop of a hat," I said without stopping to take a breath. Then I stood, dropped my cut-off sweat shorts revealing my hard five-inch dick. Yeah, I know, everyone in these stories is hung like a horse. Well, I'm a bottom, and I may not have a lot of dick to play with, but I certainly have enough muscle to make up for it. Besides, little dicks get hard, stay hard, and shoot nice creamy loads. So, get over it.

I also know that I said he wasn't my type. But, I wanted that estimate lowered, and my hole filled at the same time. He was there; I was horny; do the math.

I then bent over the table, while he fumbled around with his pants.

"Hurry up, I don't get this horny often, just grease it up and plug me," I said over my shoulder.

I then felt the cold lube dribbling down my crack. He sort of rubbed it all around, and I could tell he was nervous. I then heard the condom wrapper being opened; he cursed himself while he tried to roll it on. I clearly had him flustered.

"Are these the largest ones you have?" he asked.

I turned around and saw what looked to be a good ten thick inches of circumcised dick sticking straight out at me. There you go – a horse-hung top in a porno story. Are you happy now?

"Look in the back of the drawer. They must have slid back. There should be some extra-hungs or whatever they call them," I said as I marveled at his heat-seeking moisture missile, which is a friend's nickname for huge cocks.

"Found them," he said with delight.

"Good, slip one on and fuck my brains out," I said as I again bent over the table. "And, don't bother eating me out or fingering me, just stick that barbell up my chute ... I hate foreplay."

He did just that. All the way in, no apologies, no hesitation, no finesse, no bullshit, and I loved it.

"Now, reach around and pull my nipples as hard as you can while you fuck me."

And, he did just that. He reached around and pulled my big nipples, no apologies, no hesitation, no finesse, no bullshit, and I loved it.

He practically pounded my huge muscular ass over the moon (excuse the pun) and pulled my nipples another inch. I was in heaven. He was having a pretty good time, too. Or, he was good at faking it because he kept telling me what a hot ass I had and what a sexy motherfucker I was. And at one point, he started nibbling on the back of my neck, and that did it.

I cried out as I came. I wasn't even touching myself since I was using my hands to hold onto the edge of the table while he pounded me for points. And, right after I came, he filled that extra large rubber with his own load and yelled out loud what a "man slut" I was, and amazingly, I came again – hands free.

When he recovered, he apologized for calling me a man slut and gave me ten percent off on the windows in addition to another ten percent for the hot fuck.

I never told him, but calling me a man slut was the best part of the fuck.

The windows look great. And Allan? He is a muscle freak now, too.

I love being me.

FOOTBALL DADDIES
By Milton Stern

Dan and Bobby had played football together for close to thirty years, from peewee, through high school and finally on the same pro team and always on the offensive line. When Dan decided before he turned forty-two that it was time to retire, Bobby came to the same conclusion within minutes. He couldn't imagine playing the game without his best friend around, especially since they had been lovers for the past fifteen years. But, they didn't know what to do in retirement? A lot of football players went into the restaurant business or lent their names to other service industry venues, but Dan and Bobby had no interest in that. Their decision became easier when they heard of a gym that was up for sale in their hometown because the owner had died and his kids had no intention of running it.

They flew down to Elkhart, North Carolina, a small town most maps ignore, and made an offer on the old place. The heirs were more than happy to unload the business and accepted their price without hesitation. Dan and Bobby paid cash and found themselves in the gym business.

Once they found a place to rent until they decided where to live permanently, they began the work of renovating what would become the D&B Fitness Factory. This was one of those old-time gyms with benches, free weights, no machines to speak of, and only a couple of stationary bikes serving as cardio equipment. There were mirrors on all the walls and an open shower room that could accommodate eight people at a time.

The work began with getting rid of all the old equipment, so they donated it to an organization that sends fitness gear to developing countries. They ordered all new benches, rubber coated plates, a few basic machines and a couple of treadmills and arc trainers. Their goal was to keep the gym as 'old-school' as possible. They figured if they tried to go fancy, they would not be able to compete with the 'pretty boy' club in the next town.

Elkhart may have been a small town, but football was huge there. Dan and Bobby weren't the only former residents to go pro. Many of their former teammates bought property near the coast, which was only a thirty minute drive from where they were, and once they opened for business, the D&B Fitness Factory filled up every day with quite a few muscle daddies.

Dan and Bobby were all too happy to offer a gym their fellow gray hairs could enjoy. Dan stood over six feet and weighed over 250 pounds of solid muscle with a fifty-inch chest, nineteen-inch arms and maintaining a thirty-six-inch waist, all covered in salt and pepper fur from his head to his feet. Bobby was smooth, but no less impressive with a shaved head to match. He stood barely five-ten, weighed almost 225 pounds, but had just as much muscle as Dan with an even broader chest and bigger biceps, but he carried a few inches around his belly. He had one of those tight bellies that many a boy finds sexy. Dan loved Bobby's belly and would come on it every chance he could get. They were both also hung very nicely and circumcised with big round balls, making for a beautiful sight in the bedroom.

The gym was doing very well as they had tapped into a market that the mega-gyms were ignoring. It also helped that they did not require that their members wear shirts, only proper footwear and shorts as long as they cleaned off the equipment after each use. Dan and Bobby did this mostly for their own entertainment since they both enjoyed watching big men get all sweaty and pumped. Even with the lenient rules, the place was kept immaculate, especially the shower room, which was no small feat considering some of the action rumored to be occurring in there especially before the 10:00 pm closing time.

Dan and Bobby had not engaged in any of the antics but had witnessed a few while they were working. They had hired a college senior, who was getting a degree as a physical therapist, to work the evening hours, so they could have a life outside the business, and he was a very hard worker. Miles was also an offensive lineman in high school, who decided not to play college ball for reasons he never explained, so Bobby and Dan took a special liking to him. At twenty-two years old, Miles was already as big as many of the pros, standing at over six-foot-four and over 260 pounds with a solid frame holding a fifty-two-inch chest and twenty-inch arms. He was not only big and muscular, but he was devastatingly handsome as well with dark features, curly black hair and covered in just a touch of curly black fur. When he smiled, men and women melted regardless of their sexual inclinations.

Dan joked that he didn't care how competent he was; Miles had the job the second he applied. What made him even more appealing was his lack of attitude or ego. Miles was a damn hard worker and kept the gym spotless and in order. He never engaged in 'activities,' nor did he do anything inappropriate. He was quiet and respectful with a pleasant demeanor. He only made one request. Miles wanted to be able to work out after the gym closed for the evening since this would not interfere with his studies. Dan and Bobby suspected Miles was a bit of a loner, for he never received personal calls, was seen texting or had any buddies come by the gym to visit. They wanted to invite him over for dinner, but somehow never got around to it. What they did learn was that his parents died when he was very young and that he was raised by his grandmother, who recently died. He had no other family and lived in the apartment where he was raised.

Dan and Bobby would usually work out mid-day when the gym was the least busy, but this became a hassle as the business of running a business takes more time than people realize, so they decided to try working out at 4:00 am before they opened. This lasted only a couple of days because getting up at 3:00 am was nearly impossible, too. That was when Dan suggested they follow Miles's lead and work out after hours. This would work since they hired Bobby's nephew to open for them during the week, and they could come in around 7:00 am. Bobby's nephew was competent but not worth the trouble of describing since he spent most of his time at work surfing the net and texting his girlfriend. He was just there to occupy space until Dan and Bobby came in. Miles left the place in such order that there was nothing to do in the mornings, and Bobby told Miles that he knew his nephew was useless, but he needed him for those two hours, so he and Dan could get some rest. Miles never complained. And, Dan and Bobby would keep the place in order while they worked and tended to the business as well.

Around 10:30 pm, Dan and Bobby showed up on the first night they decided to try their new workout schedule. The gym was closed, and the blinds were drawn indicating it was closed, but they could see Miles's shadow as he worked out inside. They told Miles they would be coming in to work out, so that he wouldn't be startled when the door opened.

Dan and Bobby walked in just as Miles lay down on a bench to perform dumbbell presses with 110-pound weights. They both stopped in their tracks at the sight before them. Wearing nothing but a pair of black 2xist briefs that did little to hide his candy and a pair of New Balance cross trainers, he was pushing the weights up, and his chest was glistening and pumped.

He finished his set and sat up on the bench. "Hey, when you didn't show up at closing, I decided to get comfortable. I'll go get my shorts," Miles said as he greeted them.

"Don't ...," Dan almost shouted.

" ... worry about us," Bobby interrupted. "Stay comfortable."

"Are you sure?" Miles asked as he stood up, revealing his body to them for the first time.

"I didn't realize how hot it gets in here with the AC off. Why didn't you reprogram it to stay on for an hour after closing?" Bobby asked.

"I didn't think I had the authority," Miles the ever-dutiful employee responded. "Besides, I prefer it warm when I work out."

Dan and Bobby walked toward the locker room to put away their gym bags, and Miles dropped to the floor to do a set of push-ups. They each glanced at his perfect, big and muscular butt as it went up and down.

In the locker room, Dan took off his shirt as Bobby did the same. "Should we strip down as well?" Dan whispered.

"I might pop wood," Bobby said with a smile. "But, what the hell?!?"

They each stripped down, Dan to a pair of white Calvin Klein briefs, and Bobby to a pair of black trunk briefs of the same brand. They exited the locker room and joined Miles in the gym. Miles went about his chest work out as if everything was normal, and Dan and Bobby did the same while they worked legs.

Occasionally, they would smile at each other, but Miles was very serious about his workouts, as were Dan and Bobby, and after the initial excitement of being half naked with the college senior wore off, all were grunting and sweating their asses off.

Miles was attempting to do a set of incline dumbbell presses with 100-pound weights, but was struggling to lift them into position to begin his set. Dan noticed this and offered to help him.

"Thanks, maybe I should begin with these. I can never lift them up this far into my workout," Miles said as Dan walked over. Bobby followed.

"Lie back; Bobby and I'll hand them to you."

"I'll give you a spot, once you get started," Bobby added.

Miles lay back, and Dan and Bobby on either side of him lifted up the dumbbells and waited until Miles was holding them firmly. Bobby then positioned himself behind Miles to spot him. He managed five reps before he needed assistance, and Bobby helped him with two more.

Once he was done with the set, Miles thanked them, but Bobby remained crouched behind the bench. Dan looked at him, and Bobby motioned downward with his eyes, for he was sporting a hard-on that could not be hidden.

"Let us know when you are ready for another set," Dan said and winked at Bobby.

Miles lay down on the bench again, and was ready in thirty seconds. The kid really did an intense workout.

They helped him get a grip on the dumbbells again, and Bobby hoped Miles didn't see the bulge in his trunk briefs.

Miles did this set and another, and at that point, Bobby's underwear was soaked with precum. He quickly went to the locker room to fetch another pair he hoped he remembered to put in his gym bag. There was a pair, and by the time he had removed the soaked pair and wiped off his dick, he was no longer as hard, but still a little firm.

He changed into a matching pair of black trunk briefs, which was a relief, for he would have to explain the change in wardrobe.

He exited the locker room and the sight he saw was about to ruin another pair of underwear. Dan was doing a set of squats, and Miles was spotting him from behind. Bobby stood there awestruck at the sight before him, and his dick was now out of control, hard as a rock and leaking like a faucet. When Dan struggled for a few more reps, Miles leaned in closely to help. Two reps later, the set was done.

Miles stepped back, and Dan stepped away from the rack, and he was now sporting a rager equal to Bobby's. He looked over at Bobby, who looked over at Miles, who looked at both of them and smiled.

"I get hard when I work out, too," Miles said. And when they looked down, they noticed his underwear was beginning to stretch quite a bit. He then dropped down and did another set of push-ups, while Dan and Bobby watched.

Dan looked at Bobby and shrugged, and Bobby shrugged back. Miles then finished his set and declared his workout was done, and he was going to take a shower. Meanwhile, the bulge in his briefs was bigger than before and the head of his dick was sticking out of the waistband. Miles walked past Bobby and into the locker room. Within seconds, the sound of a shower being turned on was heard, and Bobby turned to follow him.

"Are we done working out?" Dan asked as he followed Bobby.

Bobby never answered. He stepped out of his newly precummed briefs and into the shower room where Miles was using the middle-most showerhead. Dan followed suit. Bobby chose the shower to the right of Miles and Dan decided to occupy the one on the left. They watched as Miles soaped himself up and were mesmerized by his pumped, heavily muscled and lathered body and his enormous circumcised cock that stood out and up. Dan and Bobby's not quite as big, but big enough dicks were just as hard.

Dan soaped himself up waiting for Bobby to take the lead if anything were going to happen. And, take the lead Bobby did. He lathered up his hand, reached down, and began stroking Miles's dick, and he was met with no resistance. Dan then leaned in and kissed

Bobby full on the mouth, and their tongues wrestled as Miles reached down and stroked both their cocks. Within seconds, Bobby was ready to pop, so he grabbed Miles's hand to stop the momentum, but Miles proved to be quite strong. That strength was all it took, and Bobby was shouting and shooting a load all over Miles's hand and leg.

Not even a second after that, Dan added to the spunk on Miles and shouted his pleasure as well. The hands of a physical therapist were obviously magic. Dan planted his mouth back on Miles and Bobby continued to stroke the enormous cock until it shot a load all over the shower wall – a load so impressive that Dan and Bobby almost applauded.

Once he caught his breath, Miles declared, "I've never touched a man before. I have wanted to do that with you guys since the day you hired me."

"You never touched a man?" Bobby asked with surprise.

"Where did you learn to stroke like that?" Dan asked.

"I guess from playing with myself," Miles said as he resumed soaping himself up.

Bobby stopped him, and Dan joined Bobby as they lathered up Miles, taking turns kissing him and stroking him until he shot another load – this time on the shower floor.

# # # # #

Dan and Bobby soon found a 19th Century home that suited them perfectly and settle in nicely. Miles graduated from college and landed a job at a local hospital as a physical therapist.

Does Miles still work at the gym part-time? You bet he does, and he still works out in his underwear after closing every night along with Dan and Bobby. But now, they sometimes shower at the gym or the three of them go home afterward to shower, where they live in a polyamorous relationship that has 'worked out' quite well.

Teammates for life!

THE CONTRIBUTORS

CONRAD JAMES is a psychologist, educator, and the author of a number of published short stories, which he refers to as Hard Homo-Psycho-Sexual Erotica. Contact him at drconradjames@cox.net.

DERRICK DELLA GIORGIA was born in Italy and currently lives between Manhattan and Rome. His work has been published in several anthologies and literary magazines. Visit him at www.derrickdellagiorgia.com.

DIESEL KING is the proud poppa of his first short story collection entitled *A Good Time in the Hood.*

DONALD WEBB has had short stories published in numerous gay magazines and anthologies. He lives with his life-long partner in Victoria, BC. andon402@shaw.ca.

FOX LEE is an erotic fiction writer living in the Midwest. You can reach Fox at WanChaiFox@yahoo.com.

HL CHAMPA is an extensively published writer of erotic fiction. Find out more at www.heidichampa.blogspot.com.

Residing on English Bay in Vancouver, Canada, **JAY STARRE** has pumped out steamy gay fiction for dozens of anthologies and has written two gay erotic novels. Contact: writer.brentley@gmail.com.

JESSE MONTEAGUDO is a freelance writer who lives in South Florida. Since 1993, he has contributed more than 25 short stories to STARbooks Press.

LANDON DIXON has published over 200 stories in anthologies, magazines, and on websites. A collection of his stories was just recently released, *Hot Tales of Gay Lust.*

LOGAN ZACHARY (loganzachary2002@yahoo.com) is an author of mysteries, short stories, and over forty erotica stories, living in Minneapolis, MN, with his partner, Paul, and his dog, Ripley, who runs the house. www.loganzacharydicklit.com.

MARK APOAPSIS chooses to remain a mystery.

MILTON STERN is an author of biographies, novels, screenplays, and dozens of short stories, living in Maryland with Esmeralda, his rescue beagle. www.miltonstern.com.

R. W. CLINGER writes for STARbooks Press. His novels include *The Pool Boy* and *Soft on the Eyes*. *Skin Tour* will be released in the spring of 2011.

RAWIYA is a happily married mother of two who has had nine short works accepted for publication. Visit her at www.rawiyaserotica.blogspot.com.

ROB ROSEN, is the author of several novels. Please visit him at www.therobrosen.com or friend him on Facebook at therobrosen

RON RADLE writes gay love stories in the very buckle of the South Carolina Bible Belt. His work has appeared under various names in a number of magazines, journals, and anthologies.

ROSCOE HUDSON is the author of several erotic short stories and novels. He is a full-time academic, writer and bodybuilder and lives in Chicago, IL.

THE EDITOR

This is **MICKEY ERLACH**'s seventh anthology for STARbooks Press. He once got caught having sex in a gym shower, and instead of kicking him out, the manager joined the action.